THE WAY OF UNITY

VELSPAR - ELEGIES
BOOK 1

SARAH K. BALSTRUP

First published in 2023 by Burning Mirror Press, ACT, Australia.

Copyright © 2022 Sarah K. Balstrup. All rights reserved.

Illustrations by Andy Paciorek.

Celtic Garamond Pro © Levente Halmos.

Sarah K. Balstrup asserts the moral right to be identified as the author of this work.

ISBN Paperback 978-0-645474-70-1

ISBN E-book 978-0-645474-71-8

Full map of the Seven Lands of Velspar available at www.sarahkbalstrup.com or via QR code.

See end matter for detail maps of Avishae, Brivia, Lindesal, Maglore, Seltsland, Vaelnyr and Nothelm.

For Alex
1985 - 2020

CHANT OF REDDENING

readying the

red flesh

blood flesh

shiver flesh

hot flesh

Siatka the

red flesh

blood flesh

shiver flesh

hot flesh

Kshidol the

red flesh

blood flesh

shiver flesh

hot flesh

Velspar the

red flesh

blood flesh

shiver flesh

hot flesh

CHANT OF CONCEPTION

ah   ah   ah   ah

spa   spa   spa   spa

ah   ah   ah   ah

vel-spar ah   ah   ah

drifting   in   darkness

V   E   L   S   P   A   R

drifting   we touch

V   E   L   S   P   A   R

chasing   we gather

V E L S P A R

we circle   and spin

V E L S P A R

we press we enter

V E L S P A R

without within

V E L S P A R

VELSPAR

ah ah

VELSPAR

spa spa

VELSPAR

ah ah

VELSPAR

ah ah

BIRTH CHANT

Siatka   Kshidol

    ah ah   ah ah

    Siatka   Kshidol

      ah ah   ah ah

        Siatka   Kshidol

         ah ah

         ah ah

CHANT OF RETURN

Great   Stream

V E L S P A R

stream   spin

V E L S P A R

dissolve   among us

V E L S P A R

as   one   again

V   E   L   S   P   A   R

bright   and   shining

V   E   L   S   P   A   R

the   brightest   star

V   E   L   S   P   A   R

gather   together

V E L S P A R

V E L S P A R

V E L S P A R

VELSPAR

ah   ah

ah ah

ah

BADEN FOREST, AVISHAE

One Year Before The Fire

"Intercessor Camis?"

"Yes..."

"Shall I extinguish the Alma?"

"Yes."

"You are shaking. Is it too strong? I will open the tent."

"Please."

"Can you open your eyes?"

"No. Pass my Meridian, the vision is too strong."

"Your hands aren't moving. I will position it for you. The first stone is at your forehead. Now the second is in place, at your crown. You will feel the nape stone as I tighten the band. There."

"Thank you." Intercessor Camis felt the sensations return – flesh and hair and earthly scents. His heart dully thudded. A rasping dryness in his throat.

Camis opened his eyes.

Landyn Raeburn was with him, and Camis looked about the tent, regaining his bearings. The swept earthen floor, the sacred instruments, the parchment and ink set out, ready to record his vision.

Camis wiped the sweat from his aged hands, his white robe

smudged with dirt, the leather pouch of dried Alma still hanging open at his waist.

Landyn secured the flap so the smoke funnelled out, and looked down at him nervously.

"I am well, Landyn. Sit down," Camis said with a gesture of his hand.

The two men sat on stones either side of a small fire pit, and Landyn smothered the coals with a copper dish, placing a lantern amongst the ashes. Twilight had fallen since Camis had arrived at the Raeburn camp, and Landyn's eyes pursued him in the dim grey light.

"What did you see?"

Intercessor Camis regarded the man. "I am curious to know what you saw. Were you able to penetrate my vision?"

Landyn's throat clicked as he tried to swallow. His brow furrowing as impressions coalesced in his mind. "I felt my heart being torn from my chest. Some great tide stealing my daughter away." He tried to smile. "Such is a father's grief when his daughter marries."

Camis saw real terror in the man's eyes. "Rebekah is a Skalen now and I am sure you feel the distance of her new station, but the dread that hovers about you in this moment, it is stronger than that. You do not fear simply for your daughter."

Landyn frowned, then rose suddenly to close the tent. When he returned to his seat, he leant forward and whispered. "What did you see? Please, Intercessor."

Camis met Landyn's stare. "Around the seven-pointed Skalens' Star is a circle. At its heart there is a circle. My vision clothed itself in the Chant of Conception, drawing my attention to these circles, to the cycles that purify, to rebirth, and the eternal spirit of which we are part."

Landyn gathered the parchment and began to write. "Would you recite the Chant for me?"

"Only High Initiates are allowed to hear the sacred chants. I am sorry, Landyn." Camis drew a long breath and exhaled. "I believe we are approaching a time of great transformation. A difficult time, as you have sensed." The Intercessor paused. "Landyn, I came here not simply to teach you the principles of Intercession, as you have asked, but because I have seen you in my visions."

The man looked up.

"You are connected to Velspar's fate, as is your daughter, but perhaps not in a way you will like. There are parts...that are yet to become clear, but I must impress upon you that whatever sacrifice you are asked to make, it will be for the glory of Velspar."

Landyn licked his lips. "What type of sacrifice?"

"There is blood in it. And that blood will open The Eighth Gate." As Camis spoke, an image arose in his mind. The self-fertilisation of a holy seed. The absorption of Mother and Father into an eternal child. An image of actualisation, of perfect unity. An image that this man before him would not understand.

Landyn's quill scratched out the words and hovered there, a drop of ink falling from its tip, spreading dark upon the page.

"What is the Eighth Gate? I know of the Seven Gates of Wisdom. Is this for the Intercessors alone to pass through?"

Camis nodded. "Those blessed by Velspar will hear the call." The Intercessor laid his hand upon the wiry muscles of Landyn's arm, that twitched, giving off waves of heat. He siphoned the redness out until the man's spirit grew calm.

"You will not be among them," Camis said. He absorbed the flicker of anger as it issued from somewhere deep in the man's gut. "We each have our holy purpose, and yours is to be our sentinel."

Landyn's mouth formed a grim line.

Camis shivered, a feeling of lightness coming upon him. "You must protect this place for our return. Will you do it?"

The man set down his parchment and drew a shaking breath. Camis sensed his thoughts twisting this way and that, searching for a way to be counted among the elect.

Landyn drew his ink-stained hands to his forehead and bowed. "Yes, Intercessor."

Camis stood, readying to depart, for already he had stayed too long. "Velspar's blessings upon you."

"Velspar's blessings," Landyn murmured as he stared, transfixed, at the words on the page.

PART I
THE FIFTH GATE

1

WALDEMAR

The Year of The Fire

THE WAY OF UNITY must not be lost. When you read my words, slow first your breath, and open your inner eye. Among them is a silver thread. Follow it, and you will find Velspar. Return always to Velspar.

We are the threads that together form the Great Stream.
Before Velspar, we were fragmented.
Death desiccated the spirit,
And we were lost to the wind.
The light in us scattered, ever outward.
Like so many bright stars, we separated,
And other forces held us at their mercy.
We were mixed with the dark spaces between the stars, and we remained unconscious.
Then, Velspar, the eternal,
Called the silver threads of spirit to gather,
In one place: in Velspar;
As Velspar.
When the Holy Ones were revealed,
The Stream was purified, and fortified, through our unity.
Mother Siatka, serpent of sea,

3

Father Kshidol, bird of sky,
Opened their mouths,
And guided us home.
And so opened the eye.
It opened in the earth, beneath and among us,
and within our own minds.
All who are lost – in vision – may find Velspar.
All who are lost may return to Velspar.
Turn inward.
You have passed this way before.

Intercessor Waldemar Rasmus of Brivia, *700.*

2

SYBILLA

Six Years Before The Fire

HER FATHER WAS YOUNG. He was Reyan Terech then, and nobody's
father. He was just out of boyhood and there at his mother's behest.
Reyan was running down the Temple stair, slipping on blood as he
tripped, but the Intercessor drew him back into the room. Reyan was
afraid. He had passed the First Gate of Wisdom – sympathy; the
Second – to know a vision's source; and the Third – to instil a vision.
The Fourth was to administer blood rites, and these he had
performed, but to pass through the Fifth was to follow red thoughts
right down to the base of the stem. To know the substance of evil inti-
mately, so one might recognise its symptoms in others. The necessity
of the Fifth Gate was to be alleviated by the promise of the Sixth –
where red thoughts were drawn out; and the Seventh, where one
learned how to cause evil's dissipation.

The Blood Call had ended for the day, and with the sealing of the
door, smoke rose thick around Reyan, stinging his eyes. The Intercessor was still there, the soft flesh of his cheek quivering as it rose
into a half-smile. Was he the only one there? No, there were others.
The Intercessor's fingers were greasy with oil of Alma as Reyan's
wrists were bound. He could not run now if he tried. Reyan's tongue

grew heavy in his mouth and could no longer form words, but he knew the binds were to prevent the initiates from clawing their eyes.

Reyan's name swung back and forth in the gloom. The smoke was so sweet he began to drool. *Reyan*. They were checking whether he was still there, or if he had passed through. All parts of him swelled, as if he were an overripe fruit, the animal essence rising in his flesh, showing itself. The pain in his head was unbearable, his fingers like sausages, and his other part deformed past imagining.

In a shocking surge of will, he prised open his eyes. A momentary breeze passed through the window. They stood there, motionless and trembling, naked of their robes, their faces naked of skin, their eyes seeking some forbidden place at the back of their skulls. An excretion pulsed from their bodies that stank of pack animals and rutting, of raw flesh ripped with the teeth. Reyan could not bear to look at them, and with all of his strength, he moved his eyes to the wall.

The wall was white.

He stared at it, refusing to close his eyes. Smoke coiled and shifted and, in a flash, he saw something concealed there. A scaled form liquefying the marble, pushing up against it as if encased in an egg sac. She split through. Siatka's scaled body emerged from the wall, first in relief, then fully formed. She slithered low across the floor so the others wouldn't notice, moving quietly around Reyan's legs, encircling him – his ribs, his neck – cracking his bones into splinters. She smelt of soured milk, of bloodied rags. She squeezed until the world turned white – Reyan's thoughts exploding into stars.

He was almost gone when he felt Her release. Her scales whispered across his skin, Her body slick with spiritual blood. She moved away from him, leaving the throb of his injuries, the chill of his nakedness.

He could hear Her, a sound all meaty and wet, but he did not want to see. It went on and on, Her fevered presence circling, waves of terror emanating from the bodies in the room. They were there, the others – on some level he knew that – but when he opened his eyes, the space was empty, bone white and blood stained, a forsaken place where they had left him to die.

Only then did he see what had become of Kshidol – The Father –

the winged one. His belly had been full to bursting with the flesh of the dead. So heavy was He that He could not fly. So sated was He that He fell drowsy and slept. His eyes were glossed with Alma, skyward in ecstasy, even as She gorged herself, ravaging the swell of His belly.

Her eyes fixed on Reyan, sensing the rousing of his consciousness. She tasted the air, yearning for the oil at his wrist, the sweet smoke in his hair, and his flesh that was suffused with it where it had got in through his mouth and nose. The Alma. She neared, and nobody came to help him. She slid through his spirit like a knife–

Sybilla gasped for air.

Her body was drenched in sweat and the sheets stuck to her skin.

The vision had come again. She stared at her hand as if it were on fire, a prickling sensation running up and down her arm.

Sybilla considered lighting a candle but did not want anyone to know she was awake. The sick feeling lingered, drawing menace into the darkened rooms of the Skalens' House. Unable to withstand the intensity of her own imaginings, she slid out of bed and crept across the flagstones to find her sister. In the hallway, one of the night lamps spluttered, a mouse darted, but all else was still.

She opened her sister's door. "Lucinda," she whispered.

Nothing.

"Lucinda," she said, louder this time.

The mound of sheets groaned as she tiptoed into the room.

"Sybilla? What are you doing?" Lucinda mumbled.

"Can I sleep here till morning?" Sybilla perched herself on the edge of the bed.

Lucinda sat up, glaring in the grey light.

"I just..." Sybilla could not find the words.

"You had a dream."

Sybilla nodded.

"Why don't you just put on your Meridian and sleep in your own bed?" she said, pulling the covers around her.

Sybilla hugged her knees, emptiness shivering at her back.

Lucinda sighed. "It's alright. Take mine." She reached beneath her pillow and offered the Meridian.

Sybilla traced the leather straps, determining which way it should

7

go. She positioned the blinding stone at the three points – forehead, crown, and nape – then tightened the band. The stones exuded their cool serenity, their obliterating numbness spreading out to encompass her.

"Thank you," Sybilla said and lay down beside her.

"Don't be like that, you can come under the covers," Lucinda said, turning on her side to face her.

Sybilla shuffled in, staring at the ceiling. "Did you go to town today? I could hear the drummers practising from here. I don't know why they start so early, Festival is more than a month away."

Lucinda exhaled sharply. "Do not wake me in the middle of the night to talk of trivial things. What is going on? This is the second time this week. You are too old to fear your dreams."

Sybilla remained silent. She'd bothered her sister too many times with this, but she preferred Lucinda's lectures to a night alone in her chambers.

"Siatka and Kshidol are symbols, not gods, Sybilla. You have to trust in this. The creatures that come to feed at the altar do so because they are hungry. They hold no power over the living or the dead."

Sybilla looked at her sister. In the soft light, she could just make out the curve of her cheek, the gleam of her eyes. She wanted Lucinda to understand. "Are you telling me that you feel nothing at Blood Call?"

Lucinda sighed. "I don't like to be near them, but that is because they are dirty animals. If they were anything more, then Mother would have told me."

She must have felt the sting of her own words, the favouritism they implied, because when Lucinda spoke again it was in a more careful tone. "I'm sorry, Sybilla. I know it is hard, but they are only distant with you because you feel things so deeply. They don't want you to worry. Mother is preparing me and I want to tell you everything, but I must also keep her confidence. Just know that things are going well. Father is making progress."

Sybilla shifted away from the pressing warmth of her sister's arm.

"You know what scares me?" Lucinda gave her a half-smile. "That horrible guard from Maglore. His face would give anyone nightmares."

Sybilla let out a snort of laughter.

"See? Things are not so bad. We are safe here," her sister said. "Now try to get some sleep."

Sybilla turned to face the wall. As the smile faded from her lips, a familiar disappointment settled around her. Lucinda seemed to live in a different world. The one person Sybilla could have confided in about her dreams was her grandfather, and he was gone. She remembered how he had looked up at the Intercessor at his bedside when he was days from death. How the flick of his hand told Sybilla to conceal her thoughts, and quickly.

The Intercessors had their tendrils everywhere, and her grandfather did all he could to arm her against them. Ever since she was a child, he had set aside his duties in the Skalens' Guard to train with her. Most afternoons, Sybilla and her sister would go down to the barracks to see him, and there he would be, staring into the middle distance, waiting for their silence. He'd present a cup or a leaf or a stone, and ask them to fill their minds with it, to become nothing but the thing they saw. They'd practise with sounds, with feelings, with nothing itself. Then they would test one another. *What am I thinking of now?* To Lucinda it was a game, and she enjoyed it even though she rarely won.

For Sybilla, the silence preceded a yearning to spill out of herself, to be taken by the flood of images and sounds that shook from silver threads. This was not Hiatus, her grandfather told her, but the first stage of Intercession, and his look told her that she should not pursue that path. He wanted his granddaughters to learn Hiatus, the Guard's principle – the remedy he had taught his son – to make them impervious to harm. For if the spirit was silent, it could not be heard. If it was protected, as if by a shell, it could not be breached. And that was his gift to them.

The day he died, his body was washed and wrapped in white cloth. The Intercessor held her hand above her grandfather's forehead and closed her eyes, listening for the call. Numbly, Sybilla watched the woman's eyelids flicker and the reddening of her hands.

Mother Siatka hears his call, she said, and so it was decided that her grandfather would be buried at sea, to be reborn as a girl-child.

The next day, Sybilla and her family arrived at the Gulf, making their way to the front of the crowd. The Intercessors had cleaved his body into seven pieces, wrapping each in fine muslin, anointed with oil of Alma. They had built a raft for him, chanting softly as they sent him out upon the waves. The shore was thick with mourners and Sybilla was thinking of the tumour at his throat, wondering whether the Intercessors had cast it out, or whether they had wrapped it up with the rest of him.

The first of the siatka rose from the waves, tipping the raft. She saw one of the white-wrapped parcels lodge in wide jaws before it disappeared beneath. Her father gripped her arm. A sickly pulse went through her and she glanced up. She looked into her father's eyes, and that was when it happened. The vision coursed through her, every part of it – from him to her – in a surge of anguish. It could not be undone. And when they roused Sybilla from her faint, her father looked upon her in shame.

The vision lay between them like a burning chasm, the horror of what had been done to him, and he would never let her in again.

3

SYBILLA

Six Years Before The Fire

SYBILLA SHIFTED IN HER CHAIR. All day she had been troubled by feelings of unaccountable dread, but when she saw her father, she knew he felt it too. Something had happened – was happening, would happen – and its darkness would run all the way to their door. She tried to catch Lucinda's eye, but her sister chose that moment to pour the wine. A sweet, sharp tang filled the room, but no one reached for their glass. At the head of the table, Sybilla felt the charge of her father's silence, and the rushing torrent beneath.

Her mother's thorn-bitten hands fussed over an arrangement of crimson roses at the centre of the table. They were the first of the season – impressive in number – and arranged lengthways in a glass vessel that showed the cleanness of their stems. With petals pursed, the newly opened buds sat atop one another, fringed by dark leaves. One was too long and had to be pushed down, another unfairly shaded by foliage. A wet smear needed to be polished from the vase. And all the while the Attendants waited, the evening meal growing cold as they stood with their silver trays along the far wall.

Finally satisfied, her mother sat, smiling briefly at her daughters. Her father signalled the Attendants, and the white-capped procession advanced. Dinner was roast fowl, pale carrots, nubby potatoes, and turnip. The Attendants ladled gravy into their trenchers. Lucinda took a single spoonful, her mother slightly more, but her father did not notice till his meat was drowned.

With a clatter of plates, the Attendants filed out, closing the door behind them.

Finally, they were alone.

Her father rubbed his face, groaning slightly, but his frown did not shift.

Sybilla drank deeply of her wine, willing the muscles in her jaw to relax.

"The roses are beautiful, Vivienne," her father said, lifting the fork to his mouth.

"They are indeed," her mother said, smiling.

Sybilla could hardly bear their conversation. She could feel the half-formed words, the restlessness of her father's thoughts as he maintained his inner focus, his barrier against her. But her mother's arrogant displays of normalcy were especially tiresome. The way she fawned over her flowers, wasting her mornings in the garden as if the future of Vaelnyr did not hang in the balance.

Her parents were in talks with the Greslets of Maglore, that much was obvious, but every ally her father brought over to their cause widened the web of trust, leaving them vulnerable. The Intercessors' psychic tyranny was subtly woven, impossible to trace, and every move her father made to prepare a force against them laid a greater weight of culpability on her family. When he disappeared for days, forging allegiances, whispering with her mother in the dark, he drew their enemies closer. Soon they would notice, soon he would make a mistake.

Sybilla's gaze was drawn by the movement of Lucinda's hand smoothing a lock of blonde hair behind her ear, and she could tell her sister was thinking about Bryden. It showed in the quirk of her mouth, the dimple forming on her cheek. She just carried on as if life would be a fine adventure. Did their father not see that Lucinda was unfit to rule? That she was pliant and easily led astray by dark-haired men? That Sybilla was the only one who could see the devils among them that hid in human skin?

She tried to think of the right words to say, each unspoken impulse leaving her throat a little tighter. She needed to know what her father was doing.

Sybilla swallowed the piece of carrot she had been chewing. "I saw guardsmen from Maglore in the training yard today."

Her father raised his eyebrows. "We welcome guardsmen from all the Seven Lands."

Sybilla reached for her glass. "Will he be sharing a banquet with us at the Skalens' table?"

"He has dined with us already," her father said, the firm set of his shoulders reminding her of a stone wall.

Her mother gave her a pinched smile. "Guardsman Rayhmer has just been appointed Head Guard of Maglore. This is his first tour of Velspar and he brought a small contingent with him, but he is not a cultured man. Not much of a conversationalist."

Sybilla exhaled slowly, cutting the gristle from her meat.

Her mother moved forward in her chair so the lower half of her face disappeared behind an effusion of flowers. With eyes downcast, her mother's cheeks flinched with the action of chewing. Her father scooped his gravy to one side, scraping a skinless section of breast against the lip of his trencher.

Sybilla nudged her food about, separating the turnip from the potatoes, the carrot from the meat, the meat from the fat, until she had five equally unappetising portions.

There was a knock at the door.

Her father turned in his chair at the sound of the bolt and Peran appeared in the doorway. The Head Guard of Vaelnyr strode toward her father and whispered in his ear. The colour seemed to leech from her father's face.

"Yes, I agree, it would be best," he said, "make all the necessary arrangements." He looked at her mother first, and then at his daughters. "Skalen Jagoda Hirvola is dead."

Her mother's face went still, calculating.

For the first time since their meal began, Lucinda broke from her daydream. "How? Was she murdered?"

"She died of pneumatic flu, and yet her husband and sons were not afflicted," their father said, pushing out his chair.

Her mother's eyes sought his and her father's gaze darkened in reply.

"Peran tells me the Intercessors have decided on sea burial," he said.

His chest rose and fell, a tense exhilaration building in him. He glanced at Sybilla pointedly and with a jolt of shame, she withdrew her mind from his. She stared at the roses, willing their colour to fill her, along with the shape of their repose. To immerse herself in Hiatus to give them the privacy they sought, but her heart was pounding too hard for her to concentrate. Under the table, she reached for Lucinda's hand. A childish habit but one that worked when nothing else would. She concentrated on the softness of her sister's hand, the fine bones of her fingers, the place inside her that was unharried and free.

"When will the burial take place?" her mother asked.

"Peran did not say, but we should leave tonight. Best that we offer our condolences before the other Skalens arrive. The situation is far too sensitive."

Lucinda shook Sybilla off, and stared at their father with incredulity. "Can they not wait until morning? What are we to do with Guardsman Rayhmer?"

Her mother stepped in. "Skalen Cerek is grieving, as are his sons. We would not want the wrong words to be spoken into susceptible ears."

Lucinda pressed her lips together in frustration. "Can you not wait until the Skalens' Council is called?"

Sybilla knew Lucinda would only bite back with such keen irritation if her parents' absence affected her plans with Bryden. The absurdity of her sister's perspective might have amused her if she did not feel as if the world around her was falling apart.

Her mother held her hands together and stared intently at the floor waiting for Lucinda to regain her composure. "We must go because it is our duty," she said quietly. "Your duty, Lucinda, is to remain here in our stead."

Lucinda met her mother's gaze before offering a conciliatory nod.

Her mother's eyes flicked back and forth between her daughters. "While we are away, you are to remain here, in the Skalens' House. If anything happens, Peran will know what to do. He will be keeping watch, and will convey our apologies to our guests."

Her mother cradled Lucinda's head in her hands, pressing their foreheads together.

"Goodbye, Mother," Lucinda said, softening at last. "Velspar's blessings upon you."

"Velspar's blessings," her mother whispered.

As they embraced, Sybilla watched her father, his shoulders hunched as he paced, the name *Karasek* teeming about him like a plague of ants.

"Farewell, Sybilla," her mother said, her face oddly expressionless, her thoughts already on the journey ahead.

They touched foreheads, and her father approached to say his goodbye.

Sybilla looked up at him as he bent down, not wanting him to go. When their foreheads touched, she felt the firmness of bone, smelt the homeliness of his hair, but his movements were absent of feeling.

Tears rose in her throat, and as the door closed behind them, she felt the distance between them widen.

Sybilla looked at her sister with reddening eyes. "I hate this."

Lucinda shrugged in sulking resignation. "It will be a month, nothing more."

4

SYBILLA

Six Years Before The Fire

SYBILLA PEERED DOWN at the figures in the training yard, comb gripped tight in her hand, concealing herself behind the thick velvet drapes. As the guards went through their drills, Peran and her father walked, locked in focused conversation, her father shielding his eyes from the sun. Peran spoke with a placatory tilt of the head, his gestures imploring, or apologetic – she could not tell. Her father paced, his hands on his hips. The two looked at one another and nodded, some decision being made, then walked out of sight.

In watching them, Sybilla had stopped brushing her hair. She daubed oil on her fingers, smearing it along the teeth of the comb, setting to work on a stubborn knot that had been bothering her all week. She didn't like the Attendants touching her, but her mother would send Anlyn with a comb and shears if Sybilla made a habit of leaving the Skalens' House unkempt.

Finally, the knot gave way, and she relished the smooth path the comb made through the dark waves of her hair. Parting it neatly down the middle, she swept the length of it down her back. She wore black britches and a belted maroon tunic adorned with Alma blossoms of appliqué silk, an ensemble respectable enough for a Skalens' daughter, but plain enough to allow her to melt into a crowd.

Sybilla was to meet Lucinda at the front of the Skalens' House at midday to accompany her on an errand in town. She strolled the empty hallway with time to spare, the sweet aroma of Alma incense wafting past, but soon she heard voices, and the creak of the council room door. The Intercessors must have just finished their audience with her mother. Sybilla froze, listening as their footsteps grew faint, the Intercessors descending the stairs, her mother crossing the entry hall on her way to the East Wing.

In the silence that followed, Sybilla's heart thumped and she stared at the hall's end, breathing the fragrant draught as she continued onward once more. She turned the corner, finding the council room door ajar, casting a splinter of light upon the flagstones. A gentle push, a quick glance behind her, and she went inside. Honeyed light filled the room, streaming in through diamond-shaped windows, illuminating the bluish smoke that still hovered in the air. It was as she'd suspected – on the copper dish at the centre of the Skalens' Table, the Alma still burned. Her arms grew heavy as she breathed, but she fought the feeling, reaching for the bell cover that should have been used to extinguish the spark.

Nothing else was amiss. The Skalens' Table and its fourteen chairs were perfectly aligned at the centre of the room, the floor swept clean. Still, her eyes skimmed every surface, as if she might discover some necrotic stain, some foul residue the Intercessors had left behind. Chewing her lip, she considered opening the window but thought the better of it. Her mother would be furious if she knew Sybilla had been in there.

Sealing the room behind her, she went down to wait for Lucinda.

The carriage was ready and the horses stood at attention, but she would have much preferred to ride in the saddle, she and her sister side by side. Sybilla lifted her hand to the gelding's black muzzle, his breath warm on her skin as he watched her with deep brown eyes. His chestnut companion had a stiffer temperament, and she moved her hand along his coat in firm strokes.

A moment later, her sister appeared dressed modestly in grey, her loosely braided hair shining like cornsilk. Seeing her, the coachman advanced.

"Ready?" Lucinda called.

"And waiting," Sybilla replied.

Lucinda laughed, hitching her skirt as she climbed into the carriage.

Sybilla jumped in beside her.

When her sister did nothing but stare out the window, Sybilla gave up any hope of conversation. She could sense the nervous thrum of Lucinda's pulse, her floral perfume heavy in the air. Sybilla folded her arms, pressing her thumb to each finger, working her way back and forth, just to pass the time.

As they moved into town, the streets branched into laneways, the grey stone terraces standing wall to wall, their lower floors caught in perpetual shade. The Krigers' shop had a red door, and when it came into view, Lucinda pressed her eyelashes with her fingers so they feathered brightly about her amber eyes.

A faint breeze was blowing and the door sign squeaked on its salt-rusted hinge.

Sybilla followed her sister, and the coachman departed, promising to return in an hour.

Mrs Kriger was poised for their arrival and smiled broadly as they entered. "Miss Ladain!" she said, only once, as if Sybilla were not there. "I have your order just here." Mrs Kriger presented a small item wrapped in silk, peeling back the folds for Lucinda's inspection.

Sybilla looked about the room, ostensibly admiring a set of framed scrolls on the far wall that recounted the Visions of Skalen Karasek. She wandered back to the counter as Lucinda drew out the fine silver chain, laying its gleaming pendant on her palm. A Vaelnyri woman had recently given birth to twin baby girls, their birth date coinciding with Lucinda's own. The pendant was for the mother, who'd received Siatka's blessing, twofold, and whose daughters would forever have the honour of taking pilgrimage with the future-Skalen of Vaelnyr, now that they were Birth-Kin. The front of the pendant featured two rubies nestled between the paired mouths of Siatka and Kshidol. On the back, their birth date was inscribed.

"It is perfect. Thank you, Mrs Kriger."

Sybilla noticed Bryden waiting in the back room. With a reflexive smile, he moved out of sight. A moment later, he reappeared with a tray of biscuits, glazed fruits and a pot of spiced tea. His hands looked awkwardly large as he set out the shining teacups, pressing a finger to the lid of the pot as he poured. He placed a Kshidol-shaped biscuit on the side of Lucinda's saucer, but Sybilla held up her hand, taking the tea on its own.

Bryden disappeared out the back and his mother proceeded to show the sisters about the shop. Lucinda dipped her biscuit into the tea, and sipped, complimenting Mrs Kriger's fine taste, speaking of the mother and her infants and what a glory it would be when they were old enough to join her at Blood Call.

Bidding Mrs Kriger good day, the sisters walked two blocks before Lucinda squeezed her hand and departed down a side street, covering her hair with a grey kerchief.

Sybilla took a great breath of air and exhaled, making her way to the main street. She did not want to imagine what they were doing. Crammed in an alleyway somewhere, tugging at each other's clothes, Bryden's hot breath on her sister's neck. No.

As she rounded the corner, she heard voices in their steady murmur, the caw of sea-birds, the splash and draw of the sea. People passed her, going about their business, paying her no mind. A cart squeaked along with its jostling cargo, and she could smell the acrid tang of potatoes brown with earth. She did not know why her sister took such risks. One night, in the dark, when Sybilla could not sleep, Lucinda had told her that she wanted to make a few choices of her own before a political marriage was forced upon her. That was all very well, Sybilla had said, but what if he got her with child? Her sister had laughed at that. *Don't let your Temple lessons scare you, Sybilla, or you'll miss out on all the fun.*

But her Temple lessons did scare her. The sharing of spirit, through touch or by other means, brought the Holy Ones close. When a child entered a woman, the spirit was put there by those same entities that consumed the dead. Lucinda dabbled with forces she did not understand – that is what instinct told Sybilla. But perhaps her sister was right. The siatka and kshidol were animals, their etheric bodies nothing more than an Intercessor's trick.

Sybilla wandered past street vendors with their trays of cooked clams and merchants of all stripes selling Seltslandi water chestnuts, Maglorean spiced sausage and preserved roots from the forests of Brivia. She drank it all in, the sun warm on her face. As long as none of them spoke to her, she could enjoy this.

She passed a sweet shop where she used to buy candied aniseed for her grandfather. The door opened and the heady scent of peppermint and cinnamon brought her back to a simpler time, but she did not go inside. The Bindery next door was still closed, she saw. There against the glass sat a lopsided sign, 'Apprentice Wanted', written in Mr Watson's confident hand. The Intercessors had taken him a while back. Sybilla liked the man and had looked up his name in the execution tally, knowing what she would find. *Red thoughts, unrepentant*, it read. If only they knew the contents of her own mind.

By the dock, a man plucked out a tune on the lyre, and people from the tavern gathered to hear him play. A group of them peeled away from the crowd, stumbling as they sang.

Moving to avoid their path, she almost bumped into an old man who'd crouched to take his turn in a children's game of knuckles.

Sybilla slowed, pretending to examine lengths of cloth laid out in baskets beneath a billowing awning. The man wore a threadbare shirt and a faded leather cap. The children stared at him apprehensively as he took the knuckles in his fist and put them to his mouth. A moment later, he coughed, pretending to spit the knuckles on the ground. "Gah! Me teeth! Quick, help me put them back in!"

The children laughed, their faces full of glee.

"Again!" the youngest boy cried after he'd repeated the trick three or four times.

The old man got up with some difficulty. "Oh no, no, I need to keep a few. I won't be able to eat my supper."

Sybilla smirked, the man ambled on, and the children returned to their game.

Without the man there to make them laugh, the children seemed suddenly remote.

At Festival, the little ones tugged at Lucinda's skirts, wanting to dance with her, or steal a flower from her hair, but Sybilla, they left alone. Sensing the darkness in her, or the fear.

She stopped, having reached the end of the harbour, and sat on a low stone wall. From this vantage, the Temple loomed, dizzyingly white, making the clamour of the street below seem small and insignificant. For a while she stared out to sea, watching the bright waves whisper toward shore. The chiming of the Temple bells brought Sybilla back to herself. The pilgrims must have reached the Sky Altar, and in the distance she saw the kshidol circling like black sickles in the sky.

Here and there, families were arriving, claiming a spot close to the Long Pier so they could greet their loved ones when they came down from the mountain. A group of Intercessors joined the throng, emerging from the dormitory gate. It must have been the fine weather that drew them out; they did not normally come so early in the afternoon.

Sybilla started back, quickly, and with her head down. She sidled past a group of sweaty fishermen only to get stuck behind two men arguing over a mess of smashed glass and mustard seeds.

"Excuse me," she said, stepping around them.

There was a back route she could take, and once she found an opening in the crowd, she slipped down a side-street, sighing with relief. She needed to calm herself. If she was calm, they would not notice her.

Sybilla kept the rhythm of her breath. Thought of the old man spitting knuckles, the burst of laughter that made her smile. She renewed the thought over and over. It worked, at first, but then it didn't. It was not strong enough. Sybilla exhaled, held her breath a moment, and brought to mind her grandfather's face, his weathered hand holding a haloed dandelion. She inhaled, and with her breath's release, the dandelion seeds took flight, dissembling her thoughts... on the wind she was, unknowable, untraceable – nobody at all.

"Sybilla?"

A hand on her arm.

Blankly, she followed the white of his sleeve to a face that she recognised.

His smile was warm, his blue eyes bright.

"It is nice to see you here," he said, when she did not respond.

He removed his hand, his expression hesitant now.

"Intercessor Caleb," she said breathlessly. "I didn't see you, I was walking so fast, I am late to meet my sister." Sybilla looked down, noticing his robes were still grubby at the hem from walking with the farmers at dawn.

"I will see you at the Temple then," he said.

"Yes, of course. Velspar's blessings, Intercessor."

He held her gaze a moment longer. "Velspar's blessings."

The smile slipped from her face the moment she turned her back. She sensed that he still watched her as she walked, his curiosity casting hooks, but she would not be caught.

When she emerged from her detour, Lucinda was talking with the coachman.

"Dammit," Sybilla cursed.

The coachman saw her first, and looked her over with a mild expression.

Lucinda clapped her hands together. "Sybilla, there you are! Did you find the bracelet that I dropped?"

Sybilla held up her hands, shaking her head.

"Never mind," Lucinda sighed, her face flushed with the lie.

On their way home, Sybilla began to feel the creeping sensations of regret. It was not like her to lose track of time.

Lucinda's back was very straight, her jaw stiff with fury. "If you ruin this for me, Sybilla, I will never forgive you."

The silence stretched, and then it was too late to reply.

When they reached the Skalens' House, her mother was waiting at the entrance and she waved, smiling. Sybilla got little more than a nod before she took Lucinda on her arm, eager to see the pendant for herself.

Sybilla wiped her damp palms on her britches and stood there a moment, not wanting to follow too close.

As the coach drew away, she noticed someone standing in the

doorway of the Guard's barracks. Peran had watched them arrive and was watching her still. There was no place for secrets, no deceit that would not be discovered in time.

Lucinda was not free, but if she believed it was so, then Sybilla would not take that from her sister.

5

SYBILLA

Five Years Before The Fire

THE ATTENDANTS STOOD in line to wave them off. In her lap, Sybilla held a basket of oranges that Anlyn had packed for the journey. The Ladains would be gone three days, hunting at Lake Nanthe. The Guard gave escort and Sybilla busied herself peeling an orange, the skin's sharp spray filling the carriage. Pasture extended in its endless monotony, but when Sybilla turned to point out a field of bright flowers, she saw Lucinda's chin had fallen to her chest. For a while, Sybilla ate her orange in silence, collecting the seeds in her hand before tossing them out the window. An hour or so later when Lucinda woke, the sisters looked nervously at one another but did not speak, keeping their eyes on the horizon and the thickening treeline.

When Lake Nanthe came into view, the sun was low and there was a chill in the air. Sybilla stared out the window for passing farmers or people from the Lake town, but there was no one in sight. She tapped Lucinda's knee, and they put their Meridians on, concealing the band beneath dusty-brown kerchiefs. In the clearing, Peran and his men made camp, starting with the Skalens' tent. Sybilla and her sister waited in the carriage until they were done.

Once the fires were lit, the Ladains went quietly to their horses, for their true destination was a cave high in the Mountains of Jokvour. On horseback, her father led the way with her mother at his waist, and Sybilla behind with her sister. Peran assured them the people of Maglore did not travel the mountain paths often, and never by night. Still, they disguised themselves in shabby cloaks. As darkness fell, Sybilla could almost hear her father rehearsing the words in his mind. Her mother's body obscured sight of him, but Sybilla watched for a glimpse of his face within the hood, his eyes like shining coins.

The mountain path wound upward, and finally her father pulled on the reins. Sybilla could not see how this cave differed from any other. Once inside, her mother set Sybilla the task of preparing the fire while Lucinda swept out the entrance with a thatch of dry leaves. The cold wilderness took on a purposeful air as the fire settled into a steady glow, illuminating Lucinda's fine brushwork and the circle of stones their father had gathered as seats.

Her father called it a meeting of Council, and he was correct in calling it such, for any meeting of Skalens was a meeting of Council, but her father did not wish to speak with the Hirvola or the Karaseks, the Askier or the Elshenders. This Council drew allegiance from Vaelnyr's neighbouring lands. The Braedals of Nothelm in the north, and the Greslets of Maglore in the south. To the others, the truth would be given more gently, the temperature slowly changing so that when the time came, they would recognise the kinship of Skalens, and the Intercessors' treachery.

Sybilla looked out into the night. The wind came in waves, but through the rush she heard the thin whinny of a horse. She tensed. Her father called out in greeting. Sybilla edged closer to her mother at the sight of the lone horseman. It was Domhnall Greslet of Maglore. He was not yet a Skalen but would be soon enough. The man's black eyes appraised her father from a height. In the midst of his black beard was a soft mouth, his skin youthful and unblemished. Descending his mount, Domhnall secured the reins and moved stiffly after her father.

Her mother emerged in the firelight holding clay cups of water, her eyes glassy with sleeplessness, her hair lit up like the setting sun. Domhnall's attention was on her father, and he barely glanced at the women, but soon realised his mistake and bowed deeply to Skalen Vivienne and her fine daughters. Important business rolled from his tongue, and her father received it with knitted brows, giving the Maglorean heir deference, for he needed much from him in return.

Moments later, her father turned from Domhnall to the entrance where Skalens Damek and Lenna Braedal of Nothelm stood unsmiling, shaking off their riding furs. Lenna's reddish hair was braided high and tight, accentuating both her graceful brow and angular jaw. She was a full head shorter than Damek, whose broad shoulders and wolfish beard gave him a predatory appearance. Lucinda took their garments on her arm, laying them on a stone ledge in the shadows.

"Skalens, it is good to see your faces after a long journey," Damek said, looking at her mother and father as he removed his gloves.

Domhnall's face soured as he waited for the introduction that never came.

"Skalen Vivienne," Lenna inclined her head and her mother returned the gesture.

Damek looked at Sybilla, who stood in the corner with her hands behind her back, and then pointedly at Domhnall. "I did not know this was a matter for living heirs. We would have brought our Voirrey."

"Skalen Nevis is gravely ill and would not have survived the journey to Jokvour. Domhnall will be Skalen of Maglore soon enough. My daughters accompany us as a precaution," her father said.

At her mother's signal, Lucinda took Sybilla by the arm, and led her outside. The wind blew wildly, making the horses restless. Sybilla sat close to her sister, huddling for warmth, the two of them listening, just out of sight.

"Let us begin our Council," her father said.

Inside, they were silent for a time, the sweet Alma smoke wafting from the mouth of the cave soothing Sybilla's nerves. Time stretched, so that she noticed only rhythms for a while – Lucinda's breath, wind rushing over stone, the throb of her toes as she squeezed them and let go.

Then came her father's voice. "We bear the title of Skalen as a demonstration of our clan's faith in the visions of Skalen Karasek, the First Diviner. Skalen Karasek revealed the name of spirit, and in Velspar we discovered the common thread that enjoins the living with the dead and the unborn. The thread that enjoins the Seven Lands in eternal friendship.

"But Skalen Karasek's vision said nothing of Intercessors. He did not command that we set people apart and clothe them in white. He did not say their visions should be the arbiter of truth. He did not ask us to build Temples or to give blood sacrifice on the anniversary of our birth. He did not decree that people be condemned for their red thoughts before they have committed any crime. He did not name a priesthood impervious to the Skalens' judgement, who should rule the people by stealth, encouraging the view that Skalens are best suited to the measure of earthly things – to matters of administration – and they the measure of spirit."

Sybilla glanced at Lucinda, who stared back, wide-eyed. It was one thing to know their father despised the Intercessors, but quite another to hear him pontificate in the presence of others.

"The Intercessors speak often of heresy," he went on. "In the execution lists it is by far the most prevalent crime. My reflections on this matter have led me to but one conclusion. I say that Skalen Karasek had one vision and one vision only. It was of Velspar – of seven clans united as one. That vision was true. But who was it that claimed the divinity of Siatka – a sea serpent, no less – and Kshidol, a foul-smelling carrion bird? These are not the words of Skalen Karasek. This is the corrupt vision of some other – some vile whisperer – perhaps the first Intercessor. It may have been his brother, a servant, a trusted advisor. Their name may never be known to us, but we know the import of that vision, we know what it has done to our people. It is our sacred duty as Skalens to remove the leech from the heart of Velspar. To pull out the weed that has grown up beside us, intertwining itself so that it would not be seen. We must put an end to the First Heresy."

Sybilla's heart thumped in her ears. She could hardly stand the silence that followed and pressed her fingernails hard into the flesh of her palm. Her father spoke of heresy, but by the laws of Velspar, he would be the one cast as a heretic. How could the Braedals be trusted with this? How could Domhnall Greslet? A son who would leave his dying father's side to collude with strangers. Or were they in on it together? Had they drawn the Ladains of Vaelnyr to this desolate place to end them?

Lenna coughed and spoke in a high, thin voice. "That was a rousing speech, Reyan, but I must confirm something before we commit the weight of the Nothelm Guard. You have come to this through *reflection*, yes? We have not come this far to name you the 'Second Diviner'."

"I understand that it discomforts you to know that I entered training at the Temple when I was a boy, but I assure you it was nothing more than my mother's fervour that sent me there. I have never been partial to vision. Yet, being among the Intercessors opened my eyes to the extent of their corruption, and for that insight I must thank her."

"In all seriousness, Reyan," Damek said, "the Skalens of Nothelm have awaited this day. We abide the Intercessors and their rites but it is high time our society progressed and left these primitive customs behind. You well know that I believe the lands of Velspar extend beyond the continent. The Nothelm Guard have sailed beyond the places where the siatka swarm, and there is free ocean out there. There is no telling what we will discover once they have been eradicated. And the first step toward this is the removal of the Intercessors. I do not believe the people will mourn their blood rites when they have the hope of new horizons."

At those words, Sybilla felt relief's softening glow. They would be allies. She closed her eyes and pressed her head into her hands.

"I can see you are hungry for this, Damek," her mother said carefully, "but we should not begin until we have the weight of numbers."

"Do not condescend to me, Vivienne." And by Damek's tone, Sybilla could imagine his sneer. "You speak indirectly, but I will lay your message out for the one to whom it is intended. Domhnall: we must not seek to prove ourselves too early, your lands share a border with the Karaseks, so your task is to remain faithful to our cause, to keep quiet and to stand aside when the Karaseks put their noses to the wind. They will think you young and easily manipulated, and that is best, for they will count the Southlands as entirely within their control."

Domhnall was quick to reply. "But what of the Elshenders? It makes strategic sense to establish a new trade route from Maglore. If the Greslets can keep the islanders in supply of food, they will not be so reliant on Port Innes."

Damek scoffed. "It may look well on a map, boy, but the Karaseks will see your ambition and will have you surrounded. Do not think this alliance is forged to provide backing for another Greslet conquest."

A tense moment followed. It was a horror from the history books that the original clansmen of Maglore had taken to consuming their own dead, believing they could absorb the spirit by mouth, thereby fortifying their bloodlines with the power of Velspar. The Greslets and their people's army had ended all that, rising from obscurity to the holy station of Skalen. Domhnall's imminent reign would herald the fourth generation of Greslet Skalens, but still, the Braedals did not seem inclined to welcome him on equal footing with the ancestral clans.

"Damek, please," her father said, his voice barely audible.

Damek's low chuckle echoed from the cave mouth. "I am just testing him, Reyan. Seeing if I can get his temper up, seeing what the Intercessors can get out of him. I'm impressed."

Her father responded in a measured tone, turning their talk to other things. "Now that you are satisfied, can you advise of your brother's progress–"

Just then, a strong gust of wind came, making it impossible to hear, and when it died down, they had moved on to the closing prayer.

Sybilla and her sister jumped to their feet, brushing the dirt from their clothes and moving to the horses. From the corner of her eye, Sybilla watched the assembly as they pressed foreheads, giving their oaths. The Braedals departed first, leaving her father to pat Domhnall on the back, whispering some final confidence to see him home.

When her parents came near, they smiled. Despite the Braedals abrasive manner, all had gone as they had wished and they were happy. Sybilla burned with questions she could not ask. Behind her Meridian, a storm of words tumbled and swirled, places and names and the myriad ways in which their fates could proceed. Her father could not have perceived this, but perhaps it showed on her face for he reached into his pocket and set his own Meridian in place. Only then did he put his hand on her shoulder, giving her a reassuring squeeze.

The way back down the mountain was treacherous, and moonlight shone fitfully upon the path. Her parents were seasoned riders and took one daughter each, Lucinda at her mother's waist, and Sybilla at her father's. She felt his focus entirely on the task at hand, on wrangling the reins, so the horse did not try to forge its own way down. And so, Sybilla's thoughts returned to the cave, considering what had changed. They had Domhnall Greslet now and the future promise of their southern neighbour, Maglore. They had Nothelm to the north. But more than that, her father's vision for the future of Velspar had a name. The First Heresy. He spoke it like an accusation, but she knew – more than anyone – what that accusation meant.

6

SYBILLA

Three Years Before The Fire

SYBILLA HUMMED, LOW AND DEEP, in breath's slow rhythm. She kept her eyes downcast and moved nearer to the others to hide her fear among their faithfulness. Each time her note ended, she gasped, sucking grey air that was sweet with smoke. Each inhalation softened her, welcoming her let go, to join them: her Birth-Kin.

The Intercessors swayed, the chains of their censers clinking as they ascended. Sybilla followed them, this year as every other, up the spiralled stair that wound the inner dome. She passed the fifth floor of the Temple without incident, as she had mastered that particular spur, but each time she found Hiatus, some flash of the Council meeting at Jokvour would return to her, and she scrambled to conceal it. If she did not, she wouldn't live to walk this stair again. Her name would join a different procession: *Sybilla Ladain – heretic.*

The echo of their footfall, the breath and the humming swirled around her. All about her, she saw her Birth-Kin, old and young, fair and afflicted, how they gazed at one another, their faces gentle with comfort. Sybilla ached to join them in the growing ecstasy of their breath as they moved higher, above the town. Within the humming she eventually found her cold place, the point of unthought, cleaving to it as they reached the top of the seventh stair.

They stood in the Temple's holiest part, and all went quiet. The Intercessors came, one at a time, and Sybilla's hand trembled at the thought of the dagger. Intercessor Maeryn came toward her. Without wanting to, Sybilla met her eyes. Maeryn's pupils were black with Alma; they seemed to suck Sybilla down, like a rock into a chasm.

The Intercessor's warm hands held hers. "Speak your prayer, Sybilla."

She sweated hot and cold, unable to keep herself from the Intercessor's mesmerism. Sybilla's face fell heavy and the words spilled out of her, ringing in her ears as all the others recited theirs, starting moments before and after one another, blurring and overlapping in the hiss and clack of words that held magic but no meaning.

Siatka of sea
Kshidol of sky
Life bringers
Gatherers
Hear my Blood Call
At last breath
Guide me to Velspar
Return me to the Stream
Pure is the Stream
Clear and bright

With the cut, Sybilla flinched. Intercessor Maeryn pressed the cloth into her palm to soak the blood.

"Three drops for sky and three drops for sea, that is all they need, my dear," she said and smiled.

As the Intercessor took the cloth to the offering bowl, Sybilla glanced around at her Birth-Kin. Their faces were passive, hands dangling as droplets fell on the white floor. The Intercessors tore the white rags in two, mixing them in copper bowls with meat paste and Alma.

At the ringing of the bells, they descended, red drips smearing underfoot. They followed the bowl carrier and the Intercessors with their drums, on and on in an endless trudge, out of the Temple, toward the Atilan Mountains and the Sky Altar. The pilgrimage was long, and the sun rose high above them, making the skin of her forehead sting. She drew the veil from her satchel and wrapped it about her head. Though she wore soft woollen socks, her boots rubbed blisters on her heels. She walked steadily, ignoring her Birth-Kin. Sybilla did not want their words of encouragement, their cloying hands or sympathy. She was one of them, yes, but she was also a Skalens' daughter. They all knew Lucinda was destined to rule, but remained wary of Sybilla, the sullen, dark-haired sister who could whisper things to change the tally or to turn their fortune.

The pilgrim's trail was well-worn, and there were places where they rested along the way. A little boy smiled at Sybilla over his mother's shoulder, sticking his fingers up his nose. A lad behind her laughed and patted her back. His touch scalded her, but Sybilla gave him a look mirroring the one he gave, a look of solidarity, of fellow feeling. Sybilla found the strength to walk faster then. She could not stand the child's eyes on her. Passing a man she recognised from the tannery, and a pretty maid with freckled skin, she tried not to notice the scent of their flesh, the unique story their sweat made known to all who came near.

Then the wind swept up from the mountainside, bringing heat from sun-drenched stone, and the whisper of reddening leaves. Sybilla loosened the sash about her waist and breathed. In the sunlight, the blue silk of her robe was mottled with stains. Insufficiently scrubbed stains. Anlyn always made a fuss over her birthday, pressing Sybilla's robes between hot irons, steaming the outer silks, airing the garment, smoking it in myrrh. But her sentimentality made her reluctant to scrub the blood, to completely remove its memory. It was disgusting.

Up ahead, Sybilla glimpsed the Intercessors, their censers in pendulous swing. The wind brought a meaty waft from the offering bowl, laced with wisps of smoking Alma. Upon the rise, the Intercessors began to chant. They had reached the Sky Altar. Sybilla stood at the back, her feet tight and throbbing. There, they smoked down the kshidol. Four or five of the great birds hovered above, hanging lower on the air before they came to land on hulking claws. Even as she hated them, their presence paralysed her. Their plumage shone silvery black and their hook-knife beaks opened just a little at the scent of blood. The kshidols' eyes knew the Birth-Kin. Black breasted and ungainly in their movements, they walked like men, cloaked and ruffed. And then, stalking toward the bowl, the hunch-necked beasts began to eat. The Intercessors recited the Hymn to Kshidol, beating the drum.

Kshidol!
Swift feather
Traveller
Blood beaked
Kshidol!
Hear the call
Heralded by blood
Birth Call
Kshidol!
The flesh it wilts
Carry the spirit
Of our dead
Kshidol!
Bright wing
Deep eyed
Consumer of our dead
Kshidol!
Return to our kinfolk
Boys
Of bright flame

When the bowl was empty, the kshidol took wing and the procession walked by drum down the mountain. It was quicker on their return. Sybilla gazed at the vista of Vaelnyr, imagining it free of the Temple's white obscenity. Time at home in her father's presence had filled her mind with sharp fantasies. In the years following her grandfather's death she had felt prey to everything, but now she saw her father's mission as a glinting knife, and their allies the fist that would drive it home. She had dared to wish that this year she would not have to perform the Blood Call, but the months had rolled by, and still they were not ready. Things were delicate in Seltsland. The Askier could not be pushed. Cerek Hirvola was not in his right mind, and it was likely Lindesal would be ruled by his sons. The Karaseks... the Elshenders... the Braedals busy with their boats.

Sybilla willed herself to concentrate, to heed the danger of letting her thoughts wander onto dangerous ground. She focussed on the scene before her. A tessellation of grey roofs split by rivulet paths, running down to the Gulf, and on to the endless sea. As the pilgrim's trail passed the curve of the mountain, the Temple disappeared from sight, replaced by mottled trees that sheltered fonder memories. Swinging from branches. Diving into the cool stream. Shouting secret words to her sister beneath the surface. Listening through the echoes for her reply.

She kept her mind in that forest as the sun sank low, harnessed to the sound of her breath, the ache of her muscles, the sting of her blisters, and away from thoughts of what awaited her there. Nonetheless, with one foot after the other, she and her Birth-Kin made their way down, past the Temple, over cobblestones, past well-wishers with eager smiles, to the Long Pier at the Gulf.

At the end of the pier sat the Sea Altar. The wooden boards were strong. Blessed with smoke and infused with prayers. But there were cracks between them that showed the water below, and each gleaming gap threatened the sureness of her step. *They were nothing,* she told herself, *they could not harm her. They were nothing.*

Up ahead the Intercessors poured the Alma wine, and soon dark shapes gathered in the water beneath her feet. Black scales slithered to the surface, twinkling green with moss and plunging deep again, beyond sight. Dusk was falling and Sybilla shivered beneath the thinness of her robes. A jet of water shot up, leaving droplets on her skin. The siatka circled, undulating in their hidden tidal dance. They opened their jaws, anticipating the Blood Call, breaching the surface with red eyes fixed upon the Intercessors and the Birth-Kin. The

Intercessors scooped out the meat paste with their hands, tossing it high in the air for eager mouths that swallowed and resurfaced, again and again. The Intercessors raised their voices to drown out the wind as they recited the Hymn to Siatka, and with each word Sybilla felt an imperceptible tightening.

Siatka!
Large mouth
Glinter
Of deep places
Siatka!
Salt one
Keeper of dreams
Hearth eyed
Siatka!
Hear the call
Heralded by blood
Birth call
Siatka!
Womb giver
Milk one
Purifier of spirit
Siatka!
Return to our kinfolk
Girls
Of bright flame

At this final word Sybilla's heart nearly burst and she wanted to run ashore where her parents and sister were waiting. A band of Intercessors led the procession landward, as others gathered behind to nudge the Birth-Kin along. She was surrounded on every side. Sybilla counted her steps, counting loud in her mind to stave off their ever-attentive gaze. The blue-robed boy in front of her walked too slowly. With mounting anger, she watched his blood-smudged hand dangling at his side. He shuffled forward, smiling at the lights of Vaelnyr.

Then finally, underfoot, she felt stone.

She searched the darkened faces of the crowd. With a rush of relief, she saw Lucinda walking briskly, jostling past proud fathers and beaming nervous mothers.

Sybilla smiled, her eyes watering of their own accord. Her sister embraced her, a mutual squeeze, tight and brief. Later, Lucinda would comb out her hair and they would talk, but not here.

Linking arms, they made their way to the Skalens' carriage. Inside, her father gave Sybilla a hesitant smile. But there was pain in his eyes. The wound was there in the palm of her hand, and he did not protect her. It had happened again.

Her mother reached over, placing Sybilla's hand in her lap and set to work. Wetting the cloth, she scrubbed the redness that grimed the lines of her daughter's wrist. Gently, she dabbed at the gash till it shrunk to the shape of this year's scar. Sybilla stared at it. Flexed her fingers. Curled her hand into a fist. The carriage had already started moving, and soon she would be back at the Skalens' House. She would not do it again. She swore it.

They would have no more of her blood.

7

MAERYN

One Year Before The Fire

IT WAS A COOL EVENING and the little house was hidden behind a copse of trees. Intercessor Maeryn's hair and neck were bound in muslin, her hands protected by long gloves, her robe hanging to the ground. Across her plump face she wore a veil so the man could not mar her with his spittle or his blood. It was important she did not have any physical contact with him, for the vital fluids were both potent and contagious.

She walked in the company of four guards, their faces hard and ghostly.

"He will kill me this night," the woman had said.

Intercessor Maeyrn had laid her hands upon the woman; had taken her guilt, her doubt, her shame, and promised her a remedy, but Maeyrn would not end his life to save her. She would save them both.

As they neared the house, lamp light shone between the branches. Maeryn could feel them in there. The woman, her three young children, and the man. From within the house a storm was about to break.

Maeryn signalled the guards, and two of them moved off, circling around to the back of the house.

The Intercessor plodded onward, a full head shorter than the guards at her side. One of them opened the gate for her, its squealing hinge drawing the man's face to the glass. His eyes widened at the sight of her, the unmistakable figure of an Intercessor, all dressed in white. He barked something at his wife, and Maeryn saw his teeth flash within his black beard.

A second later he was gone.

Inside, there was shout, the smashing of glass, and a sound like a bullock trying to free itself of its pen.

Slowly, the front door swayed open; the woman, listless and thin, her children clutching at her skirt.

The boy caught Maeryn's eye and his voice issued into her mind.

Don't kill him! Don't take my daddy!

She crouched before him, though it hurt her knees, and removed her veil.

Outside, they heard grunts and a low thwacking sound that roused the hens.

The boy's hands were tight fists, and she took them in hers. She looked at him as a grandmother would, though she was not much older than his ma. With the warmth of her expression, she willed his hands to soften, and drew him into a memory, where he lay atop a hay bale, summer wind upon his face. ...He could feel it now, a smile forming on his lips. The hay prickled his back, and white clouds scudded the sky. The dry, horsey scent of the bale mingling with the smoke of some distant fire.

Your father is sick, my dear. I am here to heal him.

The boy strained weakly against her words, but then accepted them like a long drink.

Maeryn took the woman's face in her hands and drew their foreheads together.

I will deliver him to Kshidol's sight and he will be cleansed. Do not go near him. He will lay in the field for three days and then return to you, anew.

As they drew apart, the woman looked at her with pale, bleary eyes. "Yes," she murmured. "Thank you, Intercessor."

Maeyrn nodded and went out the way she had come, her heavy figure swaying as she walked.

The door clicked shut, and among the shadow of the trees she felt the carnal heat of him, the tightness of his sinew, the way he coiled like a snake, just waiting for his chance to strike. He was doubled over on the ground. Writhing this way and that as they bludgeoned him with their clubs.

At her approach, the guards stepped back and stood at attention.

Maeryn smiled at them and repositioned her veil.

She walked close to the man, who panted, the sack over his head making it difficult for him to determine the direction of the next blow.

Then slowly he turned to Maeryn, hearing the light crackle of her footstep.

He tried to stand, but his hands were bound behind his back, and one of his legs appeared to be broken.

He cried out, his breath steaming through the sackcloth.

Be still, she commanded.

"Fuck you!" he roared. "Aaagh," he cried out in agony, and collapsed on the ground.

She stepped closer and crouched beside him.

The man's body was rigid and his limbs twitched spasmodically.

Maeyrn filled her lungs with holy light and slowly exhaled. She held her hands above his abdomen and made room for him inside herself. Making herself a vessel for his animalism.

Her hands grew hot as it began to flow from him, feverish with predation. Beneath her long gloves, the hairs on her arms prickled as if she stood in the shadow of a great black bear.

The man whimpered and voided his bowels, giving off a sickly stench.

The Intercessor's eyes leaked as she held the connection, drawing hard on his essence.

His body shook, his pelvis rising toward her outstretched palms. Maeryn had that familiar feeling of drowning in flame as she fell into

40

rhythm with his laboured breath. The air heaved in and out of her lungs, in and out of him, like a bellows, sweat and mucous soiling her veil.

Gritting her teeth, she reached for that last part, the part hidden like a worm at the base of his spine.

She could not get it.

"Guards!" she spat, and they knew what to do.

One of them belted the man across the face.

As pain pierced though the man's eye, something in him released, the animal essence losing hold on his spirit.

"Again!"

Maeyrn readied herself for the next blow, which landed on the man's ribs. When the pain sparked, she reached in as far as she could go without killing him.

"One more..." she panted.

As they broke the man's nose, he keened, and finally she got it. He was empty now, his body falling slack.

"Stop," she said. "Stop, it is done."

The Intercessor staggered back, shaking her hands as if they were sticky with tar. She tore at her veil just in time, removing it from her face as she collapsed on her knees and vomited into the grass. She rocked back and forth, moaning like a beast in labour, vile fluid pouring from her mouth.

When the sickness had passed, one of the guards brought her pack, and behind her she could hear them tending to the man, who was unconscious as a doll.

She stared at the golden light of the cabin, the way it leaked around the curtains, seeming very bright. First, she removed her head wrappings, and then her robe. She used the water skin in her pack to wet a cloth, and with firm strokes, she cleaned her face and neck.

Maeyrn thought of the woman inside, of the boy, and the two little girls – what this would mean to them – but still she felt defiled.

Putting on a fresh robe, she bundled her soiled garments into her pack. She could see where the guardsmen stood in the centre of the field and with a sigh, she followed them.

Beyond the copse, the grass grew high and Maeyrn stumbled

forward, her legs weak as a new lamb's. She stared down upon the sleeping man; how peaceful he looked now. The guards had removed his clothes, washed him the best they could. They had wrapped him in bandages and covered him in furs, for it was cold in the field.

A guardsman passed her a bundle of dried Alma he'd lit on her behalf. The smoke drew off in whorls, marbling the air.

Though her face was numb and her lips did not want to move, she spoke the prayer.

> *"From vastness preserve,*
> *In continuity,*
> *In holy unity*
> *I enfold you in Velspar's light."*

And with this last, she unstoppered the vial of Alma oil in her hand and dripped it onto his tongue.

Maeyrn glanced at the guards. "Let us go now."

"Can you walk, Intercessor?"

"Yes, thank you."

She started for the carriage that waited for them at the edge of the pasture, aware of nothing save the rasping of her robe. Maeyrn was weightless and hollow, and her body felt strange.

The guards woke her when they reached the Intercessor's dormitory. She must have fainted out there in the field.

A guard escorted her, taking her on his arm as she staggered through the archway, through the main doors, and down the hall to her room. Inside, three solemn-faced initiates awaited her.

When the guard had gone, the girls commenced to remove Maeyrn's garments, peeling them gingerly from her pale, blotched skin.

A kettle of salt water steamed in the fireplace, and they poured it into copper urns, scrubbing her skin with linen, kneading the loose flesh of her arms and thighs. Wringing the cloths, rubbing until her skin felt raw.

With closed eyes, she let them do their work. In her mind she saw the bearded man, the wild look in his eye, the redness of his spirit. His sickness was still in her and would not be gone in the morning.

When finally the girls had dried her and put on her smock, they tucked her into bed and put out the candles. She stared above, a censer of Alma burning softly in the dark, laying upon her the heaviness of sleep.

8

MAERYN

One Year Before The Fire

In the morning, Maeryn dressed and headed to Intercessor Rankin's apartments to be cleansed. She felt diseased. Her veins prickled with the grit of impurity, her body eager to sweat it out.

As her slippered feet traversed the hallways and the stairs, she imagined they left stains of blood and dirt, and she hung her head so the other Intercessors would not have to see her this way.

When she approached Intercessor Rankin's door, she caught the strong scent of wood polish.

She knocked.

"Enter!"

Intercessor Rankin had flung the curtains wide and the brightness of the sea beyond made Maeryn squint. He had the same simple furnishings as she, the same table and chairs, the same cot and cupboards, the same fireplace and desk, but everything in this room gleamed, the instruments of his station on full display, not hidden away in some dark cupboard.

Rankin greeted her with a broad smile. He was a tall man with straight dark hair and hazel eyes, and the mere sight of him normally put Maeryn in good humour, but not today.

"Oh, Maeryn. You look ghastly." Intercessor Rankin wrinkled his nose. "Take a seat and we'll get started."

She sat on a wooden chair in the centre of the room, her motions automatic. Intercessor Rankin stood behind her and breathed slowly, in and out, before placing his hands on her shoulders.

At first, she felt an almost irrepressible desire to slap him away but mastered the urge, reminding herself where the feeling came from. Rankin snorted with amusement and intensified his will. He was a powerful Intercessor, his hands growing hot as forged iron, sucking at her wounded spirit, drawing the poison out. The process was intense, but Maeryn had been through it many times before and knew it would be over soon.

As redness began to flow out of her, a profound sense of relief blossomed in her chest. Her jaw relaxed, and she felt like herself again.

"*Pure is the Stream. Clear and bright,*" Intercessor Rankin intoned, and tapped lightly at the three points – forehead, crown and nape.

Maeryn shivered and opened her eyes.

Intercessor Rankin went to the corner and spat in a copper pot before cleansing his hands in a bowl of salt water. He looked a little ill.

He sat in the chair opposite and gave her a weary look. "You keep yourself busy, Maeryn."

She smiled, her heart serene. "I feel good. It feels good to help them, Rankin."

"You serve in holiness, that is certain, but it ages you beyond your years."

It was true, Maeryn's hair was streaked with grey, her knees ached, and she had the fleshiness of a grandmother who cooked all day and never sat down to a meal but ate often from the wooden spoon. In truth, she was only forty-five, and Rankin her junior – in age, at least.

"But you, Rankin, you look so young," Maeryn chided.

The Intercessor stared at her, his expression grim. "I respect you, Maeryn, but do not think yourself a lonely bastion of wisdom in a foolish world. Sometimes, the spirit is best cleansed by death. It is an absolute cleansing. I prefer to welcome the spirits home upon their return. To give my energy to the children and nurture them in their faith. A happy childhood is the best preventative of red deeds."

Maeyrn looked at his hands, wondering if they had ever been dirty in the way hers had been. Whether he had ever tried to help someone who was not already saved by their own volition. "I think sometimes we condemn them too soon." Maeryn searched her friend's eyes but saw her words had not moved him. He was so very stubborn.

"Be careful you do not cling too tightly to personhood, Maeryn – yours, or mine, or anyone else's." Rankin leaned back in his chair. "*I am Velspar*. That is a superior knowledge. Do you know it?"

She nodded. "I do, Rankin."

He held his arms wide. "I am Velspar. Every spirit that has been or will be. And this is why we must respect the sanctity of Velspar with harsh judgement. You would not forgive yourself what you forgive in others. The animal in them will perish with the passing of time, do not let it distract you from what is pure – it is the spirit we must shepherd."

Maeryn's eyes narrowed. "I wonder, Rankin, are you trying to draw me into an argument? Because it will not work. I feel there is something else on your mind. Will you tell me what it is?"

"Ah, I see your wits have been restored in full." Rankin rubbed his knuckles across his lips and then folded his hands in his lap. "The High Intercessors have conferred, but I do not have answers, only suspicions. It is too early to know what is to come."

"Of course." Maeryn bowed her head. She sat there, sensing he wanted to say more, but the moment passed. "Well, thank you, Intercessor. Best I leave you to your meditations."

Rankin went to the window and traced his fingers along the leadlight design, the encircling curve of the Skalens' Star.

She was about to leave when he held up his hand and ushered her to return.

"Maeryn," he said in low tones. "There have been developments in Brivia."

She met his eyes, the sunlight accentuating the dark spots about his iris. Maeryn nodded. "Emryl and Medard have passed the Seventh Gate?"

Rankin laughed. "No, no. But they have passed the Third." His smile faded. "It is a dangerous business. If they become full initiates of our order, they will be at odds with the other Skalens. But if they are not capable of passing through the Seventh, the outcome will be far worse."

Maeryn considered. "What do your visions tell you?"

He stared out at the waters of the Gulf. "Like you, I see rivers of blood. I hear the ancient women of Jokvour calling to the battle dead. I find myself drowning in the tears of Siatka and being reborn, but the world of my birth is hazy and mutable." He sighed. "I do not know what it means. But I feel we must ready ourselves to enter the Great Stream. We have all felt its pull, and it gets stronger every day. It calls to the Intercessors alone."

Maeryn stroked his arm and he turned his face to her. She gave him a gentle smile. "This Festival, Velspar will reach its seventh centenary. It is a sacred time. But it is not a time of certainty. Imagine how the First Diviner must have felt when he walked the mountains of Jokvour, surrounded by blood and desolation. His first vision, strange as it was, has bound these Seven Lands in peace. We know its truth, and we live it each day, but there was a time when he did not know – the time before the vision – and that is where we stand."

They fell into thoughtful silence.

Maeryn reached forward and drew their foreheads together. "Do not be troubled, my friend," she whispered. "I will know your smile, in this life and the next."

9

SYBILLA

The Year of The Fire

SYBILLA SAT ALONE IN THE DINING HALL, eating strange meats that stuck in her throat as she swallowed. The air was thick and grey. Clouds from outside wafted in, passing through the walls, and through her skin. She went to the window and opened it wide, but the smoke was thicker there. Sensing it was not safe to remain inside, she jumped, swimming blindly through the choking mist.

Though she strained her limbs to move forward, the smoke dragged at her, the clouds circling as if they might form a whirlpool.

Swoosh.

Something moved. Sybilla felt Siatka's muscular form as She parted the air.

Sybilla's legs tingled, her body rigid with fear.

Siakta drew close, wreathing Sybilla in the heat of Her breath, the ache of Her hunger.

Swoosh.

The serpent's black scales slipped like a ribbon around her ribs. A second time. Now it was a ribbon drawn tight.

Sybilla screamed for her body to move.

Siatka loosened, and Sybilla felt the blaze of those red eyes as they turned upon her, the opening of Her jaws.

Sybilla wheezed. There was no way out of the smoke, no way other than that evil, beckoning mouth. Sybilla took in a great breath of air, and dove headlong into the cave of Siatka's gullet, wanting to kill Her from the inside, wanting to disappear.

She drove herself deep, to a place where the black walls of the Mother squeezed and squeezed and squeezed–

Sybilla awoke, coughing, burning with sweat and could not understand why the clouds of her dream remained. She hacked involuntarily and threw herself to the floor sucking at the clearer air, only to hear her sister's muffled screams through the wall. Sybilla stumbled to the door. She turned the handle, but it was locked. Why was it locked?

With shaking hands, she wrenched open her dresser drawer and felt for the ledge where she had hidden a spare key. She turned it in the lock, but the door was blocked on the other side. She threw her body against it, grunting with frustration. Moments later, she tried again with a chair, smashing it against the door until finally it gave way.

Through bitter smoke, she saw fire. Flames licked the rafters, and half-way down the hallway a beam collapsed in a rain of sparks. She ran toward it.

"Lucinda!" she cried, through wracking coughs. "Lucinda!"

The fire thundered in full plume, blocking the passage. Her sister was not screaming anymore.

Her eyes were streaming, there was no way through. Above her there was a loud crack and with a startling burst, sparks shot through her hair and nightdress. The flames quickened to her scalp and she ripped the clothes from her breast. She tore a great tapestry from the wall and threw it over her body, smothering her burning hair as she dropped to the floor.

She had to get out.

Dropping the tapestry, she ran down the passageway and away from the fire, bursting through the heavy wooden door, down the Attendants' stair, and through another passage, slipping on something wet and scrambling on. Then she was outside, the gravel biting her feet.

She tripped, falling hard. Her lungs rasped and she lay there, her back pinned to the grass, unable to tear her eyes away. Soaring flames engulfed the entire eastern side of the Skalens' House. Windows shattered in the hot roar, glass falling like stars, with her parent's bedroom at the centre of it all.

The ache went to her marrow, so that every part of her seemed to contract, recoiling.

She was up on her feet, staggering toward the building.

Somebody grabbed her and held her fast.

She screamed. A shrill and lacerating sound.

"Sybilla, no," he said.

His breath was laboured, smelling of potatoes and boiled meat.

She twisted her head around. Peran. "Please, please..." *Save them!* She screamed somewhere inside.

Sybilla struggled against him but could not break free. Her fingernails drew blood from him but still he would not let her go. A wave of helplessness descended, and she went limp, his grip on her relaxing.

Peran's voice spoke in distant tones, giving instruction to a body that seemed not to be her own.

"We must go, it is not safe for you here. Take my cloak," he said, removing it from his back and draping it over her, threading her arms through its sleeves as if she were a child.

As she followed him, she noticed that her breast was showing, and she stopped, staring down at her torn nightdress.

"Sybilla!" Peran's sharp whisper startled her and he grabbed her arm, pulling her into the stables.

His hands shook as he tied the shredded fabric in a knot, fastening the cloak at the neck.

He helped her onto the horse and placed her feet in the stirrups. And when they were both in the saddle, he fastened her arms about his waist with a length of rope.

They rode. Gathered speed. The horse huffed, galloping on and on, Sybilla's eyes pressed tight as they careened through the dark.

She could smell the leather of his vest, the sweat of middle age, and mud, and leaves, and fire.

Something seethed, black and rotten. *No. Not this.* She was about to be sick.

Sybilla opened her eyes a crack. How did they get here? This far? Lake Nanthe. Her thighs were bruised from the saddle. The horse's reflection charged through black space and shattered moonlight, then vanished in the reeds.

Their mount was growing tired, and Peran stopped to let the gelding drink.

When he lifted her from the horse, she found she could not stand. So she sat, her legs tingling as he scuffed about in the shadows. Sybilla covered her face with her hands. She could not sleep, but could not bear to look at him. At anything. The horse chomped and tore at the grass for a while, and then made its way to the river's edge.

After a time, Peran returned and they kept riding.

The mountains crested and fell on one side as trees thickened on the other, the river disappearing from sight. Her mouth was dry and her skin was sour with smoke. Terrible images bit at the edges of her mind, but she willed them away, as if the horse could outrun them. Her body thumped against Peran's back. She did not care where they were going. There were mountains and more mountains; there were trees thick with shadows.

"We will pass the border soon," Peran said.

Maglorean land.

They slowed, following a winding path she had travelled long ago.

Ascending the black mountains of Jokvour, they saw the first light of day. When they stopped, Peran carried her into the cave, but it was not the one she knew. She remembered the shape of its mouth, when she and Lucinda had peered round to listen to the Skalens speak, her father giving name to the First Heresy.

The day grew bright and hot. The day grew cool and slipped into night.

Peran went out and she did not know how long he had been gone.

She must have fallen asleep because she awoke screaming as smoke filled the air. Fire!

Peran stamped on the small fire he had built. "To warm you..."

She stared at him with savage eyes. "Let me outside."

Sybilla stood at the mouth of the cave where a ragged, leafless tree quivered in the wind.

Eventually he came to her side.

"It is better if you come in," Peran said.

"Why can't I stand here? These caves are made of blinding stone."

"Yes, Skalen, but if an Intercessor came close, they would still perceive our presence. I can make Meridians for us to wear, but I need time to prepare the stone."

She stared at him in shock, words dying on her tongue. He had called her Skalen. He had called her *Skalen*.

Her eyes narrowed. "How dare you."

Peran frowned. "I'm sorry, Skalen, but you must wear the Meridian. It is not–"

"How dare you call me that. I will not do it!" The air was cold in her lungs as she tried to breathe, but still she felt that she was suffocating.

He let out a sigh. "Sybilla, come inside. Please."

When she did not respond, he gave her a pointed look.

Sullenly, she nodded and he turned, leading the way. Walking behind him, she stared at his ash-streaked arms, and the thick muscles of his back.

He gestured for her to sit on the ledge beside him. "Sybilla, I know this is hard. But if we let ourselves fall apart, then the Intercessors will win. I promised Reyan that no matter what happened, I would continue his mission."

"The Intercessors did this?" she said.

Peran nodded. "They brought fire to your House, and now we must bring fire to theirs."

A kinetic sensation started in her legs, and with it came an image. Her parents screaming in their beds, the fire all about them. Their bodies stiffening like spiders, flesh bursting, frozen in an agony that would not cease.

"I am not ready. I don't know what to do. I don't know anything about Father's plans," she said, tears rising in her throat.

Peran's mouth kept moving, his words sounding strangely about the confines of the cave. "We are never ready for such things. You must think, Sybilla. What will they do when they find you? They can drive you to madness with the power of their minds. Your father saw it, he *knew* it, even as a boy of thirteen. We kept him safe, in the Guard–" Peran's voice broke. "Sybilla, I tried to save him, I couldn't get past the door, there was no way in." Tears gleamed at the corners of his eyes, but she could offer him no comfort.

She swallowed hard, feeling lightheaded.

He wiped his face and coughed, his thoughts retreating into silence.

Eventually he left her, making his way to the back of the cave where he set about making their Meridians.

Despite his warnings, Sybilla moved out into the open, letting the night winds assail her. Her mind drifted and snapped like the sapling at her side.

Fire. Father. Her grandfather's body, parcelled, and slipping beneath the waves. The vision of the Fifth Gate.

Mother Siatka hears his call...

Sybilla's mind sharpened, becoming white-hot. She listened, as if Siatka might find her there.

Siatka, wet with birth-slick, wet with death, slithering up the rock face, gravel-crusted and hungry.

She was not real, *She was not real.* An animal. An Intercessor's trick.

Sybilla remembered her father's words then, like holy scripture.

"The Intercessors believe that fire destroys the spirit," he'd said. *"That they burn away what is evil, and so, protect the purity of the Stream. But the Hymns tell us otherwise. It is those of 'bright flame' that are indeed holy. Fire frees the spirit from its slavery to flesh. Not to be scattered and lost among the stars, but to come back, whole, of its own volition. Those consumed by animals are brought low, and made filthy in Velspar's sight. Knowingly or unknowingly, the Intercessors have done this, our brightest spirits sent to the wastes."*

"Bright flame," she whispered to the night and the stars, her hands pressed to her heart.

When she returned, Peran looked at her with great sadness.

She stared back at him. Hating the choice he put before her, for it was no choice at all.

With roughened hands, he passed her the Meridian he had fashioned with his knife and the cloth of his back. Positioning the blinding stone, it was as if she had closed the door behind her where the fire had raged and found herself in some cool chamber. Her own feelings were still there, but the pitch had changed. In the dimness, a fragile peace arose within her. She breathed carefully around it, knowing that it would not last. That it could not quench a horror this immense.

She thought of her family, the three faces that had joined her at the dinner table all the years of her life. Tried to imagine their uncorrupted spirits slipping between clumps of ash and into the air. It thrilled her to think of it, as if they had found a secret door hidden from the Intercessors. The way past the Holy Ones, and on into eternity. But the thought disintegrated easily in the sickening tide of all that had happened, and all that was to come.

Peran lurked like a shadow at the edge of her vision. *Skalen*, he had called her.

What would become of her if she refused?

10

SYBILLA

The Year of The Fire

"I wish to return to Vaelnyr," Sybilla said.

Peran gave her a long look.

Sybilla began to sweat. There was nowhere for her to go. She wanted to go home.

"Skalen, you must eat." Peran passed her a lump of stale bread from his pocket.

She waved him off. Her body fairly shook with rage. If Peran wanted her to be Skalen, then she would start with the Attendants. Those weak-minded, weak-willed traitors who had let themselves grow soft in the Intercessors' hands. Which one of them lit the fire? Who locked the chamber doors? She thought of them each in turn, of striking them in fury, of them breaking down sobbing at her feet. Which one of them? She would kill them with her bare hands. She would make them tell her the names of the Intercessors who had breathed their devil's breath into their naked ears. Then she would destroy the Intercessors one by one. String their bloodied corpses to every post on the road to Vaelnyr. She would pile their bodies in the streets and let them rot in the sun.

Her hands trembled, frail and white as she finally took the bread.

It felt like a stone, a rough and inedible thing. How could Peran possibly eat at a time like this?

Anger flared in her stomach – the acid of it causing an audible gurgling. Peran had sat there all night, his brow smooth, his breath tranquil as the lapping tide, in Hiatus. She could not do it. Did not want to. She wanted to slap him, to tear at his beard, to scald his face with the smouldering branch of their small fire.

"Skalen, we cannot return to Vaelnyr, it is too dangerous. We must get word to Maglore and Nothelm, and return with the combined strength of the Guard. The people of Vaelnyr are not ready. They still believe the Intercessors holy. They believe the Intercessors do the Skalens' will. If we are to say otherwise it will cause great unrest. It may work to the Intercessors' advantage. In truth, we do not know what they have planned," he said.

Her eyes narrowed. He kept calling her that. *Skalen.* She had not yet agreed. And who was he to tell her she could not return to her homeland?

Sitting on the floor of the cave, Peran rested his elbows on his knees, eating slowly.

His words irritated her. His logic and his plans. She wanted to exact justice upon those who had murdered her family. And if he did not know what the Intercessors had planned, what good was he?

She needed to say something. "We must call a meeting of Council."

Peran gave her a brief and exasperated smile. "Of course – in time."

Her heart raced and she carried on talking, ignoring all the subtle ways in which he was telling her to *be still.*

"I want it to be held in Vaelnyr. The Council will see what the Intercessors are capable of. They will fear their own deaths. They will be forced to admit what the Intercessors have done," Sybilla said.

"The other Skalens will take more than a month to gather," he said, "and that will give the Intercessors opportunity to act. You are flesh and blood, Sybilla." He looked at her. "And you are not in full command of your emotions. Your mind is unprotected."

Sybilla's stomach flared with renewed malice, but she offered no retort.

He sat a little straighter and closed his eyes. "Let us find Hiatus."

She glared at his silent form, at the expansion of his ribcage as he breathed. Sybilla fumed, but after a few minutes, she felt the futility of her protest. He would not take her seriously if she could not demonstrate mastery of her emotions. He would not let her leave Jokvour.

Sybilla tightened her makeshift Meridian, giving the stones better contact. Bitterly, she closed her eyes and focused on the stone. At first, her vision pulsed, the silence a prickling scream that drowned out the wind. But eventually, she began to feel the tranquillity of the stones. They drew the heat out of her; lessening, easing, creating distance.

In the quiet came her sister's muffled cry, smothered by fire, entombed in stone. Sybilla listened to her sister's pain. It opened the fruit of her heart, and where her love flowed, the pain got in, but she could not make it stop. Her face contorted around the memory, around what it told her, the tears coming steadily now, her nose running as she gasped for air.

Warm arms surrounded her and she leaned into Peran's embrace, wanting to disappear into him and never return.

He held her until the tears dried upon her cheeks and at last, she opened her eyes to gaze vacantly at the ground.

"We must go to Maglore," he said gently.

"I cannot do it, Peran." Sybilla's voice was flat. "It was never supposed to be me."

"You are the Skalen of Vaelnyr. And I am your Head Guard. You will not be alone. There is no decision you will be left to make alone. The Guard is prepared for what is to come."

"Then what do you need of me?" Sybilla said, listening to the beating of his heart.

"The Intercessors exist because of the First Heresy, and it is a heresy that only a Skalen can undo. Do this for your father, if you cannot do it for yourself. We must all make our sacrifices to Velspar. Do not let his be in vain."

11

SYBILLA

The Year of The Fire

IN THE MORNING THEY DESCENDED the mountain, Sybilla holding listlessly to Peran as they rode. They avoided the settlements that fringed the River Nanthe, crossing at a little-used bridge that took them into the barren Fields of Marain. In the afternoon, they steered closer to the forest, through pasture purple with heather. But it was not until they reached the crest of the dirt road that Sybilla caught her first glimpse of central Maglore. Beneath white clouds, the hills kindled green, until all was emerald, distant buildings gleaming beyond the stately form of the Skalens' House.

On the road, Sybilla spotted the silhouettes of three riders, and straightened herself. The frill of her nightdress was clearly visible beneath the maroon cloak Peran had given her, and she adjusted it so they would not see.

Peran saluted the approaching men, who wore the peaked helmets and brown leathers of the Guard.

"What is your business, Guardsman?" the first of them asked.

Peran's clothes were dirty, but the maroon, black and gold of Vaelnyr was unmistakable.

"We come bearing grave news for Skalens Inry and Domhnall Greslet. Your escort would be most welcome," Peran said.

Sybilla could not tell if they recognised her, but they were not questioned any further.

As they rode, she stared resolutely into the distance, not meeting the guards' eyes. Eventually, they were led up the hillside where the Skalens' House sat, unblemished and glowing in the golden light of the slipping sun. The building was squat and square with crenelated turrets that looked to the four corners. In all ways it resembled the other Skalens' Houses of Velspar that were built at the same time in the agreed style. But to this house, the recently wed Skalens of Maglore had added touches of their own. The four roads that led to the House were framed by a fantastic array of flowers that curled and burst open in pinks and reds, fizzing with bees and blossoms. Starflowers jostled for attention amidst crisp white lilies that arched toward the sun. The scent of them made her stomach turn.

When they dismounted, the guards led them on foot through the central archway and Peran gestured for Sybilla to enter first. She held herself tall, so that they would listen to her, despite her state of undress. When finally, the guards pulled open the door of the main chamber, she saw the familiar face of Domhnall Greslet – saw him as he had been five years prior, a man of twenty-five, full of pride, speaking on behalf of his dying father, but speaking truly of his own vision. A lump rose in her throat as she remembered her mother's face, appraising him in the fire-light. The memory refracted at the edge of her mind as she advanced across the flagstones; the pressing of foreheads, the taking of oaths.

Domhnall was older now, and thicker set, but his eyes still gleamed hungrily beneath the shadow of his brows. The woman in the room she had not met, though Sybilla knew her to be Domhnall's wife, Skalen Inry Greslet. The woman was barely that, and slouched languidly upon her chair, not having acquired the stiffness of rule. Catching her eye, Inry jolted slightly at the sight of Sybilla.

"Welcome!" Inry said, finding her smile.

Domhnall placed his hand upon his wife's shoulder.

"They tell me that you come with news?" he said, clearly disappointed that the cloaked Ladain was neither Reyan nor the Lady Vivienne.

Sybilla wondered if he had forgotten her name – the Skalens' daughter who was now older than his wife, who stood there, dirty and barefoot before him. Sybilla could feel Inry's narrowed eyes trying to make sense of her, as if the Vaelnyri were a savage folk, unaccustomed to bathing. Sybilla's ears began to ring and she felt oddly separate from her body as she prepared to speak.

"Skalens of Maglore," Sybilla began, "the worst has come to pass. The Intercessors have moved against us." With a great force of will she dragged the words from a shapeless place inside. "My mother, my father, and my sister are dead."

As the blood drained from his face and Inry clung anxiously to his arm, Sybilla felt herself an artefact of anguish, a display to cleave the hearts of strangers. A powerful thing. Domhnall sputtered and scratched at his hands, pacing. Inry just stood there, looking stranded, her glossy curls shining absurdly in the light of the setting sun.

They did not know what to do. It felt so strange to be the one to speak, to be the fist upon the table. She stood tall, feeling like her father, elated, almost invincible.

"Skalens, there is little time to act, but with the full force of the Maglorean, Vaelnyri and Nothelmite Guard, we will end the reign of the Intercessors."

Domhnall looked at her sharply. "And the other Skalens?"

"I will call a meeting of Council in Vaelnyr. The Intercessors will be held to account." Her hands tingled. "And those Skalens who will not renounce them choose their fate as murderers."

She could almost see her own face, incandescent, ready to lead Velspar into holy battle. If she let this passion take her any further, she would scream until her eyes bled, she would tear the flesh from her chest, and raise a storm to drown them all.

If she did not wear the Meridian, they may have feared that she had gone mad. She trembled, a wave of nausea swelling the hollow of her belly. She swallowed, focusing urgently on the stones of her Meridian. Like a cold poultice they called off the heat, the pain,

60

urging her blood to flow softly. She found the space between things, and slipped into it, the deadness of Hiatus.

Sybilla spoke decorously now, as her mother would have done. "I pray for your assistance in preparing correspondence to the Seven Lands, and for safe lodgings for myself and my guardsman."

Domhnall stepped forward and clasped her hands. "Skalen Sybilla, the Greslets of Maglore honour your request and remain yours in loyalty."

Sybilla believed him sincere, and that was enough. She felt suddenly tired and sighed deeply.

Inry's eyes were dancing with the excitement of unfolding events. "Dear Skalen, you must be weary. Let our Attendants see to your wounds and take you to your quarters."

Sybilla's lips tightened, not wanting anyone to tend to her, much less the Attendants of a foreign land. Inry looked confused that her words did not please this stranger who stood before her with blood-encrusted hair.

"I thank you," Sybilla said, "but I would tend my own wounds. Clean water, bandages and riding clothes would be most welcome, but I ask that these be delivered by my guardsman."

Domhnall interjected. "Oh, Sybilla, you mustn't fear the Attendants of this House! They are good workers, loyal only to the Skalens."

Sybilla forced down a chuckle of disgust. "I do not wish to refuse the hospitality of your House, but it appears Vaelnyri Attendants were used as an instrument, just days past, in my family's murder. I would not wish the shadow of my grief to fall upon such faithful servants as yours. It would be a great kindness if you would bid them to leave me to my solitude."

"Of course," Domhnall said, becoming lost again in the enormous gulf that had claimed a great man and his lady, and a young maiden besides. That had nearly snuffed out the Ladain family line.

Pain seemed to have scrubbed all illusion from Sybilla's eyes and as she watched, she saw Domhnall rising up before her, as if his own father had died, fortifying himself as heir to a mission that would change Velspar forever.

12

WALDEMAR

Two Years After The Fire

LOST ARE MY BRETHREN, CAST DEEP *into the fathomless night. Have they passed through the Eighth Gate? I pray that it is so, but my heart is heavy with doubt. When in the fire's wake they spoke of blood-blessed Temples and the new womb of the Eighth, a shadow moved across my spirit, and I did not follow them. Through wisdom or fear, I could not abandon this life. I could not turn my eyes away from once-holy Skalens that shun the light of consciousness to follow the fire's red light.*

How small these 'Skalens' are. Their eyes are red-rimmed, and red are their deeds. Red are their hearts as they bestow their cruelties, as the animal in them grows strong. How sure they are of their earthly dominion, twisting the holy rites to their own ends. That they should accept Skalen Karasek's second vision, but not his first. That they should call the faithful, heretics. Without the Holy Ones, the spirit of Velspar will dissipate. Even those bright ones whose faith is strong – I fear that they will not find their way.

And yet here I stand, in Jokvour – among blood-blessed mountains, and grief-blessed mountains, among mountains of holy yearning – and I remember the First Diviner. For if he listened and could hear, then that must be my mission. I must honour him, preserving his teachings for those who may yet survive this time of darkness.

You, who have come, thirsting for truth — may your spirit be quiet, as Skalen Karasek was quiet when he heard the unheard name. May your mind be like the stuff of creation, ready to become, but not determining, for it is then that you will understand.

THE VISIONS OF SKALEN KARASEK

Let it be known that in the beginning the earth rose from the sea. Mountains blistered, and became tree-furred, giving rise to birds, low-walkers, the tall, and the loping. Our ancestors flourished, but their blood was foul with animal instincts. Dreams came, and with them, so many false gods. The clans came, not in friendship, but with rattling shields, casting chalk circles to mark the reaches of their dominion.

It was in the mountains of Jokvour that three circles touched. There, three clans, equal in strength, performed a triple sacrifice. For seven days and seven nights the Brivians, Magloreans and Lindesali fell into a fever of bloodlust. The reddened soil shot up with new flowers, and the earth was pleased.

But over the dead, the women were wailing, and their lamentations drew yet more to their song. They plucked the strings, and shook the silver threads, until all were shaking, until all were singing.

ON THE SEVENTH NIGHT, AFTER BREATHING OF THE ALMA, SKALEN KARASEK OF BRIVIA HAD A VISION.

He saw the great winged Kshidol birth a baby boy, that fell from the sky into the sea. Beneath the waves he watched the serpent, Siatka, consume the bodies of the battle dead. And when he took his dagger to her belly, a baby girl emerged, rising to the surface.

The next morning, Skalen called upon his people to bring the bodies of their kinfolk down from Jokvour. He brought them to the Holy Ones, for he understood that Siatka would be as their Mother, and Kshidol would be as their Father. That they alone could shepherd the spirits of the slain. They would draw the silver threads from dead flesh, salvaging spirit from the hunger of earth.

The Karaseks gave of their dead, and prayed. With the passage of the moon, the women among them felt the spark of life in their bellies, and Skalen gave thanks. For he saw in the little children, the look of the ones who had perished. Those that had been gifted to the Holy Ones were given back, anew.

AND THEN, FOR HIS FAITH WAS TRUE, SKALEN HAD A SECOND VISION.

In it, he saw into the earth, into the beginning. A place of endless ocean, where the seabed came to swelling. As it grew larger, Skalen saw that the earth contained something else within. A silent presence regarded him. It was as a closed eye, deep in vision, where voices escaped in fissures, crystallised by the weight of Seven Lands.

The word 'Velspar' came upon his lips and he spoke it to his kinfolk. The name of spirit. The living essence within them, that bled in streams through the stuff of earth, though the earth itself was unholy.

The earth sent pestilence and famine, and storms of ash from the east. Villages were swallowed by the sea. In the north, the clans of Vaelnyr, Seltsland and Nothelm huddled tight as their number dwindled, and their people grew old. In the southern isle of Avishae, the starving ones came to Brivia to plead for grain. In Maglore and Lindesal the people stroked the dry bones of their dead, and bore no children.

But still Skalen talked of Velspar. Of the Holy Ones, that would protect the spirit, drawing it back from the reaches, gathering it together as one.

It was then that the clans came, in their poverty, to Brivia to seek Skalen's counsel. It was then that the Holy Ones were honoured with the septuple sacrifice of the Skalens' Pact. When all Seven gave the flesh of their dead for the promise of rebirth. For the promise of unity.

And so it must be that all who bear the title of Skalen are holy. The Great Stream spins around them, comes back to them, finding their light in the darkness.

INTERCESSOR WALDEMAR RASMUS OF BRIVIA, 702.

13

SYBILLA

The Year of The Fire

WHEN NEWS OF THE FIRE OF VAELNYR reached the north, Skalens Damek and Lenna Braedal did not swoon or stutter as the Greslets had done. They offered their condolences and their plan of attack in the self-same breath. It seemed they had already taken measures against the First Heresy in Nothelm. Where Sybilla thought merely of execution, Damek gave flourish to new ceremonies of faith.

The Nothelmites had already slain many of the water serpents, and once salted and dried, the siatka served both as a nutritious meat, and as an unequivocal renouncement of heresy. Those who would eat their own deities could be considered worthy of a future in Velspar, Damek said.

The Vaelnyri Guard milled about the Gulf, greeting the Nothelmites with nods of kinship and the slapping of backs. They had come to slay the siatka, and Sybilla was there to bless the proceedings. She stood back from the throng, staring down the Long Pier.

Sybilla gathered her nerve, hardly believing what they were about to do. The siatka were there, she knew. Their tongues had known the taste of her blood. At Birth Call, and in dreams, they had coiled about her, moving in and out of vision, drawing her one step closer to death. Their otherworldly eyes were an abyss, a promise, that one day she would be consumed, in body and in spirit.

The Braedals insisted they were easy to kill, but she would not believe it until the deed was done. Sybilla looked about her, unsettled by the scent of so many men, the charge of their readiness bringing stiffness to her arms. The Nothelmites brandished hook-spears that gleamed as they turned them this way and that, letting their Vaelnyri brothers try their hand.

She walked the cobblestones, catching the musk of other creatures recently slain. Though the Nothelmites had not turned their attentions to the kshidol that shadowed the mountains along their southern border, the Vaelnyri Guard had amassed twelve carcasses in recent days. Of course, the hunt had only just begun, but arrows found their mark easily enough, for the beasts were nearly tame, accustomed as they were to the sweet smoke that preceded the filling of their bellies.

Sybilla beheld the headless carcasses and the dutiful Attendants that had commenced the plucking. The kshidol looked even more grotesque in death, and she saw truly that they were beasts. Their downy underwings showed the reddish joint where knives would separate wing from belly. They were grey-skinned and dirty, but the Attendants would salt them well enough that they would taste like any other meat.

Behind her, footsteps neared.

Peran approached with a tall, blonde-haired man. From the burnished green Skalens' Star embossed on his breastplate, Sybilla knew him to be Edric, Head Guard of Nothelm.

Edric did not wait for Peran to introduce him, greeting Sybilla with a half-smile. "Honourable Skalen," Edric said as he bowed. "I see that the Vaelnyri Guard have made an impressive start." He gestured toward the kshidol carcasses.

"They have indeed," Sybilla said. "I trust you will keep my Attendants occupied for weeks to come if your hook-spears are as effective as your Skalen suggests."

Peran glanced between them, apparently irritated by the shirking of formal introductions. There were days when Sybilla cared about such things, but today was not one of them.

"We are most grateful Nothelm has come to our aid," Peran said, glancing at Edric.

For Sybilla, Peran attempted a smile. "We may yet see clear waters in the Gulf."

Edric grinned. "Of that I am certain. By Festival, little children will be paddling in the waves. Skalen, will you join us on the Long Pier?"

At first, she hesitated, a bloodless sensation rising in her legs, but she could not rightly refuse, and so she nodded.

Sybilla kept her distance as the Guard assembled at the shore, Edric demonstrating the action of the hook spear, and passing out weapons. She took the time to reach into Hiatus, for she could not show any signs of weakness. Other guards did the same, becoming still, closing their eyes, and when they opened them; they were different. Smoothed, plain-faced, capable. In such moments, it warmed her to be among them.

She walked tall as she approached the pier. One of the Vaelnyri Attendants joined them with the Alma wine, her hands trembling. The girl wore her Meridian, as this was now a requirement for all who worked in the Skalens' House, but it did not seem to calm her. Sybilla watched her with concern, expecting her to lose her footing at any moment. She would not let the Attendants ruin this as well.

Sybilla called out. "To mark this occasion, I will carry the Alma wine." The Attendant turned uncertainly, her eyes flicking up and down as she bowed.

"Yes, Sybilla – Skalen," she corrected herself, blushing deeply as the vessel was passed into her hands.

Holding the wine above her head, Sybilla addressed the Guard. "On this day I will call the demons up so that they may be slain. Together we will suck the poison from the wound, that Velspar may be purified. I bless this day as we continue to fight the First Heresy."

The roar of the men was fierce. Sybilla turned and faced the pier, and then she walked. At first, she could not see them, though she felt their eyes beneath her. Watching. It did not take long to glimpse their coiling shadows. There were more of them than she expected. They had not been fed for months now, and they were hungry.

In the glassy depths they swarmed. Their bodies longer than seven guards measured head to foot, their jaws seemingly built to accommodate the width of human shoulders. Nevertheless, they were tame. She told herself this as she walked, not robed in white as they were used to seeing, but clothed in crimson, the colour of Vaelnyr, the colour of Skalens.

The unhunted ones were placid as they breached, proving themselves to be exactly what she knew them to be – creatures devoid of both intelligence and foreknowledge.

Approaching the altar, she raised the urn for all to see, and then poured – without hymns, without calling them by name. They came thick and fast, their powerful tails creating churn and a great splashing about the pier. Briskly, she retreated the length of the pier, standing well back as the Guard moved in. Edric signalled them, and all at once, the Guard launched their spears into the water. The siatka writhed violently, covering those closest in cold water. A mournful lowing erupted where their mouths reached the surface. Sybilla's heart raced, transfixed by the confusion of bodies, the grunting and screams, the jutting of spears into flesh.

She looked past them. At the headland, the Braedal boats strained to hold the braid net between them, where the siatka were becoming snagged. If some swam deep and escaped the nets, then all the better, Edric had said. For each culling, only half of those that survived would return. Deprived of their usual diet, they were more savage at the second cull, but succumbed more quickly. At the third, they could simply gather them up by the tails like so many slint lizards.

The Guard worked as one, sweating and straining to hold the nets, spears flying, one after the other. As the boats advanced toward shore, they dragged the bodies with them. A few of their ghastly heads were lodged in the upper nets, their limp, muscular bodies floating flat against them. Those that had fallen to the seafloor would not be easy to dredge and would soon foul the water if they were not removed. Still, she was pleased to be filled with thoughts of their stinking corpses for it meant that they were gaining the upper hand.

Suddenly, a huge tail slapped the pier, sending splintered planks high in the air. Sybilla clasped her mouth in alarm. There was now a gap in the pier that would require the guards to swim or be carried by boat to shore.

A guardsman ran past, and turned to her with a reckless chuckle. "That was a near one!"

Something in his daring restored her conviction and she chuckled breathlessly in return.

The killing seemed to go on for a long time. Several guards fell into the water and were dragged on long poles back to the pier, but one did not resurface. He was a guardsman of Vaelnyr. After that, the exhilaration of the hunt sank to laborious butchery and hauling. Where she could, Sybilla pulled nets with the others, but she had not trained with the Guard since her grandfather died and was little help. It did not matter. They would see her blood-spattered and dripping, and they'd know she was one of them.

She remained among the Guard until the sea grew quiet. The nets creaked as the Braedal ships lurched toward shore with their hideous cargo. She stayed with them until the first of the siatka had been dragged to shore. With their hands gripping the jaw at the gill line, two men called for four more to pull the slippery thing onto the sand. She was grateful for its closed lids, and that the slit in its belly bore no child. The Attendants marched down, tools readied for the gutting.

The shore foamed pink with blood, and the sea was like wine.

14

SYBILLA

The Year of The Fire

THE SKALENS HAD BEGUN TO ARRIVE. Sybilla peered from her window, noticing figures of unfamiliar gait passing through the forecourt. A smile tugged at her lips as she watched them turn their eyes to the carnage, their faces full of horror. The Attendants had begged her to let them commence repairs before the meeting of Council. For months they had sought her approval, eager to wash the smoke stains from the walls, to replace singed furniture and drapes, to set the masons and glaziers to work on the East Wing.

"*No,*" she had told them.

At night, cold winds blew through the hallways and birds found clear entry into the sitting rooms. The mouth soured at the smell of charred wood, scarred stone, and somewhere in the middle of things, black bones still lay beneath the rubble.

"*No,*" she had said.

The Attendants were under the strict watch of the Guard, but that did not prevent Anlyn from interfering. As Sybilla's personal Attendant, it was her duty to ensure the wellbeing of the young Skalen. Wherever she went, Anlyn would follow, placing unwanted food before her, muttering, fussing. She was always there, wanting to launder her clothes, trim her nails, powder her face, to anoint her with the sickliest of oils. But it was Sybilla's hair that bothered Anlyn most of all. In places, the fire had burned it down to the root, and the skin, now slick, shined white. Anlyn presented her with a hairpiece harvested from a village maid.

Sybilla had laughed. "*No.*"

She wanted the other Skalens to see for themselves. To see her. To imagine themselves and their Houses, mutilated by fire. She greeted them, a ghostly apparition in an Intercessor's Meridian – the younger one with the dark hair. But where were the others, the Skalens Ladain? The question trailed in their eyes...

In the council room, the Skalens took their seats around the table, each sitting before their point in the Skalens' Star. She felt them focus in on her, all of them at once. For a moment she wavered. Then, bracing herself, she removed her Meridian. At the centre of the table, a small fire burned upon a copper plate. She looked down, thinking only of her hands, of their motion as she scooped the Alma and scattered it on the fire. *One, two, three...* the scent was powerful; her mouth pooled. She swallowed... *four, five, six...* her limbs warmed like honey, she almost dropped the spoon... *seven.*

The fire leapt, brightening their faces, and as Sybilla looked up, she saw that their lids were closed. Her breath caught in her throat, her body stiff as if readying to plunge into a river of ice. She wanted this. She would show them.

Pressure mounted, boiling up beneath her skin.

Sybilla let go.

A distended moment. Then the feeling came.

Her heart screamed. A foul stench, the clearing of rotten blood; her pulse delivering more. Showing them – these strangers – letting them see.

After a time, her own feelings quieted enough that she could discern the others, their presence like shades. She felt their personalities, shifting and filtering through the stuff of their bodies, subtle scents, the feeling of close coarse hair, warmth, dryness, wetness of eyes, and among all of that, feelings humming, songlike and constant, many-textured and blending, revealing themselves from the fog as her breath took her deeper.

She intended to show them the horror, to make them admit their complicity in a corrupt regime, but she did not imagine she would recall her mother's thorn-scarred hands, and wet her cheeks with tears. She did not expect to feel the others as she did. In a swirl of confused impressions, Sybilla felt Cerek Hirvola, greyed and broken, calling for his darling Jagoda.

Domhnall was there, black furred and crouching in the shadows, eager for what was to come. She saw the small of Inry's back, felt her smooth fingers grip the bow of her father's merchant ship as the water turned rough, half wishing it would crash.

In the corner of some distant hall Ulric Elshender stood, stony and silent, sword held in a frozen posture. Behind him, his wife Rebekah waited, hair wavering against the sun, her hands covering her belly.

Lenna stood upon a high mountain, peering down at the devastation of things wrecked and fallen, regarding all with cool acceptance. Damek's eyes appeared close before her as they squinted hard into the crack of the horizon, as if the sky would separate from the sea at the force of his prying.

In the corner of the council room in which they all sat, Emryl and Medard Karasek burned like twin flames, their elderly eyes unblinking, their bodies anchored in statuesque posture, two faces upon a single coin that dizzied her with its ceaseless spin.

In a thicket she found Kalet Askier, her bodice all stuck with feathers, with something hidden in her hands. The drum of her heart beat loud in her chest. The eastern sea boiled deadly in the distance. Her husband, Magnar, was there – a small figure on the beach, collecting things that gleamed in a flash of lightning.

She started to taste them in her mouth, to feel them overlapping her spirit with the pre-existing structures they held within them. Their strategies, like hieroglyphs, presented themselves in cryptic formations and she felt a pang of fear as if they would overwrite her altogether. Then a wellspring of rage bubbled up, clearing her consciousness.

Sybilla started to ignore them; whatever secrets she might ferret from them in their cascading openness were irrelevant to her. The Intercessors would pay for their crimes and there was no weighing or consideration that could change that. She did not need to know the contents of their hearts, as long as they made the right choices and took the right oaths. She willed herself to stand firm, pouring herself into Hiatus. The dew of curiosity that had formed on the surface of her attention evaporated, and once more she felt her awareness held within the familiar shell of this breathing, glowing being, *Sybilla*.

When the Attendants outside sounded the gong, she heard the small details of breath moving in and out of them, this their quietest voice, and opened her eyes. Their faces were confronting in all their fleshy reality, and stranger now that she had seen them through the soft layers of the Alma. She looked around, reckless in her recent nakedness of spirit, possessed of a defiant courage.

She opened her mouth and spoke, "Skalens of Nothelm, Maglore, Seltsland, Lindesal, Brivia and Avishae. I have called this Council so that you may bear witness to a great evil that has been committed in Vaelnyr. The Skalens' House is sacred. This House, and the station that my mother and father held, are symbols of unity. And who would desecrate it? Who would work against us?" Sybilla looked at them each in turn.

She did not expect them to answer, but Damek spoke on her behalf.

"The Intercessors."

"Yes," Sybilla said slowly, noting the sharpening tension in the room.

"My father knew the Intercessors for what they were. Because he had the courage to resist their advances, they silenced him with fire. We Ladains knew their nature and they would have finished us all. But Velspar spared me for a reason."

Emryl's voice came, age-roughened as a cat's tongue. "Sybilla, it is with a heavy heart that I hear of your parents' deaths and the passing of young Lucinda, but the Council of Skalens does not meet to decide matters of guilt or innocence. This is the rightful role of the Intercessors. And if there are guilty parties, surely those individuals will be made to atone for their red deeds, or face execution, if that is found to be the just course."

Medard joined his wife against Sybilla. "Indeed. The Intercessors will be able to discover the truth of it. But here we must pay our respects to those honourable Skalens now past, our friends, Reyan and Vivienne Ladain, and their daughter Lucinda."

Sybilla watched with disgust as Cerek gave the elder Skalens a nod of assent.

At last, Domhnall threw himself into the fray and Inry observed him with anticipation as if he were her very own fighting dog. "I think the Karaseks should show a little more respect for Vaelnyr's present Skalen, who has just survived an attempt on her life. The deliberate snuffing out of the Ladain line is an open act of war against the Skalens."

Cerek's eyes narrowed. "Emryl and Medard are the wisest among us, and you would do well to heed their counsel. Your blood runs hot, Greslet, now that you call yourself Skalen, but we cannot simply abandon our customs when ill fate touches us."

Domhnall glared at him, and it was obvious that he itched to snap Cerek like a twig.

Magnar smiled bitterly. "Cerek, your blind loyalty to these over-puffed meddlers only serves to demonstrate how much power you have ceded to them. Skalen Jagoda is mourned by us all, but you must take back the reins before Lindesal slips from your grasp."

Cerek's face burned crimson. "You dare to speak her name in the same breath that you cast insult against me?"

Kalet ran her tongue over her teeth in snide silence, keeping her eyes fixed on the table.

"And where do the Elshenders stand on this?" Magnar asked, looking the younger Skalens up and down.

Ulric's jaw flexed as he wrapped his hand around his wife's. Rebekah touched him lightly with her free hand and he released her.

Rebekah looked to Sybilla with an even expression. "Sybilla, if murder has been done, then all who are guilty should pay for their crimes. There are Skalens of old that have committed red deeds and we have cast them out. If the Intercessors have evil doers among them, we must do what we can to ensure the truth comes to light."

Lenna regarded Rebekah with her imperious gaze. "We all know what mud is mixed with truth when we call upon the Intercessors for their testimony. This deed of murder is as Domhnall described, an act of war. If one, or ten, or a hundred of them knew of this plot and did nothing to stop it, then all must be held to account."

"I think heresy is about to show itself," Emryl muttered.

Sybilla could feel the crack forming; secrecy's veil torn by the spectacle of murder. At last, she would stand in truth. She felt all of her father's clandestine teachings welling up within, ready to be spoken. "You have the measure of this, Emryl," Sybilla said. "Before his death, my father spoke of a dark heresy. The First Heresy. And it was your ancestors who brought this upon us."

Medard's eyes blazed and Emryl's mouth went slack.

"Restrain her – she has gone mad!" Medard cried.

Cerek looked poised to move, but Damek held him with his livid gaze. "Do not touch her," Damek said.

Sensing that things could go either way, Sybilla spoke her piece. "Before you leave this place, you will choose the side of the Skalens or the side of the Intercessors. But know that the guilty shall receive their due."

She felt the animal rage rising in them. Some of them wished to strike her, while others wished to lift her up as the sword of battle.

"The siatka and kshidol are beasts. They separate our dead from Velspar. It is fire alone that will free them. We are the children of bright flame!"

The smouldering Alma sparked then, as if holy fire were speaking through her. They were words of resurrection, and they had power. She would not stop at killing the Intercessors, she intended to undo their every action. She would salvage all those who had been denied holy burial. The burnt ones; the unforgiven and the unforgivable, her parents and her sister.

Out of the corner of her eye, a shape came toward her, and then

Domhnall tackled Cerek to the ground. She felt Medard's shining eyes on her as he drew up to strike, but Damek came up behind him and held him fast about the throat.

"Guards!" Sybilla called, and seconds later, six guardsmen entered to restrain the traitors. One of them pushed her to the wall and stood between her and the other Skalens with his blade drawn.

"I know what you plan to do, Sybilla," the old woman shrieked. "I have seen your heart. Guardsmen, you are sworn to Velspar and she is moving against us!"

Sybilla sweated cold, but the Guard stood firm and did not betray her.

Magnar's mouth twisted into a smile, and Kalet stared at Sybilla with admiration.

The Elshenders held hands, their faces stiff.

More guards entered the chamber, and all stood stock still, weighing their chances, considering their next move. She had to act now.

Sybilla pushed the guardsman clear of her and addressed the room. "The Guard will escort you to your quarters, but on the morrow, I will ask for your decision. The Intercessors are being held in the Temple dungeon, and those among you who wish to perish with them will have their final chance to look upon the moon this night, and the rise of the sun."

Peran entered then with the Meridians.

"Your prayers will not reach them in dreams," Sybilla said, "The time of whispers and plots is over. From this point on, you will think only those thoughts that are your own, and you will use your mouth to speak."

Sybilla and her allies put on their Meridians, which was signal enough for the others. When Peran applied a gentle hand to fit Magnar and Kalet's, they took them readily, if not awkwardly. Rebekah and Ulric did not move or speak as Peran fitted theirs. It was, after all, their first Council, and their decision was one of great consequence.

Next were Emryl and Medard, who would have readily bitten the fingers from Peran's hand if they thought they would survive it. For them, he added the chinstrap and tightened it just enough to leave them breath. Cerek took his with fear in his eyes, only now aware of how little chance he had of returning to his blessed homeland and his sons, and how little power the Karaseks wielded when the magnificence of their name failed to adorn them.

15

SYBILLA

The Year of The Fire

SYBILLA DRESSED HERSELF IN HER MOTHER'S maroon ceremonial gown, fastening it at the waist. Around her neck she hung her father's chain that bore the Skalens' Star, placing her mother's quietly in the drawer. The seven-pointed star represented the Seven Lands, with Vaelnyr glowing in red carnelian. For each of the Seven Lands, two V-shapes signifying the twin mouths of the Holy Ones enjoined to form a diamond. The seven diamonds formed the star, so that each Skalen would know they ruled but a fragment of Velspar. Sybilla wanted to erase all symbolism that might tempt her people to revere unholy deities, but Peran assured her there were other ways to interpret the diamond. They were not mouths, he said, they were the outstretched hands of the twin Skalens of each of the Seven Lands. And by this she knew that he wished her to marry.

The centre of the Star seemed to behold her in judgement, and she stared right back. The eye of the pendant had witnessed seven centuries of peace, and would watch the events to come with its back to her breast. She was the last Ladain, and when her time came, she would take the twin pendants with her, for she still believed the Star to be a symbol of the past. Those who outlived her could forge their own symbols.

The bindings felt awkward, like an unwanted embrace, the scent of roses infused in the fabric. In the looking glass Sybilla combed her hair this way and that, covering the bald patch rising from her left temple. She thought of the last time she had seen her mother wearing this gown, considering her own reflection in the mirror. But Sybilla was not soft of mouth and her eyes were not pale or gentle. Her jaw was strong, like her father's, and her eyes were dark, deep set, and fringed by heavy lashes. There was a weight to her look, a certain nakedness of emotion that her eyes gave away. She looked nothing like her mother. Bitterly, Sybilla exposed the scar, braiding her hair in a path across her skull so that it twisted like a snake, showing all.

Sybilla went down to the kitchen; she did not like to eat in the dining hall. It made her ears prick up and hear footfall where there was none. Instead, she ate what she needed to sustain her at the cook's table. The Attendants served her, and performed their duties well enough, but she could sense their fear. When she came near, they called her Skalen, bowing low, hiding their eyes, or, as it was this morning, they heard her approach and scattered. The bell of seven chimed and she called for the guards to escort the visiting Skalens to the Temple. She would be waiting for them, to receive their oaths.

From the carriage window, the low gleaming water was clear now, and she took solace in the green shoots she had seen in days past, nibbling their way into the mountain clearings where the Sky Altars had been. The guard sat beside her in silence, his back very straight.

As they approached the Temple, her heart fluttered dangerously in her chest. Though she knew the Intercessors were secured below, she half expected to find them there, white-robed and unshackled, awaiting her arrival. But when they stepped inside, the Temple was hollow, harbouring nothing but the sea's solemn roar, the dungeon giving off neither sound nor odour.

"Thank you, Guardsman," she said, shocked by the amplification of her voice. "Please ask the others to prepare the offerings, then bring them to me."

"Skalen." He nodded, departing.

79

As clouds passed the sun, shadows fell, resembling robed silhouettes, putting her nerves on edge. Her eyes returned to the stairwell and doorway, then came to rest upon the floor. She wore her Meridian, and they did theirs, but somehow she could still feel them beneath her feet. The floor was white, and they scrubbed it so after the daily smearings of the Blood Call. She wondered who had scrubbed it since their imprisonment? Probably the Attendants.

She fancied that she heard their urgent prayers – felt them mounting furious incantations that rattled impotently about their skulls as the people of Vaelnyr went about their day. She could not discern any individual among them, though together they exuded a distinct presence. Their thoughts, collected in nearness, were like a dense substance, harder and heavier than other things, harbouring excessive depth. Hearing the scrape of approaching footfall, she put them in the substratum of her mind, where they would keep, for she would need all of her strength for what was to come.

Guards stood behind her, and below, more monitored the preparation of the execution line. Her father had told her the Intercessors felt honoured to perform their executions. They thought it the letting of poison, for evil showed itself in the blood, in the foul stuff that flowed from the guilty. The Skalens' Guard did not take to the role as easily, being accustomed to the kind of violence that erupted in trade skirmishes. It was not easy to kill as they did, slitting the throat from behind. Sybilla watched the guards on her way in, taking slow inhalations, sinking into Hiatus. She wondered if it was possible to go so deep that one felt nothing at all.

"Bring them in!" she called, and the Skalens were led in, hands unbound, but still shackled by their Meridians. Those who had already extended the hand of friendship looked unruffled, if not a little excited, but the others had a misshapen look, as if each one had sent their weaker twin as a substitute.

"Skalens," Sybilla began. "The crime of murder is but one of the reasons we must act against the Intercessors. Take a moment to remember those who were condemned here, behind closed doors. Who never came home to their families."

She paused. "By what authority do the Intercessors act? By

Velspar? No. Skalen Karasek, the father of all Skalens, spoke truth, but heresy is also attributed to his name. We are Skalen's spiritual descendants and we must trust our faculty to know what is good from what is corrupt."

Sybilla turned to the guardswoman behind her holding two ceremonial bowls. She picked up a flake of dried meat from each and presented them in turn.

She raised the first in her left hand. "Siatka." And the second in her right, "Kshidol." She placed both on her tongue and swallowed. Their ghastly looks strengthened her resolve. "We must renounce what is unholy, so that Velspar may be cleansed," Sybilla said, approaching the Braedals. "And now, I call upon you to honour the spirit of the first Skalens' Pact, so that we may bring unity to Velspar, once and for all."

"Lenna and Damek Braedal of Nothelm, will you take your oath to Velspar in the name of the Skalens?"

"I give my oath," Damek said in a clear voice, placing the salt-meat on his tongue without hesitation.

Lenna regarded the brown flakes with some distaste but gave her oath unflinchingly.

"Inry and Domhnall Greslet of Maglore, will you take your oath to Velspar in the name of the Skalens?"

"Yes, Sybilla, I give my oath," Domhnall said, sweat beading on his forehead. Though the meat was thin enough to require little chewing, his jaw worked at it in a determined muscular movement.

Inry lengthened her neck. "I give my oath," she said solemnly and closed her eyes as she ate.

"Cerek Hirvola of Lindesal, will you take your oath to Velspar in the name of the Skalens?"

Cerek paused, his bloodshot eyes shining an iridescent blue. His mouth quivered. Sybilla tensed with disgust but could not afford to have any of them turn against her. With effort, she softened her expression, showing that she would accept him should he join her, but his gaze fell to the floor and he began to sob.

After a moment Sybilla spoke again, searching for the tone that would call him back. "Cerek... will you join us?"

Finally, he raised his head, but he had set his vision on the far window where the sky's horizon met the sea. "You will not have my oath," he said. "I remain faithful to the Intercessors and will not pass beyond my station as Skalen."

She thought he had finished, but then, more words came from his mouth. "*Velspar, alone in endless ocean... Velspar, singular and miraculous...*"

Sybilla's warmth dissipated, and once again, she was of stone. She glanced at the nearest guard and with a firm hand he led the weeping man across the room and down the stair.

Still, they heard him. "*Siatka preserve us, Kshidol preserve us, Distil the holy essence...*"

Sybilla grit her teeth. As she stood before the Karaseks she could sense the venom gathering on their tongues. Quickly she uttered the words that represented the rope that she flung to them, even as they wished her dead.

"Emryl and Medard Karasek of Brivia, will you take your oath to Velspar in the name of the Skalens?"

Medard spat and Sybilla shook her head, smiling wryly.

"Emryl, will you be joining your husband in the fire pit?"

"Yes!" she hissed, jutting her livid face toward her as the guards secured her arms.

Sybilla took a moment, looking to the door to stop herself from shaking. She tried to gather her thoughts, but all anyone could hear was Cerek, shrieking out the Hymn. "*From vastness preserve, In continuity, In holy unity...!*"

Then, the Karaseks joined in, their voices hoarse and guttural. "*In Alma we call to our brothers, In Alma we call to our sisters, As one in Velspar, As one in holy dominion...*"

Sybilla went on, grave of face, approaching the Elshenders, uncertain of which way they would turn.

"Rebekah and Ulric Elshender of Avishae, will you take your oath to Velspar in the name of the Skalens?"

"We will," Rebekah said quickly, reaching for the offerings. Her cheeks were hot, and her hair had begun to curl at the scalp where sweat crept from beneath her great auburn mane.

Ulric glared at Sybilla, but he reached into the bowl regardless. As he chewed, his stare followed her, but she walked on.

Sybilla had come to the last, and her breath tightened, fearing they might join with their southern neighbours. "Kalet and Magnar Askier of Seltsland, will you take your oath to Velspar in the name of the Skalens?"

Kalet narrowed her eyes, regarding her for a long moment, and then smiled. Her bony fingers fossicked in the bowl as she chose the morsels she liked best, before placing them on her outstretched tongue.

Magnar stared down at Sybilla, seeming to enjoy the way his height forced her neck to crane. "Sybilla," he said. "You have our oath."

Sybilla looked intently at those who remained. Inry and Domhnall Greslet of Maglore, Lenna and Damek Braedal of Nothelm, Kalet and Magnar Askier of Seltsland, Rebekah and Ulric Elshender of Avishae, and herself, Sybilla Ladain of Vaelnyr. Five of the Seven Lands. It would be enough.

"On this day, I, Skalen Sybilla Ladain of Vaelnyr hold prisoner the Intercessors of this land, and the traitorous Skalens of Lindesal and Brivia. I put forward that they be executed in the traditional manner for their involvement in the murder of the Skalens of Vaelnyr and their daughter Lucinda. What is your will?"

"It shall be done," the voices intoned.

"And so it will be."

16

REBEKAH

The Year of The Fire

WATER LAPPED AT THE BOAT as the rowers dipped their oars, the thick forests of Brivia receding in their wake. The Skalens Elshender sat at the front of the craft, their cloaks tight about them. The boatman had laid out a meal of cured meat and cheese, but the sight of it made Rebekah weep. Confused, the man had returned with two pitchers of warm spiced wine that had since gone cold, the purplish liquid spilling in droplets with the rise and fall of low waves.

Rebekah reached for Ulric's hand. They were almost home. The people there, the people of Avishae, awaited their return. They would welcome them at the docks, hopeful their Skalens' had smoothed things over, that they could forget this business in Vaelnyr and go back to their fields, their families, their lives, as they had done at the time of Jagoda's passing.

Rebekah's stomach convulsed, she hiccupped acid, and swallowed it back down.

"The baby?" Ulric murmured, his face grey with fatigue.

She shook her head.

The baby was fine, but the world was not. She was not.

High Intercessor Camis had told her to think of nothing but the safety of her children. To agree to anything the other Skalens' wanted, and to do so without guilt or hesitation.

She did not know it would come to this.

Rebekah tried to catch her husband's gaze. He stroked his blonde beard, tugging at the hairs as if it might stop the tears. The cloud about him was thick and impenetrable. She missed his easy smile, and knew that the mainland had already taken its due. She would never see her husband again, not as he had been, and she hated them for it. Sybilla's justice would break them all.

"We can't do this," she whispered.

Ulric sighed. "The Intercessors do not fear death. They have permitted this. They wish it," he said. "This is bigger than us, Rebekah."

He was repeating the words of the High Intercessors who had come to them almost a year ago to tell the Skalens of their visions. Rivers of blood, smoke and flame. A sacrifice that would usher in a new and enlightened age. What was she to make of it?

The Intercessors promised they would return. That their spirits would flood the wombs, and all the children would wear their faces. A cleansing that would draw the power of Intercession into every home. Into the Skalens House itself. Rebekah did not understand them.

She could not do this without them. How could they ask her to? When all was done, would the newborns arise to wash the blood from her hands?

"We are not initiates. How can we do what they ask? I can hardly bear the pain of it, I–" A sob escaped her, tears flowing down her face. "I do not want to live in a world without Intercession. Where the Holy Ones are butchered for their meat."

Ulric held his head in his hands. "Camis says it is necessary. We have to have faith."

Rebekah looked at him, the way his body cowered under the weight of their task. She knew what he felt, but he would not admit it, could not say it out loud. Still, she could not stop the words from coming. The time for talking would be over the moment they stepped ashore.

"What if we chose to fight?"

Silence trailed.

They had spoken an oath, they had scrawled their names in ink... that is all they had done.

But even as she said it, she knew that they could not.

Domhnall Greslet had chosen his sister, Olinda, and her husband, Jemryn, as the Regents of Brivia. If she and Ulric did not hold true to their oaths, Avishae would be at the mercy of the Maglorean Guard. They'd met Guardsman Rayhmer upon their return journey and knew that he would not hesitate if it came to killing them.

She wiped her face, a wince of fear sharpening her senses.

Ahead, the Caulmont Range came into view, the kshidol hovering above snow-capped peaks. She thought of flesh, then, of bloodied carcasses. The sweet grasses of the valley burned black, the poisonous stench of the execution pyre.

With a sharp breath, she stood, taking her thoughts to the end of the boat. Behind them, the Brivian coast was nothing but a dark smear upon the water. But then there was Rayhmer and his men.

She imagined what she would do with Zohar and little Ambrose if the Maglorean Guard crossed the straight to take Avishae. They would hide in the bowels of the Skalens' House. Ulric would take Ambrose, and she would take Zohar, holding her hand as they ran... But what of her father, out there in the forest? What of the people in Haydentown, and the Intercessors in the Temple?

The Magloreans had been cannibals once.

She pressed a trembling hand to her belly. *Velspar, bless this child. Mother Siatka, please, bless this child. Protect my children. Protect Zohar and Ambrose and this little one, yet to be born. Protect my Bethany. Mother Siatka, be with me at the birth. See her safely into this world.*

17

SYBILLA

The Year of The Fire

Sybilla vomited through her fingers, the hot fluid turning sickly wet on her skin, her eyes streaming as she watched.

"Get her out of here!" Peran called.

She stared at the bodies. Their flaccid limbs atop one another, their unseeing eyes, the deep red gashes at their throats.

The guardsmen brought in more from the cells, a black-haired woman breathing through flared nostrils, eyes glazed with prayer. A foot pressed the back of her leg and she knelt. A fist grasped her hair to expose the throat, and – gush. The neck spasmed, chugging that redness out, joining the flow of the others, beside her, up and down the line.

Sybilla wiped her shaking hands on her cloak, unable to close her mouth.

They dragged the woman off, her hair a paintbrush made of sable in a mess of spilt ink.

The next one almost slipped on the blood-slicked floor. A young man with fawn coloured hair. *No.*

Intercessor Caleb. Of course he was among them. All of them, and every one, without exception: the Intercessors would die. By nightfall they would all be gone. It would be over.

His blue eyes pierced her. His look so full of questions, as if he might implore her, as if justifications meant anything here. She felt the heat of his spirit like fire's haze. Her bones began to ache. Behind Caleb, a High Intercessor stood, his eyes closed, looking utterly resigned. But she saw it – the old man's red hand, outstretched and trembling, lending strength to Caleb's plea, and Caleb's spirit, leafing the scales of her armour, searching for the place he had found in her, all those years ago.

Sybilla's wails joined the cries of the dying, the air thick with transitional energy and viscera.

"I said, get her out!" Peran shouted, pointing to a guardsman by the door. Peran was covered in blood. It matted the hair of his arms and soaked his leathers black.

Sybilla pressed her hand to the blinding stone at her brow and shut her eyes. She willed her Meridian to shield her, to shield her *now*.

A gentle hand pulled at her elbow.

"Skalen, please, follow me. I will take you outside."

Keeping her eyes closed, she let the guard lead her away, a high-pitched sound in her ears.

She leaned into him as the air from above rushed through the dungeon gate. The lock turned with a clunk and he held her awkwardly as he returned the keys to his belt.

"Skalen, if you could just open your eyes." The guard put one hand to her cheek. She let her head fall against his hand, tears streaming. She would never open her eyes.

She wanted Lucinda. Her face contorted. *Lucinda*.

In her mind, Sybilla crawled into her sister's bed and slept. Together, on that fateful night, peaceful as they slept, never waking, never knowing what was being done to their bodies. Peaceful as the heat of Intercession encircled them, flames urging their bodies, first by smoke – to sink deeper in their dreams; then by sweat – to loosen the spirit; then by bubbling – to split the skin, the flesh of their cheeks melting, tightening, their teeth cracking in a fury of flame. Peaceful as their flesh released them, sisters, escaping on the wind.

She swallowed dryly, tasting ash. Opened her eyes.

The guard slowly removed his hand and smoothed it on his trousers. Gavril. That was his name.

A sharp breath hit the back of her throat, and another, the scent of blood too rich in the air. With difficulty she nodded and he put his arm around her waist, supporting her as they moved up the marble stair, Sybilla's breath coming in wheezing gasps.

"Let us leave this place, Skalen. You do not have to remain here." His clear green eyes held hers, and she felt the urgency in his grip.

At the top of the stair, the entrance seemed a hollow tomb, but the business of it was still being done, the feverish sound of their moaning, the grunts and shrieks betraying the animal within, the thing that wanted to live.

"Put up your hood," Gavril whispered, as he peered out at the street outside.

She did as he asked, keeping her head down as they rushed to the carriage. She heard his breath, smelt the bile on her hands, her eyes fixed on his feet as he led her out.

There would be witnesses to her failure. Oath-takers curious to hear the screams. Those who needed to know when the job was done. They would have to kill them too.

She blundered into the carriage, Gavril falling in beside her. They moved off. Travelling fast.

When they reached the Skalens' House, Gavril took her not through the main doors, but to the Guard's barracks. Inside, it was musty and dim, smelling of sweat, leather oil and hay mattresses. They were the only ones there.

"You can come in here to wash. I will get you something clean to put on before you go up to the House."

Sybilla went to the washroom and closed the door. Along the wooden bench, clay pitchers and basins were laid out with a folded cloth beside each one. The slatted timber platform she stood upon was dry and mould-stained and would surely soak up the blood on her shoes.

Numbly, she yanked at her boot laces and freed the clasp of her cloak, letting her things tumble where they would. Her remaining clothes she peeled off one at a time, finding pinkish smears on her skin where the blood had soaked through.

"Skalen, do you need help?" Gavril called.

She poured water into the basin and picked up a cloth, dipping it in to make a splashing sound.

"Leave me," she said.

And as she washed her arms, her thighs and her feet, it reminded her of their death rites, the washing that came before the cutting of the corpse. Seven pieces. The head, the upper torso, the lower torso, each limb bound as one, folded like a wing.

She wiped the salt-crust from her eyes, skirting a rag-covered finger along her teeth before dropping the cloth into the water. The white shape sank down, undulating at the bottom.

She stood there, pale with gooseflesh, a droplet of water slipping down her arm.

"Skalen?" Gavril called.

After a long moment she responded.

"Yes?"

"There are clean clothes outside the door. I will move where I will not see you, but I will be right here when you are ready."

She heard his footsteps recede and went to the door. She opened it carelessly, feeling that she might walk naked into the training yard and shove one of their swords right up under her ribs.

But instead, she dressed herself in a guard's tunic and britches, slipping on boots that had bumps in all the wrong places. She emerged, wandering to the nearest cot. She sat, running her fingers over the cotton slip, feeling the coarse fibres of the hay beneath.

She looked up to find Gavril standing there, wearing a new set of clothes.

"If you want to sleep there, I will keep the others away," he said, gently.

Sybilla held his gaze. His green eyes seemed to glow against his sun darkened skin. He wore no beard, his shaven jawline bluish where one would have grown, his cropped hair dark and thick.

"They will not forgive my weakness today," she said gravely, shaking her head. "They will not follow me now."

Gavril crouched so his face was level with hers. She felt the closeness of him, his muscled forearms, his breath a whisper over her hands. How did he dare come so close? Her head swam, feeling the structure of things dissolving.

He glanced across the room. "I remember when you used to train with us, when your grandfather taught us out in the field." A smile touched his lips as he held up his hand. "With his rocks and his flowers."

She knew it must be true, but did not want to admit that she'd never paid much attention to the striplings that sat behind her. And even now, she did not know all of the guards' names. The world was full of people with unknowable motives, their seeping influence poisonous to an open heart. But now that she was Skalen, she could not be so indrawn. All of them looked to her now, and they expected her to look back with recognition, with a superior knowledge of their fates, and the wisdom to lead them.

"He was a patient man," Gavril went on, searching for the right words.

Sybilla felt a pang in her heart. She could not think of her grandfather now.

"I am sorry, Skalen," he said, finally.

Dust motes meandered in a stream of sunlight by her feet. "If I call for death, I must be able to witness it," she said resolutely, her fingernails pressed into her palms.

"No one is born with mastery. Sometimes we fall off our horse. That is all that has happened today. You fell off your horse and I helped you up so you may ride again."

Gavril shifted into a cross legged position.

By his posture she saw what he offered. He would sit with her in Hiatus before they returned to the Skalens' House. If it had been Peran, she would have resented the gesture. She reminded herself that for members of the Guard, this was a daily practice, and no member of their retinue was expected to persevere alone.

She gave a small nod, closing her eyes as she folded her hands in her lap, allowing herself to melt into the musky scent of the barracks, to become the soft creak of the great wooden door, the distant sound of swallows in the training yard. She followed Gavril's breath as it slowed, letting go of everything, feeling the cool weight of her Meridian now sufficient to the task, heat and terror drawing off her, realities receding, the cool moment growing wide.

18

SYBILLA

The Year of The Fire

Sybilla awoke in her chambers, harsh sunlight fringing the heavy drapes. All about her she could smell the nauseating stench of their bubbling flesh. The ash becoming airborne, making its way into her mouth, filling her lungs, so there was nothing clean anywhere. She rang the bell at her bedside and a few minutes later a young Attendant appeared in her doorway.

"Skalen?" the girl whispered, searching the gloom.

"It stinks in here. Please, do something to keep the smoke out, I can't stand it."

"Of course." The Attendant bowed and disappeared.

As she waited, Sybilla found herself wishing the girl hadn't closed the door, but she did not have the strength to get up and open it herself.

When the Attendant returned, she entered with a basket of linens on her arm, a jug of water in one hand and a lit candle in the other. She dripped a little wax from the tip and fixed the candle in the sconce by the door. Among the linens were posies of sharp smelling herbs. The girl kept her eyes down and extended her arm, careful not to touch Sybilla as she placed one on the sheet. Sybilla reached down and took it, drawing it to her nose. Rosemary and lemon peel, lavender and pine needles. Sybilla averted her gaze as the girl tied more posies to the bed posts.

She stared at the bleeding light that danced on the wall as the girl disappeared behind the drapes, pressing wet rags into the window crevices.

Taking up the empty basket and jug, she paused. "Shall I leave the candle, Skalen?"

"Take it with you, but make sure you extinguish it outside. You don't want to undo your good work." Sybilla tried a smile. A pointless gesture.

The girl removed the candle with a clunk, her serious face ablaze with light as she slipped out, and closed the door.

Darkness.

Sybilla pressed the lavender, crushing it lightly between her fingers, closing her eyes. At some point she drifted back to sleep.

The drapes whispered on the flagstones, the brass ends of the draw-cord clinking. Thick, fatty smoke wafted in. It travelled with purpose. Perhaps it had opened the window? But that was impossible. The smoke moved slyly, unspooling into wide sheets that settled over her pale, sleeping body. Layer, upon layer.

She coughed. The smoke distended, mimicking the spasms of her lungs. Her arms were so heavy she could barely lift them. She thrashed the air, but the smoke did not dissipate, it gathered, sculpting itself before her, becoming rhythmic, a heaving thing that she clung to, for it was below her now, or was she upside down?

A sharp gust of wind stung her face and she was riding. Her father was a horse that breathed fire. And she was tied to him, her flesh seared by the furnace of his lungs, his scorched flank splitting, the hide rolling back to show his blackened bones. He was disintegrating. *Father! No!*

She clung to his neck, burying her face in his mane, trying to cover him with her body, to calm his heart with her hands. To calm her own heart. A red thing that throbbed in her hand, that dripped, dripped, dripped...

Sybilla's eyes snapped open, her palm sticky with pine resin as she slowly opened her shaking hand. She could still hear it, the dripping, and as she shook herself awake, realised that the sound came from the wet rags on the windowsill.

She sat up, her muscles sluggish from months in bed. The bones of her wrist were just visible in the reddish dark of midday, and she wondered how long it would take for her to die. If she wanted that to happen, she could not give in so easily when the food tray came. There were quicker ways, but she could not face the prospect of setting them in motion. Of ringing the bell and commanding them to do it. Of choosing the way it should be done and making it so.

She massaged her scalp, trying to release the tension of her dream. Her nightgown stank of stale sweat, and she traced the greasy terrain of her forehead and chin, wondering if she could bear the task of washing her face.

There was a tap at the door, and Sybilla looked up to see Anlyn with her dinner tray.

"Ah, you are awake," Anlyn said, reservedly, placing the tray on the dresser.

The bowl of broth steamed softly, illuminated by the hall lamps outside her door.

Anlyn pulled a set of candle sticks from her apron and stepped out to light them. One after another she set them about the room, fourteen candles in all. Anlyn whisked past her, casting her cloth over sooted surfaces, reaching under her bed to remove the fouled chamber pot, cleaning the water that had pooled beneath the windows.

"I will speak to the Attendant that served you this morning, if this water infuses the drapes, you will get damp in your lungs."

Anlyn did not turn around as she spoke, and Sybilla kept her silence resolute, knowing that if she gave any reply, the old woman would see it as an opening for discussion.

Eventually, Anlyn approached the bed, placing the wooden tray carefully over Sybilla's shrouded thighs. The soup was tepid, and Sybilla swirled the spoon through it a few times before placing it beside the bowl. She wanted Anlyn to go, but the Attendant was rustling around in her bedside drawer, counting under her breath.

The old woman stopped and looked up at Sybilla with suspicion. "Are you late with your monthlys?" she whispered, her brow creasing in anxious accusation.

Sybilla sniffed. "I do not know what day it is, Anlyn."

"Nobody has... come here?" She leaned in to put her hand on Sybilla's arm as she would have done when she was a girl, but stopped herself, her fingers recoiling into her palm.

Sybilla shook her head, almost laughing in disbelief.

Anlyn nodded. "Then you must eat!" She gestured impatiently at the untouched broth.

Sybilla glared at her.

Anlyn took in a sharp breath. "Sybilla, we are all waiting for you. Do you know that next month it will have been a year? What was this all for?" The old woman held up her hands, her face growing tight with the words she could not say. Then through gritted teeth she muttered, as if Sybilla had grown insensible and could not hear. "Your parents would not have stood for this. You have abandoned them, and you have abandoned this House." She clapped her hands to her mouth.

Sybilla flung the bowl. "Get out!" It smashed against the wall, and Anlyn jerked backwards.

The Attendant straightened herself, glanced at the shards on the floor and stalked out.

Sybilla's breathing came hard. She tore at the sheets. Freeing her legs, she tried to stand, the sudden movement making her queasy. She drew herself up, anger surging through her muscles, and grabbed the nearest candle, smashing the wick into the wall. She staggered the circumference of the room until all fourteen candles were out.

Darkness.

She fell to her knees and began to sob, crushing her knuckles against the cold flags. Strange keening sounds emitted from her, and little hitching gasps.

A fist rapped at the door.

"Sybilla?" Peran's voice was firm. "Do you need a physician?"

Her ribs convulsed silently, tears dripping onto the floor.

"Sybilla? I am going to come in."

She let out a rasping scream.

"Okay. Okay. Can I open the door? I will not cross the threshold."

"No!" The word tore from her throat, and sobbing returned in its wake.

A pause. Murmuring behind the door.

"Who then? Will you let one of the Attendants help you? Mara, who came this morning?"

"No Attendants," she called, tonelessly. She wanted none of them.

She imagined herself curled on the hay mattress in the barracks, and that guard who had been so kind to her. Gavril.

"You must allow one of us in. Do you trust me, Sybilla?" His voice had grown quiet, his face right up to the door. They would not leave her alone.

"Gavril."

A thin voice – Anlyn's perhaps. "What did she say?"

"Gavril!" Sybilla called, louder this time.

The people behind the door went quiet.

"I will send for Guardsman Gavril now," Peran said. "Is there anything else you need?"

"Water," she said, and rolled onto her back, the floor icy through her nightdress.

Gavril. Her heart thrummed in immediate regret as she braced for this newest humiliation. Why Gavril? What had she done?

19

SYBILLA

One Year After The Fire

"What do you think you will see if you open that window?" Gavril gazed down at her, candlelight dancing across the contours of his cheekbones and jaw.

Sybilla touched her own face to reassure herself that she was clean, that her hair did not fall in rank clumps as it had done the first time he had come.

"A wasteland," she murmured, the image clear in her mind. A place of charred remains where horses wandered with maggots falling from their open wounds.

He looked down, sadness infusing his smile. "Not a wasteland."

Why was he so kind to her? She did not understand it.

"The only way you will know for sure, is if you look with your own eyes." Gavril reached for her hand, pulling her gently from the bed.

Sybilla fought the urge to pull her hand away.

He reached for her gown and draped it around her shoulders, and she pulled it tight about her chest.

Gavril stepped slowly across the room, as if she were a wild animal that might startle. "I will open the north window first."

Sybilla watched, rigid as stone, as his hand dipped into the pool of light on the wall, and pulled the draw cord.

Brightness knifed her senses, the cord drawing like a noose, until it was all the way clear. Sybilla blinked quickly, seeing only sky – a pale blue sky, rippled white.

"Come closer," he urged. "Look upon your homeland."

She shuffled forward, making out green pasture, the town buildings curved about the Gulf, and a glittering sapphire sea. A laugh escaped her, and Gavril grinned. "See? There are sheep. And look, the first blossoms of spring. A man riding a cart, just there."

His smile faded as he beheld her face.

"It still stands," she said.

Tall and iridescent. A beacon of heresy.

"It will fall at your command." Gavril's jaw flexed as he squinted down at the Temple.

Sybilla came closer to the glass, swivelled the lock free, and pushed the window open. A glorious gust of air hit her face, fresh with salt and meadowsweet. She let it wash over her, taking it into her lungs, feeling strength and purpose returning to her blood.

"Tell Peran that I will meet him in the council room the day the Temple falls."

Gavril pressed his hand to his breast, bowing his head. "Yes, my Skalen," he said, full of gratitude. "Yes. It will be done."

The breezes of early spring blew freely as Sybilla worked at her desk, unfurling scroll after scroll to read the tally of the dead. She pressed her quill to points on the map where rebellion had flared, and those places where it had been staved off, finding their position strong. The toll was great – there were more executed in Velspar than those who yet lived – but life went on. Children were still being born, the crops came in, and trade continued.

As she gazed from her window, watching the great Temple crack, hope grew in her that the people might still look to her as their leader, that all was not lost. The hammers clattered, relentless in their beating as they bruised the Temple grey. In places, the surface buck-led, and wounds opened, showing the dark flesh of the hammerers inside. Each morning she arose to find the thing deeper in its death throes. And when the upper floors fell, she knew that the end was near.

The dungeon's gurgling throat remained as a warning, an open reminder. In its impotence it could glug only rain. Some days it gleamed with high water, for its drains were built for the thinner streams of human blood. She imagined it choking, unable to splutter, and in her mind, she held the Intercessors in eternal torment. The Holy Ones were dead. Intercession was a crime. There would be no new initiates, no blood rites, no Gates to separate the seers from the seen.

Her father's mission had been fulfilled, and the future was in her hands.

She told herself this as she dressed, winding her braids about her Meridian. The day had come.

Her footsteps resonated as she approached the council room. The door was open and she saw Peran seated at the table. Her pulse flick-ered at her neck, and she released a shaky breath, drawing her mind into the cool heart of Hiatus.

Peran turned. "Skalen."

Sybilla entered the room, aware that he was taking in her appear-ance, judging the health of her body and mind.

"You are looking well," he said.

Sybilla pulled out the chair beside him, for she could not rightly sit in any other. With a cough, Peran stood, running his hands awkwardly along the circumference of the table, deciding how much distance was appropriate when they had not looked upon each other's faces for a full year.

Peran settled on the seat of Lindesal, and regarded her across the table. "Thank you for coming. I know things have been... difficult."

She had rehearsed this moment many times in her mind and knew that it would be best to keep things brief. "Peran." She smiled. "Your stewardship has been invaluable over this past year, but I am ready now to take that burden from your shoulders."

The Head Guard's expression remained carefully blank.

"I read your report regarding the incident at Lake Nanthe and the family who warned us of the traitors' plans."

Peran nodded.

"As a gesture of my personal gratitude, I would like to gift them our finest Attendant, so that they might enjoy care and comfort, just as we enjoy their loyalty."

Peran looked baffled. "Anlyn?"

"Yes. Give them Anlyn, along with my thanks."

Peran opened his mouth, closed it again.

"The second matter I would like to discuss is my appearance in public. I must make myself visible. I know this. I will need to travel and meet with the other Skalens."

"Of course," he said, quickly.

"But I think we both know my safety is not assured. And it is for this reason I have appointed Gavril as my personal guard. I want someone who can accompany me in Council, and Gavril has proved himself both trustworthy and capable."

The words settled between them, Peran's darting eyes revealing the idea was new to him. For a moment he gazed out the window. Sybilla's breath tightened as she steeled herself, unsure of him after their time apart.

"Gavril has taken an oath to the Guard, and the Guard exists to protect its Skalen," he said, searching her with his eyes.

"That is right. Now, you must excuse me." Sybilla stood. "It has been such a long time since I have felt the sun on my face."

"Sybilla, before you go," Peran said, lowering his voice. "You understand Gavril will be looked upon differently if you set him apart like this?"

She gave him a curt nod, not wanting to share confidence.

"If he breaks his vows," he said, carefully, "he will not be permitted to serve as a member of the Guard. Decisions concerning Gavril's future will not rest only with me."

Tension gathered like a stitch in her side.

"He will continue in his duties," she said, lightly. "I am simply informing you of his election as the most suitable guard to attend me in matters of diplomacy."

Peran smoothed his beard. "Yes, I must agree with you there."

Sybilla pushed her chair in and took a step toward the door. "Well, now that is settled, I would like to go and visit my mother's garden. Mara mentioned the roses are in bloom."

Peran extended his hand in a gesture of dismissal. "Go. There will be time enough to discuss the tally at our next meeting."

"Good day, Peran."

The Head Guard looked at her again, taking her measure. "Good day, Skalen."

20

SYBILLA

Three Years After The Fire

GAVRIL RODE AHEAD OF HER, winding a path through the abandoned quarter where the Temple once stood. The day was bright, and for a moment Sybilla closed her eyes, the light throbbing through her lids. Two years had passed since her convalescence, but still, her chambers felt stifling. She wanted always to be outside, to be out riding. To distance herself from the Skalens' House, with its grimy western façade and the clean-finished stone of the revived East Wing.

A warm, salty breeze moved across her braids and bare arms and, sensing the light change, she opened her eyes. Ahead, Gavril's horse ambled past rows of boarded-up terraces, the scene bleached grey. As her eyes recovered, she saw that not all of the houses here were uninhabited. A woman flicking her broom sharply across the steps glanced at Sybilla, inclining her head before disappearing inside.

She had become used to the dull silence, the shadow that hung over everything. After a few zealous months of speeches and decrees, the truth of things had settled around her. The Guard had used her grief to shift the pieces into place, and now her job was done. She had been the tip of the spear, but now they required a figurehead, and they needed only for Sybilla to keep her mask in place.

She took in a great breath of sea air and sighed, steering her horse toward the left-hand side of the road. Gavril turned to make sure she was still behind him, his smile framed by the cropped black beard he had grown to match his elevated status as the Skalen's personal guard. She followed him onto the main street, slowing to allow a wagon to pass. In the distance, children shrieked in the waves, just as Guardsman Edric had prophesied.

The water gleamed, and fishing boats bobbed on the tide, roped in lines on either side of the Long Pier. The main street was busy, but nothing like it had been in days gone by. The merchants had returned, their wares tinkling quietly as the people of Vaelnyr shuffled by, sour-faced as they haggled, holding tight to their remaining coin. The hawkers that had once been famous for their fresh roast meat were nowhere to be seen. In their place a skinny man peered up at her between ropes of dried fish. The fruit seller beside him doing her best to pretend she had not seen Sybilla, polishing her apples with a striped rag.

All about her, Sybilla sensed them waiting for her to pass. In the bakers and the cobblers, faces hovered at the window, choosing their moment so they would not have to come too close. Women laying reams of woven cloth upon the cobblestones, gave nods of deference, the incense they burned sweetening the air. Out on the water, a fisher boy crouched in the bird's nest, the boat's mast creaking in the falling wind.

The senior guardsmen had sent her to town this day to be among her people. To smile and shake their hands, to reassure them she valued their oaths, and that soon would come a time of plenty. But the Guard did not understand the flint-eyed populace who had sent their friends and neighbours to the pyre. They were not sentimental. They wanted a Skalen who kept goods flowing and fences in place, who abided the unbending rule, and did not seek to rouse them with high ideals and rallying cries. She cast her gaze about, riding slowly so they would see her, so she could say she'd done her duty.

Finally, they turned off the main street, wending their way down quiet laneways where the horses' hooves clattered on with the fading of the sea. They passed the burned gates of the Temple dormitories, where the high windows shone with shards of broken glass. The path once thick with pilgrims, now a place for darting rats.

They rode on, toward Atilan, passing slowly out of town and onto a wide dirt track. Skirting the base of the mountain, they took the northern fork where the trees leaned in, the path growing fainter on the ground until it disappeared completely.

Gavril stopped and tied his horse, stretching his stiff muscles and rolling his neck from side to side.

She smiled down at him. "Let us go down to the river." Her throat was parched.

He squinted at her, shading his eyes from the sun that shone hot on her back. "Very well," he said, and waited as she dismounted, leading her horse beneath the shade of a drooping elm.

Sybilla drank half the water in her skin and wiped the perspiration from her face with the back of her hand. "The shortcut we took last time will do well."

Gavril nodded and started off, stepping over ancient roots that split the earth, and saplings that sprouted among the rocks.

The air was damp, the soil wet from night rains, and soon enough Sybilla's boots were muddy to the ankle. Cool sweat trickled down her back, the bowing trees sheltering them from the heat of the day. She loved it here. Listening to the birds' liquid call, the crunch and rustle of living things. This place did not think or reason, it did not yearn or regret. Through everything was a pulse of water, a living essence that spread from the deep earth to the tips of the highest branches above them.

Ahead of her, Gavril moved gingerly across the cracked grey boulders that blocked the path. She remembered them from last time, and knew there was no easy way to avoid them. "The rocks are slippery today, Skalen, best I take your hand."

Sybilla climbed halfway across and then reached for him, his hand warm in hers. She braced herself and leapt across the void between rocks, letting go of him once she was across. "I'll be fine from here."

The way was steep, but small trees anchored their descent until they reached the shining water below. Their footfall startled a family of rabbits and she laughed as they shot, one after another, into a hollow log. She crouched on the bank and plunged her hands in, her grazes stinging. Sybilla rinsed her water skin and refilled it, coming to sit with Gavril on the soft grass.

After a while, she spoke. "Will you tell them that we came here?"

Gavril's green eyes glimmered with reflected light as he held her gaze. "I do not see any reason that I should."

She smirked and leaned back, stretching her legs. "What will you tell them of our hands and knees?"

"I will tell them that you stumbled near the rocks while playing with the children at the Gulf."

"I like that story."

Eventually, Gavril stood to wander along the rocks where a tree had fallen in the water, leaving Sybilla alone with her thoughts.

She lay back on the grass, closing her eyes to the current's burbling song. But even here, she could not maintain the feeling of the place – of solitude with Gavril close by – without drifting to thoughts of their return, and how she would present herself to the senior guards. Her jaw tightened, Peran's voice filtering down, fleshing out the details of the latest tally. In Vaelnyr, red thoughts were no longer a crime, this she had decreed. But men still stole each other's pigs, women still drowned their newborns, swords and short daggers still found their way into vital organs, men still dealt roughly with their women, and those men, in turn, still took to choking on supper's broth.

She could not help thinking of the people she would pass in the street on their way home. People easily ignored when she had an afternoon to look forward to, but who weighed upon her when she was the one that had to answer for their crimes. Problems in the tally were Sybilla's problems, and they reflected badly on her rule.

"You look troubled," Gavril said on his return, and his dark brow furrowed as he waited for her to speak.

"I am tired of the executions, Gavril. I thought that once the Intercessors were gone, that the threat of death would be enough to deter them from red deeds. I wanted their minds to be their own, to give them the freedom to think and feel without reproach, but still..."

Gavril sat and twirled a stick between his fingers, watching the patterns it made. "You have endured more than anyone could ask, Sybilla, and it is your strength and decisiveness that saved Velspar from the Intercessors. If you had not acted, where would we be now? The dawn of a new age is a time of dimness when the light has not yet flooded the darkness away. You must not lose faith in your mission."

Sybilla ran her fingers beneath the leather strap of her Meridian, massaging her forehead. "They are defenceless," she murmured.

Gavril peeled leaves from the stick, clearing it of imperfections. "What do you mean?"

"The Intercessors can no longer enter their minds, but the connections are still there, among families, and enemies and lovers. It is those connections we must break. Think of the passion it takes to kill out of anger. If they wore the Meridian, it would be different."

Gavril smiled but held his tongue.

Her heart leapt, a charged silence falling between them. They both wore the Meridian but still her passion flared. Could he feel it? She turned her reddening face away. "We had better head back."

"Of course, my Skalen," Gavril replied, swinging the stick as he strolled toward the rocky escarpment.

Now that his back was turned, she wished she had not ended their day so early. What did that smile mean? The things she wanted for the people of Vaelnyr were not what she wanted of him. She longed to see behind his reassuring words, his artful turns of phrase that showed only the surface of his thoughts. What she wanted was there in his movements, his look, in the words he did not say.

Sybilla brushed herself off and followed him, going back the way they had come. She fixed her gaze on the firm line of his shoulders as he stretched and clambered over rock and crevasse. Watched his fingers moving over mossy stone, seeking purchase. Whenever the breeze picked up, she caught the smoky scent of his skin and wondered what it would be like to run her hands down his back, for the day to grow so hot that they'd have to leave their clothes on the bank and swim. Oh, how she understood her sister then. Gavril's presence made her body shimmer, her Temple lessons turned to dust. But still, she could not touch him, could not tell him what she wanted, and he was bound by her command.

The slanted afternoon sun was thick and hazy, casting golden shafts through the trees. She imagined the canopy dripped a nectar of fire oil, a drop upon her neck, upon his forearm, promises like kisses, the flicker of leaves falling. Her heart beat steadily, reminding her of a reddening coal, and all around her was the stuff of kindling. She followed him, the forest unfolding, and she would follow him on through the town, and along the water's edge. She would follow him up the path that led to the Skalens' House, and she would follow him though its halls. She would find a place where they could exist, a place of sanctuary.

21

SYBILLA

Six Years After The Fire

SYBILLA WALKED BY THE STABLES intending to take one of the horses for a ride along the Atilan track. A female guard pushed past her.

"Beg pardon," the woman muttered without turning, stalking into the Guard's quarters.

The murmur of clipped conversation bled through the doorway, and moments later, four half-dressed guards followed the female guard out.

Only then did they recognise their Skalen, dressed as she was in her riding clothes.

"Skalen." The first of them bowed, the others inclining their heads one after another like puppets worked by a common set of strings.

More guards emerged, fastening doublets and leather surcoats, others fairly running to the horses.

"What is it, Guardsman?" Sybilla asked.

Andrin came over to her, wincing in the sunlight. "There is trouble in Lindesal, Skalen. It is not for you to worry."

"Am I not your Skalen? You will tell me of this incident and I will give the order," she glared at him, but felt nothing more than an impertinent child as she stared up at the man, a full foot taller than her.

He wet his lips in irritation at the delay. "Of course. A regrettable turn of phrase. Forgive me, Skalen." He led her to a nearby bench, giving one of his brethren a look that told him to continue preparations. "Skalen, you will remember in our last briefing, Peran spoke of the Sisters of Jagoda."

Sybilla had some hazy recollection of the words. "The Skalens' Attendants," she said, remembering that much.

"Yes. It seems on the day that Festival would have taken place, the women took themselves to the Sea Altar, drunk on Alma wine and danced there – naked – calling out to 'Mother Jagoda'. They had converted a surprising number of women from the town, and fighting broke out between the Lindesali Guard and the townspeople. Some of them wanted the women arrested, but the other part of the crowd won out, forming a barricade around them."

"Mother Jagoda," Sybilla repeated.

Andrin took this as a question and went on to explain what Sybilla feared she had already been told in the council room. "They believe their lady Skalen became one with Siatka when her body was consumed, for she was a bright spirit. They say she foresaw all that was to come, and chose the moment of her death so the siatka would take refuge in distant seas. The Attendants – the 'Sisters' – say that when Jagoda's sons performed the Blood Call, they were acting according to 'Her' will. They drowned themselves so She would be sure to consume them." Andrin pursed his lips, as if this would hold back the effect of his words.

"Do you travel there to execute them?" Sybilla asked wearily.

"No, Skalen," he said, averting his eyes.

"What then? Hasn't Domhnall the forces to assist if the Lindesali Guard are insufficient?"

"The Regents of Lindesal did send for reinforcements, but it appears Kalet refused her sister Seltsland's aid."

Sybilla looked at him in disbelief. "Kalet appointed Haldi as Regent. On what basis did she refuse?"

"It appears the sisters quarrelled – the exact nature of their disagreement has not been reported to the Guard."

Sybilla frowned. "This is completely unacceptable. Kalet will explain herself at Council."

Andrin shrugged, as if he thought that unlikely.

She would not discuss Skalens' business with this man. "Please continue. What is the situation now?"

"When word reached Maglore, Domhnall sent his Guard to settle the matter. It seems..." Andrin coughed. "It seems the Maglorean Guard have not acted according to our sacred laws."

Sybilla scoffed. "This seems to happen every other day. Of which sacred law do you speak in this case?"

Andrin did not smile, nor offer her a response, but tapped his foot irritatingly against the leg of the bench.

"Are they all dead?" She looked hard at him.

"Yes," he said, but did not go on.

Sybilla's heart thumped, imagining that they had committed the same atrocities that had seduced the Maglorean Guard before the Greslets came to cleanse their ranks.

Sybilla spoke in a hoarse whisper. "They have eaten of their flesh?"

Andrin inhaled. "No, Skalen. But they have conducted themselves in a manner unbefitting to the Guard. The women were violated, most grievously."

"I see." There it was again, that feeling. A slipping sensation in her gut. She should not have asked.

"The Guard have been tainted by this act. We must confer with those involved, and exact punishments where necessary. Velspar stands or falls upon the honour of the Guard."

Sybilla raised her eyebrows at this.

Andrin coughed again, several times, his eyes watering. "Apologies, Skalen. Is there anything else? I really must be getting along."

Sybilla tried not to register his dismissive tone, her insignificance in these affairs, and though she knew her question would not land well, she asked it anyway. "Does Gavril travel with you on this mission?"

She kept her face plain, her heart still.

His eyes flickered, watching the guards loading provisions onto the saddles. "Is it your wish that he accompanies us?" he asked, looking down at her.

"There is a matter I would have him attend to in Vaelnyr," she said, the words coming like mud, thick with guilt.

"Very well, Skalen," he said, and bid her good day.

Sybilla watched him walk away, sweating as she searched the throng for that one familiar face. She remained there, watching the guards go out, the musky scent of horses and leather sharp in her nostrils. And with the clang of the gate, they were gone.

She stared at the empty stables, the white remains of a dandelion clinging to a spider web above the water trough. In the distance, she could make out the line of the road dotted with mounted guards flying the scarlet flags of Vaelnyr. She imagined them riding roughshod over naked, hogtied men, stripped of their rank. It sickened her, but also satisfied some other impulse, as if Andrin had discovered a nest of vermin in her chambers and had offered to remove them for her.

All the pieces floated about her, seeds of danger, spreading out and thriving wherever they fell. The foul urges of the Maglorean Guard disgusted her, but without their barbaric acts, she would have shuddered nonetheless at report of the Sisters' heresy. By refusing to take their oaths Neilan and Orane Hirvola had done nothing but abandon their people, leaving behind them an orphan land. The Sisters made magic of the pneumatic flu, resurrecting the First Heresy and making it new by exploiting the love that all Lindesalis felt for their lost Jagoda. It would keep happening, she knew.

At the muffled sound of voices, she turned to the doorway. Peran walked with Gavril, their voices blending uncomfortably in her ears. She waved, straightening herself.

"Good day, Guardsmen," Sybilla called.

She wondered whether Peran spoke with Gavril simply to inform him that he would not be joining the mission to Lindesal.

Peran walked slowly but acknowledged her with sagacious eyes.

Gavril offered her a fleeting glance, then kept his gaze to the ground as he listened to the last of Peran's words.

"Sybilla, I understand you are acquainted with the situation in Lindesal?" Peran asked.

She knew he phrased the question so he could secure his quick departure. But she did not feel well about this business and determined that he should not brush her off so easily. "I am. It is a matter of great concern," she began.

"I can assure you, Sybilla, that it is all in hand," he said with a fatherly smile.

"This is not an isolated incident. But I expect the Guard to behave in a civilised manner and perform the executions with appropriate solemnity. The people must see that the Guard are not like ordinary folk. They must remain in control of their passions." Sybilla was not sure of the point she was making, for surely Peran shared this view, but she wanted him to remain where he stood and listen to her speak.

Peran gave her a deferent smile. "I have written to Rayhmer to discuss the possibility of retraining some of the Maglorean contingent here in Vaelnyr."

Sybilla's stomach turned at the thought. "Would it not be better to send some of our own into Maglore?"

"But then I would have no oversight. And they would be dominant in number," he said.

"What of the women in our ranks? I would not have them sleep under the same roof as such animals."

"We would establish a second barracks in the abandoned quarter. The Magloreans would not be permitted to move about Vaelnyr. They would be properly secured."

Sybilla did not like the idea but felt suddenly tired. "Thank you, Peran, I expect you will walk us through all the details in our next Council meeting."

Peran nodded reassuringly at this. "Of course. Now, Sybilla, it is a beautiful day. Put these troubles far from your mind. Take a walk about Vaelnyr and remind yourself of what we have achieved here, of what is possible elsewhere." He gave her a little push in the small of her back. "Gavril, would you be so kind as to accompany our Skalen?" Peran said, moving away from her and toward the House.

Gavril bowed in assent and came beside her, obscuring her view of Peran's departure.

When they had walked long enough to convince her that they were alone, she let her body relax. Gavril did not try to start conversation. He stared thoughtfully across the field, watching the sway of yellow flowers peeking through long grass.

Sybilla wondered at the air of calm that surrounded him. She had trained in Hiatus as a girl, but Gavril possessed a serenity equal to that of her late grandfather, and she could not fathom how he had attained it. There must be further stages in the training of the Guard that took them deeper into that silence, so that it permeated body and spirit. For Sybilla, life was impossible without the Meridian, and those times when she called on Hiatus, it was with great conscious effort. She had no intention of joining ranks with the Maglorean outcasts, but Peran's plans had made her curious. What lessons would he subject them to? How would he turn them back to the path when they had strayed so far?

She longed to question Gavril, to make him her teacher, but that would not be in keeping with their silent bargain. They did not remind each other of their oaths, or their titles. They did not speak of Peran's nudging hand, and Gavril's elevation. For Sybilla had decided. The rules of rank and ritual did not apply to them. Their love was a hidden thing, and better it stay that way.

"Shall we walk in the mountains today?" she said.

"We still receive reports of kshidol by the Atilan altar," Gavril said, looking skyward.

"Let them come," Sybilla said. "It is fair weather for a hunt."

Gavril shook his head and chuckled. "To the armoury, then. I will fetch my longbow."

"And I my gutting knife."

22

WALDEMAR

Six Years After The Fire

Four years I have scavenged in these mountains, isolated from the sickened Stream. Winter has come and there is little sustenance here. The day of my Blood Call comes but once a year, and long do I prepare for it.

Alma grows in the valley, but for Mother Siatka there will be no more Alma wine. I steep the leaves for Her, and my blood reddens the mixture. I whisper Her hymn, and pour out my cup into the gentle current. She does not traverse the rivers, but the rivers flow to the foaming shore, and the shore stretches to the dark places, out there, where She resides.

I raise the smoking Alma above my head and look skyward. My prayer swells in my lungs, it reverberates and rises on high. How my face grows wet with tears as the echoes return to me in song. The Mountains of Jokvour surround me with voices, but they are not the voices of my Birth-Kin. When I call Father Kshidol, blood exudes from my hand. I have made a paste of Alma mixed with the flesh of the lesser birds.

He does not come.

My eyes are closed, His shadow pulses behind my eyes, a memory of my first Blood Call in this place, of my elation when I saw Him, the wind buffeting Him sideways, solitary and sunken with hunger. How He drew His head back close to His wing, His look injured, His movements timid. It shames my heart, what they have done. What have they done? And how could the enlightened among us allow it?

Still, I prepare my offerings, though for a time, I did so in despair. In my wanderings I wished to stop counting the days, for they ran on and on, meaninglessly, endlessly...

But one of faith found me when I was lost to myself.

I was in twilight when he came. Intercessor Amand Angenet of Selts-land. How my heart resounded when I saw his bright face. When I held out my hands to a brother of Velspar and pressed his forehead to mine.

Praise Velspar, the eternal.

When we spoke, I asked him of High Intercessor Salma, who had initi-ated the Skalens Karasek, for I knew that she too had felt the uncertainty of the Eighth Gate. With tears in my eyes, I asked of Intercessor Ultreia, so young in her training, who was the purest of heart. He could tell me nothing of their fates. Word no longer travelled north from Brivia.

But Amand believes there are others. When he came by river, he felt a soft presence, a stray thread – especially bright – not taken, as yet, into the Stream. We will call with our silent voices, and if there is one to hear us, we shall find them.

I feel hopeful, for Amand's faith is fresh and urgent. These years in the wilderness have not harried him. It is a great blessing, he says, that his faith met my wisdom in this deserted place. And so we tend to each other's spirits, finding where agony and vengefulness reside, to bring the peace of silvering. For that is our everlasting mission, to be a balm to the soul of the world.

INTERCESSOR WALDEMAR RASMUS OF BRIVIA, 706.

23

SYBILLA

Seven Years After The Fire

IT WAS A FAMILIAR SCENE. Alma smoke rose in fragile wisps as Sybilla
and Peran sat side-by-side in the twin seats of Vaelnyr.

The senior guards occupied the other seats. Sybilla stared at the
markings of the Skalens' Star that divided the table. The Star was
prophetic indeed. She was but a fragment of the whole, and desperately outnumbered if they wished to thwart her wishes. But she had
thought long about her proposal, and had sown seeds in the mind of
each man so they might truly consider it.

The Meridian Decree would ensure the citizens of Velspar wore
the Meridian, night and day. Intercession had poisoned them, she
argued, and they could expect no end to red deeds if they could not
offer a cure. If a man wished to know the will of his brother, and
made fantasy of a passing glance at his wife, would it not cause his
hands to clench? Would not his brother feel the keenness of his
hatred? Would his wife not be shamed? The Meridian would offer
them protection. They would not delve so readily into each other's
minds. They would not be so sure that they knew what was meant by
a passing glance, by a clenched hand, or a downcast gaze. They

would have to ask one another. And in the asking, passes human reason, she said. In the listening comes human understanding.

Did she believe the Meridian could do all this? She prayed that it would. Sybilla could not bear to hear of another man crippled in a tavern beating. The way they gathered in packs to hunt one another. It only took one of them to claim that they knew the true will of their neighbour. It was the arrogance of the Intercessors that fortified them in this. There could be no protestation, no evidence sought, the pack justified itself, the false vision, and the conviction it gave them, bleeding from one mind to the next.

When these things got out of hand, it was the Intercessors the people would turn to. When the mob finally realised the vision was false, they would bind the one who spoke it and drag him to the Temple. The Intercessors would be there to purify the spirit. But for every red thought they drew out, some sediment would remain in them, to be infused in the balm they administered to the souls of others. There was only one way to end it, for the people could not cure themselves. The Meridian would ease them, protect them, would stop the flow of red thoughts, and in turn, red deeds. The Meridian, she argued, would bring peace to Velspar.

The senior guards nodded approvingly. But then they spoke of her father. How he was one of the weak ones the Intercessors selected for training. She grit her teeth as they told stories of a man they had never really known. They spoke of the night he stole a Meridian from the Temple to protect himself from the dreams. Though Peran knew the truth, he did not correct the others. The tale was useful. The Guard could keep their teachings – their gift of Hiatus – within the barracks' sanctum. The commoners could have the Meridian.

She left it to Peran to strengthen her point, to unfurl the logistical plans that would see three discs of blinding stone and straps of fine leather adorned the heads of every citizen. In the north, supplies of blinding stone were insufficient, but the Southlands held ample deposits. Sybilla would travel to Maglore, Brivia and Avishae, then back up to Lindesal before returning to Vaelnyr. She was to secure trade deals that would guarantee a dependable supply of blinding stone, both now and in the future. Peran assured her the Skalens of

Seltsland and Nothelm had already confirmed their allotments from Maglore were sufficient to the task, and required no emissary. In her absence, Peran would arrange for the apprenticeship of young workers who could prepare the leather, work the stone, and become adept at fitting, so the Meridian could work as intended.

The largest inland deposits were located in the mountains of Jokvour that stood abreast the Maglorean-Lindesali border, seconded by Brivia's Aldberg Range. In Avishae, deposits of blinding stone lay off the coast in The Bay of Knives – so named for the jutting blade-like formations that created an impassable corridor from the Sea Altar on Brivia's south coast, to the tip of Avishae. The Elshenders had more than enough blinding stone to supply their populace, but mining was made impractical by sea, where divers chipped away at the rock with hand tools. The Aldberg and Jokvour Ranges were plentiful but would one day be exhausted. Avishae's Bay of Knives, then, must be safeguarded as the vault by which Velspar would be sustained for generations to come.

Gavril accompanied her as they rode into Maglore to break bread with the Skalens there, and to speak of the stone and how it must be chipped. Perfume wafted on the breeze, transporting her to days gone by, to memories of grimy petticoats and war cries. Inry met them at the door, a great white lily in her hair. Domhnall greeted her warmly and shook Gavril's hand like they were fast friends. When she outlined the reasons for the Decree and how it was to be implemented, Domhnall was as a fat black mole, well satisfied with his winter horde. He knew that of all the lands of Velspar, his held the richest share of blinding stone, and she could tell that he was going to enjoy his new position as the generous benefactor of the Seven Lands.

Sybilla allowed Inry to indulge them in tours of her orchards, taking them to many beautiful sites, where swans dipped their heads beneath the water, and elsewhere to the town, where merchant ships gathered sociably at the docks, and music made its way across the rooftops. They departed with their wagon full of oranges, honeycomb, fresh bread and cloven wine. They followed the River Nanthe along its west bank, leaving the mountains of Jokvour to their ancient silence before the miners came with their incessant tapping. They slept under the stars, sharing the Alma pipe and drinking Maglorean wine. There were things to laugh about, and much to say about the places and people they had seen.

After several days' journey, they crossed a stone bridge at the Brivian border that carried them to the east bank of the Nanthe. People worked the fields. Old men hunched like curled leaves, toiling in the bracken and the dust. There were so few of them out there working. It did not look at all like the Brivia she imagined, but as they moved east, the landscape changed, becoming greener and more wild.

A stone arch marked the entrance to Thrale Forest, and there they met a company of guards who were to escort them on the road that led to the Skalens' House. The path wound this way and that, obscured by snaking branches and low hanging vines. The forest held a damp serenity, but seemed a haunted place, the dripping leaves causing Sybilla's head to turn, half expecting to find the spectres of Emryl and Medard Karasek lying in wait. But they were gone. She had witnessed their executions in Vaelnyr. Still, she approached the Skalens' House with trepidation, sensing traces of the Karasek line all about, their trails criss-crossing the House and its surrounds with a ghostly vapour that clung to the leaves of every tree.

They passed a second archway, and a third, but by the sixth Sybilla understood there would be yet one more. The seventh arch featured carvings of the Holy Ones, and a wave of disgust hit Sybilla as they passed beneath. As they tied the horses nearby, she felt poised to give an order to have the archway demolished, but decided she must ingratiate herself to the Skalens' Regents first. After all, she had taken this journey to gain allegiance in support of the Meridian Decree. The destruction of artefacts could wait.

As they neared, Sybilla noticed the wrought iron gate barring the Skalens' House door was ajar. In the dappled shade there stood a woman and man dressed in simple clothes – Olinda and Jemryn Greslet, the Skalens' Regents of Brivia. A third figure appeared behind them – a boy of ten, perhaps – in a leather cap.

"Greetings, Skalen Sybilla, I am Olinda Greslet, sister of Domhnall." Olinda bowed in greeting. "Jemryn Greslet, my husband," she said, gesturing to the man, who also bowed. "And our son, Illiam." The lad stared up at her as if to hide himself beneath his small, smooth brow.

"I thank you," Sybilla said. "Gavril, my guard, will be accompanying me and will be present at our meetings."

"You are most welcome." Olinda smiled and turned to lead them down the darkened hallway. "I am afraid that in Brivia, the Skalens' House is not staffed by Attendants. We have closed many of the rooms and have some of the woodland folk visit during daylight hours to see to the essential tasks. And some members of the Guard have discovered a hidden talent for cooking and other house duties." Olinda peered round to see if Sybilla found this to be disagreeable.

But Sybilla was not so particular as Inry, who had no doubt visited Brivia in the intervening years. "Your work in Brivia is of service to all of Velspar, and I think it wise that your efforts are concentrated elsewhere. The House will stand with or without Attendants."

Sybilla and Gavril were given time to refresh after their journey and were invited to take supper with the Greslets in one of the reading rooms. The central chamber had been shut up for it required too much upkeep, too much dusting. The many closed doors blocked out the fading light of evening, and lanterns were set sparingly at intervals. Jemryn held out a chair for Sybilla and the four of them sat at a small table laden with dried fruit, cured meat, and cheese. Sybilla presented a bottle of cloven wine for them to share.

Olinda took the bottle in her hands, turning it over. "A gift from my brother?"

"Yes," Sybilla said, noting her wry expression.

Jemryn opened the bottle, pouring the fragrant purplish liquid into four glasses. "Domhnall must think that if we drink enough wine, we will come to love this place," Jemryn said, gesturing to a cache of wine that filled the bookshelf in the far corner of the room.

"What do you make of Brivia?" Sybilla asked, and it was odd that she must ask it of a Maglorean native, for this House should have been as a second home.

In days gone by, the Skalens' Council met in full every two years, each land playing host in a running cycle that had continued unbroken for centuries. The host would choose the day of proceedings according to its namesake – Avisday, Brivisday, Lindesday, Magsday, Seltsday, Vaelsday and Nothsday – the week, a chant in honour of the Seven. But following the Council of Vaelnyr, and the 'Purge of the Intercessors', as it was now known, the Skalens discoursed via the Guard in envoys and by letter, but seldom in person, and never with all Skalens present. Perhaps it was because none wanted to bring permanence to arrangements in Brivia or Lindesal. It was not wise to bestow eternal right to a new clan when so much remained unsettled. Or would it one day be the Five?

Olinda sipped her wine and looked out the window and Sybilla could see why they chose to keep this room in use. The Aldberg Mountains were blue in the distance, the foothills laced with twilight's mist. All the other rooms were tinged with green, set as they were beneath the forest canopy.

Jemryn regarded Sybilla and Gavril before answering. "There is little chance of rebellion. The Brivians who took their oaths to the Skalens did so against the instruction of Andsen Karasek. He had rallied them to put themselves to death rather than to renounce Intercession. If you had witnessed the early stages here, you would have seen that the Brivians were fierce. A force to be reckoned with. It is thanks to your father that much of the Brivian Guard were ready when the moment came. They were victorious and I am sure they have not told us the half of what they did to achieve this. When we arrived, the people were decimated."

Jemryn glanced uncomfortably at Gavril and seemed as if he would end his story there.

"Please go on," Sybilla said.

Jemryn took a deep breath. "Every Brivian who survived lost somebody close to them. They are all in mourning. But they are also in mourning for their Skalens. They were heretics and chose their fate, this is true, but it was more difficult to see the Karasek brothers in their struggle for faith, for the people to watch their downfall as well."

Sybilla nodded. "Sidney Karasek yet lives. I have heard the reports, but what do you make of him?"

"Sidney will not set foot in the Skalens' House," Jemryn said. "He walks the woodlands, eating scraps, and finding shelter in caves. He wishes to live out his days there, as a hermit, and he has offered us no trouble. He took his oath, and in doing so has earned the right to his life, but he will not rule as Skalen. He is not able or willing it seems."

"Can you tell me of his elder brother's death?" Sybilla asked.

Jemryn's expression grew introspective. "We were not in Brivia at that time, Skalen, but those who have come to share their stories with us say Andsen never turned toward the light. He got the villagers into a frenzy, telling them they must make their final Blood Call or the Holy Ones would never find them. He knew the old death rites would not be observed. They were soaking rags with blood of their wrists and sending young boys to the mountains and sea, so their offerings would reach the gods before the hour of their death." Jemryn licked his thumb and rubbed at a wine stain on the table. "After that, they started to kill each other with rocks, drowning their children in the river. Sidney tried to stop them. He told them to take the oath. Andsen struck him and harsh words passed between them. That night, Andsen climbed to the tower across the hall from where we are sitting, and fell to his death. It is said that one of the faithful took his body to the Sky Altar before perishing there himself. When we arrived in Brivia, Sidney was gone. The Skalens' House all but abandoned. It took us months to coax the survivors out of the forest, and for them to tell us where Sidney was hiding."

Sybilla's stomach fluttered and she set down her glass. She looked at the table. "Thank you, Jemryn, for speaking so freely. The suffering of Velspar pains me greatly. I know more than most that it is not enough to cut off the festering part. Over time, one learns to love what is rotten; it becomes part of oneself, and a part of our loved ones. This is why I have come here. I want to help the people of Velspar. They are sick. They are still caught in the briar of Intercession, but the Meridian will soothe them, it will set them free."

Jemryn looked to her Meridian. "I know there are blinding stone deposits in the Aldberg Range, but there are none left who would know how to mine it."

"Not here, perhaps, but the techniques can be taught," Sybilla assured him.

"You will send people?" Olinda asked.

"Gavril and I are yet to travel to Avishae and Lindesal, but between the Seven Lands we will find the labour and craftsmen required for the task. Those who support us in Brivia will not be abandoned. They are the future of Velspar."

Jemryn nodded. "Will you have an audience with Sidney during your stay?"

"If he is willing. I will speak with him and thank him for his service," Sybilla said. "I think it is fitting if he be the first to receive the Meridian, for his bravery in the face of such horror." Sybilla stood, ripples extending across the surface of her unfinished wine. "Now, you must excuse me, it has been a long journey."

"Yes, of course," Olinda said. "It is getting late. Thank you, Sybilla."

Sybilla and Gavril followed the Regents into the dimly lit hallway. "I must say, I am pleased Domhnall sent you here," Sybilla said. "Brivia is in good hands. But it occurs to me that you have not mentioned the Elshenders. Have they not offered their assistance?"

Olinda frowned. "The Skalens of Avishae have not travelled to Brivia, if that is what you mean. But they have asked nothing onerous of us in the way of resources. They must be using up their existing stores, and perhaps this is how they have chosen to help us. Though, they cannot continue this way for much longer. Avishae will not survive without supplies from the mainland."

Olinda spoke with a certain weary foresight. The trade of goods had become fraught after so many deaths, but Sybilla felt a surge of surety for the first time in years. Her past was behind her now. And the suffering they carried, she'd lift it all away with the blessed peace of the Meridian.

24

SYBILLA

Seven Years After The Fire

Though Sybilla had felt apprehensive on the road to Brivia, by the end of their stay, she felt much revived. The Greslets took Sybilla and Gavril on forest walks and on a hike through the Aldberg Range. The boy, Illiam, came too. When they reached the summit, Sybilla looked down upon the sweeping expanse of Brivia, and Gavril smiled, for he must have felt it too. There would be no uprising here, these lands did not teem with resentment; the people had taken well to their Regents. It was lush and green as far as the eye could see, a beautiful place that needed only some small spark; a nudge in the right direction, and it would bloom.

She felt better after seeing it, after being there, not realising how the Karasek homeland had lurked within her mind as a place of danger. As they set off for Avishae, Sybilla sincerely thanked Olinda and Jemryn for their hospitality but was quietly relieved when they failed to locate Sidney Karasek. Let him live out his days as he wished, it was not for her to tell him that a Skalens' House was better than a cave, or to compel him to lower his head and take up the yoke of the Skalens' Star.

The local Guard loaded their carriage with Maglorean wine and jars of a sweet-seeded paste derived from the Brivian orchid, as gifts for the Skalens Elshender. The road from Brivia to Port Innes was long, and several times the guards were forced to alight the carriage to cut branches from the path so that they might proceed. When they emerged from the forest after two days on the road, they did not come upon a thriving port town but a quiet, windy place where thatch-roofed houses hid among the rocks, and only a few small boats sat at anchor.

A Brivian boy helped them aboard a weathered barge with simple accommodations that was to ferry them to Port Fallon. The hazy shape of Avishae was visible across the strait and it did not take them long to reach it once aboard. At Port Fallon, a local guard checked the boat before nudging the craft down the Selbourne. All around them the trees grew thick and wild, rising up into inhospitable mountains, the tallest of which were dusted white. The river snaked its way through the silence, broken only by the occasional crack and rush of leaves as creatures moved beneath the canopy. When the trees thinned, the mountains flattened out giving way to scattered houses. As they rounded the bend, the quaint stone buildings of Haydentown glowed golden, and people moved about the streets in flashes of colour.

At the dock, Sybilla spotted an Avishaen guard standing at atten-tion beside a hooded carriage. Gavril walked close as they made their way to meet him, ignoring the townspeople that stopped mid-motion to watch. The guard bowed and held open the door, securing the latch with efficiency once they were inside. As the carriage set off, they left behind the many eyes that followed them. The town reminded Sybilla of Vaelnyr, though it was a fraction of the size and the people seemed less accustomed to receiving visitors from other lands. They looked at her as if she might covet the life they had here; as if any mainlander would. But she would not be the one to tell them that on the mainland, 'little Avishae' seldom featured as a topic of cultured conversation.

They soon moved into farmland and Sybilla had a good view of the snow-capped mountains in the north. She could not see the Temple, and she whispered as much to Gavril. Eventually he spotted it. The people of Avishae were a practical folk and needed it as a storehouse, they said. Sybilla had read the letters, had seen the signatures of the other Skalens, and added hers alongside, but the mark of her hesitancy was clear on the page in a drop of black ink. It did not seem a convenient location for a storehouse, she thought, trying to measure its distance from the valley. She turned away, pained by its whiteness, and looked down at her hands where the afterimage throbbed at the centre of her vision.

Gavril grasped her hand, enveloping it in his steady warmth.

The path to the Skalens' House was flanked by a wide meadow on one side that led down to the sea, and thick woodland on the other. Sybilla focused on the pleasant sight that unfolded around them, of soft grass and sheep with their heads low. A proud dark horse made its way across the pasture, moving jauntily, and Gavril laughed at the lad who tried to ride him. It broke the mood but Sybilla found that her stomach clenched the way it had the last time she'd seen the Elshenders. When she had gone into their minds and screamed in primal agony – when she had demanded their loyalty, knowing nothing of them, and they had given it.

As the path ascended, the Skalens' House came into view. It was set upon the cliff edge and surrounded by a stone wall. The path led them to a wrought iron gate revealing the salt-eaten House with its faded blue flags that shivered stiffly in the wind. Rebekah and Ulric awaited them in the forecourt. While she recognised them, they looked to her like strangers. Both appeared taller than she remembered. Or perhaps it was that they now looked like Skalens, regal and full of grace, but with faces aged beyond their years.

Those years had aged them all.

As they exchanged their greetings, Sybilla noted that Ulric's beard had filled out, and his sandy hair had its first streaks of silver. Rebekah's smile was tarnished. She had the look of someone with no more tears to cry, and her embattled beauty was heightened somehow by the freckles that stained her cheeks and the fine lines about her eyes. Rebekah's twilight-coloured dress shone between the folds of her cloak, and Sybilla could see why the Skalens of Avishae chose this as their clan colour, it was the mixture of sea and sky, a colour of distance. The Elshenders guided them into the House, where the halls were cold, even in the firelight.

Sybilla suddenly felt very far from home.

First, they were to meet the Elshender children. Zohar, a girl of ten with cheeks like the breast of a dove, curtseyed and looked at the floor. She nudged her younger brother Ambrose, who could not help himself from fidgeting. Sybilla could see from the whites of the girl's eyes that Zohar feared her. Sybilla had made the effort to speak to children more, of late, but they did not seem to like her. She was relieved when it was over, and the young Elshenders disappeared through the door. Sybilla thought then of Rebekah with her hands across her belly, but there was no child here of that age. Of course, she could not expect an Alma vision to have substance. She was not such a fool as the Intercessors. The Alma cleansed the mind as a precursor for true speech. To share the Alma was a gesture of trust, nothing more.

They moved into the council room and took their places. Ulric gave spark to the Alma, a sweet grey mist filling the room. "Bless this meeting of Skalens, by the grace of Velspar."

"Bless us, Velspar," Sybilla whispered along with the others.

After a brief pause, Ulric tapped his fingers on the parchment in front of him. "Sybilla, shall I read the Skalen's Tally?"

"That will not be necessary, Ulric. Pass it to Gavril. I will have him relay its contents after we have discussed more pressing matters."

Ulric obliged, and Gavril began reading as Sybilla spoke. "As I understand it, you will be requiring significant resources from the mainland in the near future."

Rebekah smiled uncomfortably. "We did not wish to burden the Brivian Regents until absolutely necessary."

Sybilla met her eyes. "Rebekah, I can assure you that Brivia is rich in resources, and in Maglore they have luxuries to spare. The Seven Lands are equal in Velspar. We are one family, one clan."

Gavril tapped Sybilla's arm and she turned, his finger set beneath the executioner's tally. Sybilla frowned. "I see your execution rates are very low. How do you account for this?" she asked, eyes narrowing.

Rebekah clasped her hands. "We are a small community. The people know the consequences of their actions."

Sybilla leaned back in her chair. When she had first encountered the Elshenders, she had attributed their silence to inexperience. Now she was not so sure.

"I would credit it to the persistence of the Guard," Ulric said. "They make house visits every week. They speak to the children. They check people's stories against each other. With a population as small as ours, it is possible to work in this way. The people know there is no room for red deeds, and that heresy will not be tolerated."

Sybilla glanced at Gavril; she would have to make sure he became acquainted with the local Guard, so he could confirm Ulric's version of things.

"It is not so easy in Vaelnyr, I assure you. And this is the reason I have come." Her eyes rested unconsciously on Ulric's naked forehead. "You will have noticed that Gavril and I wear the Meridian."

"Yes," Ulric replied.

"On the mainland there has been an upsurge in red deeds," Sybilla said. "These are not deeds of outright heresy, rather crimes of passion. We have found that wearing the Meridian changes these figures somewhat. We hope widespread use of the Meridian will prevent such crimes."

Rebekah inclined her head. "Well, as you can see, we do not have that problem here. Why should we impose the Meridian if our people are innocent?"

Sybilla was quick to assure her. "It is not a punishment, you mistake me. The Meridian soothes the spirit. For Velspar to be at peace, every spirit must become peaceful. Without change of this kind, we will never be able to move on."

Ulric exhaled audibly.

As silence filled the room, Sybilla tried a different angle. "You may say your people do not need the Meridian, but they do need food. If your people wear the Meridian – at all times – then I will ensure your stores are replenished."

Rebekah's eyes flashed for a moment, but when she spoke, her voice was measured. "But you have not the blinding stone for all the people of Velspar. You must also have come to seek stone from our Bay."

Sybilla was impressed. Rebekah had changed much since the Council of Vaelnyr, of that, she was sure. "There are plentiful deposits in Jokvour and Aldberg, but you are right, in the future, we require access to the Bay."

Rebekah breathed deeply, her shoulders visibly relaxing. Sybilla felt it too. Though there was tension between them, the Alma was softening their muscles, and as their eyes became languorous, their words flowed with greater ease.

"Sybilla," Rebekah said gently. "I respect your intentions here, and we will do as you ask but I, too, have a proposal for consideration."

Sybilla did not expect this but nodded, bidding her to go on.

"Our execution numbers are low, it is true. But this does not mean our people do not suffer," Rebekah said. "As in all of the Seven Lands, we have had to develop new ceremonies around execution. I understand that in Vaelnyr they perform them in the mountains and that you have your citizens cast the final judgement."

"Near the mountains," Sybilla corrected her. "We do not wish to draw vermin."

"Of course. And we perform ours in the valley," Rebekah said. "This Meridian Decree of which you speak, it is to soothe the suffering of your people. In our way, we have done the same by weaving Alma fronds into the pyre."

Sybilla imagined the scene with arms folded, for it sounded dangerously similar to Festival.

Ulric added, "We find that when loved ones tend the pyre, and breathe its smoke along with the dying, their hearts are at ease. They do not seek to avenge their dead for they understand fire's holy function. They know we all must do our part to protect the purity of the Stream."

His words reminded Sybilla of those her father had spoken, long ago. But her father was gone now. He did not have to rule over a land haunted by the pyre's 'bright flame'. She and the Elshenders did, and the burden of it was relentless.

Rebekah continued. "I am proposing, Sybilla, that we honour the Alma as our people have always done. It is time that we reinstated Festival."

Sybilla raised an eyebrow.

"Sybilla, I implore you," Rebekah said. "The Alma burns here, in this very room. Why should the people be denied it? And with your Meridian Decree in place, things will be different."

This gave Sybilla pause, but before she could speak, Ulric caught her eye.

"There is one more thing Rebekah has not mentioned." He placed his hand upon his wife's. "In Avishae, the villagers have a tradition of making effigies from corn husks. I imagine they do the same in Vael-nyr. In days gone by, they'd burn them the night before Festival."

"You want to make Shush Dolls?" Sybilla laughed.

Ulric's expression was deadly serious. "We do not call them that here, but it seems you are familiar with the custom."

Sybilla frowned. "All I know is that children whisper their secrets to the dolls, and if they are truthful, they will find yellow corn by their bedside. If they lie, the corn will be black."

"Now Sybilla," Ulric said. "Do not dismiss this as child's folly. If our people could cast their burdens into the flames and never have to speak of them, they might be able to let go of the past; to move on."

"But you said you wanted to reinstate Festival. Are you suggesting we celebrate the corn harvest along with the villagers?" Sybilla asked.

"No," Rebekah said. "It would be a celebration of the ripening of the Alma, just as it had always been, but it would be a solemn event. The people would bring effigies to commit to the Alma fire. We would be bringing the community together and putting the past where it belongs."

Sybilla stared. "This was your idea?"

"Yes," Rebekah confirmed.

Sybilla marvelled at the sentimentality – the naivety – of these provincial folk. They wanted to make dolls to ease the burden of their guilt? It was ridiculous. "I am not opposed to it, exactly, but I do not know if these practices would be readily adopted on the mainland."

"All I ask is that you consider our proposal as we have done yours; in good faith," Rebekah said.

Sybilla saw Gavril nod out of the corner of her eye and was surprised at his ready assent.

"Very well," Sybilla said, at length. "I will put your proposal forward in Vaelnyr and will convey your request to the Skalens of Maglore, Seltsland and Nothelm."

"Thank you, Sybilla," Rebekah said and bowed her head low.

The next day, the Elshenders took them through the town to observe the industry of Avishae and to meet the common folk. It was a long day, where one smiling, bowing citizen blended into the next, and Sybilla's head ached from the persistent reek of fish emanating from the boats at the dock. She felt much relieved when it was suggested she and Gavril might enjoy a walk upon the beach, while Rebekah and Ulric retired to the House before supper.

Sybilla let the ocean's roar deafen her, washing away the pain at her temples from too much smiling. Gavril left her alone, but she knew he was waiting for her to speak, and this might be the only time that they'd be alone.

Sybilla sat beside him on the sand. "What do you think of this place?"

Gavril considered. "The locals seem overly aware of their separation from the mainland. It makes this place seem distant, when in fact it is not."

Sybilla stood and gestured for Gavril to follow her. She preferred speaking where the waves could obscure their voices. "Gavril, do you think it is wise to allow Festival to return?"

He looked thoughtful. "It will never be like it was."

"How do you remember it?" she asked, looking at him as she often did, as a quiet mystery.

Gavril looked up. "I think that if I had not been trained in Hiatus, I might have found it frightening as a child. But when I was older, I enjoyed it. It was exhilarating. I didn't have to hold myself back like I did the rest of the year. At Festival, I was just like anyone else." Gavril held her gaze in a way that made her heart race. "Did you enjoy it?"

"I dreaded it. Father would prepare us before we left the Skalens' House. It was like going into battle."

"Still, there is merit in the Elshenders' proposal."

"But this effigy idea. I don't know..."

"That man – Sidney Karasek – there are many in Velspar that suffer as he does. If there are too many, it will be dangerous for us."

The whole thing set her ill at ease. She had done many evil things for the sanctity of the hard line, to protect Velspar from the contamination of the past. She did not want to risk any permeation between the old ways and the new. But she also knew things were beginning to fester. She believed the Meridian Decree would solve this, but after seven years of rule, she understood the necessity of trade in the Skalen's bargain.

"Sybilla, you may find peace in solitude, but there are many who will not. Reinstating Festival after the Decree has passed will prevent many of the dangers you fear. You know that when you wear the Meridian, the Alma does not work the same way. There are no visions." Gavril took her hand. "Only closeness."

Sybilla pulled away, wrapping her cloak tighter against the wind. "I will think on it."

She stared off into the distance where the waves were making mist along the shore. At her feet were seashells. She picked one up, brushing off the sand, and wandered closer to the water. Gavril left her to do as she wished, walking up to where the grass grew in dry ropes along the ground. She felt him watching her as she walked, felt him waiting for her, patiently, quietly, sitting there upon the ground.

25

SYBILLA

Nine Years After The Fire

PERAN SMILED AT HER. "You have done well, Skalen."

Around the Council Table, the senior guards gave nods of approval. Andrin had just read out the list of those executed since the last new moon. The numbers were stepping down, and Peran was determined they should not rise again.

"Sybilla has shown great leadership in instituting the Meridian Decree. Crimes of passion have lessened in number, and now we see that blinding stone alone can achieve what Intercession could not. On the matter of Festival, I will admit that I was in error when I argued against the Elshenders' proposal. As we pass the second year of this reformed celebration, I see that a new age must have its rituals."

Sybilla listened to Peran's words, but her mind was elsewhere. The storms of late autumn had kept her indoors for almost a week, and through the diamond panes of the council room she watched full-bellied clouds hanging low above the pasture like so many huddling sheep. Inside, though, the hearth fire was warm and her thoughts drifted to places protected by ancient trees, where she and Gavril walked.

"Tomorrow, Sybilla will attend the opening of the new Guard's barracks–"

At the sound of her name, Sybilla looked up.

"–where the Temple dormitories used to stand. This change is of great symbolic importance to the people of Vaelnyr, who no longer wish to look upon the abandoned relics of a troubled past."

Sybilla let her mind wander again. She had heard it all before.

Beneath the stones of her Meridian, she brought Gavril's face to mind. His eyes. What were his eyes like? Green, like silvered leaves... with gold, at times, the colour of a brook where branches had fallen. His lashes were black, but it was the expression of his eyes she was after. For a moment she touched upon that look, then lost it once more.

This time she started with his voice. Something he said – a laugh – no, she couldn't capture it.

"Skalen?" Peran said, and she realised they were all looking at her.

"Yes, Peran – I'm sorry – I was just running through what I might say at tomorrow's speech."

"Very good. I have also taken the liberty of preparing a few ideas for you to consider." Peran passed her a scroll held fast with twine.

"Thank you, Peran."

At the close of the meeting, Sybilla bid the guardsmen good day, walking down the chill hallway to her chambers where a low fire burned behind the grate. She closed the door and sighed, running her fingers along the crimson veils that hid her bed from view. It was too early for sleep. Rain still pattered against the window, but beyond, the town shone in the late afternoon sun. Was it too late to call for Gavril? They had ridden in weather worse than this.

No. It would attract too much notice.

Then, Sybilla had a novel thought. She could call him here, to her chambers, to discuss the morning's ceremony. To discuss what about it exactly? She paced the room, biting her fingernails. He could help her with her speech? But she had never asked him to do so before. She could ask him to deliver some part of the speech. Could she? He would likely refuse. She would ask, and he would refuse, but she would see him.

Before she could change her mind, Sybilla rang the Attendants' bell.

Her stomach twisted as she made her way to the chairs beneath the window. Remembering that they were to discuss her speech, she doubled back to retrieve the parchment from her dresser, sliding Peran's scroll into the drawer. She placed her speech on the small table beside her chair and checked her hair with her hands. Lately she had taken to looser braids, and today, her hair was swept to one side, smooth beneath her Meridian, plaited only where she wished to hide her scar. To her great surprise, she had seen young women wearing this same style in Vaelnyr, and laughed to think that she, like Inry, could attract such interest.

A few minutes later, one of the newer Attendants entered. "Skalen?" The young man bowed.

Sybilla smiled, but he did not raise his eyes. "Please ask Guardsman Gavril to attend my chambers. There has been a change concerning tomorrow's schedule."

"Of course, Skalen. I shall send for him directly." The young man nodded with utmost seriousness, and departed, closing the door softly behind him.

The lad's shoes went clip, clip, all the way down the hall as he went to deliver her message, his ceremonious manner causing a giggle to rise in her throat. Then there was silence. A silence that made her hot in the chest. Sybilla removed her woollen mantle and hung it carefully with her other clothes. Her mind danced, running through the different things she might say.

Just then, there was a heavy knock at the door, and a squeak of hinges as Gavril entered.

"Guardsman, please sit. We have much to discuss," Sybilla said with instinctive formality, but of course, there was no Attendant accompanying him.

Gavril closed the door and already she felt the danger of his presence.

"I was told there have been changes to tomorrow's proceedings?"

Sybilla held out her hand, indicating that he should sit with her by the fire. "Yes." She paused, unsure if she should actually say the words. "I was hoping you might stand beside me at the ceremony and, perhaps..."

"Perhaps?" he asked, a smile tugging at his lips.

Sybilla's mouth went dry. "Perhaps, you might say a few words yourself?"

Gavril frowned. "Peran suggested this?"

"No," she said slowly, "he does not know of it. I wanted to speak with you first."

Gavril broke into a broad smile and leaned back in his chair.

His reaction surprised her. He wanted this.

"You would do this, Sybilla? Truly?" he breathed.

His expression was so open, so full of gratitude, that she immediately regretted her request. What was she thinking? Unlike her secret imaginings, an act such as this would have consequences. Irreparable consequences, she thought, with growing agitation. It would be an affront to the Head Guard assuaged only by marriage, an admission to all that she had chosen Gavril as her Skalen, and soon enough she'd have no place at all.

Gavril had grown quiet, his eyes appraising her, the joy she had just witnessed leaching from his face.

She was cruel. How could she do this to him? She wanted to hold him, to apologise for words she had not even uttered. "Yes," she said. "I want you there." Of course she did. It was Peran and his blank-faced retinue that were the source of her misgivings. If only they could leave them alone.

"Then that is where I will be," he said, his warmth returning.

She passed Gavril the slip of parchment where she had written her speech. "I will have to perform the blessing, but if there is a particular part that calls to you, I am happy for you speak those lines." Sybilla watched his eyes flicking back and forth across the page. "Or, you can add a line or two, if there is something you feel I have missed."

He looked up. "Thank you, Sybilla."

Gavril continued reading, his eyes tracing some point on the ceiling as his thoughts took shape. At length, he returned the parchment to the table. "I think I have decided on what I will say. I will tell a story, a humorous one that should not ruffle too many feathers. And then, I will introduce you. Is that what you had in mind?"

She let out a long breath, and smiled. "That sounds perfect."

Why had she expected anything other than his usual quiet diplomacy? She was letting her nerves get the better of her. And that was the real reason she needed him there, she realised. In the morning she would have to walk through that wooden arch, and pretend she was not stepping into the past. Though its rooms had been transformed, in her mind, it would always be the Temple dorm.

"I wonder. Is there any other reason that you asked me here?" Gavril slouched sideways in his chair, his eyes fixed upon the parchment, as if inviting her to look at him. He ran his thumb across his lips, his informal manner so unexpected that for a moment, she had no breath in her lungs.

"No, that is all," she insisted, but suddenly her heart was pounding.

Her mind went blank, seeking desperately for small talk, for some word about the weather, or preparations, or the timing of their arrival.

He nodded to himself. "You have not dismissed me." He looked at her, a questioning eyebrow raised.

Sybilla opened her mouth, blush rising in her cheeks, but there was nothing to say. He knew what this was all about, the elaborate ends to which she would go to see him. But this time, they were not out walking, and there was no destination for her to rush away to.

"I can stay a little while if you would like," Gavril said.

"Yes, we can run through tomorrow's speech." At this, she ran out of words, and turned her eyes abruptly to the window. There, the Gulf glittered orange with the fading sun, but soon enough they would be alone together in the full of night. If she had lit more candles, she could continue the pretence, but the fire had burned right down to ashes, and even now there was not light enough to read by.

In the wordless quiet, air hissed at the window's edge. The

moment went on, the silence intensifying, becoming intimate and unbreakable.

Sybilla rose and opened the cabinet beneath the window, her every movement magnified. First, she placed two tinkling glasses on the table, then drew out a bottle of Alma wine, its cork coming free with a pop. Purple liquid glugged from the bottle with agonising slowness, the sound narrowing as it reached the mid-point of each glass. Together they sat, drinking deeply of sweet and spice as the sea-wind blew, rain tapping at the windowpane.

As the Alma made its way through her limbs, a luxurious calm came over her. Sybilla felt her eyes soften and exhaled. The room was tranquil now, a holy sanctuary, where they could be together always. Gavril's hand reached for hers. He had done this before, and it was not so strange. But then he sat forward in his chair, and moved toward her. Before anything could happen, Sybilla closed her eyes, her pulse rich with Alma.

She felt his breath coming hot and cool upon her face. She could taste the desire in it, the metallic charge of his scent. The closeness of him was unbearable. When she dared open her eyes, his gaze struck like small lightning, snaking the length of her. Sybilla gripped Gavril's hands, drawing them into her lap. He shifted closer, coming to kneel between her thighs. His mouth found hers, and she drifted, his lips soft among the peculiar texture of his beard, his tongue searching. Her head fell to the side and she kissed him deeper, her fingers discovering his cropped hair, his smooth temple, the grit of his shaven jaw, and the place where his beard began.

Her heart thundered like the crashing of waves. Already his hands were on her, unlacing, seeking skin. She pulled at his doublet, her fingers trembling as she unhooked the buttons, getting no further than the third. Suddenly he stopped, his fingers snagged on the stubborn loops of her bodice. Taking her hand, he led her to the bed and drew the curtains back, removing his outer clothing with practiced efficiency. She rushed to free her laces, disliking the distance between them.

When she was down to her undergarments, Sybilla slipped beneath the covers. Coming in beside her, Gavril kissed her so she would not notice them coming free. So she would feel only the heat of his skin against hers.

She twined herself around him, drawing him closer, stroking the thick muscles of his legs as his fingers found the well of her desire.

"Let us take off our Meridians," he whispered into her hair.

Sybilla's breath stuck in her throat and it was as if someone had thrown a pitcher of cold water over them. She turned her legs away from him. "I can't," she croaked.

He looked at her in the bluish twilight. The room was cold. Gooseflesh spread across her skin. He watched her, waiting for her to meet his eyes. When she did, her throat grew tight, afraid the spell had broken.

Leaning on his elbow, Gavril stroked her forehead, tracing the straps and the stone. Then he glanced at her naked breasts, the curve of her waist, places that no man had seen. He moved over her, placing kisses like stars upon her breast. She could smell the musk of his hair, and as she ran her fingers through it, his kisses lingered, the hair of his beard prickling her skin, the wetness of his mouth setting her body aflame.

Her hands moved down his back, his ribs, the hard planes of his stomach. Hungrily, she drew his face to hers, pulling him tight against her, wanting his hands, his heat, and felt the burning weight of him as he pushed himself inside. She tightened her thighs around him, feeling the blood rise beneath her skin, wanting, wanting, grasping his flesh, drowning in the scent of him.

She craned her neck to find his mouth again, cool sweat upon her brow. She cried out. He was everywhere, oh Gavril, inside her spirit, drenching her like rain. She throbbed around him, and his muscles tensed, his body full upon her as he moaned, the sound muffled in her hair.

Cradled in his arms, Sybilla floated there, at peace. She listened as his flickering pulse grew still, giving way to the sounds of the storm.

But little thoughts crept into her mind. Small worries about how things might be between them, and a different thought. Of wet scales slithering beneath marble walls, Gavril's seed slick upon her thighs.

Of a child pressing hard against her groin, coming in heat and blood, small red hands reaching for the Skalens' Star, for a place among the Seven.

Gavril turned his head to kiss her, then stared amusedly at her forehead. "Next time, you will have to tell me first, so I can join you."

Sybilla's hand shot up in horror to feel that her Meridian had slipped. Sitting bolt upright, she fumbled to refasten it, looking at him accusingly.

"Have I done something wrong, my Skalen?" he asked, a bitter spark entering his voice.

She scanned the room, finding the darkened shapes of cabinets and chairs, the candles' undulating light upon the wall. Sybilla closed her eyes, rubbing them with her palms as the mattress shifted beside her. She would need a remedy. She tried to remember where Lucinda had bought her tonics, the one that made her stomach loose after careless afternoons with Bryden. Was it the old woman in the farmhouse by the river? Surely, she had survived the executions.

When she looked up, Gavril had dressed himself and seemed ready to depart. "Gavril, wait, I am sorry..." Sybilla trailed off.

He pulled his boots on, fastening one and then the other.

"I want you by my side," she said.

Letting out a breath, his posture softened. "I will do whatever you ask, Sybilla, but one day you will have to speak the words you keep hidden there," he said, pressing the stone of his Meridian.

"I will," Sybilla said, her expression pleading for more time. "I promise you that I will."

Gavril stood but did not come to kiss her. "I will wait for you, then," he said, and made directly for the door.

With the squeak of the hinge, her dresser shone in the hallway light. Then it was dark, and he was gone.

26

WALDEMAR

Ten Years After The Fire

Praise be to Velspar, for once I was alone, and now we are three. After Amand came, we searched the mountains, finding no one.

On a high cragged peak, Amand assisted me in performing the Blood Call. We sang the Hymn to Kshidol, our feet stamping the earth.

The skies were untouched by cloud or shadow, and only in our hearts could we see the shore. The Alma smoked about us, and our spirits were raised up in joy, in faith that the Holy Ones would hear.

It was then that we heard a new voice, one that we did not expect.

She did not call out her name with the breath of her lungs but spoke gently within. Her soul reached out to us in sweet silver, in a voice of love, as she joined our Hymn. Blessed Intercessor, Maeryn Rosemond of Vaelnyr.

Her smile was peaceful, as if she expected our coming. And that night, she warmed us with The Visions of Skalen Karasek, as rendered in the Temple books at Vaelnyr.

Looking upon her, I was awash with gratitude. I felt the heady pulse of Velspar, the vibrancy of an oncoming vision. All in a rush, the well-worn ruts I had formed for myself were laid bare. How different her reading was! The stultifying labour of my own recitations brought a smile to my lips.

The word that ended her rendition was: Velspar.

It seemed to turn in the air, refracting with new meaning, unveiling, and I watched it birth itself, over and again. The marvel of it, filling me with hope.

INTERCESSOR WALDEMAR RASMUS OF BRIVIA, 710.

PART II

MERIDIAN

27

ZOHAR

Ten Years After The Fire

Zohar and Ambrose rode out with their parent's blessing. As the Guard closed the Skalens' House gates behind them, they followed an unfamiliar path. Today, they were not to ride westward to the beaches of grey sand. They had spent enough time collecting shells and making seaweed skirts, enough hours playing like children for two who were almost grown. Today, they were to ride northwest into the heart of Baden Forest, where the Raeburns held camp – the place where their mother, Rebekah, was born. Their mother rarely mentioned her family, and when she did it was through tight lips. Sometimes, Zohar and Ambrose saw their grandfather, Landyn Raeburn, up on the hill or among the faces of the peasants in town. Bald and wiry he was, with weathered skin and piercing grey eyes that made the stomach jolt. They would meet him today.

Zohar sat at the front of the saddle with her brother behind.

"Why do you keep slowing down?" Ambrose asked with irritation.

"You're not holding onto me tight enough," she said, and could almost see her brother roll his eyes.

When the trees grew thick and the brambles snared Silvey's

hooves, the siblings alighted from their horse and tied the mare to a great oak where they were sure they could find her again.

Continuing on foot the way their mother had told them, Zohar plodded on. Ambrose ran ahead whacking tree trunks and shrubbery with a switch. She glanced regretfully at the plant life dishevelled by her brother, as leaves shuddered back into their original formations. Soon, Zohar caught the scent of smoke and stew on the wind.

"Ambrose – come here and stand by me, we need to look respectable when we meet Grandfather."

Her brother gave her a mischievous smile, but trudged through the ivy to where she stood, taking her arm in his. "Is this respectable enough?"

Zohar glared at him. "Aren't you nervous to meet them?"

Just then, she heard the crunch of footsteps in the distance and fell into an embarrassed silence.

Ambrose saw him before she did. "Grandfather!"

As the tall man emerged from daylight shadows, Zohar searched his face and found a misshapen likeness of her mother, but much more there that scared her.

"Welcome, blood of my blood," he said, bowing his head.

Zohar bowed in return. "Grandfather."

"Zohar, you look at me strangely, as if you do not know me."

Turning to her brother, he frowned. "And you, Ambrose. You took your first steps in this forest, do you not remember?" Ambrose looked at his feet. "No matter," he said with an unconvincing smile, "there are many who do not remember those years."

He turned and began to walk, and so they followed.

For a little while they proceeded in silence, and then they came upon a high wooden fence where their grandfather clanged the bell-string, and a gate was opened. Zohar's eyes darted around to take in the scene, and it took her a moment to notice that the people inside did not wear Meridians. As the gates were fastened behind them, she felt suddenly afraid. Her mind raced, thinking her mother must not know the Raeburns shunned the Meridian Decree. Zohar didn't like wearing hers but was accustomed to it now.

Her grandfather looked at her and laughed. "Is it this that bothers you?" he said, removing his Meridian and hanging it upon the fence, where many others hung from their leather straps.

She looked at him with wide eyes.

"Your parents are Skalens, and Skalens do not deal in truth, but I do." He watched them, reading their reactions.

People did not talk like this and Zohar did not know whether it was a joke or some kind of test. She moved closer to her brother, bumping into him, and grasped his hand.

"Your parents cannot show themselves here. They have much to atone for. But I would not begrudge you that. You are Raeburns, and as Raeburns, it is your duty to learn something of your heritage. After all, it is you who will wear the Skalens' Star. And if my kinfolk must bow to you, it would be well if you were made wise. As for Skalen Sybilla's Meridian Decree, we do not see the need for such displays of mistrust among family."

Zohar did not like the way he held her gaze. She was not at all sure they were safe with this man, whether or not he had held them as babes. Internally, she regretted bothering her parents with endless requests to visit the Raeburns, to meet her family, to make friends. She felt then it was one of those lessons her father liked to administer after being subjected to a sibling chorus of nagging. *You want to taste the mead? Then by all means, here you go.* And the sour taste said more than a thousand admonitions. She imagined the look her parents would give – *now you understand why we kept you away from them –* and she felt the fool.

Zohar was about to tell him they would take their leave when Ambrose spoke. "What will you teach us?" he said.

Zohar could have kicked him.

But if her brother were to eat the bitter fruit, then she would not let him do so alone. She met her grandfather's eyes. His arrogant smile vexed her, but she did her best to hide it.

"First, remove your Meridians and hang them over there," he said.

Zohar tried to catch her brother's eye, but he had already started to take his off. Her heart thudded in her ears. This was something she and Ambrose did alone, not in front of people that might wish them harm. Zohar stared at the mark the disc of blinding stone left on her brother's forehead.

Ambrose came close to her and whispered, "Don't worry, the Guard won't come here."

Zohar looked into her brother's eyes, unaccustomed to him acting the elder. Gently, he slipped off her Meridian and her resistance melted as if she were warmed by sunshine.

Her grandfather led them to a tent, and Zohar felt all eyes upon them. As they entered, she immediately recognised the powerful scent of the Alma. She and Ambrose used to steal it from the council room, little bits here and there, so their parents wouldn't notice. The Alma was strictly reserved for Skalens' meetings, and for Festival. Zohar and Ambrose went to great effort to breathe of the Alma in the privacy of the sea caves where the Guard were least likely to catch them. The ceaseless wind washed the scent from their hair long before they returned home. And because her parents wore their Meridians, they could not sense that their hearts had recently flowered, or that their thoughts had traversed both the inner and outer realms, gliding through water and air, she and him.

Zohar did not want to enter the tent; did not want to show her spirit to her grandfather, or any of these strange people. But Ambrose walked right in.

Her grandfather looked at them more gently in the reddish light. "It saddens me to see that your parents have taught you to fear what is as natural as breath. But I am glad they have let you come." He gestured for them to sit upon the stones that circled a small hearth of glowing ash. Already Zohar could feel herself softening as she breathed the air's compelling fragrance.

Ambrose's eyes had darkened and he looked up at his grandfather like a cat to the moon, drinking in his words.

"The heart of Velspar has tiny veins that reach up through the earth to find us. This is the Alma. It is a gift from Velspar, and it connects us. I know you have breathed of it before, but you must learn to follow the pathways, to sense them all at once. I will teach you how to become still and to listen – to find the silver threads and to follow them."

Brightening the coals with a stick, he continued, "Close your eyes, and breathe long. This is all you need to do."

Zohar wanted to grasp her brother's hand but felt she was not supposed to do this here. Ambrose's presence hummed beside her. The walls of the tent hung close and then expanded, like lungs. Beetles nestled dumbly in a half rotten log at her grandfather's feet.

Then she noticed him as if seeing him for the first time. He stood before them, an owlish being, ushering them onward into the unknown. She followed.

Out of the long rhythmic silence of their breath, his voice entered, reverberating through their bodies, through the trees outside, through the earth.

"Can you see the silver thread?"

A curious glimmer emerged from the tree branches and Zohar could almost see it, winking in and out of sight, from the corner of her eye. Then with a start she felt Ambrose set off, leaving her behind. She tried to keep up but realised she could not fly. She roused herself, opening her eyes to the sight of him sitting there, still and silent, her grandfather on the other side of the tent in self-same repose. She focused on them, trying to find them again, but her inner gaze flitted in the shallows, where the light of day refused to diminish its persistent glow. She sat there for what seemed an age, vacillating between the desire to scratch the various itches that prickled her skin and moments when she became anxious for the lesson to end.

Finally, her grandfather spoke. "Draw your spirit back to this place. The tent you entered on this day. Baden Forest." His voice came dreamily, like gestures of a broom upon sand – not speaking, so much as causing vibration in the position of speech.

She opened her eyes in the half-light and saw Ambrose gazing into the warm ashes.

Her grandfather stood. "Let us eat."

Zohar and Ambrose brushed themselves off, and followed him to the opening of the tent where the afternoon sun burned bright. Outside, she squinted, feeling strange. She wanted to ask her brother what had happened to him in there, but she could not.

Nearby, a woman stood beside a pot of stew, ladling its steaming contents into bowls. The smell hit Zohar's stomach and she realised she was ravenous. The woman smiled as Zohar approached, and handed her a serving. She drew her lips to the bowl, relishing the rich, peppery flavour. Around her, several others ate, and it felt odd to sit near them when no one had yet exchanged greetings. Her grandfather did not look at all inclined to introduce them, but everyone knew who they were – Skalens' daughter, Skalens' son. She felt safe enough among them now to sit and eat, but not so well at ease as to trust them.

A girl that looked about her age entered the circle and received her helping, and Zohar watched her with curiosity. This was, after all, why they had come. She dared not stare at the girl, but she noticed her simple hunting clothes, her serious face, and mouse-brown hair. The girl refused to acknowledge her and sat on a rock farthest from where she and Ambrose sat. When Zohar's parents allowed her to travel to town to accompany them on Skalens' business – trade and such – she felt quietly pleased by the occasional admiring glance of the workers, the merchants, the women and their shy children. But here, she felt that her fine clothing and comely face set her apart in a different sense. She had never felt so unworldly or unwise.

But Ambrose seemed quite at home. She could imagine him walking in step with the girl, impressing her despite his age as he gutted fish or showed her some other rough skill he had acquired en route with their parents. She envied him the quickness of his tongue, the way he could leap from the wagon and persuade his parents to let him look at the crops, the back rooms of the leather shop, the well that had turned sour. In full sight of his parents' supervisory gaze, he managed to meet and charm the folk of Avishae, no matter their station. He seemed not to care if they were dirty, if they had the cast of a murderer, or whether they were selling spurious lies. He craved their presence, and wanted to know what things felt like, without care for the consequences. She, on the other hand, recoiled when she caught scent of danger, and was well attuned to the subtle signs of unwelcome. She thought it would be different with the Raeburns, but here again she felt her younger brother running ahead of her.

The sun was beginning to set and her grandfather took their

bowls. "Well," he said with a sigh. "I am pleased to have spent this day with you. I hope you will return to us." The old man that looked like her mother, smiled. "With Skalens' blessing, of course."

Ambrose grinned, staring up at him.

"You have shown us great hospitality," Zohar said, grasping her brother's hand.

Her grandfather led them to the perimeter, unhooking their Meridians from the fence, and gave the signal for the gate to be opened. Bouncing the stones in his hands a moment, he hesitated. "You may feel different once you put these back on," he said, finally handing them over.

Zohar fitted her Meridian and Ambrose did the same. Bowing their farewells, the two walked in slow crunching footsteps as the gates were fastened behind them. Her grandfather was right; she did feel different. With her Meridian on, quietness enveloped her, and her brother seemed so very far away. She guessed that he must feel the same, as he walked with eyes downcast, which was not his usual way. She did not want the silence to go on too much longer, or it would follow them all the way home.

"Ambrose?"

Her brother looked over in reply.

"Do you think Mother knows the Raeburns do not wear the Meridian?"

Ambrose frowned. "I don't think we should mention it."

"Then, what will we say?"

"I thought that was your job to figure out."

Zohar gave him a sharp look. "What happened in there?"

"What do you mean?" Ambrose said, refusing to follow her lead.

Ahead of them, Silvey stood, flank twitching as she chewed at a clump of grass. Ambrose ran ahead and mounted the horse, sitting himself up front.

"Hey!" Zohar shouted, running after him.

"It's not fair that you always get to ride up front. I am a good rider, and my legs are longer than yours now." He made out as if he were speaking in jest, but in his eyes, she saw that he was serious.

"Fine," she said in her best impression of good humour.

Climbing on at the back, she put her arms around her brother's waist and he started off, riding at a rollicking speed.

"There's no need to show off," she said, her voice jolting to the clatter of hooves.

Ambrose laughed and rode harder until all she could do was hold on. In the straining of his muscles, he seemed different somehow. Perhaps the Alma had made her senses keener, or perhaps it was the smell of the smoke on him. They had never breathed so much at one time, and suddenly she feared for him. She was supposed to be looking after him and now she was letting a smoke-addled boy of eleven ride a full-grown horse.

The gate reared up before them and Zohar felt a twist of regret in her stomach. Slowing Silvey to a trot, Ambrose waved to an amused party of guardsmen. Zohar looked up, and saw her mother's flowing auburn hair moving in the hollow of the high balcony, and a figure behind, that moved out of sight. The pair alighted and Silvey was led to the stables as they made their way toward the House. Moments later, their parents appeared to greet them.

"Hello children," her mother said, the shape of a smile forming on her tense and troubled face.

She approached Zohar and embraced her, holding her very tight, as her father clapped Ambrose on the back.

They exchanged nervous smiles and made their way up the stairwell.

Her father looked around to check that no one could overhear. "Did your grandfather treat you well?"

Ambrose smiled. "Very well. He showed us the camp and fed us a fine meal."

"Anything else?" their mother asked.

Zohar felt her ears reddening.

Ambrose chewed his fingernail. "We were not sure whether we should tell you, but..."

Zohar looked at him in horror.

"Yes?" their mother said, staring at Ambrose intently.

Ambrose looked at his feet and then to a place on the wall.

"Grandfather told us that sometimes they use the Alma for their own meetings – like family meetings," he said.

"I see," their mother nodded slowly. "Zohar, let us take a walk before the sun sets. We so rarely spend time together as mother and daughter. Ulric, take Ambrose to help the guards light the night lamps."

Zohar followed her mother numbly, wondering what corner she was about to be trapped in.

Her mother took her by the arm, and they walked through the meadow as small, winged creatures buzzed about the clover. "Zohar," she began, "one day you will be Skalen."

Zohar looked up at her mother, trying to hide her trepidation.

"When your grandparents died, your father and I had been courting for less than a year. We thought we knew what it meant to be Skalens, but after the Council of Vaelnyr, everything changed. I do not think you can understand how close we came to death, and not just our family, but everyone in Avishae." She paused, chewing her lip. "We did what we had to do to survive."

Her mother's words did not make sense.

"I pray that you will not have to face such choices, but you have to be ready."

"Mother, I don't understand," Zohar stammered, the day's events taking their toll.

Her mother's face softened. "I know. How could you? I wish I could speak freely, my love, but Velspar is not safe. That is the one thing you must remember."

"Yes, Mother."

Unaccustomed to feeling the grip of her mother's hand, Zohar clung to it, afraid to say anything that would make her let go.

"The Raeburn camp is protected. As long as this is the case, you may go there. Ask of them all the questions you would ask of me. They will answer you truly."

"But why can't I ask you? Or Father?"

"It is not possible," she said, her face taking on its more familiar stony cast.

Her mother steered them back toward the Skalens' House, and Zohar took that to mean that the conversation was over.

When they were in sight of the guards, her mother whispered, "Your journey is the Skalen's journey, but this is not so for your brother. You will need to keep some things to yourself from now on. Do you understand?"

Zohar nodded, but in truth she did not.

28

ZOHAR

Ten Years After The Fire

ZOHAR SMOOTHED THE GRAZE on her palm as Ambrose clambered into the cave. The guard below knew where they were, and though the cave heightened their voices, the crash of the waves scrambled the sound before it could reach the ears of their long-suffering sentinel. Zohar wondered if Elis volunteered to mind them on their morning climb because he loved the ocean's roar. He did not fiddle with a toothpick in his teeth as some of the other guards did, but seemed to notice how the waves clutched at the shore, sucking back through the rocks, reaching for land again.

Zohar and her brother did much the same thing whenever they came here, but on this day, conversation did not come easily. She felt questions readying themselves to leap from her tongue, but they would have to wait. Ambrose pulled himself to stand and stretched his arms, breathing the sharp sea air. Zohar laughed, somewhat nervously, waiting for him to sit. Walking to the back of the cave – where it was darker and sheltered from the wind – she sat and placed a stick upon a notch in a small log, rubbing it fast between her palms. It was not the easiest way to make fire, but she liked the challenge of it. Today she was determined to make it spark.

Ambrose sat beside her. Pulling a leather pouch from his pocket, he prepared the Alma. In smooth motions, he gathered it up with his fingers, chopping it into a fine crumb. Zohar watched her brother hunched over with his dark, lazy curls moving among his Meridian. They were about to cast off the shackles of the past week and let their minds drift together, but Zohar felt her brother was a world away. She wondered if he would feel the tension of her mind as she rehashed their visit to the Raeburn camp, desperate to ask him what he had felt, what he had seen. Her palms were hot and damp as she worked the stick, trying to funnel all her nervousness into the task. Heat pooled inside her coat and her muscles began to tire, but she would not give Ambrose the satisfaction of watching her start again from scratch.

"Ah!" she called out in triumph as a wisp of smoke curled out. Zohar blew softly on the spark and Ambrose helped it catch. Carefully, she nudged kindling into the tiny rose of heat that spread and gathered, steadily transforming into flame.

Once the two of them were laughing, Zohar felt more at ease. She would simply ask him what had happened. Once the Alma smoke gathered around them, he would tell her anyway – he would want to.

"Ready?" he said, his hand poised at his Meridian.

"Ready." Zohar smiled and removed hers in unison, shaking out her fair, reddish hair and massaging her scalp.

Ambrose crumbled the Alma into the flames and as it filled the air, Zohar felt her brow relax. She would put her queries aside for now. She would wait until they were deep enough for the question to flow out of her, and for the door of his mind to fall ajar; because they loved the Alma, and they relished it in long, luxurious breaths that harmonised with the rolling of the waves.

The breeze tousled clouds across the sun's great eye. It scalded the firmament with its song. As she watched, its white heart cast off veils of red, veils of blue. It hummed, and she listened. It was rising, almost imperceptibly, ascending to the roof of the sky. She imagined it moving, as the hours passed, above the lid of the cave, so she would not see it.

She chuckled, finding the humour in it, that thousands of shattered suns still shined upon the waves, still delivered light into the cave. But the thought also scared her. When she closed her eyes, the light was there too, drawn unceasingly into her mind. Its all-seeing light would consume the shadow things, the things of shape and form, until nothing remained.

Zohar focused on the crackling fire before her, warming her feet. She became aware of Ambrose sitting beside her, staring miserably at the scuffs and smudges that marked the cave floor. She could almost make out the shape of his handprint, where he had pulled his body in.

"Brother..." Zohar said, her voice resonating in the cave's cupped hand.

"Brother?" she said, more directly, feeling that it was time.

After a moment, Ambrose replied, sounding very far away. "Yes, Sister?"

Zohar fixed her mind and called the sound-shapes from the places where they slept, so that they might go to her brother, and wrest answers from him. It was not easy.

"Where did you go?" she said.

Moments passed. "I remained here."

She shook herself and tried again. "With Grandfather."

Zohar felt a hot gust, like fire's breath, lift from him and drift across her chest. Its weight bruised her. Ambrose let out a small groan and reached for her hand. "I do not want to tell you."

Zohar's mind swam. Where was the answer? It was hidden beneath storming sands and mists, bracken and briar. "Did he do something to you?" Zohar's muscles became hot.

Ambrose looked at her with dark, unfocused eyes. "You are so angry, Sister. He showed me a way out. I was lost, before."

She could not grasp what he was saying, her brow furrowing as she met his eyes.

"He will help us," he said with finality, turning to face the fire.

Zohar grew quiet, watching as flames lipped along the blackened branches. The Alma turned to ash, and as the fire winked out, Zohar felt cool wind wakening their faces, calling them to return. The sun had made its climb, and soon enough, they would have to make their own. It was becoming much easier to think, as impressions scurried into position, and the cave itself began to appear exceedingly normal. Ambrose shifted his legs wakefully, and Zohar knew that if she did not ask him then and there, the moment would be lost.

"I want to talk to you," she said, a little too loudly.

Ambrose looked uncomfortable. Closing off the same way he did when her mother asked him things. A desperate feeling rose in her throat and she wanted to grasp his mind and fix it there until he softened and listened to the words of her heart. They had always shared everything with each other. And she was the first-born; she was the one who should walk first into the unknown. But he had gone somewhere without her and didn't look like he was about to turn back.

Knowing he would sense her vexation, she steadied her voice. "I'm sorry, Brother, but I fear for you. The Raeburns are kin to us in name, but not in our hearts. We do not know them."

Ambrose laughed, but there was a note of resistance in him as his eyes slid past her, looking elsewhere. "How will we come to know them if we keep them at arm's length? All these years we dreamed of this. And by some miracle Mother and Father have allowed it." As he gathered up his leather pouch, he still would not meet her gaze. "What did Mother say to you in the meadow that night?"

His look was a challenge and though she wished to parry, her face soured with her swallowed retort.

Ambrose nodded; they both had secrets they were keeping, and they would keep them still. As if to make a point of it, he chose that moment to put on his Meridian. Reluctantly, Zohar gathered hers and smoothed her hair behind her ears before tightening the band.

She was about to try another approach when Ambrose moved to the edge, lowering himself down on his belly, dropping below her sight.

"Wait!" Zohar called out.

"I'll race you!" Ambrose shouted and let out a mad laugh.

Grinning despite herself, Zohar scrambled over the edge, gripping familiar stones. Gaining on him, she jumped off the rocks and onto the sand, breaking into a run. He was just out of reach and she screamed out taunts in little gasps that were quickly stolen by the wind. Just before he reached the grass, Ambrose cried out, clutching his foot and rolling across the sand. Moments later, Guardsman Elis appeared.

"Are you hurt, Ambrose?" Elis said with a frown.

"Are you alright?" Zohar gasped, pushing past.

Ambrose grit his teeth, still grasping his foot with eyes squeezed shut, letting out a groan of annoyance.

"Fine," he puffed, "I'm fine. Thank you, Elis, I can walk."

After that there was no getting rid of the guard, and it seemed their time was up for the day.

The three of them walked together in silence, red of face and alone with their thoughts, rounding the path that led to the Skalens' House.

29

ZOHAR

Eleven Years After The Fire

ZOHAR AND AMBROSE MADE THEIR WAY to the Raeburn camp in long strides. It was Guardsman John's habit to eye them suspiciously as they departed, but the Guard were under orders to let them explore the forest as they wished, each and every Magsday. When they entered the gate, they practically threw their Meridians in their haste to be free of them, sometimes missing the fence-hooks entirely. Ambrose slapped her on the back as he ran off to see their grandfather. Zohar supposed she was used to it now.

She scanned the camp to see who was about and noticed Ma Bet digging twisted potato roots from the garden patch.

"Zohar," she said, without looking up, "help an old woman with some digging, would you?"

Relieved to have something to do, she sat by Ma Bet and took up a spade. Though she had come around to the Raeburns, Zohar still couldn't understand why they insisted on producing their own food when the farms of the valley were plentiful. They seemed to find reasons to be busy – too busy to leave the camp. Her grandfather and a few of the young men travelled to town selling pelts and forest herbs, but they always returned nattering, in a gruff sort of way, about all the things they had seen that displeased them.

As Zohar dug in the soil, pulling at the rust-coloured potatoes, she watched some of the Raeburn kids across the way, arguing about the best way to manoeuvre the wagon they were loading.

Ma Bet regarded her. "You want to tell them how you think it should be done?"

Zohar flushed. "No!" Then in a more measured tone, "No, thank you, Ma Bet. I am happy to help you with your work. We don't have a garden at the Skalens' House, so this is a rare treat for me."

The old woman flinched slightly, and Zohar regretted reminding her of her life outside the camp. Sometimes she wished she could forget it herself. Ambrose seemed to shake off the name Elshender as a dog shakes off the rain, but it clung to Zohar, and all of them saw it.

Ma Bet had turned her attention elsewhere. "Edith!" She beckoned the sour-faced girl Zohar had noticed on her very first visit.

Silently cursing the old woman, Zohar made to absorb herself in the task of prising out the stubborn roots.

Edith approached with her arms folded, the straight line of her mouth showing no sign that it would curve into a smile.

"Edith, thank you, my dear. I know you have some chores to attend to up in the mountains today. Zohar would like to accompany you."

The girl threw her arms down and gave Ma Bet a withering look as if she dared to refuse her.

"Zohar would like to see the mountains." Ma Bet spoke slowly, fixing Edith with a meaningful stare.

It was humiliating. Not only had she failed to make friends with the Raeburns, they had to be forced to spend time with her against their will. She grit her teeth, hating Ma Bet and her stupid grandfather for their love of embarrassing the young.

Edith looked down at her without smiling, turned and strode toward one of the huts. "Be waiting over there, and make sure your hands are clean," Edith called over her shoulder.

Ma Bet smiled at Zohar. "Have fun, dear!"

Zohar brushed the earth from her skirt and went directly to the well. Scraping black grit from under her fingernails with a twig, she rinsed her hands in the cool water.

When Edith reappeared dressed in her hunting gear, she did not even look at Zohar's hands.

Edith traipsed on ahead, and Zohar followed in silence. To calm her nerves, Zohar tried to immerse herself in the sweet forest smells, noticing tiny purple flowers and the flick of lizards along the way. The canopy shuffled above them, awash with light. Edith climbed confidently, crouching and clambering over uneven terrain, but Zohar still wore her dress and had much more trouble. She sorely wished she had drunk the water back at the well instead of wasting it on her hands. Zohar could see a full waterskin hanging from Edith's belt but did not dare ask her for it.

It was hard work and the two girls were sweating, filling the forest with the small sounds of their labour. They had ascended high above the camp, but it was difficult to see where they had come through the thickness of the trees. As they rounded a steep section of the path, a large boulder came into view. Edith sat there and gulped at the waterskin.

"We will stop here for now," she said, catching her breath.

Zohar joined her on the far side of the rock, her bodice damp with sweat. Edith held out the waterskin and surprised her with a smile.

"Thank you," Zohar said and drank deeply.

"The place we are going is just over there." Edith pointed to another steep rise then looked Zohar in the eye. "When we get there, I need you to do exactly what I say. Will you do that?"

Zohar nodded.

Once they had made it over the rise, the view from the top of the mountain opened up before them. Zohar had never seen Avishae from this angle and she gasped at the sight. One day she would be Skalen and she felt suddenly that she knew nothing of her own lands. Far below, wooden houses clustered about the edge of a golden valley that gave way to taller buildings of grey and black in the east. Haydentown looked very small from here, and the gushing

Selbourne was but a sliver of light, disappearing into the Caulmont Range.

There, at the very edge of her vision, the Temple sat, white and shining among the pines. To the west, Baden Forest rose thickly, swallowing the horizon. And over there, to the south, was the Skalens' House, sitting stoutly above the broken rocks of the Bay. In her excitement she turned to Edith, but the girl had little interest in the view.

Edith laid out a number of items on a large slab, and Zohar watched as she mixed something vigorously in a bowl. Smoke rose in a mist about Edith and when the breeze hit her face, Zohar recognised the Alma. But there was another smell that she did not expect.

"If you must look, come quickly, because you will need to take shelter in a moment," Edith said.

Zohar came nearer. Edith had set fire to a bundle of Alma that stuck out of a cleft in the rock. In a small wooden bowl was a foul looking pink paste, lumpy with herbs and shredded rags.

"What is that for?" Zohar asked, hoping that she would not be expected to eat it.

Edith ignored her question. "I want you to crouch over there, beneath that tree. Get as close to the trunk as possible and stay there."

Zohar was growing tired of her manner and was about to say as much when Edith caught her with an urgent look. Zohar made her way to the tree and shuffled backward under the foliage.

Edith took the smoking thatch in her hand and raised it high, waving the bluish smoke across a shaft of sunlight. Zohar then heard rhythmic thumping and saw that Edith was using a small hand-drum, flicking it forward and back so that the rocks struck the skin.

Suddenly a huge black shape passed overhead, and the clearing flickered with shadow. Zohar's eyes widened but she could not fully comprehend what she was seeing. It looked to be a cloaked spirit falling from the sky, charred black, its long fingers caressing the wind.

It stepped down the sky, arcing its terrible wings. As it came to land in front of Edith, it spread its talons wide. Edith met its eyes and spooned out the paste for it to eat. Zohar felt the prickle of twigs against her skin as she tried to hide herself, but she did not look away.

Just then, another shape hovered above them, to be joined by two more. Edith's voice, normally so tight when Zohar was around, was soft and throaty as she called them by their god-name, "Kshidol."

Edith called them, guiding them down in graceful movements, totally unafraid. Before her eyes, Edith transformed from a humourless, mousy-haired girl into a kind of priestess. The kshidol crouched about her feet, tilting their heads to lick and gobble at the offerings. Zohar's hands tingled as she watched them eat. They were so powerful.

Her mind flashed this way and that, to the silent skies she had known for most of her life, and the memory trying to push through. Hadn't they been there, a constant presence above the Caulmont Range? Hadn't she stepped close to them as a child? She must have. They were right here – the smell brought it back – they were here in front of her as they had been at Blood Call.

Her memories faltered, *Blood Call* sounding strangely in her mind. The words were trapped together with others in a secret place she was not supposed to visit. They were untouchable, but touched too often, and when she sought them, they sounded not like real things but like things she had invented. The smell of their musky black feathers, the undulation of their necks, it drew her in and out of time, here and now, and long ago.

Then suddenly it came.

Vividly.

Zohar was five years old. The air stank of ash, had done for months. Her mother was not there but her father crouched before her, devoid of laughter. This year they would be doing something different for her birthday. She would put on her blue robes and they would go to the garden. Her mother had made birth cake. It was very nice. A special treat. Her father helped her dress, and then held her hand as if they were about to walk off the edge of the world. He kept smiling and explaining that things were going to be different, but all would be well.

It was cold in the garden and Ambrose scratched at his knees as he looked up at her. There were strangers standing on the far wall, a man and a lady, wearing Skalen's Stars as her parents did. Her father sat her on his lap and then her mother appeared holding a tray.

Her mother's eyes sparkled redly as she chuckled. "Let us celebrate your special day."

Steam puffed from her mouth as she spoke and Zohar shivered, looking at the small brown cake in front of her.

"Eat it, dear," her mother said.

Her father hugged her tighter on his lap, stroking her hair. "Your mother made it especially."

Ambrose gave her a look that told her there was no way anyone was leaving that garden until she ate it. Although he was younger, she trusted his instincts.

She picked it up. It smelt of dried berries, but something else as well.

Her mouth pooled with saliva even before she had taken a bite. Chewing slowly, she tried not to taste it, tried not to notice its texture or anything about it. There were berries in it, that much she knew. There were salt-parts too, tough and chewy. When she was finished, she imagined them burning in her guts, becoming globules, growing into toads and bursting right out of her stomach.

"Good," her father said and kissed her, but she did not feel comforted.

Her mother stepped forward. "Now, I just need you to say something for our visitors, to show them what a good girl you are."

Zohar stared at her mother.

"Say: I give my oath to the Skalens."

Zohar's mouth was frozen shut.

Her mother gave a strained laugh. "Don't be shy dear. Your brother said it just before, and he did such a good job." She ruffled his hair.

Ambrose shuffled nearer to Zohar and held her hand. He leaned his head on her shoulder.

"There's a good girl," her father said.

She looked up at him wanting to cry.

He mouthed the words: *I give my oath...*

"I... give my oath... to the Skalens?" she said, shrugging nervously, scared she'd said it wrong.

"That will do," the woman said.

Her mother nodded. "Well done, Zohar."

Hiding in the scrub in the mountain light it hit her with dreadful certainty what her mother had put in that cake. One of the winged ones looked at her with knowing eyes and her stomach convulsed. Fluid came from her mouth in little retches. Doubled over in the dirt, her eyes blurred with tears, and all she wanted to do was disappear from their sight. From the majestic ones who had known her as a child – who had vanished but who were here, now.

Edith came over, but Zohar could not find the words to speak, and when their eyes met, Edith seemed to flow around her like honey. Zohar's heart swelled, sensing the unique quality of Edith's kindness, a fruit unusually tart, but also sweet, in its way. Edith extended her hand and smiled, but this time the smile was real. She took the stick of Alma, and held it between them for a moment as they bowed their heads. The smoke softened her grief, and her thoughts expanded beyond the memory. Expanding until they were too wide to hold it.

Edith turned to the kshidol. "They will go now," she said, extinguishing the Alma.

The food was almost gone and the kshidol bounced about, buoyed by their ungainly wings as they hunted for scraps. With a few lurching steps, one took flight, and then the others followed. Black spirits, crawling back into a milky blue sky.

30

ZOHAR

Eleven Years After The Fire

IT WAS THE DAY BEFORE FESTIVAL and Zohar sat upon her bed applying the finishing touches to her effigy. She remembered the previous year, collecting wildflowers from in and around the Raeburn camp to form the figure, having many red thoughts to confess to it. But after seeing the kshidol, her other concerns seemed of little consequence.

Her thoughts were a staircase missing stones. Childhood memories crumbled at her touch, but new knowledge laid down by the Raeburns proved flimsy beneath the weight of her questions, or otherwise too lofty to reach. As she placed the pieces of her effigy across the surface of her quilt, she feared that each passing year would be like this. New truths calcifying around her, making her heavy until one day she would stiffen and become a maiden of stone, slowly entombed by the horrible things her parents had done.

She wanted her effigy to contain all that she felt, and climbed the mountain once more, finding that same clearing where Edith had taken her. There she took a small black feather that glowed green in the light, dipping it in seawater, in mourning for Siatka, The Mother, who, in truth she still could not clearly recall. The feather was secreted at the effigy's core, and around it she placed lengths of Alma, clover from the field where she and her mother had walked, a hair from Ambrose's head, a hair from her own, and a length of thread she had used to mend her father's tunic. Touching these precious objects with her fingertips, Zohar selected threads of grey and blue to bind it together, but only the Alma fire would know what was hidden within.

The Raeburns hated Festival, and Ma Bet never tired of expressing her distaste for what had once been the holiest of days. Zohar listened, and sometimes she thought she remembered the way it used to be. Voices, clamour; the sound of drums. Sweat smells. Red hands that shook, loosing demons into the night. Village children grabbing her by the hand, laughing, spinning around and around, losing Ambrose, then finding him again with grass stuck in his hair. Perhaps these memories were her own, but as Ma Bet spoke, the past gathered detail, and became a place she could visit in her mind.

Before the Purge, the people came to Festival to confess their red deeds to the Intercessors. The making of effigies was a new custom in Avishae. It was her mother's notion, and because of that Ma Bet liked to ridicule Festival, calling it 'Rebekah's Pantomime', when everyone was made to play with 'little dolls'. Winding thread around the legs and torso of her effigy, Zohar thought she preferred her mother's way. Her shame at having eaten the flesh of the Holy Ones was private. She liked the feeling of being made free of it, of the flames devouring all that was bad in her, cleansing her spirit for the new year.

Zohar wrapped her effigy in blue silk and hid it in her drawer. She wondered what Ambrose was doing. Eventually, she found him, armed with a wooden sword, parrying with Elis in the yard. The day was unusually humid, and they were fighting bare-chested. Across the way, she saw her father. He leant forward on the railing, watching Ambrose, though she doubted her brother knew that he was there. It was unusual to see him at all during daylight hours, for he was always in the Tower.

Down in the yard, the men's bodies were drenched in sunlight, but her father stood pale in the shadows. She waved to him, wanting so much to see his smile, but she could not catch his attention. Slipping back into the corridor, she made her way to the opposite side.

She scanned the area where he had been, but by then, he had gone. Faintly, she heard his footsteps ascending through the Tower door. She dared herself to touch the handle, to turn it, but her arms remained at her sides.

"Zohar?" Her mother's voice rang down the colonnade, making her brother look up.

"Hello, Mother."

Her mother approached, frowning, and took Zohar by the arm. The guardsmen returned to their swordplay. Ambrose looked at her a moment longer, then brought down his wooden sword upon Elis' shield with a great thwack.

"Let us have some tea," her mother said, releasing her.

Zohar managed a smile and followed her back inside.

The scent of dried Alma that filled the House became striking and intense in the sitting room. It was dark, and the hearth unlit, surrounded as it was by woven lengths of Alma. The Attendants had spent weeks crafting fronds into decorative shapes. The Hall below contained their most impressive creation, an Alma effigy the height of two men that would form the heart of the fire.

Her mother drew up a chair and called for one of the Attendants to prepare tea. Zohar gazed at the ocean beyond the window, her hands folded in her lap.

Once the Attendant had placed their tea upon the table, he left them, closing the door.

"Have you finished your effigy?" her mother asked.

Zohar felt protective of her small creation, so kept her answer brief. "I was putting the finishing touches on it earlier. And you?"

"I've yet to add the binding, but the rest is done." Her mother took a sip from her cup as the scent of steamed lavender and wood herbs joined the Alma's heady aroma. "Are you looking forward to Festival?"

"I am," Zohar said, sounding brighter than she felt.

Her mother paused. "It must be hard for you, after spending time with my family. I am well aware that they do not approve of our Festival reforms."

Zohar smiled wryly at that, but her mother's face grew serious.

"Have you been asking questions of the Raeburn elders, like I bid you to?"

Zohar shrugged, an uncomfortable heat rising in her cheeks.

Her mother inhaled sharply. "So, do they mention me at all?"

"Sometimes," Zohar said, seeking some safe example to relay.

"And what do they say?"

She tried to think, but every anecdote contained something that would be taken as an insult. "I'm sorry, Mother, I–"

Her mother waved her hand. "Never mind. Do they speak of the other Skalens? Of the future?"

"Grandfather has mentioned Sybilla." Speaking the woman's name sent an icy sensation through Zohar's stomach.

Her mother leaned forward in her chair, so close that Zohar could smell the lavender on her breath. "Keep your voice low, Zohar."

She nodded.

"What does he say about her?"

"He calls her the Red Skalen," Zohar whispered. "And not because that is the colour of Vaelnyr."

Her mother leaned back, looking thoughtful.

Zohar was sweating, she wanted to open the window and feel the cool breeze on her neck but knew her mother would think it rude.

"My father will teach you about the past, but do not let him cast his own vision over your future. He is but a citizen of Avishae and it is very well to be high minded when your power extends the span of a village. Your power will surpass the borders of Avishae, touching all the Seven Lands – if you want it to. Every decision you make will leave a reddening stain on your spirit. That is why they call it the Skalens' burden. And you will have to bargain with Skalens like Sybilla. You will have to offer them something of value to turn them to your side."

Her mother paused, running a finger along the dusk-blue embroidery of her skirt. "That is what my father does not understand. Festival would be banned entirely if your father and I had not negotiated with Sybilla. She wanted the Meridian Decree, and I wanted Festival reform." Her mother took a sip of her tea.

"Yes, Mother." Zohar gave her a weak smile.

"Zohar, you may speak freely, as long as you do not raise your voice. The Attendants are busy with preparations. It is just you and I here."

Zohar looked to the crack beneath the door. She thought of her effigy, and the way she would feel on the morrow when she threw it into the roaring flames. "The Raeburns may not understand Festival – the way it is now – but I do. We all must have our chance to move on from our mistakes, to let go of the past," Zohar said, feeling oddly relieved to have spoken something true.

Her mother nodded. "And what does your brother think?"

Zohar looked at the fireplace, choosing her words.

Her mother did not wait for her to answer. "I see," she said. "I imagine my father has taken him in with his stories, he probably finds it all very exciting." She paused. "But you still take care of each other, don't you? Ambrose still seeks your counsel?"

Zohar swallowed awkwardly, her emotions too close to the surface. She had no words for the unaccountable distance that had grown between her and her brother.

The moment went on too long.

Both of them were silent for a time.

As the minutes passed, Zohar's discomfort rose.

Her mother's eyes had become unfocused as she gazed into her cup. Without warning, dark spots appeared on her skirt, and Zohar realised she was crying.

"Mother..." Zohar made to stand, but her mother shooed her away.

At the sound of passing footsteps her mother faced the window, hiding her face.

Zohar sat there, unable to leave. She reached for the teapot to have something to do with her hands, filling her cup with cool water that spun with lavender buds.

"Thank you for sharing tea with me, Zohar. You have not displeased me and I am not upset with your brother." She gave Zohar a watery smile. "Putting together my effigy, I have been recollecting moments from the past that are difficult to bear."

Zohar stood and placed her hand on her mother's shoulder.

"All will be well, my darling. Tomorrow we will be lighter," she said, giving Zohar's hand a squeeze.

Zohar walked hesitantly toward the door, then glanced behind, wondering who her mother had once been, this woman whose shoulders crouched around her heart.

31

ZOHAR

Twelve Years After The Fire

Zohar's cheeks glowed red as apples. The Alma fire had taken, its flames reaching for the sky. Ambrose stood beside her and she followed his eyes northward, where the Raeburns emerged like so many wolves from the shadows of Baden Forest.

"I see they have dressed up for the occasion this year," Zohar said.

Ambrose's mouth tugged at the edge, but he did not smile.

In the roaring light, Zohar noticed the hair on his upper lip had darkened, and stifled a chuckle.

"What?" he said, irritated.

Her father gave her a stern look from the other side of the blaze, where he and her mother stood.

Zohar calmed herself and looked about the sea of faces before her. It felt strange that she did not know them. They came like ants, in trails, from the town. Fishermen brought their little ones upon their shoulders. There were shopkeeps and farmers and an old woman who walked with a stick. There was a well-dressed man with a lady on his arm, her great round belly drawing smiles from even the roughest of dockhands. Zohar's heart sank and swelled as she watched them. How they greeted one another with pats upon the back, children hugging knees, heads bowed in friendship. She wondered if she would ever know what it was like.

The Raeburns advanced down the hill. Ma Bet ambled grumpily beside Zohar's grandfather who surveyed the scene with his shrewd grey eyes. Rowan walked with his head down alongside the other lads. Zohar looked for Edith, but her meagre height made her difficult to spot. But when one of the aunties bent down to pick up her dropped effigy, she saw Edith behind her, at the centre of the group, her face a mask of contempt. Zohar swallowed, feeling cast out, unable to greet her family as she stood beside the dais, a Skalens' daughter in full regalia.

When the last of the stragglers had joined the flock, her mother ascended the dais to give the Skalens' address.

"People of Avishae. Your Skalens welcome you this day. We come together each year, at harvest time, to remind ourselves of what binds us. The Alma is a gift from Velspar, and it connects us all. On this Festival day, we mark the 712th year since Skalen Karasek's first vision; a vision of unity, of the Seven Lands joined as one. Though you have suffered much hardship these last years, we must hold tight to one another, and cast all doubt, fear and hatred into the flames."

Zohar watched the faces of the crowd. The way their eyes gleamed in the firelight. They did not cry out or clap their hands. They did not grin from ear to ear, or spin in circles, dancing. The wind blew. Zohar's gaze was drawn to the Temple nestled in the mountains, its whiteness still pristine, its presence ominous as it kept silent witness.

Her father stood beside her and called over the fire's roar. "Cast off the heaviness in your hearts! The new year begins!" He held his arms wide and turned to the fire. Guardsman John handed him the ceremonial knife. Zohar watched as her father pressed the blade into his palm, his head cast back as if in rapture. Holding his effigy in one hand, he squeezed his other fist high, blood dripping down upon the face and body.

"Praise Velspar!" he cried, casting it deep into the flames.

"Praise Velspar," the voices intoned.

Her mother went next. Holding her palm close to her belly, she made the cut, wrapping her hand about the effigy. She brought the doll to her forehead, whispering under her breath, and threw it into the fire.

Zohar looked at her brother, because it was her turn, but he offered her no encouragement. Irritation helped her push the blade. She found it easier to cut the flesh of her thumb, and slit the skin, wincing. Marking the outer silks of her effigy with a single drop of blood, Zohar thought of her stupid brother, and flung the figure through a gust of Alma smoke.

As she stepped to the side, her limbs grew heavy, the breeze pleasant upon her face, her anger suddenly gone. She turned to smile at Ambrose, preparing to embrace him when he passed the fire, but his expression made her start.

Ambrose dragged the knife across his palm with gritted teeth. Her heart leapt as dark streams flowed down his wrist and elbow. He had cut too deep. Blood soaked the red cloth that bound his effigy, and when he pressed it to his forehead, the veins of his arms bulged with the force of his confession.

He looked up, his forehead smeared red, his eyes livid as fire, as the Attendants came with their bandages.

32

WALDEMAR

Thirteen Years After The Fire

OUR DAYS ARE SIMPLE, *and each cave that we make for our home, we imagine as our Temple. I hoped that we would find others, but we have wandered the mountains of Jokvour for thirteen years and found no one. Maeryn has pain in her knees, and Amand has silver in his hair. The dust of age has fallen upon my hands, in sunspots and darkspots, in climbing scars and the yearly etch of the Blood Call.*

I think of the children, peering over the crest of adulthood with not a single scar upon their palms. I fear for them, and for the spirits that have already turned to dust. It seems they all wear the Meridian now. We need only to step into the shadows to avoid capture, for the Guard are now blind. The cowherd wandering by the foot of the mountain is blind. The fishermen of the Samlae, and the drunken man lost in the Fields of Marain, are blind. They hear only the sound of their own voices, ringing with self-certainty. They are unguided and bereft of wisdom.

They mine the blinding stone, but they do not do it well. There are none left who know how to find the peace within it. They come to the outermost caves, taking great boulders on carts, or rolling them by hand to the valleys. They do not know that blinding stone must be buried in the earth, made to rest with stone of its kind for many moons if it is to perform its sacred duty.

We hear the buzzing of the spirits, as if they were speaking through water, but they are not silent.

We hear many things.

Maeryn spends long hours listening for Sybilla, for she knew her as a girl, and knows her still. There are changes in her, she tells us. The hot white fire of her sun melting into sunset's blush. She tells us such things, but my retort comes like a barb in my throat. I want her to speak of extinguished light, of a sun that traverses the darkness but does not return. Amand helps me to dissolve the feelings that burn in me, helps me to have faith in Velspar.

In vision I search for those who yet have ears to hear. For there are cracks in the stone, and bands that are loosened in the night, and stones so dry they hold no vigil.

I show them the primal image: the mouth of Kshidol above, the mouth of Siatka below, and between them the eye of Velspar. I show them so they will know that the Holy Ones keep spirit alive, as hands around a flame. I show them this symbol and nothing more, so that it may become as the beat of their hearts − as the flow of their breath − ever returning, and ever renewed.

INTERCESSOR WALDEMAR RASMUS OF BRIVIA, 713.

33

AMBROSE

Thirteen Years After The Fire

AMBROSE ARRIVED AT THE BAY just before midday, accompanied by Guardsman John. Leaving the horses at the crest of the hill, they strode toward shore. The sky was overcast and the wind was up but the air was warm. Mr Sherburn emerged from a weathered shack, holding his hand up in greeting. As John waved, Ambrose chewed his thumbnail trying to make out the three figures slouching on wooden crates at the water's edge.

John turned to Ambrose. "Shall I leave you here?"

"Thank you, Guardsman."

"Expect my return at the set of the sun," he said, and departed.

As Mr Sherburn approached, Ambrose pushed his curls from his eyes and smiled, "Good day, Mr Sherburn."

The old man was thin-haired with blotched, leathery skin, the wrinkles around his mouth showing Ambrose that the grim expression he wore was his usual one.

"Good day, Mr Elshender." Mr Sherburn appraised Ambrose, his eyes sharp with scrutiny. "I suppose you are suitably dressed. You can swim, can't you?"

"Yes sir."

"Alright then. My sons are preparing the raft over there. Go on and introduce yourself." As he pointed, and one of them looked up, rousing the others to their feet.

Ambrose walked toward them, sand-grass stinging his ankles with the whipping of the wind.

When he neared, he saw that he did not know them, and that all three were older than him, the youngest by several years. They were salt-crusted and sunburned, with tufted ash-brown hair. They turned toward him, like a pack of dogs.

"Hello there," Ambrose said with a wave.

The middle one broke into a broad grin. "Hello there, *Skalens' son*."

The eldest approached. "My name's Rob," he said, "and these are my brothers, Gwyn and Allen."

Allen, the youngest, gave him a smile.

"Pleased to meet you," Ambrose said, sucking in a shallow breath, "and thanks for agreeing to take me out. I've always been fascinated by blinding stone."

Rob pulled a small pickaxe from his belt and handed it to Ambrose. "I'll show you the basics first, and then we can head out."

As Gwyn and Allen readied the raft, Rob sat with him at a low bench shielded from the emerging sun by a series of roped planks. He showed Ambrose how to cut a shard of blinding stone without shattering it, along with the proper methods of chipping and prising. Ambrose watched him intently, practising the movements and taking his corrections.

They worked at it for close to an hour, but every now and then Ambrose looked up to find Gwyn smirking at him and would fumble the strike. When Ambrose cut his finger Rob finally told his brother to piss off and things went better from there.

"Well, you're no expert, but that should be enough for today," Rob said, finally.

Before they went out, Allen brought a pitcher of cold spiced tea which they shared between them.

Rob gave Ambrose a tool belt to wear and handed him the pickaxe. "Now, you can dive with us if you're confident you can handle yourself."

"Thanks, Rob," he said, and followed him to the water.

When they boarded the raft, the brothers fell into their natural rhythm. Allen manoeuvred the craft with the wading pole, Gwyn paddled, and Rob selected the best diving sites, calling out commands.

This was the first time Ambrose had traversed The Bay of Knives by sea, though he had gazed upon this stretch of coastline often from the sea caves. He had learned to swim in the sandy part of the Bay, where the waters were clear, but was not permitted to go beyond the shadow of the Skalens' House. Avishae's eastern shore was littered with shards of black rock, such that no boat had ever passed the southernmost tip of Velspar. The peaks that jutted from the shallows were mostly slate, but beneath the churning waves, deposits of blinding stone could be found in blistered patterns upon the rock's surface.

Ambrose hung back, keeping out of their way so they might forget he was there. He studied their every move, hiding his curiosity behind a blank expression that twisted only in response to the glare of the sun. Ambrose gripped his pickaxe and adjusted the toolbelt at his waist. As the raft slowed and the brothers moved toward the edge, he readied himself to jump, but then thought the better of it. The water was extremely choppy and a hard slap against any of these rocks would knock him unconscious. He'd watch them do it first.

"Afraid of getting wet?" Gwyn said.

Rob smiled. "If you think this is bad," he said, keeping his balance effortlessly as the raft rollicked in the spray, "try doing it when a storm comes in."

Gwyn peeled off his tunic and stood beside his brother.

"Come and look," Gwyn said, with devilish innocence, and Ambrose worried he'd be pushed in.

When Ambrose remained where he was, Gwyn turned with a shrug. "Suit yourself," he said, before diving off the side and disappearing beneath the surface.

A moment later, Ambrose did come and look, watching Gwyn

vanish beneath the fizzing bubbles. Before his excitement turned to fear, Ambrose dove off the other side of the raft, and swam as deep as his breath would take him. Down there, the movement of the waves was not so violent, and though it stung his eyes, he could see where the rocks were.

Tight chested, he pushed toward the closest rock, groping the stone as he reached for his pickaxe. With a rush of dread, he realised that it was gone. He felt about the sand, and clouds of it rose to obscure his vision. Blood beat hard in his ears and he cursed himself, knowing he was out of time. Ambrose shot himself up toward the shadow of the raft. When his head cleared the surf, he gasped for air, taking in a great mouthful of seawater. A wave pushed him back down. Desperately he clawed toward the surface, and he was almost there when he felt a searing grip on his arm.

Rob yanked him up and Allen reached for his other hand, the two of them dragging him out of the water. His chest scraped against the edge of the raft, but once his legs gained purchase, he pulled himself the rest of the way. Ambrose shook, on all fours, as Allen pounded his back to bring the water up. It came up all at once, a gush of fluid that burned his nostrils with salt.

"Are you soft in the head Skalens' son?" Rob shouted, breathlessly. "I can't have you dying out here."

Too humiliated to speak, Ambrose lay there panting.

He could feel the three of them watching him. He stared at the sun-bleached timber and the dark water stains spreading from his hands. What would they do when they realised he'd lost the axe? Damn it! Ambrose decided it best if he played dumb.

Slowly he came to sit and turned to face the others. He expected to meet their disapproving eyes, but all three had their backs to him. Rob was talking to Allen, who appeared to be steering the raft back to shore. Gwyn sat at the centre of the raft emptying the stones from his belt-pouch into a bucket.

As the waves pushed the raft high between the crest of two rocks, Ambrose braced himself to keep from sliding off the edge. Following Gwyn's lead, he shifted to a central position, but farther down, and sat there hugging his knees, looking out beyond the blades toward the open sea.

The journey went on in silence, and after a while, Ambrose let his thoughts wander. There were two other families that collected blinding stone on Avishae's eastern shore. It would be a longer ride, but he could train with them. Why not? His parents might even let him stay overnight in Haydentown.

When they reached the pier, Rob extended an arm so Ambrose could climb ashore, but would not meet his eyes. Mr Sherburn approached, casting a questioning glance to his eldest.

"The boy fell in," Rob said by way of explanation.

The old man appraised Ambrose's dishevelled clothing and dripping curls with amusement. "Well, we can't lose a day's gathering. You three go back out. I'll mind him."

Ambrose eyed the brothers guiltily but none of them gave him a backward glance.

34

AMBROSE

Thirteen Years After The Fire

Mr Sherburn's workroom was dark, and it took Ambrose a moment to adjust to the dim light.

"Sit here." Mr Sherburn pointed to a broad workbench littered with assorted boxes of stones.

Ambrose smiled uncomfortably.

"Come now, let us concentrate on your lesson." Mr Sherburn presented three boxes of charcoal-coloured stones. "I want you to look at these and tell me which ones are fit for a Meridian."

Ambrose assessed them, but they all looked the same. "May I take them to the window?"

"By all means."

Ambrose took the three boxes and placed them under the windowsill where the afternoon sun cast unhelpful shadows. They contained shards and chipped discs of stone, all of similar size and colour. He picked up the cool fragments and examined them closely. He looked for patterns, textural changes, holding each stone up to the light.

Time elapsed, and Ambrose felt his cheeks burning with frustration. At last, he closed his eyes and touched the blinding stones of his own Meridian, as if they might tell him something he had missed. *They're smoother* – was all he could think, and he sighed.

Coming to sit beside him, Mr Sherburn picked up a stone in his fingers, turning it over, stroking it with his thumb. "I can see what this work means to you, boy. I don't imagine they let you out much."

Ambrose was surprised at the old man's apparent insight, considering the morning he'd had.

Mr Sherburn's hands moved ceaselessly on the stone, as if it were a small creature in need of comfort. It was a curious mannerism. "I learned what I know about blinding stone when I was about your age," he said.

Ambrose set his eyes on the scene outside, as if to follow the old man in his thoughts. Out there, wisps of sun-bleached grass flicked about in the wind, and he caught the movement of a sand mouse among the knotted roots.

At length, he continued. "You may wonder why we still dive for the stone, and why there are so few of us that perform this work when blinding stone is in high demand."

Ambrose had not given it much thought.

"It responds to us, you see, and we respond to it. It is a living stone. If you had not fallen off the raft out there you may have been able to stay long enough to see my boys at work. We have permission from the Skalens to remove our Meridians so that we can feel the stone." He tapped his forehead. "Inside our minds."

Mr Sherburn took off his Meridian and lifted the stone to his forehead, touching it upon his crown and nape, pausing at each point. Ambrose watched his every movement with intense interest.

"This one has been handled well and will be taken to the carver later this day." Picking up another stone, he repeated the process. "This one is older, and will need to be returned to the sea."

"Can I try?" Ambrose asked.

Mr Sherburn nodded and passed him three stones. Ambrose removed his Meridian hesitantly, clearing his mind before steadying his focus on the stone. Breathing slowly, as his grandfather had taught him, Ambrose closed his eyes and drew it to his forehead. It felt similar to the one he usually wore, but in and amongst the cool silence of the stone, he heard – or felt – a slight crackling. He picked up another, and immediately noticed the crackling sensation. The third one, however, was silent, and gave away nothing unusual.

He held it up. "This one is ready."

Mr Sherburn smiled. "The others have been away from their birthplace too long and out of human hands. This is the law of blinding stone. If it is handled often, it becomes attuned to us, but if it is left, it will become as any other stone – deadened to human concerns."

Ambrose nodded.

"If we are to make Meridians that will act as an impermeable psychic shield – as the Skalens wish – they must be chipped with hand tools and taken to the carvers within the week. The carvers need to work them as soon as possible, and if they cannot, they must handle the stone regularly, otherwise the process must begin again."

Ambrose found a disc-shaped stone. "Is that what happened to this one?"

He took the stone from Ambrose and ran his finger over its surface, then passed it back again. "Why don't you tell me?"

Ambrose lifted the stone to his forehead and closed his eyes. The stone imparted its coolness, shrouding Ambrose in a familiar feeling of detachment. Placing the stone on the crown of his head he felt nothing unusual, but after he had held it to the back of his skull for a minute or so, he began to feel a slight dizziness, a distracting feeling.

Ambrose placed the stone on the bench with a sharp click and stared at Mr Sherburn. "What is wrong with it?"

Mr Sherburn's mouth rose in a half-smile. "Can you find that feeling again? Without the stone?"

Ambrose looked at him suspiciously, and then closed his eyes. The sensation was elusive, but eventually he found it. It was masked by its constancy, its steady hum. It seemed to disperse his strength, to quietly erode the very act of concentration. Ambrose drew his attention to a single point, and the feeling broke.

When Ambrose opened his eyes, Mr Sherburn was nodding.

"Very good," he said. "It seems I'd underestimated you, Ambrose. You have a talent for this."

"But I don't understand–"

"It is not the stone you felt. It was that the stone contained a flaw. Do you see this crack here?" He held the stone for Ambrose to see. "It weakens the stone's power. The will you felt was mine."

Ambrose felt a shiver of unease.

"It is an ancient technique," he said.

It is an Intercessor's technique, Ambrose thought. The danger of it excited him. This was why he had come. "Can you teach me how to do it?"

Mr Sherburn laughed and began to pack the stones away. "You young folk do not know how to be, and it is because you grew up wearing the Meridian. It was never intended to be worn as it is now. The Intercessors made it so they could relinquish their inner barriers and be kept safe by the stone. If you are to master blinding stone, you cannot allow your mind to go slack, to have it held in place by some external device. You must train yourself to open and close your mind according to your will." Mr Sherburn's steely eyes beheld him with expectation.

Ambrose nodded. "I understand," he said. Ambrose wanted to say more. He wanted to thank this man – this stranger – for pulling back the veil and showing him something real. His grandfather acted as if he were the last living Intercessor, but he always kept Ambrose at arm's length. But Ambrose had seen past his grandfather's psychic fortifications, and it was not some great secret kept hidden, but the man's inadequacy. He knew his grandfather feared him, because Ambrose was a born Intercessor, and one day he would usurp him. That is what Ambrose saw, that first time in the tent, when his grandfather opened the way.

Mr Sherburn was still staring at him, scrutinising his face. "I know what you want, Skalens' son," he said, "and if you can keep the secret I have shared with you this day, then there will be more to come."

"You have my word."

From the corner of his eye, Ambrose noticed the horsed silhouette of Guardsman John and his heart sank. He wanted to stay, to learn more, to master the techniques of the holy Intercessors.

Mr Sherburn followed his gaze. "Your escort awaits."

Reluctantly, Ambrose followed Mr Sherburn out the door, the salt-wind cool upon his face.

Guardsman John dismounted and ushered Ambrose to make haste.

As they rode toward the Skalens' House, he took one last look at the Bay, where the brothers hovered on the waves, watching sunset fall.

35

AMBROSE

Thirteen Years After The Fire

Mr Sherburn must have spoken to his sons because the next time Ambrose visited, they referred to him by name. They forgave him the lost axe when he gifted them a selection of tools fresh from the smithy, but he promised also to return the original. The brothers told him not to bother himself, but each time he dove, he searched for it on the seabed. The taunts continued, though it seemed they now made fun of his daring rather than the taint of his lineage. While it felt natural to remove his Meridian at the Raeburn camp, he relished it even more when he could swim among the stones with only a single span of breath to carry him.

With the Sherburns, he was allowed his opinions and off-hand comments, something he seldom experienced with his sister, the Raeburns, or his friends in the Guard. Down at the Bay he could be a right ass and the brothers would relay nothing to his parents. Ambrose suspected they hated his parents, and he soon learned not to mention them at all when Mr Sherburn was around. If they had pressed him, he would have said he understood little about his parents, and even less about their reasons for joining Skalen Sybilla's crusade against the Intercessors. There were black holes in the

Skalens' House, rotten parts where he and Zohar had learned not to tread.

Ambrose only ever saw his father late in the evening when he plodded, waxen-faced, from the Tower. Did he sit there all day staring at the names of those he had killed? Ambrose could not imagine what else would make his father's face look like that. The man was like a ghost. Ambrose got more out of his mother, but she only ever spoke of inconsequential things. Weather and horses and how the meat tasted today. Ambrose hated the constant sneaking and second-guessing he and his sister had to endure at home. His grandfather had made it quite clear. No one in the Skalens' House could be trusted. So, he stopped making small talk with the guards, and tested his words before he spoke them. Sometimes he did the same with Zohar.

Upon the waves, surrounded by blinding stone, it was easy to keep their secrets. But one day, when the three of them were aboard the raft, Allen broke this unspoken pact.

"Ambrose, we've heard that Skalen Sybilla will be visiting Avishae."

Ambrose rolled chips of blinding stone in his hand like dice, trying to decide what he should say. Of course, it was pointless to deny it when she would be walking the countryside and making her tour of the town. "Skalen Sybilla will be lodging with us, yes."

"What does she want here?" Gwyn asked, sharply.

"I – ah, I believe it is a trade matter."

Ambrose could tell the brothers had been discussing this before he arrived, and it felt as though the walls of kinship were rising against him, turning him into a stranger.

Gwyn opened his mouth, then seemed to taste the salt of his bitten tongue as he pushed the words back down.

Ambrose knew if he didn't let them in on something, the thin cord of friendship between them would snap. "Mother said Sybilla is interested in the transport of blinding stone to Vaelnyr."

Rob snorted. "It would be next to useless by the time it got there. What about the caves at Jokvour? I thought the Ladains and Greslets were thick as thieves."

Allen steadied the raft with the wading pole. "She could be lying."

"My mother, or our guest?" Ambrose asked, more aggressively than he intended.

Rob's mouth twisted into a sneer. "In all, we do not know what to think of your mother, but we are sworn to the Skalens Elshender, so that is that. We are sworn to all Skalens. But Sybilla is a rare breed. The turning of her temper is like a strong tide, and we can keep ourselves afloat if we know when it will rise, and when it will fall."

Ambrose nodded.

It all sounded reasonable enough, but in it Ambrose detected some dark purpose. He had felt his grandfather's hatred for Sybilla, the one he called the 'Red Skalen'. Had felt Grandfather pulse in vision, possessed by savage desire. He wanted to kill her. No, not just to kill her, but to beat her until her bones were but shards in the bloodied pulp of her flesh. His grandfather showed Ambrose this so he could learn Intercession. Ambrose was to reach into the sensation, as if plunging his hand into a fire. He was to take the heat into his own being. Be a vessel that drew off poison but swallowed none. Now he knew that feeling as if it were his own.

Gwyn shuffled a little closer to him. "Ambrose," he said, with uncharacteristic warmth, "will you tell us everything you know about Sybilla?"

Blood beat in Ambrose's cheeks. "I can – I will, but I really don't know very much about her."

"But you've met her before?" Gwyn pressed.

"She visited once when I was eight. I don't remember much about it. Zohar and I just wanted to get away to the beach."

"Come on," Gwyn said. "You can give us more than that."

Allen turned to his brother. "How much do you remember of your eighth year, Gwyn? Ambrose will tell us what he knows."

Water lapped at the raft.

The tension grew and Ambrose just started speaking, saying anything that came to mind. "Ah... she travelled with a Vaelnyri guard, Gavin or something like that, and he stayed in her chambers. She kept to herself, didn't talk much to us, but I remember her hair was very thin on one side, like she was going bald. She wore the

Meridian, even back then. My parents didn't, so I suppose she persuaded them to."

Rob seemed pleased by this. Gwyn flashed his elder brother a meaningful look, and Rob cleared his throat, coming to sit directly in front of Ambrose. "You are like a brother to us now. We have your back, and you have ours, right?" Rob said, leaning close.

Ambrose nodded.

"There is something that you can do to help us, but you need to keep it to yourself." Rob stared into his eyes, taking his measure.

"Don't tell your sister, either," Gwyn added.

Ambrose's head swam. All he could think was that he finally had real friends. Friends he could have secrets with, and he wanted that more than anything. He and Zohar shared enough, what would it matter to keep just one from her?

"Okay," he said.

Rob produced a small knife from his belt. A ceremonial knife, not a tool made for fashioning blinding stone. In a deliberate motion, Rob cut his own thumb so that a jewel of blood rose and trembled there. He grasped Ambrose's hand firmly and by his manner, Ambrose knew that he was about to do the same to him. He let Rob cut him but could not imagine what it was all for. Allen fastened the wading pole and Gwyn shuffled in beside Ambrose. The two younger brothers presented their thumbs, and Rob slit them each with gentle precision.

The four of them pressed their cuts together and Ambrose felt the sting of their blood. The brothers began to hum softly and closed their eyes. Ambrose copied them, the cut on his thumb pulsing, a soft, breathy sensation moving up his arm. He tried to ignore it, concentrating on their voices instead. The melody was old, yet he knew it somehow. It tugged at something buried deep in his memory, a serpentine hymn, of dark shapes and liquid Alma. Hungrily, he pursued the sound, reclaiming it, and joining them, his voice vibrating strangely in his ears. His heart pounded, and he felt the warmth of the brothers next to him, their bodies extending from his own, their personalities diffusing into his hair, moving closer, flowing into him. His jaw relaxed, and he began to unfurl, to let himself be seen.

Their voices fell still, and in the silence they flowed unhindered. The sensations came in hot waves. Gushing out of him. Fear and joy and humiliation. His private thoughts unaccounted for, unprotected, and entrusted, it seemed, to the brothers. Should he trust them? He felt a shadow of predation, a warning moving near. His eyes flickered open. The brothers sat motionless, their faces passive and unseeing.

Ambrose closed his eyes once more, wanting to keep this moment of closeness, where no look, no scoff of laughter, no small act of betrayal could undo it. He wanted to go back there and for it never to end. He breathed deeply, allowing his thoughts to dissolve, his fears a shoal of fish dispersed by the current, until all was clear before him.

The rocking of the raft had never sounded so peaceful. He explored the water sounds. Slap, patter, whoosh, slap – amidst the burr of the constant wind. Below the surface of the water were other sound-feelings. He sensed them, black whisper and moss green, glittering salt-diamonds, soot silting down to the sea bed – and then, with a snap, the *eye* found him.

It was red. It expanded, seeing him. *Siatka*. The god-name unpeeled itself from the rock as from the inside of his skull.

Gasping for breath, he willed his own eyes to open.

The brightness hurt him and he trembled uncontrollably, recoiling toward the edge of the raft, where he nearly upended it.

"Ambrose! Ambrose – look at me!" Rob shouted.

Allen and Gwyn were closer and reached to steady him. Ambrose fell to his knees, his ribcage heaving through the shirt of his back.

"Ambrose, there is nothing to fear, we are with you," Allen said, placing a hand on him.

"Take... me... back... to shore," Ambrose managed. "Please."

"Of course," Rob said softly.

Allen turned the craft, and they began their passage back through the blades.

The journey proceeded in fits and starts as Allen guided the raft backward, forward, sideways and on again to harness the tide.

When enough time had passed for Ambrose to catch his breath,

Rob came to sit beside him. "I should have told you what it might be like before we started. The sensations can be strong, or confusing. For that I am sorry."

Ambrose took a deep breath and looked at him. He did not have the words to explain what he had seen – was it real? Instinctively, he drew his legs closer to his body, desperate to feel the certainty of dry land.

Rob continued, "I wanted to show you what it can be like to step into the Stream, with others at your side." His words were stilted as if he wasn't sure what he could say in front of a Skalens' son. "There are connections between us... they are still there, even though so much has changed."

He did not like the way Rob was tiptoeing around him, and this time the words would not stay down. "You are talking about Intercession," he said and looked him plain in the eye.

Shock registered on Rob's face, but he quickly recovered.

Ambrose looked around at the three of them. "You do not need to worry. I will say it. I wish the Intercessors had not been executed. I wish I could have learned from them. I would have everything the way it was before the Purge."

Rob looked down. "You mean that?"

"If you deign to call me Brother," Ambrose said, "I will be as blood of your blood and I will renounce the laws of the Skalens."

The words hung in the air, charged with too much feeling.

His mouth felt dry. "If you will have me, that is." Ambrose tried to laugh but could not make light of this.

Rob squeezed Ambrose's shoulder, and Allen gave him a nodding smile.

"Right then – Brother," Gwyn said, in good humour, "before we get to shore, we have some things to discuss."

36

AMBROSE

Thirteen Years After The Fire

GWYN AND AMBROSE SAT ON THE GRASS drinking Alma wine. Ambrose suspected Gwyn had stolen it from his father, but didn't much care. It filled his chest with warmth, and it made his muscles feel like honey. Down by the shore, Rob and Allen were hard at work sorting the day's specimens.

The Guard seldom bothered to patrol this particular stretch of the Bay, so they drank long without their Meridians.

Gwyn upturned the wineskin and squirted a stream of red liquid into his mouth. "You forget that I can read your thoughts, Brother," Gwyn said, with a sly grin.

Ambrose frowned. "What do you know?"

"I know that even though you've stopped asking about blood magic, you're still burning to know how it works."

Ambrose shrugged.

The two of them stared at the waves a while longer, and Ambrose felt his limbs grow leaden in the sun. Gwyn lay down on the brittle grass and slung his arm over his eyes to block out the glare. Ambrose was about to close his own when a sharp gleam caught his attention.

Rolling on his side, he saw Gwyn idly twirling his pocketknife. Then Gwyn pressed the blade into his palm, drawing blood.

"What are you doing?" Ambrose said.

"Tear off a piece of your shirt, I'm going to let you in on a little secret."

Ambrose tore off a piece and handed it over.

Gwyn took it, and soaked it red. "Catch a few drops, and that is your hook," he said, passing it back.

"But what do I *do* with it?" Ambrose asked, becoming tired of the game.

"Go home, find 'the quiet place within' or whatever you Raeburns call it. Put it to your tongue, then hold it to the three points – one after the other – until you feel something."

Gwyn was almost never serious, but Ambrose saw that he was not joking now.

"That's it?" Ambrose said.

"That's it." Gwyn nodded. He stood and sucked in a breath of air. "Want any more of this before I finish it?"

Ambrose shook his head, pocketing the blood-soaked cloth.

"Okay, Little Brother – keep this one between us." Gwyn winked and ambled off in the direction of the beach shack.

Ambrose sat for a moment, his heart racing with anticipation, then started off for home.

The next day when Ambrose arrived at the Bay, Rob was waiting for him. Gwyn busied his hands with his head down, and Allen remained at a distance. It was obvious what had happened, so there was no lying about it.

"Come and help me with the raft, there is some damage on the left side that needs repairing before we can head out," Rob said.

Ambrose followed him out of earshot of the other two.

"Do you know how to tie a bowline knot?" Rob said, throwing him a length of rope.

Ambrose nodded. Rob was on the other side of the raft, removing the splintered timber and throwing it aside.

"So, tell me about last night."

"Last night?"

Rob shot him an impatient look. "You know what I am talking about. Don't tell me that you didn't try it."

Of course he had tried it, but he couldn't really say what happened. "I don't think it worked."

Rob threw the last of the damaged wood onto the grass. "Really?" He walked over to where Ambrose sat. "Nothing happened at all?"

Ambrose felt a surge of irritation. "What did you expect?"

"Tell me exactly what you did." Rob said, sitting beside him.

Ambrose smoothed the frayed rope-end, deciding that he may as well tell him. "I started sitting on the floor, breathing as Grandfather taught me, letting my thoughts disappear, and then I followed the silver thread. Gwyn told me to taste the blood first, so I did that, then I held it to the three points. I did it for a while until my arms got tired, but nothing happened, so I went to bed."

"When you went to bed, did you wear your Meridian?"

"Yes," Ambrose said, feeling like an idiot.

Rob smiled. "Did you have any dreams?"

Ambrose was about to tell him no, it was a stupid question to ask, but then a memory began to dance at the edge of his mind. A girl... she was milking a cow... Clara? "I think I might have," Ambrose said slowly, trying to catch the image. "How is that possible?"

"What did you see?" A slow smile creased the corners of Rob's eyes.

"A girl. I think her name was Clara. She was milking a cow, and her legs were... showing," Ambrose said, his cheeks growing hot.

Rob let out a roar of laughter. "Gwyn, you dog."

Ambrose began to smile, not sure he understood the joke. "Of all the things he might share, he chose sweet Clara's thighs." Wiping away tears of laughter, Rob continued. "Ambrose, I know it is hard for you to understand how these things work. You were only a boy when we lost the Intercessors. I can't explain, but it was as if the whole world went quiet and when we reached out to one another, there was this thick fog separating us."

Ambrose kept his eyes down.

"When I was your age, I had the misfortune of catching sight of my brothers' dreams, and they mine. If we tried hard enough, we could learn each other's feelings, and thoughts. If Gwyn were to think about Clara too long, *she* might feel it. But most of the time, we didn't do things like that. It is not something that can be done without notice."

Ambrose remained silent, for it was obvious he did not have a similar story to share.

Rob was careful with his next words. "I know you remember something of what it was like before we wore Meridians, but its been six years now. We all start to forget. Even when we remove them, there are so few of us with our toes in the Stream. When the Intercessors were here, it was a different world. They opened the doors for us; our spirits flowed where they wished. People could not hide their red thoughts as they do now."

Ambrose sighed, aching to know what it felt like. It wasn't fair. His parents had taken everything. All because they feared Sybilla. "But how did I see Gwyn's dream? How does it actually work?"

Rob stared at him. "Blood crosses every threshold."

"And that is why you need Sybilla's blood."

Rob nodded slowly.

"What will you do with it, once I have the blood-tie?"

Rob gave Ambrose a crooked smile. "Well, I can say one thing for certain. I do not care to learn the content of Skalen Sybilla's dreams."

"You can do something more?" Ambrose asked, thoughts darting.

"We need to gather our allies. We need to stay focused and prepare for our moment. There are no heroes in Velspar, Ambrose. It will take all of us to turn the tide."

Ambrose grit his teeth. After everything they had shared, the Sherburns still treated him like some bloody farm boy, sending him on errands, never showing him the whole picture.

"You are impatient to act, I can see that, but you have already made inroads with Illiam, and now we are allied with the Brivian

Regents. He will be visiting Avishae again soon, and we are relying on you to obtain his report. You are important to our plan. Your lineage guarantees that."

"My lineage?" Ambrose stared at him. "I want to know what we are going to do about Sybilla!"

Rob held his thoughts close and would not relinquish them.

"Why won't you tell me?"

Rob tilted his head, his gaze one of challenge. "When the time is right, we will seep into her like smoke and force her spirit out," Rob said, making a flinging motion with his hands. "The rest is not for you to know right now."

Ambrose grew hot with anger. "Why blood magic? Why can't we just kill her?"

Rob shook his head. "It is not her body we are trying to kill. If you kill the body, the spirit can survive."

"Can't we use fire?"

"There will be no more burnings in Velspar," Rob said, his voice flat as if he were reciting some long-held refrain.

"Why?"

Rob's look was so dark, so blatantly accusatory that Ambrose fell silent.

Ambrose's fingers grew taut with frustration. Who was Rob Sherburn to keep this from him? He wanted to say as much, but Rob got to his feet, whistling for Gwyn and Allen.

Ambrose caught up, walking beside him in silence.

Things remained tense as they loaded onto the raft, but then Rob mentioned Clara, and the brothers howled with laughter. Ambrose was glad of their talk, as they goaded each other with stories of this girl and that. But his own thoughts were elsewhere.

Sybilla was coming to Avishae.

37

AMBROSE

Thirteen Years After The Fire

AMBROSE STOOD BEFORE THE LOOKING GLASS dressed in his ceremonial vestments. He squinted, trying to imagine the ash-blue coat he wore as an Intercessor's robe. He could not quite see it. It was his hair, he thought, it made him appear young. He smoothed his curls and repositioned his Meridian.

Sybilla had arrived in Haydentown and was on her way to the Skalens' House.

There was a loud knock at the door. "Ambrose, let me in. It's me!" The handle rattled frantically.

Ambrose's sighed and unlocked the door.

Zohar burst into the room. "Why is your door locked? She will be here any minute! I feel sick."

A moment later she started, looking him up and down. "You look like Father."

"Really?" Ambrose considered his reflection.

Zohar stood beside him, admiring her own sky-coloured gown with its bodice of silver coils and turned to inspect the lacing at her back.

"I am quite sure you have your own looking glass." Ambrose said, impatient for her to leave.

"Can't we go down together?"

"Soon, but I am not quite ready, I will come past and collect you when I am done."

Zohar glared at him. "Done with what? Powdering your nose?"

Ambrose nudged her toward the door. "I just want to be alone right now, I will come and get you."

She gave him a look of disbelief, realised he was serious and stalked out the door.

Zohar would forgive him later. Sybilla would arrive any moment now, and Ambrose needed to prepare himself. He turned the key in the lock and laid out his tools on a piece of canvas. He'd already sharpened his pickaxe and blades, and now it was just a matter of rubbing off the oil without staining his robes.

Through the window, he heard the distant sound of horses.

It was time.

Ambrose sheathed the knife he had been cleaning and hid his tool belt in the drawer.

At Zohar's door, he knocked softly. After a moment, her face appeared through the crack. She gave him a heavy look. He held out his arm, and she took it. They were friends again and he was glad.

When they reached the entry hall, their parents were waiting, rigid as game pieces sat upon a board. Glances of greeting passed across the room, but all were focused on the main entrance where their guest would soon stand.

They heard the crunch of gravel, the creaking of an ancient hinge, and there she was, a retinue of Avishaen Guard surrounding her at a respectful distance. She was a woman adorned in blood velvet, with the white sun behind her, and a shadow for a face.

Once she had passed through the doorway, the light from the upper windows illuminated her.

"Skalen Sybilla Ladain of Vaelnyr, we welcome you," his father said.

Sybilla gave a small bow. "Skalens Rebekah and Ulric Elshender of Avishae, I am most grateful for your hospitality."

His mother walked to Zohar's side. "Sybilla, I would like to reacquaint you with our children. Zohar," she said, gesturing to his sister, "and Ambrose."

The woman looked at him fleetingly, with nothing more than politeness, and Ambrose felt himself bow.

The meeting – that he had gone over many times in his mind – felt quite unreal. She stood there before him, talking about all manner of mundane subjects, from crop yields to the distinction between the spiced wines of the various regions she had passed through on her journey. No matter how her lips changed shape, her eyes remained heavy and unmoved, like birds weathering a storm. She was not as ugly as he wanted her to be, nor was her manner as coarse. His memories of her as some hideous balding creature with hunched shoulders seemed ridiculous now. Her dark hair was thick and elegantly braided. Ambrose tried not to notice the way her bodice of deep crimson accentuated her breasts, her fine blouse threaded with gold.

There was a book in his parents' library Zohar studied with great interest, and had stolen away to the sea caves. Little had he cared for its illustrations of dresses and laced boots, cuffs and collars. *In the Northlands, they wear their skirts long so that they drag upon the floor*, she would say excitedly, and show him the pictures. Ambrose was forced to endure this subject over a number of weeks. As this memory passed through his mind, he could not help but notice Sybilla was dressed more like a guardswoman, with her riding leathers and long boots visible beneath the decorative trim of her blouse.

The conversation had turned to Meridians, and any moment now they would mention blinding stone. Out of the corner of his eye, Ambrose felt Sybilla's guard watching him, and knew that if he met the man's cool stare, he would lose his nerve. A floating feeling began in his legs, as he waited for the right moment to speak.

His mother was talking, "...we have three families who work the blinding stone, much of it is beneath the water, as you know. Ambrose has been accompanying the Sherburns on their sea voyages." She glanced at him, her face softening in a smile.

"I could take you out there, Skalen," Ambrose said in a rush. "If you are interested to learn the techniques of sea mining," he added, suddenly feeling ill equipped to offer such services.

"That is very kind of you, Ambrose," Sybilla said, her mouth curling in surprise. Sybilla had answered before his parents could protest, but he could see they very much wished to.

His mother looked at her hands. "Ah, this will change the order of things somewhat, it might be best if we visit the Bay following our existing engagements."

"We will need the light–" Ambrose interjected.

"– at the hour of three," his mother continued, cutting him off.

His parents then ushered Sybilla and her guard toward the eastern door where Ambrose and Zohar were not to follow.

As the door closed behind them, their voices grew muffled, and faded down the hall. Ambrose sighed, relaxing somewhat as the Attendants left the room, but Zohar was still there, arching her elder-sister eyebrows at him. He smiled, trying to ignore her expression, and made to leave.

"Brother!" she called. "Let us walk."

His look said, *do I have to?* And hers said, *yes.*

Taking his arm in hers, Zohar led him out into the sunshine. When they had walked far enough from the guards to speak, she harried him with sharp whispers.

"What were you thinking? Why would you volunteer to take her out with you? Why haven't you taken me out on the Bay? What do you do out there anyway? Why can't I learn sea mining? I am the eldest!"

Ambrose remained silent as her questions came at him, but then she questioned him with her eyes, and that was the most dangerous question of all.

He held her gaze and said the only thing he could say without lying. "The Sherburns asked me to bring her. She would have gone there anyway."

"Is that it?" Zohar appeared deflated.

"Afraid so."

They walked side by side for a long while, the wind hissing

through the grass. Each getting lost in thought and finding nothing to say to one another.

When they were young, silence didn't feel like this. His mind traced the course of things backward, erasing the Sherburns, hunting trips with Rowan, time spent with his grandfather in his tent. And that was where he stopped. His memory poised at the moment he and Zohar mounted their horse to meet their long-lost kinsmen in the wilds of Baden Forest. She had known it in the sea caves, but his desire for initiation was not the first secret he had kept from her. There were others, and one in particular that stuck in his mind.

It was seven years ago, the day that Ambrose snuck out of the Skalens' House, leaving Zohar sick in bed. He was bored. She was sleeping. It was a misty day, so the guards didn't see him go. His shirt clung to his body, damp with fog, but it was not until he was halfway to the village that he felt the first droplets of soaking rain. Ambrose took shelter in a barn until the shower thinned, but as he went to leave, an old woman appeared in the doorway. She brought him in, putting a thick blanket around his shoulders. She offered him tea, but the tea made him sleepy, and time disappeared for a while.

As he walked now with his sister, he could taste the soot rags that they stuffed in his mouth. Could feel the rasping sting of the ropes that bound him to the chair. His grandfather had helped him to leech the power out of the memory, but it would always be there. The old woman with her face red, her eyes intent, and beside her, two men and a lad with black hair. They knew who he was. *Skalens' son.* Those were the days before Meridians, and Ambrose knew they wanted to hurt him. Their guilt clung to them like a foul slime, and their hearts hammered in rage, in their wish to be clean. One of them wanted to light a fire, to show him what it felt like. Another wanted to butcher him slowly, starting with his arms. Ambrose felt the piss running down his leg, his chest tight with terror, and in his mind, he screamed for his sister. He remembered frantically conjuring whatever patchwork fantasies they had woven of the Holy Ones, Siatka and Kshidol. Would they meet him at the jaws of death? Which of the two should he call? The Mother or the Father? It had always been the Intercessors who chose a spirit's path of rebirth.

Then there was a knock at the door and they froze. It was a man, their neighbour, Patrick Milwain. They tried to put him off but he would not leave, and in his mind, Ambrose pushed himself into a single thought, directed at the man beyond the door – *hear my call*. He heard Patrick's wood-muffled voice. There was a wagon that needed lifting and would they get their lazy arses out there to help him pull? But within, Patrick's voice said – *I will not let them*. One of the men opened the door, and Patrick was there, a farmer, tall and fair haired with a large stick in his hand.

Ambrose awoke, slumped beside a moss-lipped well, just by the road that led to the Skalens' House. Ambrose's throat was raw as if he had breathed strong smoke, and his tongue tasted bitter, but there was no injury upon him. Then Ambrose snuck back into the House, finding the bed where his sister still slept, and crawled in beside her. For a long time, Ambrose stared at her. Her cheeks were red and she frowned as she whimpered. He clasped her hands as tears slunk round his temple and into his ear. He should never have left her. He should never have left.

He had laughed when she had recounted her fever-dream, and he reshaped his own recollection so the two stories matched. If Zohar searched for him, she'd find nothing that was his, for it had not happened. It was a dream born of her worries, made sharp by the fever's heat. Ambrose looked over to his sister, trudging through long grass, staring determinedly at the distant mountains. She was jealous. He knew she burned with questions for Sybilla. She wished to ask her of dresses, and customs, and fruits that grew only on the mainland. He fought the scowl forming on his face. His grandfather had shown Ambrose what Sybilla was—the pin upon which the whole of Velspar turned and she needed to be plucked out.

Zohar lifted her head, and they shared a passing smile. It was easy now – as they both wore their Meridians – to walk together and to be utterly separate at the same time. He could look her in the eye, recall the gag in his mouth and she would perceive nothing of it. He could spite her frivolous obsessions – still love her – and not make her cry. He could eat his supper, retracing his grandfather's words, the Sherburns' plans. He could think openly about whatever he pleased and it did not matter if the guards were about. The thought exhilarated him. And so he turned his thoughts to Sybilla, to the blade at his belt, and the brothers, who were waiting for him.

38

AMBROSE

Thirteen Years After The Fire

AMBROSE STOOD WITH HIS BACK to the shore, peering into the distance. Sybilla's hooded carriage advanced toward them in a cloud of dust. With a hand shading his eyes, Mr Sherburn came to stand beside him. The carriage jutted along the road, growing louder, until the glistening ebony horses that drew it came to a stop. The Vaelnyri guard emerged first, catching Ambrose with unsmiling eyes. Then Sybilla stepped out. She wore a light crimson tunic, black stockings and soft leather boots. She meant to swim, it seemed.

When Sybilla came close, Mr Sherburn inclined his head. "Skalen Sybilla, we are honoured to have your company this day."

"It is a pleasure, Mr Sherburn," she said.

"As I am sure you are aware, blinding stone must be mined without our Meridians..." Mr Sherburn trailed off.

"I am familiar with the practice. I will accompany Ambrose on a tour of the Bay and will remove my Meridian at sea, if it pleases me."

Her guard stood stiffly beside her.

"Very well," Mr Sherburn said. "I will leave you in Ambrose's capable hands."

"This way, Skalen." Ambrose presented his hand, and her touch was like cold fire.

On the water, the raft wavered between two black wedges of rock. Rob grasped Ambrose by his forearm to help him down, then moved aside with head bowed. Allen held the raft steady as Ambrose aided Sybilla's descent. Once on board, she made her way to the raft's still centre. Allen passed the wading pole to Ambrose before alighting onto the rock. Gwyn unwound the rope that yoked them to shore and tossed it to Ambrose. Glancing back, he saw the Sherburns, their rough clothes shuddering in the breeze, and that guard, menacing as a bow drawn taut, watching him.

Ambrose moved to the front of the raft, using the pole to nudge them into the nearest sea corridor. He was not accustomed to doing this alone, and it took all of his attention to negotiate the space between the rocks. Behind him, Sybilla remained a silent shape that he caught in glimpses at the edge of his vision. Once they were deep enough, the water flattened, and Ambrose turned. Her heavy eyes met his, and Ambrose felt his heart leap.

She smiled at him as if he might be scared of her. "Have you been sea mining long?"

"Almost a year, Skalen."

"Do you enjoy it?" she asked as if he were a boy trying his hand at fishing.

The conversation should remain in the shallows, Ambrose reminded himself. "Blinding stone is important to Velspar," he said, ending things there.

The wind pressed her tunic tight against her shoulders, and when the breeze shifted, he caught the scent of her. Her smell reminded him of pine trees and red roses, horses and ash. He felt the pull of curiosity and stopped.

He needed to focus.

"Would you like to join me beneath the surface?" Ambrose asked.

Sybilla looked amused, and this irritated him, but she was unlacing her boots, so he supposed that meant yes.

Ambrose took the small pickaxe and blade from his tool belt.

"We use these tools to remove chips of blinding stone from the rock, but down there, all the stones look black. We can only identify the blinding stone if we remove our Meridians."

She listened, but neither of them wanted to expose the three points in the other's company. Ambrose continued the lesson, drawing it out longer than was strictly necessary, as another part of his mind sought stillness. Sybilla nodded as he explained what would happen, how deep they would go, and how to safely return to the raft. Ambrose handed Sybilla a long-rope to tie about her waist so that he could draw her back if the tide was strong.

Sitting either side of the raft, Ambrose reached behind him to open a small basket, instructing her to place her Meridian within. He turned his back to her as they both loosened leather straps, reaching arms behind to deposit the clunking stones as the windows of their minds flew open. Ambrose dove in, and moments later, saw her through a frost of bubbles. He had expected to hear her, to feel her all of a sudden, within his mind. But she, too, must have completed her training, for there was only the communion of body-sense, of her arms pushing through the water, the kick of her legs, and the soft-ening of her braids. Her thoughts remained in the place before words, and Ambrose knew that if he ventured to feel them, he would expose his own.

Time was short, and Ambrose quickened behind her, gesturing to a nearby rock. Floating down beside him, she watched as he touched the rock with his fingertips, indicating for her to do the same. Taking the blade, Ambrose prized the stone at its edge. It would be seconds before they ran out of air. Ambrose's lungs held up against the thun-dering alarm of his heart as he stuck the knife deeper – and slipped. The small red cloud rose misty between them, and Sybilla's eyes widened in fear. Ambrose pointed upward in furious motions, his face a mask of concern.

Clutching the stone fragment and knife in his hands, Ambrose kicked upward. He burst from the waves taking vast gulps of air and saw parts of her rising and sinking in the churn. Ambrose dipped beneath the waves and clutched the long-rope, drawing her toward the raft as she swam, coughing. Her arms moved well enough to keep her head afloat, but she was not a strong swimmer. Ambrose pulled himself up, and then drew the wet and shaking woman from the sea. The cut was letting blood that mixed freely with the water, finding its way down her arm. Ambrose rushed to her and tore part of his shirt to bind it, using a second piece to clean the redness from her arm. Sybilla held her hand to her chest protectively and wrapped the bandage herself. Moments later, she had refastened her Meridian in a swift, practiced motion.

Sybilla caught her breath, regaining her composure. "May I see it?"

"Of course, Skalen." Ambrose held the piece of blinding stone out to her, reverently, in both hands. She picked it up, turning it slowly, examining its fine markings.

"Are yours from Jokvour?" Ambrose asked, nervous to smooth things over before they returned to shore.

Sybilla looked at him intently for a moment, and then dropped her gaze back to the stone in her hand. "Yes." When she looked up, her eyes were obscured beneath the heavy shadow of her lashes. "Yours are from the Bay I presume?"

"My first Meridian was made for me, but after I started diving, I wanted to choose my own stones." Ambrose refitted his Meridian and she glanced at his forehead as he spoke. "I made new Meridians for my parents, but they prefer their old ones."

She looked out at the horizon. "I have noticed your parents are quite traditional."

Ambrose did not want to talk about his parents. It made him suddenly nervous, reminding him that they would reprove him for this sleight.

He would handle it.

"Skalen, I want to apologise for injuring you," he said, and when she did not respond, he continued. "It is so easy to slip when working with the blade."

Sybilla regarded him. "Not to worry."

He had the impression that his apology sat upon her skin, and that she would wash it from her the moment that they parted.

It was strange to have her here, to be alone with her, and sitting so close. He looked for the evil in her, for the blood-thirst that had once inflamed her to massacre. It was obscured somewhere beneath, like the smooth skin of her scalp that now shone between ropes of wetted hair. She held tight to the raft, concealing her bandaged finger in the small of her hand.

She disappeared easily into herself, like a snake under a rock, he thought. It did not matter. He had what he needed bundled up in his pocket. Wherever she would go in the Seven Lands, he could now find her in waking and in dreams. Knowing this made her seem smaller somehow – a woman whose shadow reached no further than her mortal height. In time, their allies on the mainland would find her, and strip her of her Meridian.

Then they would act.

39

WALDEMAR

Thirteen Years After The Fire

I RECORD THIS VISION at the request of Intercessor Maeryn, who, in her wisdom, reminds me there should be no omissions. When Velspar speaks, we must listen.

In the vision, I entered a room, dim with the powdered light of dusk. Spirits wandered, travelling, passing on. The red deeds committed in life were visible upon our skin as a stain of blackened ash.

Intercessor Ultreia was about to step through the gateway into the belly of Kshidol. I stood to accompany her, even though it was not my time. A spirit told me they could see a stain forming on my right arm. I lied and told them it was a trick of the light.

I held Ultreia's hand and we walked down the stair. The flesh-coloured air changed around us as we pushed through the substance separating worlds. We entered a realm where all was anguish. Ultreia went limp against the railing as the bones of her body dissolved and I held her where she loosely clung.

"I will stay by your side," I said, knowing that I was an Intercessor, her tutor and master. I could hear ringing, heavy in my ears, of eternal pain, and desolation. Of hopelessness, absolute, and unending fear.

A spirit flew before me in confrontation. She was all red, dark and shiv-

ering. She screamed; her rank, dirt-coloured hair hanging over me as she hovered. It was Sybilla, and because we were in death, she could see all of my mind, and everything that I was able to conceal in life. Her rage was directed at me in its entirety. Great globules of mucous started to drip from her mouth and nose onto me, and I was overcome with disgust and terror.

I turned to Ultreia, watching helplessly as she came apart, little blood stubs blossoming on her gums where her teeth had been. A crushing weight descended, stealing at my will, at my knowledge of myself — salting me apart, deforming me into an unending scream, making me a vessel of pain alone.

When I awoke, I knew I had been foolish to believe I could hide from her. She was always waiting, each time I died. The horror of her presence made me flee into life, rebirth after rebirth, foolishly believing that in this life I would find a way to bring peace between us.

Believing this time it would be different.

Intercessor Waldemar Rasmus of Brivia, 713.

40

ZOHAR

Thirteen Years After The Fire

ZOHAR WAS STUCK IN HER ROOM AGAIN with nothing to do. At this very moment, Ambrose was showing the Red Skalen the ways of the sea. In Zohar's chamber, everything was unbearably still. Though she had left a twisted mess of sheets upon her bed when she went down for breakfast, they had since been straightened, her pillows puffed. She opened the window to a slight breeze bearing the persistent scent of the ocean, along with the musk of horse feed from the stables below. Across the valley, the buildings of Haydentown and the blue stripe of the Selbourne were ornamental as the trinkets on her dresser. And over the way, the Temple sat, smooth as porcelain, high and unchanging in the mountains.

She could not understand what had possessed her brother, and she was sure he had just lied to her. He didn't used to lie. But now she wondered if that was true. She thought of the kshidol. The fact that she and Edith shared a secret Ambrose did not know. She wanted to tell him, but he always seemed to be off somewhere. He didn't want to go to the sea caves. Or he did, but then it was raining, or the tide was in. Zohar was afraid that if she pushed him too hard, he would close off from her altogether. He would tell his secrets to the Sherburns, out on the waves where she could not listen in. Then there was her grandfather and his horde of hidden knowledge that he passed to Ambrose like sweets, saving none for her. Perhaps it was that she resembled her mother that the old man had not taken to her after all these years.

The thought brought heaviness to her heart. Zohar did not want to resemble her mother. Rebekah Elshender was a fettered thing, an effigy in flesh. But one day, Zohar would wear the very Skalens' Star that hung about her mother's neck. Would Ambrose leave then? Somehow, she always imagined he would be by her side. But he was not duty bound. Custom commanded that Zohar find a husband with whom to share the Skalen's burden. She ventured that some of the young men in the town thought her pretty, but as she walked among them, they averted their eyes, looked at other girls.

In the Skalens' House library, she read books about the mainland, learned all of the names, the places where things grew, the trade routes, the eternal fluctuations of the tally. But in and among the less interesting details were flashes of colour, insights that painted these places in her mind. Brivia, Maglore, Vaelnyr, Seltsland, Lindesal and Nothelm – she wanted to visit them all. Ambrose may have forgotten their plan to escape Avishae, but when the time came, he was free to leave the accursed House of his birth. He could live with the Raeburns if he wanted. Zohar did not have a choice.

She was still wearing her ceremonial gown following the morning's formalities with Skalen Sybilla. Without bothering to change, Zohar left the room, stalking down the hallway, skirt swishing. When she emerged into the forecourt, several guards turned and gave her a deferential bow. It was the dress, no doubt. For a short, exhilarating moment, she felt like a Skalen.

She waved to Elis. "Elis, please ready the carriage. I wish to go to town."

"Certainly, Miss Zohar," he said, motioning for the others to bring out the horses.

Holding herself tall, Zohar skimmed through a number of possible reasons for her urgent errand, but hardly cared if she was believed. She would be home in time for the banquet, and besides, she was old enough to go about her own business.

Soon, two fine horses appeared, drawing the same carriage that had escorted Skalen Sybilla Ladain. Elis helped her in, and she smiled. The carriage rattled along. As Zohar cast her eye across field and pasture, she thought of the people that dotted the landscape and wondered what it would feel like when she was their Skalen.

"Where to?" Elis asked, as they passed the fork that led to the Temple.

Zohar considered. "I wish to visit the leather worker," she said. It was the first shop that came to mind, but it would do.

Moving into town, the carriage slowed and Zohar could see people everywhere. Frowning men trudged about carrying heavy things. A girl in an apricot dress laughed loudly and then covered her mouth, and the lad who had been leaning in the doorway took this as licence to try another joke. An old woman yelled from the window above the monger's as a boy squinted up at her nodding *yes'm*. As they neared the water, the smell of baked bread intermingled with the stench of fish as a weathered red boat cast its catch upon the dock.

The carriage came to a halt and Zohar got out, eager to drink in all that she could before the crowd noticed her.

"I shan't be long, Elis," she said, as she started toward the leather shop.

Some did not see her straight away, dressed as she was in the colour of twilight. But once one set of eyes discovered her, the others saw the looking, and turned their heads to see. Zohar had walked among them before but those other times she had been with her parents, following them into shops, standing shyly to the side as her parents talked quantities and allocations. Even her parents did not wear their ceremonial vestments to town. She felt the fever of eyes upon her, and looked steadfastly forward, as a Skalen must.

A little bell rang as she stepped through the door. The air was cool, perfumed with leather oils. A girl with bright blonde hair sat in the back corner, her body and half of her face hidden by the counter.

The girl looked up and smiled. "Afternoon, how can I help you?"

Zohar saw her eyes glitter at the sight of her dress but was not sure if the girl knew who she was. "I would like to have a new Meridian band made."

Noticing a selection of clasped belts, she added, "and I would like a belt to match, so they are of the same design."

"Yes, Miss, we can do all of that," the girl said, nodding. Her cheeks had blossomed red, so Zohar took that to mean that she had been recognised after all. "My father, Mr Corbin, will be back at any moment."

Zohar walked through the shop examining belts and bags, straps and decorative clasps. Just then, a door squeaked somewhere out back and footsteps clipped into the room. She turned just as Mr Corbin came to stand next to his daughter, but when he saw Zohar, he was caught by surprise.

Quickly rounding the counter, he approached her and bowed. "Miss Elshender, what an honour it is to see you. What may I help you with?"

The girl's face crumpled into a frown as she had clearly missed her chance to tell papa what the nice lady was after.

Zohar smiled. "Your daughter has been most helpful. I have come to order a new Meridian band and a belt-clasp. Something more in step with the mainland style." She did not know what the mainland style was at present, but with any luck, Mr Corbin did.

"Very good, Ailbhe." Mr Corbin smoothed his daughter's hair. "Miss Elshender, follow me."

Mr Corbin led her to a cabinet, pulling out a drawer of embossed belts with silver clasps of different designs. He selected one of them, unhooking it from the display cushion so that she could have a better look. The workmanship was fine but Zohar was disappointed when she saw the clasps were the same as those she already owned, of those her mother wore.

"They wear these on the mainland?" Zohar asked.

Mr Corbin's knitted brow told Zohar that he was aware of her displeasure and she smiled in apology.

"I am sorry, I think I have changed my mind," Zohar said quietly and started for the door.

"But Papa, what about the *special* ones?" Ailbhe cried from behind the counter.

Mr Corbin's face went red.

Zohar froze on the spot, staring at the man as he nervously licked his lips. "Mr Corbin," she began in her most commanding tone, "I promise no harm will come to you or your family. Please show me."

"Yes, Miss Elshender," he said, rounding the counter.

Zohar stood in the shop and waited, hearing the click of locks, the shifting of wood upon wood. Little Ailbhe had gone quiet and was hiding behind the counter, out of sight.

When Mr Corbin returned, he leant down and whispered. Moments later Zohar heard the thump of small feet making their way out the back and up the stairs. Mr Corbin went to lock the front door, wiping the perspiration from his brow on the sleeve of his coat.

"Follow me," he said.

Zohar nodded but found his manner disquieting. She looked through the glass of the locked door. Elis was nowhere in sight.

She followed the man out back noticing the iron tools that hung from the far wall above the leather worker's bench, then crossed the room to stand beside Mr Corbin. On a small table sat a simple wooden box, illuminated by a stream of sunlight.

His hands fumbled slightly as he unclasped the box and lifted its lid.

Zohar's eyes danced, these were different to anything she had seen. She looked at Mr Corbin excitedly and he gave her a hesitant smile.

"This one is in the Brivian style," Mr Corbin said, glancing up at her. "The lines are rounded, see the graceful curves here and here? If you compare it with this piece from Nothelm, you will see the silverware is not as decorative – the design more angular."

Zohar listened in rapt silence as he described each one, nodding with appreciation.

"When were these crafted?" Zohar asked, once he had finished.

Mr Corbin pressed his lips together before answering. "They are quite old, Miss Elshender." He gave her a significant look.

She could see that they were. The patterns were subtly wrought.

Far more intricate than the current fashion. She stared at each design until it offered up the symbolism she expected must be there. Within the clustered triangles she found feathers, scales, and open mouths. The curves were serpentine, the embossed curlicues tongues seeking the centre. The circles, wherever they were placed, seemed enchanted with the power of seeing.

Mr Corbin shifted his weight from foot to foot.

"You have a good eye, Mr Corbin. I think that the Brivian clasp will do nicely," she said.

Mr Corbin closed the box, looking down. "Miss Elshender," he said cautiously, "these items are... dangerous. Do you understand my meaning?" Mr Corbin looked at her imploringly.

"Mr Corbin, I have come here personally because I understand the importance of discretion. No one will know of this exchange, I assure you."

With some reluctance, the man nodded, smoothing his hand across the box's exterior.

"Is it possible to silver the edge of the blinding stone before it is positioned in the Meridian band? I will not wear the Brivian clasp, but I would like my Meridian to be decorated in a similar design."

Mr Corbin looked thoughtful. "I am not aware of anyone doing so on the mainland, but it has been years since I have travelled. I have heard the Skalen in Maglore hangs pearls from her Meridian. But, yes, I believe I could have the edge of the stone plated... I would have to test that it did not change the properties of the stone. I will speak to the smith."

Zohar did not want to give him the opportunity to change his mind. "Very well. When can it be done?"

"For you, I could have it done within the week."

"Thank you, Mr Corbin. I will come to collect my order in person," Zohar said with a nod.

"Certainly, Miss Elshender. We will keep it for you alone." He retrieved the key from his pocket and escorted her to the main room.

As she stepped out into the street, Mr Corbin looked at her uncertainly before closing the door.

Outside, the sky was the most luminous blue. Elis did not question her and on the trip home Zohar allowed her heart to soar. She would find her own way in the Seven Lands. They could not keep everything from her. Though she did not yet possess it, Zohar treasured her prize.

As pasture opened up either side of her, Zohar found herself thinking of the Corbin girl. If little Ailbhe adored her, why wouldn't others? She indulged herself in fancy as the horses clattered on. She would travel to the mainland. Stepping from the carriage she would smile. The farmers would bow and show her the best of their crop. She would mark the tally, and her allotments would be fair. Ambrose could waste his time trying to impress the accursed Skalen of Vaelnyr, but Zohar would not allow herself to be dragged back into the past. She would not shape herself in the image of a haunted generation. She would not have grey circles round her eyes and words of death on her lips. She would win the people with kindness.

When the carriage pulled up, her Attendant was waiting for her in the forecourt. "Zohar, your mother is wondering where you are!"

Zohar put her hand on her Attendant – an action she had never tried before – and spoke calmly. "Elspeth, do not concern yourself. I am dressed, and will go to my mother directly. Where is she?"

Elspeth blushed. "Yes, Miss. Skalen Rebekah is in the sitting room by the Tower."

Elation still buoyed her step, but this did not prevent her stomach from turning over when she reached the door.

"Come in," her mother called, before Zohar had the chance to knock.

Opening the door, her mother was semi-visible in the dim light.

"Your brother's expedition went well this afternoon. I was surprised you did not attend."

"Did you attend?" Zohar asked.

"We kept our distance as they set off," her mother replied, tersely.

"Then you understand why I did not come. I did not want Ambrose to embarrass himself." Zohar still held the handle, swinging the door on its hinge. "And I had some errands of my own to take care of."

Her mother looked at her curiously. "What errands did you have in Haydentown, may I ask?"

"I wanted a new Meridian band made."

"Whatever for?" Her mother did not try to hide her irritation.

"It is only sensible to have a spare," Zohar said, evenly.

Her mother nodded but was not satisfied to let her leave. "It is not the type of errand I would expect you to undertake while we have a Skalen visiting from the mainland."

It seemed that she wanted an apology. "Sorry, Mother, I didn't think it would take long. And here I am. Where is Skalen Sybilla now?"

Her mother leaned back in her chair. "In her chambers. We will be gathering in the dining hall in an hour."

"I am ready," Zohar assured her, hand tight on the doorknob.

"Yes, well, your brother is not. I am sure his hair will be dripping onto his shoulders throughout the first course."

At that they both laughed, dissipating the tension between them.

Zohar was about to take her leave, but a sudden impulse took her. "Mother?"

"Yes?"

"You and Father work so hard. I would like to be of help, and to learn more about the allocations."

Her mother looked at her blankly.

Zohar stepped into the room and pressed the door closed behind her. "If you let me help you, perhaps Father could come down from the Tower more often."

Her mother chewed her lip, bowing her head in thought.

Zohar rounded the chair in which her mother sat. She looked so very tired. The bright light of a cloud-banked sky suffused the room, illuminating silver hairs among the auburn.

Her mother looked up at her with glistening eyes. "There will be time enough for that."

Though she could see that it pained her, Zohar persisted. "I am sixteen years old. You were only two years older than I when you became Skalen."

"I had no training," her mother said, with a trace of defiance.

"What about Father? Surely his parents taught him these things."

"You have accompanied us to town, and to the farms, and your brother is now acquainted with the sea miners."

Zohar was unconvinced. "Do you think that I am ready to attend a meeting of Council? To travel to the Seven Lands?" Zohar pressed.

At this her mother looked horrified. "There have been no meetings of the Seven since the Council of Vaelnyr. Things can be managed without travelling to the mainland."

"But Sybilla is here now. Why is she here? You know we cannot protect this island without the help of the other Skalens. We cannot be blind to their intentions."

Her mother's eyes narrowed at this. "You think you are so wise. I don't know what my father has been teaching you or what notions you have let flower in your mind, but the Skalen's burden is a curse." Her hand clenched at her stomach, and her mother continued in a low whisper. "The Guard know enough to secure peaceful trade without a single word from the Skalens. A figurehead's reign will bring the greatest peace to your heart. Discover what you must to satisfy your curiosity, but too much knowledge can be a dangerous thing. You do not want to show yourself as ambitious. It will put us all at risk."

Zohar paused. She might already have pushed her mother too far. Suddenly she felt the danger of her mother's words with Sybilla wandering the halls. Her father could keep silent no matter what happened. But her mother seemed quite out of temper. She had lost her senses before. The Guard had shut her in a room just like this one. When she lost little Bethany. The sister who was coming, but who never arrived. Zohar came to hate the name. It was the word her mother screamed as she beat on the door, shrieking heresies, cursing Velspar, whimpering like a child.

That year, her father walked the grey sand, and Zohar held her brother tight. She showed him how to make clover chains, and they collected special rocks that would protect them in the night. When she was with Ambrose, she had to be brave, and being brave kept her safe as well. But in their room, when Ambrose's slow breath told her that he had entered the realm of sleep, she found herself alone again

223

with the darkness. Her mother was in the room upstairs. Sometimes, her mother was sorrowful, oozing black oil though the flagstones and onto Zohar's resting form. Sometimes her mother cried sea scum, salty and foul. Other times she was angry.

Her mother stared at a crack in the wall; her face appeared paralysed, twisted. After a long silence, her mother spoke. "I will speak to your father."

"Thank you," Zohar said dully.

"Will you visit the Raeburns tomorrow?" her mother asked, for it was Lindesday.

"No," Zohar said sharply.

Her mother gave her a questioning look.

A lump formed in Zohar's throat. "I do not wish to go."

But her mother kept looking at her, refusing to accept this as the full story.

Then, before Zohar could stop herself, the words came spilling from her mouth. "The Raeburns do not love me as they love Ambrose." Zohar felt a rush of heat, and shame.

Her mother's face softened and she stood to embrace her. Zohar tried to laugh it off. But as her mother held her, Zohar felt her heart radiating in her chest, felt the comfort of shared pain. They remained this way for a long time, and Zohar let the tears fall, for her mother could not see her.

Eventually, her mother pulled back and regarded her, wiping the tears from her cheeks. "We are required at dinner." She smiled. "Your first duty as a Skalen will be this – make your face say nothing at all. Make sure our visitor can read nothing of what is within."

Zohar straightened herself, sniffed, and wiped her eyes.

This was the gift she had asked of her mother, and now it had been given.

Zohar gave her a conspiratorial grin. "I will not let you down."

And off they went to dine with Velspar's great reformer, Skalen Sybilla of Vaelnyr.

41

ZOHAR

Thirteen Years After The Fire

HER PARENTS HAD RISEN EARLY, the Attendant informed her, and her brother had set out for the Bay. Her oats steamed as she reached absently for the pitcher of cream. As she ate, her spoon clinked dismally about her bowl. It was an aimless, lonely sound.

Just then, Guardsman John entered the room. "Excuse me, Zohar, your father requests your presence." John furrowed his brow, pained to intrude on the privacy of her chewing. "You are to accompany him to the farms to take the Skalen's tally."

Zohar's heart skipped, and suddenly her day became bright. "Thank you, John!"

John was not accustomed to such enthusiasm and looked at his toes a moment before making his exit.

Two mouthfuls later, she deserted the bowl, making for the hall-way, where she directed a passing Attendant to fetch her coat and hair pins.

When she emerged from the main door, her cheeks were ruddy and the wind made play with her hair. Her father smiled at her. Sunlight caught his face, and he no longer looked so sallow. The

Attendants had cropped his hair and beard, accentuating his firm jaw. He wore simple clothing, as he always did when visiting the farmers, but today, his shoulders were broad, and his Star gleamed upon his chest.

Zohar jumped up beside him in the wagon and they set off at a languorous pace. She kept waiting for him to speak, for surely her mother had put him up to this, but the wagon had almost reached the Kinnon farm and he had not uttered a word. He just squinted beneath the grey thatch of his brows, his mouth expressionless.

Her initial elation flagged, giving way to annoyance. She had resigned herself to the usual way of things when her father pulled on the reins, halting the horses beneath an oak tree. Zohar watched him anxiously as he sat for a long moment, eyes set on the horizon.

Finally, he looked at her. "My girl." He smiled, tilting his head. "On the distant day when you become Skalen, you will know all the things you need to know. That is what my parents told me, and it was true enough. The rest, nothing could have prepared me for."

Zohar looked at her father earnestly.

"Mostly, you will do what you have seen me and your mother do many times before. We keep count of things, we write letters and we trade what is surplus for what is needed. That part is easy." Her father sighed, kneading the reins in his hand. "It is the interference of human feeling that complicates the job of a Skalen. In the past, we had the Intercessors to handle that."

Zohar shifted in her seat, feeling her youth, for she could never speak of the Intercessors, not to her father's generation.

"You will need to challenge people. Now that they wear the Meridian, none of them can be taken at their word." He looked at her, as if she might not be up to the task. "When necessary, you will need to use the Guard. They are there to enforce your decisions."

The last thing she wanted to hear was that it was down to the will of the Guard. They had commanded her whole life with the soft influence of their observing eyes. She could not readily imagine commanding them to do what they did not already wish to do.

"But you would be right to be wary of them," her father said.

"They have feet in two worlds. One is with their Skalen, and the other is with the Guard – a force that spans the Seven Lands. They see themselves as instruments of Velspar. They cannot move against the Guard of another land without breaking their oath."

"Is it different now that they have no common enemy?" Zohar felt quite clever at having thought of the question but was not game enough to refer to the Intercessors by name.

Her father gave her a sad smile. "Funny that you see the Guard as the natural enemies of the Intercessors. But I suppose that is all that you have known. When the Intercessors commanded the Guard as the Skalens do, they were united in service of a common ideal. Now, as you say, things are different. They are more factional."

They sat for a while, her father passing the waterskin for Zohar to drink.

Her father cleared his throat. "There is a trade matter to be handled in a month or so. Illiam Greslet will be visiting from Brivia. I want you to receive him on behalf of the Skalens of Avishae."

"Certainly," she said, though her stomach lurched. "What is to be traded?"

Her father laughed heartily and Zohar flushed red. "We can go through it together. I will show you the letters and give you our position. You are simply there to deliver the message."

Zohar nodded, trying to appear unabashed. She expected him to go on, but he had become serious again.

"I must have your word that you will not ask questions of your mother or me about the Guard. Especially in the House. If and when I can speak on the topic, I will initiate the conversation." He looked down at her. "Do you understand?"

"Yes, Father."

With a shake of the reins, the horses lurched to life, and carried on in clip-clop to the Kinnon farm, the Jones' place, and on to see the Milwains. Each greeted them with a wave as they leaned expectantly in the doorway. They'd tell them the wiles of the weather as they gave their numbers, forking hay as they talked, never tripping over the hens at their feet. Her father tested them with questions that he turned inside and out, but the figures remained unchanged. These were honest folk, it seemed.

All the while, Zohar made her observations, recording them in the Skalen's ledger.

42

ZOHAR

Thirteen Years After The Fire

ZOHAR STEPPED INTO THE HALL, sweating, as her breath did battle with the firmness of her bodice. Her father's words were there in her mind, and she returned to them every couple of minutes to check that she had not forgotten them. The Attendants would bring Illiam. He would arrive presently. Any moment now.

She felt lightheaded, wondering why she was doing this at all when she would probably just humiliate herself. And then her father would see her for the failure that she was. Her mother would scold her for endangering their relationship with the mainland and would make her do penance ladling soup in the barracks. Zohar knew the thoughts she entertained were ridiculous and they did her no good. She reminded herself that this man did not know her, knew even less of the message she was tasked with relaying. She could be, do, or say anything. She might even impress him.

Although she thought she had heard the sound ten times before, now she was sure. Steady footfall; doubled and clattering toward her. Illiam Greslet and the Attendant escorting him to the hall. She wondered which one of them it would be.

The door must have been recently greased as it opened without a creak. It was Dennis. He began formalities without ado.

"The Skalens Elshender are represented this day by their daughter, Zohar Elshender." Dennis bowed briskly. "Miss Elshender, Illiam Greslet seeks an audience to discuss trade matters pertaining to Brivia and the Southlands." Dennis lowered his eyes, and exited, sealing the heavy door behind him.

Illiam stood there stiffly and Zohar remained where she was, near the end of the long table. She could not believe that her father had omitted the most important detail of her preparation. For Illiam was not just any Greslet but her own peer, a man of eighteen, perhaps. He was tall, with the cropped hair of a guardsman, chestnut eyes, and a clipped beard that showed the dimple of his chin beneath.

Her thoughts scattered like birds. He was not the most handsome man she had seen, but he held himself with confidence, and she found him attractive. She knew he would see through her in an instant – her inexperience, her playacting. He had done this before, and at the sight of his Brivian surcoat, she felt awfully provincial. She needed to say something.

"Welcome to Avishae," she started, and hearing that her voice sounded normal, she continued. "You must be hungry after your journey, please sit and we can enjoy this meal while we talk."

Illiam obliged, and it seemed he noticed nothing unusual about her behaviour. "You are most gracious, Miss Elshender."

As he sat, Illiam smiled at her and reached for the bread. Zohar picked a few grapes, and slices of pear, eating them in small mouthfuls so as not to be caught chewing when she needed to speak. Illiam ate freely, spreading the roughly torn bread with a thick layer of butter, stuffing it with whitefish. She poured him a glass of wine so that her stumbles and imperfections might be seen in a softer light, filling half of her own glass with water.

Words were exchanged in the passing of dishes and in comments on the unique flavour of the honey, the richness of the wine. As she passed her knife through the pear, she noticed his gaze on her in the periphery of her vision. She gave him further opportunities, her eyes downcast as she folded back the bread linens for him to cut another slice.

It was not until he had eaten, that Illiam turned to his business in Avishae.

"As you may have guessed, I do not hail from Brivia but I have lived there now for more than half of my life. It is a beautiful place and has many resources. More than we could ever need. But we are desperately short of one resource – labour."

He wanted able-bodied men and women skilled in their arts, just as her father expected. She was able to offer him all that he desired, and she felt much more capable when she was able to so readily solve the hardships of their Brivian allies.

"In his letter, Skalen Ulric mentioned that the Temple is being used as a storehouse for meat and other produce. Do you think we could go there? It would be instructive to see how the Guard have utilised the building."

Zohar was caught a little off guard by this request. After all, she had not set foot in the Temple since she was a child. She almost mentioned this but stopped herself in time. She didn't want him to be escorted by one of the guards, and she was certain her parents would forbid her from taking him.

"I would be happy to take you to the Temple. How long will you be in Avishae?"

"A few days." He paused to take a sip of wine.

Now, as she regarded him, he seemed distracted, and she wondered if she had imagined his interest in her.

"In that case, we should go directly to the Temple," she said with a ready smile.

Illiam looked a little surprised. "Thank you."

Zohar rang the bell and asked for Elspeth. When her Attendant arrived, Zohar whispered her instructions, knowing that Elspeth would not complicate matters.

A short time later, Zohar and Illiam stood at the side entrance of the Skalens' House, mounting their horses. They traversed a little-used track that bypassed the main gate, dipping their heads to pass beneath low branches. They circled the village under the shadow of trees that fringed the base of the Caulmont Mountains, but after that they rode out in the open. Illiam was an able rider and went on ahead, stopping now and then to ask her the way, and before long, they found themselves at the foot of the mountain and the base of the Temple stair.

"It is a long way up," Illiam said, squinting.

Zohar noticed a particular smell in the air that took her back in time. It was the resin of the pines, the scent of Alma flowers before they were picked, and of stone wetted by the trickling of melted frost. With the smell came memories of muscles that ached with the effort of every step, of her mother carrying her part of the way while her father held Ambrose. She could almost taste the smoke of the censers, hear the voices reverberating as bees around a hive, feel the sharp sting in her palm.

The vividness of her reminiscence startled her. But it was not a singular memory. It overlapped in her mind, distinct aspects positioning themselves against a backdrop of their repetitions. Her parents would have taken her here when she could barely stand, and the next year when her legs were not long enough to climb, and the year after that when she might have made it, but still needed help after the first rise.

The memory flowered in her mind, its petals white, billowing in the mountain winds. The memory beheld her, and she felt the sudden terror of being alone on these stairs, without the tall ones, the farm boy, the beautiful lady with ginger hair, the old man who worked the iron, the colour and shape of them moving as one – her Birth-Kin.

"Miss Elshender?" Illiam looked at her with some concern.

Zohar willed herself to see the way ahead as it really was. An unpeopled staircase of stone glimmering through the pines. Somewhere above there would be guards about, lifting things, chatting as they did at the Skalens' House, for this was no longer a holy place.

"Yes, but you are right, it is a hard climb. We should bring water with us," Zohar said.

At that, Zohar started up the track and Illiam followed behind. Zohar soon felt the strain in her legs. Breathing heavily, talking became impractical, so they proceeded without words. She did not know how long it would take to reach the top but guessed that they were more than halfway there. Her heart was hammering and her cheeks were red hot. If Illiam had not been there, she might have rested earlier but she did not want to show she was unaccustomed to the climb.

In her haste to leave the Skalens' House, she had neglected to consider her clothing. Stopping made it worse, and she began to feel dizzy.

"Miss?"

Illiam rushed forward as Zohar looked over the edge of the stair, her vision swimming. Lightly, he held her back, letting go once she had regained her balance. Half staggering, she sat herself down with her back against the rock. Without looking at him, she began to unhook the buttons at the side of her bodice. Once she had taken it off, the mountain breeze danced around her heart and she sighed with relief.

Taking a sip of water, she reassured him that she was fine, but he was looking resolutely at the trees. He looked so funny she could not help laughing. "I am wearing a perfectly respectable tunic if you care to turn around."

When he did, he looked at her shyly, and as she folded her bodice, she hid her smirk of triumph.

For the rest of the climb, the silence was different. She was now intensely aware of a feverish perfume that rose from their bodies, travelling between them on the whipping tides of the mountain wind. She encouraged him to walk ahead of her just so she could watch him from behind.

Illiam turned. "I think I see it."

Zohar looked past him, catching a glimpse of white. "That is it!"

Suddenly Zohar heard the crunch of footfall behind her and wheeled round to look. Before she knew it, the guard had passed her, continuing to the top of the stair where he called out to a company of his brethren. She kept in step with Illiam as they emerged into the clearing, the great white dome rising above them. She was surprised the guard had not recognised her, but moments later, another called out from above.

"Zohar!"

Waving as confidently as she could, she smiled at Guardsman Timothy. "I am showing our guest the sights of Avishae. Timothy, meet Illiam Greslet of Brivia. He is interested to see the Temple. Would you escort us to the top?"

Timothy may have been older than her, but he was not old enough to say no. He stammered in assent and disappeared from the window.

Zohar ignored the looks of the other guards who were all beginning to notice her arrival. By the time Gareth stalked over to question her, Timothy was by her side, ready to commence the tour.

"Good day, Gareth," Zohar said sweetly. "Father has tasked me with looking after our guest, Illiam Greslet of Brivia, and Timothy has kindly volunteered to show us the Temple."

Illiam offered a small bow. "I am pleased to make your acquaintance, Guardsman. In Brivia, the locals are still fearful of the Temple, but in terms of its structure, it is a far more serviceable building than the Skalens' House. I am trying to find ways to encourage them to make use of it."

Gareth looked him over. "You must be Jemryn and Olinda's boy."

Illiam's smile slipped.

"Very well," Gareth said, casting Zohar a glance that told her she was trespassing beyond her domain.

"Timothy, show them around." He gave them something resembling a smile and then stalked away to deal with a delivery of skins that had just arrived.

Guardsman Timothy led them inside. It should have been white and gleaming, empty and bright. It should have smelt of polished timber, of Alma and copper, parchment and prayers. Instead, the space was filled with sacks, guards walking, slouching atop crates, parcels stacked and bound with twine. There was a pungent smell of soured blood, of offal and salt. The floor was dirty, a fine layer of hessian dust and stray animal hair clinging to the ceiling and walls.

Timothy led them down the stair to the forbidden level below ground. The air became noticeably cooler as they descended into a windowless room hung with carcasses, where light gleamed from air vents high on the wall. The clammy metallic stench of blood and tallow was overpowering.

"The lower temperature here keeps the rot from taking hold," Timothy told Illiam.

Zohar looked on with disgust as blood dripped from a number of carcasses in the centre of the room. The floor had seen a steady tide of blood. Her eyes followed the great rust-coloured stain along the trough to the far side of the room where it disappeared, somewhere unseen.

Timothy raised his eyebrows, and Illiam shook his head, having no further questions.

"The ground floor is used to store goods out of the rain that are due for delivery to Haydentown," he said, continuing up the circling stair.

The first floor was lined with cleaver-scarred benches and sharp tools, flesh and fat strewn about in various stages of dismemberment. Guardsmen turned, mid-task, and Zohar looked away. The second floor was crammed with wrapped parcels smelling of salt-meat and wax. A sharp-featured guardswoman lost count as they passed and started again from the top. The next floor stored fleeced pelts, the one above stored uncut leathers.

As they climbed, Zohar felt an involuntary swell of nausea, her eyes prickling with imminent tears. Quickly, she turned her head, and blinked several times to clear her vision. Illiam walked ahead of her, talking with Timothy and seemed unperturbed by what he saw. He was here to divine such practical information, after all.

Zohar's heart turned dead as a stone as they ascended the seventh stair. She dreaded to see what was up there, but when they entered the room, it was filled with endless bundles of paper and bottled ink. The dark shelves on which they sat had been brought in, sitting oddly against the rounded shape of the wall.

Timothy gave a final sigh of exertion when he reached the top. "And here we are. This is where the record-keeping supplies are kept." He shrugged. "That is about it," he said, his foot poised to return downstairs.

"Thank you, Timothy, we will make our way back down in a moment. You may return to your duties," Zohar said, trying to muster a friendly tone.

Timothy gave her an odd smile and then hurried off downstairs. The open window drew the clean air of the pine forest into the room, and Zohar walked toward it. She stared into the distance, concentrating on the tiny crashing waves that threw themselves upon the rocks, never quite reaching the Skalens' House above.

Illiam's shoes clipped behind her and eventually she turned. The expression on his face startled her. It was an impassioned look, almost of anger. Glancing away, the afterimage of his eyes remained, cutting through every other tangled thought in her mind; making her heart thump in panic. Echoes of the guardsmen's chatter rose up the stair in waves; the whistling air thick with the waft of flesh. She had to get out.

She smiled at Illiam; a polite kind of smile that shooed away whatever flirtation might have played about them in the noonday sun. Whatever sense of adventure she had previously felt had well and truly fled. Zohar did not want to see the seven rooms, a second time, on the way down. Did not want to have to explain this little excursion to her father, who would probably never trust her again.

As they descended, she looked at the back of Illiam's head, and the grey stones of his Meridian. She wondered what they could possibly have in common when this place made her sick to the stomach. And here he was on a mission to sully the Brivian Temple as the Guard had so shamelessly done in Avishae. He was a Greslet, so she need not have been surprised.

But then the obvious truth of it struck her. This was not the Guard's doing. This was a Skalen-sanctioned storehouse. Of course it was. Her jaw tightened. She could not think about such things here. Zohar held all the pieces frozen in place, just a small distance from her heart. Later, when she was alone, she would allow them to collide, but that moment was far from her now.

Illiam offered thanks and farewells to those they passed, and with so much smiling and bowing, her inner tremors subsided. Outside, as they descended the long stair, Illiam fell silent. She had expected small talk, but he kept to himself, so much so that Zohar began to worry that she had offended him.

When they reached the horses, she broke the silence. "I wonder, Mr Greslet, did you discover all that you needed to know about the Temple during this visit?"

Illiam kept his head turned away from her as he mounted his horse. "Yes, Miss Elshender. It was most instructive."

He set off, already knowing the way, it seemed, and she followed in his wake.

43

ZOHAR

Thirteen Years After The Fire

IT WAS ILLIAM'S SECOND NIGHT at the Skalens' House and Zohar could not sleep. She'd been cooped up all day with no one but Elspeth to talk to. From her window she'd glimpsed Illiam and Ambrose stepping into the Skalen's carriage, bound for Haydentown. She was burning to know what they had discussed and decided to try her brother's door.

Zohar saw light beneath the crack and knocked.

She heard fumbling and the closing of drawers. A moment later he appeared, and she saw that he was as far from sleep as she was. "Can I come in?" She smiled, her eyes sparkling in the lamplight.

Looking at her curiously, Ambrose opened the door.

She came to sit cross-legged on the rug and waited for him to join her. It had been a while since they had had one of their night talks. Looking up at her brother, Zohar noticed some imperceptible change in him. He seemed surer of himself, and it showed in the broadening of his shoulders, and the shadowy confidence of his gaze. It made her miss him, even though he was right there.

Finally, he joined her, leaning on one arm. "You have made quite a stir, going to the Temple like that," he said, visibly impressed by her daring.

"I know." She laughed. "They will probably never leave me alone with a mainlander again."

"What is it like up there?"

Like stumbling upon a dead body. "Awful," she said, finally.

Ambrose mirrored her pained expression. "That is probably why Mother and Father don't want us there."

"I can't figure them out," Zohar said. She was about to say more but knew her thoughts touched on things her mother had told her in confidence.

"I'd say it's for show. For people like Sybilla, to prove loyalty to the Skalens," Ambrose said.

Zohar considered his words, wondering if Ambrose came up with this on his own. She had not thought of it that way before.

"What do you make of Illiam?" Ambrose said at length.

In the low light, Zohar was reasonably sure he could not see her blush. "I think..." Zohar frowned but couldn't decide exactly what she thought of him. "I think he knows what it is like to grow up in a broken land."

Ambrose raised his eyebrows, breaking into a grin.

Zohar smiled despite herself. "I don't know him," she said, looking at her hands. "It is too early to know where his sympathies lie, but he seems trustworthy."

Ambrose nodded.

Zohar busied herself smoothing the fringe of the rug. "Do you know what they plan to do with him tomorrow?"

"They want to take him to meet some of the workers who will be travelling to Brivia. You want to come?"

"Even if I did, they're not going to let me go."

Ambrose shifted, sitting taller. "I will speak with Father and suggest that the whole family attend."

Zohar scrutinised her brother, who was being uncharacteristically generous. "What is your interest in Illiam?"

Ambrose shrugged. "I couldn't care less about him."

"Okay," she said slowly, cocking her head to one side.

"Do you want my help or not?" he asked, getting to his feet.

"Yes, of course," she said, not wanting to test her luck.

Ambrose stretched. "Well, we had both better get some sleep. Father will be up before dawn."

Zohar knew that she was being given her cue to leave but did not want to go. She had barely seen him lately. But he was right, morning would come soon enough. "Goodnight, Ambrose," she said with a wave.

"Goodnight, Sister."

Returning to her room, Zohar changed into her nightdress and slipped beneath the covers. She smiled in the darkness, giddy at the thought of seeing Illiam in the morning. Perhaps Ambrose was right, she did fancy him, just a little.

She thought of his flushed cheeks as she removed her bodice, his shy look, the sunlight in his hair. In her mind she continued to undress until he pressed her up against the rock wall. But then she remembered his expression as they left the Temple and chose a different scene.

This time, they rode on horseback at dusk, to a deserted barley field. The stems were heavy-laden, and she pushed the lengths apart. They found a place to hide their nakedness, his skin golden in the light of the setting sun.

She loosened her Meridian and the sensations grew rich. Hands running over smooth skin. His touch the gasp of water across hot earth. He thirsted for her, kissed her. He turned her over on the ground, stroked her haunches, the barley stems crushed beneath her breasts as he took her from behind. Rolling mists shrouded the field, a brisk wind sweeping up from the south, shuddering the grain.

She let go of her breath and the bed rose softly around her. A place of pillows, of downy sheets. She straightened her nightgown, her fingers tracing the embroidered shapes of flowers and their leaves, knowing she was alone. He had not perceived her, and she was glad of it, for she had not captured him. He was not some animal from the Kinnon's farm. She lay, toying with her Meridian, wondering what he was really like.

Reappointing the stones at the three points, Zohar stared at the ceiling. The grey feeling came upon her like a raincloud, speechless and indifferent, extinguishing the passion of her heart. Turning Illiam back into an ordinary man.

44

WALDEMAR

Fourteen Years After The Fire

AMAND DRAWS MAPS IN THE DUST *with his finger. He speaks of strategy and allegiances. He speaks of sacrifice. For we found each other to rebind the scattered souls, to draw them back to Velspar.*

As I write, my nostrils are filled with the scent of wild Alma. My feet rest upon the soil of my homeland, but my heart does not rejoice.

When I search this place for the music of life, all is silent but the stray wailing of strings, of minstrels lost in the forest.

Maeryn and Amand put their hands upon me, for my spirit courses with shame. What wounded eyes will search mine when we pass through the villages and the towns? What must I tell them?

What can I say to the abandoned ones who must give homage to the Guard? Those men who feel neither hunger, nor cold, and whose eyes are ever dry.

My old heart flutters to think of my wrists bound behind my back, of blinding stone upon my crown.

To think that they will drag me by the wrists, a stumbling old man, to the edge of the abyss. Where I should see without feeling, and hear only meaningless sounds.

Where Maeryn and Amand are gone, but Sybilla lives on. And I am alone among the burning stars.

INTERCESSOR WALDEMAR RASMUS OF BRIVIA, 714.

45

AMBROSE

Fourteen Years After The Fire

"Alright boys!" Rob shouted against the wind.

Ambrose took a moment to focus before removing his Meridian. Without looking at the brothers, he dove in, enjoying the instant lightness of his body and the heavy silence that fell upon his ears. He spied a boulder that bore the blistered pattern of blinding stone and swam toward it. He chipped off two pieces then launched himself skyward for air. This action he and the brothers repeated, passing each other like shades, upward and downward, falling and flying.

From the corner of his eye, Ambrose noticed a reddish blur. On the next dive, he swam closer, but it was only seaweed. Distracted now, he concentrated on a single outcrop of stone, using his time down there to scan the outer reaches, looking for Siatka. He remembered Her eyes like one remembers a dream, never able to make the vapour of vision solid and true. But She had to be real. The siatka had swarmed in these waters for thousands of years, surely some had survived?

That was the next thing he would ask Rob. How could they bring the siatka back? How could they bring the kshidol back, for that matter? If they were to eradicate the Ladain Heresy – as the Sherburns called it – they needed to resurrect more than ghosts.

Running out of air, Ambrose burst from the water, clattering three more stones upon the deck. Gwyn signalled for him to get back onto the raft. Ambrose hoisted himself up, and came to sit, dripping in the sun. As the brothers returned, Ambrose stared from beneath heavy brows.

"Something on your mind?" Allen asked.

Ambrose weighed his words. "Allen, do you ever feel like there is something out there?"

"Where?"

"Among the rocks… I don't know, a presence."

Allen chewed his lip, adjusting the wading pole. "No, not really. What do you mean?"

Ambrose began to sweat. "That time when I got you to take me back to shore, it wasn't that I was afraid of what we were doing. I saw something – well, I don't know if I saw it or felt it exactly – but I think I saw…"

"What?" Rob said.

Ambrose took in a sharp breath. They were both looking at him now. "Look, I know you have plans for Sybilla, but how are things going to go back to the way they were if Siatka and Kshidol are gone? I really think I felt something out there…"

As the three brothers turned to him, he felt the awkwardness of the god-names upon his tongue, for even here, they were not to be spoken.

They did not respond, but he could see them tense, their faces whitening, their hands clenching. But no, they were not clenching their hands. Their cheeks were sun-warmed, and Gwyn raked his hand through his hair, shaking water onto the deck. They did not answer him, and all went silent.

Their Meridians sat in a pile in the middle of the raft. The warmth in the air shifted.

"Why can we not speak of them?" Ambrose pushed.

Allen's brow furrowed and he looked down at his hands. Ambrose wanted to grab him by the shirt and scream, *why won't you just tell me?*

Inside his mind he propelled himself toward Allen – as Rob had said – *like smoke.* The jolt was sickening, like the faintness that follows the extraction of a blade from flesh. Close in the contours of Allen's face, in the sand that stuck to his chest, in his particular smell, Ambrose caught a flash of long knives gutting scaled bodies, a piercing shriek of inhuman pain, the Bay of Knives dyed red with blood. He felt the numbness of Allen's hands as he butchered, out there, shoulder to shoulder with the Avishaen Guard. Ambrose looked at Allen as the vision faded, and yet the knife remained in his hand. A moment later, that too was gone. Ambrose staggered backward in horror, his hands pulsing hot. His eyes darted from one brother to the next, unsure of what they would do.

"I'm sorry, Allen. I'm so sorry," he stammered. "I shouldn't have looked, I–"

"Shut your mouth." Rob was furious.

Allen stared into the distance without blinking, tears slipping down his cheeks.

Ambrose felt ill.

Gwyn looked ready to thump him. "You don't know what it was like."

"No. No, I don't," Ambrose said.

Then Allen's voice came from far away. "He knows enough."

Rob stalked from one side of the raft to the other, frowning deeply. "Well. Now you know. Mother Siatka will not forgive us. And The Father, too, has flown."

Gwyn gave Ambrose a cruel smile, "By decree of the Skalens Elshender," and bowed.

Ambrose stared right through him, determined the brothers would not see how deep Gwyn's words had cut. For the first time in what seemed an age, Ambrose longed to see his sister. Zohar alone was blood of his blood and he'd been a fool to think otherwise.

He set his eyes upon the mournful silhouette of the Skalens' House. There was light in the Tower, and in his sister's chambers.

Smoke trickled from the western chimney into a windless sky. Soon they'd be around the hearth-fire, eating and talking dully of their day. He yearned for that now. The ordinariness of boiled turnip, bread, broth and wine. His family would be there as they always were. They would always welcome him home.

46

AMBROSE

Fourteen Years After The Fire

THE NEXT MORNING, Ambrose left the Skalens' House as he usually did, but he did not go down to the Bay. His mood was dark, and all morning he'd been plagued by nerves, unable to sit still. He could not go back there. He did not want to lay eyes upon the Sherburns, and he did not feel like venturing to the Raeburn camp where his grandfather would surely question him. Part of him wanted to go to the sea caves with Zohar, but it seemed she had other plans for the day. He had walked down the hall to find her, but stopped halfway, deterred by giggles coming first from Zohar, and then her Attendant. He did not remember them being such fast friends, but then again, he'd thought the same about Edith. What friends did he have now? He had ruined everything.

Ambrose took the cliff track that led westward, peering down upon the shore, and was relieved to see no guards on patrol. He veered away from the path, scraping through untrodden scrub, pushing his muscles until they burned. The day was warm and after more than an hour's walk, his fingers grew tight with heat, his back trickling with sweat.

He didn't know where he was going exactly, he just wanted to move and keep moving. To exhaust himself of the horrible sensation that whatever he sought, it would always be maddeningly out of reach. Ambrose had worked hard to earn the brothers' trust, to make them see that he was just like them – an ally against the Red Skalen. He was sure that Gwyn, at least, would have let him in on the plan once things started to heat up. But not now. Ambrose kicked at a low branch that blocked his path, flinging it out of his way.

In his mind, the scene replayed over and over, the shock on their faces as he drew Allen's memories out, as if they could not believe he was capable of it. It was a look his grandfather gave him sometimes. When Ambrose saw more than he was supposed to see. It was in those moments he knew he was different, that Velspar had blessed him. If Sybilla Ladain had not plunged the Seven Lands into darkness, then he would have been an Intercessor. He would have joined the procession, collecting wisdom from his elders, and passing it on to new initiates in turn. His life would have held purpose. But because of her, he was a dog sniffing for scraps.

He wanted to scream, or cry, or punch something until his knuckles bled, but instead he kept walking. When he reached the southwestern precipice, he stopped at the startling sight. Two shades of blue extended either side of a cloudless horizon, as if he had reached the end of the world. Leafless trees cast shadows, but out here, there was no real shade. The sun beat down upon him. Ambrose had an overwhelming desire to be beneath the water, to dive right off the cliff and plunge into the deep. He sized up the distance, searching for rocks hidden beneath the shifting surf. It was too dangerous.

Ambrose removed his tunic and Meridian and tied them to his belt. Standing with his hands behind his head, he relished the feeling of the wind against his skin. The smell of his own sweat came to him in waves. His eyes returned to a sloping rock, and the crag that jutted out beside it. He considered the climb. It was risky, but he wanted something that would take all of his focus, distract him from the sick feeling that returned to him every time the brothers came to mind. Moving closer, he knelt and mapped the hand and footholds. Craning his neck, he spied a flat ledge halfway down that he had not previously noticed. He was good at climbing and was quite sure he could make it.

He left his shoes on the rock, the wind loud in his ears as he began to lower himself. The first part of the descent was difficult. His arms shook as he shifted carefully from one position to the next. He had one move to make before he reached the wide ledge, but the foothold was perilously thin. Keeping his body firm, he reached for it, gripping hard with his toes, pressed himself against the sun-warmed stone and pulsed to make the final leap. Landing hard on his bad ankle, Ambrose winced in pain, but after a few breaths it abated to a dull throb. From where he sat, he made out the thin line of a sandbank, and a place where the water sucked in.

Ambrose relaxed a little when he saw the rocks that led in step-like fashion to the shore below. When he reached the bottom, the sea cave was more expansive than he had originally thought. The tide was out, and the sandbank provided a path inside. Water rushed in and out of the cave along a well-worn channel but did not reach the far side. He breathed the cool air that smelt of wet rocks and seaweed. At the back of the cave were a number of tunnels, eroded by the persistent tide.

Approaching one, he peered in. Tessellated light illuminated the way, glimmering in drip trails above. Several cavities interconnected, and he could see a fair way down. The sight of the darkness beyond excited him, but it was more than that. He was drawn to it, as if listening for a voice too quiet for hearing.

Ambrose judged he had some time before the sea rose, and started down the tunnel, passing quickly through the section where it was carpeted with sand. The opening narrowed, forcing him into a crouch, but there was still light coming from some wider aperture farther down. Behind, he saw no inflow of water, only the bright disc of daylight that shone as his anchor.

Ambrose looked back into the tunnel and decided he would go as far as the light reached. He moved toward the tantalising glow that promised an alternate path to daylight, scraping his shins as he went, but as he neared, he knew he would not fit through. The hole in the tunnel wall would accommodate his head but not his shoulders.

Through the opening he saw a deep cave where muted light reflected from a pool of water. He gasped, arrested by the beauty of the place, by its uncanny stillness.

As he stared into the inky depths, the surface began to shimmer and ripple, obscuring his vision of whatever lay beneath. He had this feeling... of moving out of himself, of following, but also of being drawn towards something. The feeling was so strong that he had to force himself to remove his head from the cavern. Standing in the tunnel, he listened to the ocean roar, but could not make himself leave – not yet.

On some level he knew it was a stupid idea, but he wanted to follow that feeling, to see where it led. Ambrose turned toward the dark. He blinked, but still, he could not see a thing. The sensation was almost like thirst. His body knew where it wanted to go, and he gave himself over to it. His hands moved along moist rock, feeling its rippling layers, rough patches and broken shells – and the gloss of some other stone.

It was curious.

He stopped; passed his fingers over it once more. The stone shivered beneath his touch. Had he imagined it? But as he ran his fingers back and forth over the spot, he felt it with certainty. He wanted so badly to see it. Ambrose reached for his pickaxe, and positioned the point, pushing and levering with the utmost care. The stone was hard and did not come away easily. Sweat dripped down his temples and into the hollow of his cheeks. His legs cramped in the small space.

Ambrose took an involuntary gasp of air, his heart thrumming as he suddenly became aware of the dense rock that surrounded him. He thought of diving and of all the crevices he had swum through with less than a moment's breath, and how he always got out in time. Wiggling his fingers into the cleft he had created, Ambrose felt for the deepest spot and inserted the pickaxe, levering his bodyweight against it. He heard a clunk and grinned, fumbling to locate the fallen segment. His hand closed over the stone, and he kissed it, his laughter refracting in tight echoes.

Tucking the stone into his pocket, the feeling of want subsided, and he realised he needed to get out before he got himself trapped.

Ambrose crawled backward, shifting his shoulders and hips as he tried to gather speed. The return journey took a lot longer moving this way, and his frustration mounted. Sharp things scraped his knees, his shuffling movements the march of a man bound in a burlap sack.

His neck ached and he paused to stretch it when he felt wetness at his feet. Quickening his movements, he found his knees melting into the silt. In the distance, the network of tunnels began to make terrifying slurping noises that gurgled out again like a dying man's breath.

He forced his body to face the outer light, the rough inner wall scraping the skin from his shoulder. Ambrose clambered on his hands and knees until he found the end of the crouch space, and with his head bowed low, he broke into a bolt. Where the water washed in, it only reached his shins, but Ambrose was already reprimanding himself for misjudging the encroaching sea. When finally he was able to rise to his full height, he saw the glorious disc of daylight growing larger.

The tunnel dropped down, and the water drew heavily at his legs, making it impossible to run. With each step he pushed hard against the sandbank, pitting muscle against the leaden sea. With the next step, Ambrose howled in pain, grabbing his foot. He cursed under his breath as blood streamed down his heel and his inspecting hand. Then both were submerged by the incoming swell. Ambrose swam. The current was stronger now. The water level raised him up and dropped him low again. With each surge he held his body taut to buoy himself at the tunnel's centre. In between, he put his head down and swam straight ahead in long strokes.

At one of the honeycomb junctions, a strong wave flung him against the side of the tunnel. He hit his head, but not hard. Pushing off the wall with his good foot, Ambrose swam until all his breath was gone. Gasping at the surface, he almost cried when he saw he had made it past the entrance of the tunnel and into the wide mouth of the cave. The incoming waves made it difficult, but he felt more confident that he could make it. Thrusting himself forward, he felt the backward drag, and forward he pushed again.

At the entrance of the cave, he reached for the rock that would set him upon dry land. A chill ran up his legs as something sleek touched his foot. Water moved in its wake. Ambrose went rigid, his blood curdling. A moment later he felt it again – a muscular presence that unfurled itself as his limbs recoiled. His eyes darted all around, searching the foaming sea. Then, a small distance away, he saw the snaking form flick upward, and down again. His heart seemed to fall to the pit of his stomach, burning there, as he floated above the jaws of death.

Next thing he knew was the slimy clench of the serpent's coils around his ankle. He yanked at his foot, but its grip was strong. Splashing furiously, Ambrose's screams echoed in the waterlogged cave before the roiling silence of submersion. He was close – so close – to the rocks, and he fought desperately to break free.

Ambrose saw it happening but was powerless to stop it. The wave hurled him upwards and brought him down, striking his skull. Dizzied and disoriented, the creature dragged his body into open sea. Southward and west it went, toward nothingness, and on into endless ocean.

The sun kissed his eyes painfully, the only witness to his fate.

47

AMBROSE

Fourteen Years After The Fire

AMBROSE FELT A WINCING PAIN above his ear. The tide sucked at his legs as he opened his eyes to dirt-scudded sand; to broken barnacle shells lost in a watery swirl. He swallowed painfully, his throat raw with sea ash. Ambrose coughed salt water from his mouth. The sky was a mottled bouquet of pinks and purples that made him want to retch again. He closed his eyes and breathed deeply hearing the caw of faraway birds.

When he was able to sit, he checked his injuries. His foot had a deep gash in it, but it had been washed clean by the sea. The wound was now concealed beneath a flap of skin that he lifted gingerly, sucking his teeth at the sting. He touched his fingers to the throbbing welt near his temple. Remembering the creature, Ambrose shuffled backward, wanting to get as far from the shore as he could.

At his back, the setting sun crouched behind leafless trees. Before him, in the distance, was the western coast of Avishae. He was on some kind of islet, but it was very small indeed. Surveying the rocks above him, he judged they would remain aloft of even the highest tide, but there would be little to sustain him here.

A grave feeling fell upon him then, and he glared darkly at the faraway shore. Whatever had tried to take him would still be out there. In his mind flashed the luminous eye he had seen between the rocks of the Bay. His mind raced. It was Siatka. It had to be. The Mother – *salt one, keeper of dreams*. A chill ran through him.

Watching the current, he wondered if he could swim back without arousing Her notice. He'd swum the Bay of Knives a hundred times without incident. Ambrose regarded his ankle where She had clung to him like a vice. It did look a little bruised. He would need to find shelter for the night. Tearing a strip off his tunic, he bandaged his foot and hobbled to higher ground. Above, he spied an alcove in the rock that looked to be a good place to sleep, and set about inspecting the vegetation of the lower slopes for anything he might eat.

As dusk began to fall, he built a fire, and drank the small quantity of water left in the skin he kept tied to his belt. He felt the lump of rock in his pocket, and eased it free. It was black and rough but as he turned it over, it glimmered green and purple and red in the firelight. Taking out his knife, he chipped carefully at its surface.

His stomach lurched and he felt as if the stone were a coiled creature he was prizing apart. His hands grew hot and he felt a wet, glistening feeling, of blood melting out of the stone, trickling down his hands. He stopped, blinking to steady himself. His hands were clean. Taking up the rock again, he chiselled a line in the stone that revealed something luminous and shining beneath.

For hours he worked at it, caressing and smoothing, sloughing away its skin. His tools were not fine, but some of the impure deposits that surrounded it were coming away. Though the firelight was dim, he could not stop looking at the stone. A gleam of purple would catch his eye and lead him so far, before disappearing into blackness. He turned the stone over, searching the other side where a turquoise star winked, or an orange flower burned. The stars watched over his shoulder in a shawl of white. They wanted the stone. They wanted it and he felt he must hide it inside himself, sink it into his heart, take it into his mouth.

Then he thought to touch it to the three points, and brought it to his forehead. He opened his inner eye wider and more desperately

255

than he ever had before, wanting to merge with it, to feel it speak inside his mind. The stone shook, almost imperceptibly, vibrating in its elements and beginning to sing. At first, the voice was small and all was black within, but then it began to blossom. In the distant reaches, Ambrose felt the serpent's eye open, and the winged one gaze down upon him, white moonlight shining on His wings.

As the stone gathered him into a single point, he heard himself breathing – a heavy sighing that informed him of the labour of his heart. Some part of him was scared, but the rest of him conspired to want more, to see if his heart could trill like a songbird, to see if he could fly. Groaning, he pushed the stone upward to his crown, where it cascaded golden light. It burned brightly and his chest swelled in an outpouring of bliss so absolute that he might have cried out, but 'he' was no longer there. He had no mouth or hands, he was a vessel and he was a stone, he was flanked by serpent and by bird, and then – he *knew* their names. SIATKA. Yes, She who had carried him across the waves – and, KSHIDOL, He was also there, above. Ambrose wept tears of terrible joy; the joy of an orphan reunited with his mother and father, at long last.

A calm fell upon him and Ambrose shifted the stone to the back of his head, bowing low between his knees. He came back to himself, but was possessed by a peculiar clarity, as if he could see through to the centre of the earth and know everything between. He cast his eyes to Avishae, gazing at the dark shape of his homeland. Between the forms of things, he began to notice flecks of light, seen both within his mind, and also out there, beyond him. He felt the little voices of those who lay dreaming. He should have thought it impossible, but they were – they were dreaming! Little fragments of blinding stone floated upon the surface, but below them was a stream of silver light, a Great Stream. He smiled, wondering at the rhythms he perceived, their innermost voices interweaving and becoming a many-texture. He could even hear the lifespray of the mainland. A dust of voices, floating on the wind from Brivia and Lindesal, from beyond black mountains.

Ambrose laughed. Joyfully, knowing without any doubt that Mother Siatka would return him safely home. He knew The Father watched over him as he slept and that they would protect him as long as he held the stone. Anything was possible now, for all the doors were open. Smiling, he lay, with the stone pressed to his heart. The stars stared down at him – jealously, hungrily, and powerless in their distance – and Ambrose stared back.

48

AMBROSE

Fourteen Years After The Fire

THERE WAS A WOMAN BEFORE HIM, wholly naked, arched of back, Her head slowly turning. Her neck, once craned, twisted, lowered, and kept lowering, eyes hot as Her throat slunk along the ground, plunging Her black, legless body into darkness. There was a sigh, of breathing tides, of weightless volition as She took the whole of the ocean into Her mouth. All liquid everywhere clung to itself, converged, and was Siatka.

Then there was a man, whose flesh was bare to the radiant sun. Down, He looked, from an unimaginable height. His shoulders broadened, His mouth hardening, and with a neck now serpentine, He cast himself upon the air, drawn down to the earth. His shoulders hissed with the breath of feathers sprouting. A clustering, shadowy sound. The sound was His name, an interior whisper... Kshidol. And His canopy was vast.

Ambrose awoke to the perfect clarity of morning. When he sat up, his back was straight and before him was a manageable swim. Though when he looked down at the stone clutched in his hand, he wondered how he could hope to conceal it. Would it speak to others as it had spoken to him?

Reaching for his Meridian, Ambrose balanced the three pieces of blinding stone to cover it. He closed his eyes, and felt for its liquid voice. The blinding stone dimmed its qualities somewhat, but he would need to find more if he was to keep it from notice.

The cave where he had slept was made of blinding stone, but it had grown dull in the sunlight and there was better to be found at the shore. In the low water he crouched, chipping and prising until he had what he needed. Laying his tunic flat upon the sand, Ambrose arranged a layer of blinding stone fragments, placing the stone-of-secret-colours atop them. Carefully, he wrapped it, surrounding the beautiful one in scales of nothingness.

He swaddled the bundle, holding it close to his heart. Though it had grown quiet, still it coursed with life. Knotting the cloth to his belt, Ambrose strode into the water and dove down, casting arm over arm, kicking through the waves, toward home.

The tide determined the place where he landed. The little beach was high on the west coast, and its shore rose in a lazy incline where bellflowers bloomed among spiked leaves. With each dripping step, trees came to cover him, concealing his passing as he entered the forest. Sand became rock, rock gave way to earth, and shadow ferns unravelled, keeping low to the ground.

He was not surprised to hear the distant chatter of human voices, or to smell the roasting of meat. He would pass through the Raeburn camp, if only to change his clothes, but he could not take the stone in there. All the trees looked self-same here. They replicated, with little variety, as far as the eye could see. Eventually, a fallen log caught his gaze. He ventured there, treading softly so as not to leave the mark of his steps.

Stay here, he said to the stone, placing it deep in the hollow. He felt that it liked the darkness, and promised he would soon return. After passing some distance, he arrived at the camp where Rowan was on lookout.

"What happened to you?" Rowan laughed at the sight of him.

Ambrose had to concentrate so his exhilaration would not show, but it was difficult. He laughed. "She was sweet, at first, but then she stole my shirt and has gone to sell my Meridian to the highest bidder."

Rowan frowned with amusement. "Nice girl."

Ambrose pushed through the gate as Rowan climbed down from his perch. "Have you got any clothes I can borrow?" Ambrose asked quickly.

"Sure," he said, "do you need some balm for those scratches?" noticing the marks on his shoulders.

"Nah, salt water does the trick." Ambrose said, walking quickly.

"The perils of sea mining, ey?"

Rowan led Ambrose to his cabin and rustled through a trunk in the corner before pulling out a dark green tunic edged in brown.

"Thanks," Ambrose said, throwing it on. "Do you have any shoes?"

Rowan looked at his feet and after shifting several boxes around, produced a pair of worn lace-up sandals.

He regarded them dubiously, but then gave Rowan a wide smile. "Perfect," Ambrose said, sitting down to put them on. Ambrose eased the first shoe over his injured foot, then started on the second.

Rowan opened his mouth to speak, but Ambrose was already out the door.

Outside, Ambrose surveyed the camp, finally spotting his grandfather leaning on a pitchfork, talking to Ma Bet.

Ambrose made his way over, but when his grandfather looked up, he stepped back in surprise. "Ho! What is this? An interesting change, Ambrose. Has your sister inspired you to find a new tailor?"

Ma Bet cackled.

Ambrose puffed his chest, his hands on his hips. "You laugh, but I have caught the attentions of a fine woman, who is well pleased by the work of my new tailor." He felt a little dizzy, and wondered if they noticed his strange humour.

His grandfather raised an eyebrow then turned to Ma Bet. "Thank you for your generosity this morning. I must go and speak with my grandson."

The two of them walked purposefully toward the tent, and when they were inside, his grandfather came to sit, brushing piles of ash away from tender coals.

"Grandfather. I want to ask you something," Ambrose began.

"What is that, Ambrose?" his grandfather said gruffly. He never liked it when Ambrose started off with questions.

"The story you told me about the eye of Velspar, that is hidden in the earth. Did someone actually write it down?" Ambrose fought to keep the agitation from his voice.

His grandfather shook his head. "Well, Skalen Karasek, of course. Have you a concussion, dear boy?"

It was a joke, but Ambrose felt his grandfather's eyes linger on the wound at his temple, only partially obscured by his curls.

"Did he say anything more about it?" Ambrose said.

His grandfather reached behind him for the Alma bowl. Ambrose fortified the walls of his mind as his grandfather crumbled Alma flowers in his palm.

"You don't have to do that," Ambrose said, betraying his annoyance. "Can't you just tell me?"

His grandfather ignored him.

"Why can't you simply answer a question when it is asked?" Ambrose said.

Wrinkled hands moved slowly over the coals.

Ambrose took a sharp breath, but it did not freshen his mind. Against his will, the breath entered, caressing his throat, his lungs, his heart, and every tiny vein with smoked flowers. Soon afterward, Ambrose realised he was being impetuous. The smoke told him how lovely it was to be calm, to be kind to this old man who was blood of his blood.

"I am sorry, Grandfather. I should not have spoken to you that way."

"Ambrose, you are a Raeburn. We Raeburns are not known for tiptoeing around. If you want to know about the eye of Velspar, I will tell you, but you cannot gobble up such knowledge like a pig at the trough."

His grandfather turned and opened a chest that contained

261

leather-bound books of different shades and sizes. Some looked to be very old.

Ambrose peered into the chest as his grandfather closed it, holding a single book in his hand.

"A dear friend of mine, Intercessor Camis, asked me to safeguard these books. He was a man of great foresight, and he entrusted these to me the year before it happened." His grandfather passed his hand across the cover as if its words might pass directly into his mind without him ever opening it.

Ambrose leaned forward, wanting to snatch up the book and read its contents for himself.

"This one was written by Intercessor Janek. He was born in Brivia but settled in Avishae toward the end of his life." Finally, his grandfather met his eyes. "There are no books in Velspar that will tell you what happened in the beginning, the meaning of things, or how things will progress. The Intercessors devoted themselves to the task of navigating the connective tissue of spirit. They had visions. You and I can see something of what they saw if we breathe the Alma, and if we take time to find the quiet place within. You cannot expect to understand another's vision without first sinking into vision yourself. And even then, you may miss its subtle qualities. You may twist it to your own purposes," his grandfather said, the resonance of his words deep and musical.

Ambrose nodded. "I understand this, Grandfather."

"Very well." He leaned back, smoothing the pages open until he found what he was looking for.

"He speaks about trees and a lost maiden for a little while..." then placing his finger halfway down the page, he read aloud:

"*Veiled Eye, Eye of Stone,*
Living Stone, of Velspar.
Voices Buried in the Earth
Waking, Voyant, Heralding."

He stopped and looked up.

Ambrose waited for him to continue, but instead he closed the book, returning it to the chest.

"Is that it?" Ambrose said, disbelieving.

"You tell me." His grandfather's ashen eyes bore into him, gathering charge like an oncoming storm.

The hairs prickled on the back of Ambrose's neck, and he felt suddenly afraid. *He knows*, Ambrose thought with mounting terror. He stood abruptly. "Thank you, Grandfather. I will think upon these words."

"You will not stay?" his grandfather called after him.

"I really need to get back. But I will visit again soon." Ambrose gave him a smile and exited the tent. He felt sick.

Rowan still sat in the watch hold, hunched over and almost asleep.

"Rowan!" Ambrose called.

His friend perked up when he saw him. "Are you leaving already?"

"I need to get back, I promised Zohar I would help her with something. Do you have any spare Meridians about? I lost mine and I can't return home uncovered," Ambrose said.

"I thought you were joking about the Meridian, but yes, I can find one for you," Rowan said, knitting his serious brows.

Rowan went to the end of the Meridian row where a roughly weathered band hung upon its hook. Rowan reached for it but hesitated before picking it up. "This belonged to Arthur," he said, passing it to Ambrose reluctantly.

Ambrose didn't want to admit that he had no idea who Arthur was.

"I will take care of it," Ambrose said, holding it in his hand.

Rowan opened the gates and waved him goodbye. Ambrose walked a good distance before putting on the dead man's Meridian, shuddering slightly as he did. Then taking an elaborate detour, he looped back around to retrieve the stone.

Peeking inside its wrappings, he touched its dark, luminous surface. He considered Intercessor Janek's vision. There were voices buried in the earth, he thought, and the veiled eye had opened.

"Voyant stone," he whispered, and wrapped it once more.

49

WALDEMAR

Fourteen Years After The Fire

THOUGH I ENTERED MY HOMELAND full of fear, we have already encountered the kindness of the faithful. And in their eyes, I find my purpose once more. Of our recent travels, I will tell you all, for I know not where my path will end, and I pray that whoever reads these words will carry on this holy mission.

We had not journeyed far when a peasant woman approached. She gave us water, and a meal of rich stew. She knew me, and I recalled her face from long ago. She told us how we might find our way without rousing the Guard.

We sat around her table as she wept. The Maglorean Guard had executed her husband last spring and her tired hands could draw little sustenance from the earth. Velspar was cursed. The women were not fruitful, she said, and those who were born in Brivia succumbed before they learned to walk. It was like the old times before the Battle of Jokvour.

We took her to the barn, where we would not be disturbed, and offered her Intercession. To see her spirit cleansed, and the detritus that was upon her lift away, was a joy to behold.

On the road, we met two orphans. We told them we were travellers bound for Avishae. They warned us of taking shelter in Thrale Forest for we would surely encounter Sidney Karasek, who had gone mad.

We went to the place they warned us about. All three of us felt his presence in the woods. The tormented one whose soul cried out, unrestrained. When we found him, I saw him as he was when he was a child. He had come to me for Intercession more than once. The last time, to rid his heart of jealousy, so that he might love his brother once more. In his eyes I saw that boy of twelve, though now he was a man of middle age, dirty and unkempt, his body etched with scars.

I showed myself and bid my companions to wait behind. Sidney thought I was a shade, a spectre of vision. I removed my Meridian and reached out to him in Intercession. I felt within his mind, where Andsen stood above him, heel to his neck, calling him 'betrayer'. Emryl and Medard wavered ghostly behind, doing nothing to restrain their eldest son.

As I drew the poison out of him, the vision began to fade. Then he sat with us, and told us his story. I had not dared hope the Karasek line remained unbroken. I saw that Sidney could be saved, and that he had the power to save others. And so we confided in him our plans.

Amand spoke to him long into the night, and learned a great many things. Illiam Greslet, son of Olinda and Jemryn, came often to the forest and left food for Sidney. The Regents continued to stay their knife even though Sidney shunned the Meridian and spoke the sacred words aloud. Illiam had travelled to Avishae. The Skalens there would answer for their crimes, yet hope revived in me when I learned the Raeburns still lived. But for Rebekah, their wayward daughter, the Raeburns were people of faith.

I can see before us the path we must take. We are gathering souls, and there are more of the faithful here than I dared dream.

I know now that when our Meridians have been smashed underfoot – when the Alma re-binds us, and our red thoughts dissipate like dew in the morning sun – then the Stream will shine, and the children will return to Velspar.

INTERCESSOR WALDEMAR RASMUS OF BRIVIA, 714.

50

SYBILLA

Fourteen Years After The Fire

Sybilla picked a burr from her skirt. Gavril sat beside her.

Lilwenn and Edlin Greslet were playing by the fire. Lilwenn, the eldest, was six. She picked a card from the pack and placed it down upon the floor where they sat.

"Guess," she said, and leaned back, pointing her bare toes toward the hearth.

Edlin, a soft-faced boy of four, thought very hard, his eyes scanning the roof of his mind for clues.

"The Hare?" he asked, uncertain.

Lilwenn laughed with glee, wrinkling her nose. "Guess again."

The boy got the card wrong four more times before he gave up. "What was it then?"

"The Fish!" she cried, passing him the pack, for it was his turn now.

Gavril squeezed Sybilla's hand, and it was only then that she noticed Inry standing in the doorway.

"Such a simple game, but they do love it," Inry said, holding her arms about her as if she longed to embrace them.

Domhnall appeared beside her. "Greetings Sybilla! And Gavril, good to see you again."

Domhnall had waxed fat over the years, enjoying the comforts of home while his guardsmen attended to matters beyond the Skalens' House. Sybilla had not been able to persuade the Greslets to visit Vaelnyr since Inry had first discovered she was with child. With a glass of wine always close at hand, the hunger in Domhnall's eyes had dimmed, such that Sybilla could no longer be certain of his priorities.

He crept behind Edlin to discover the card that he was holding. The little boy looked annoyed and shadowed his card with his shoulder. Lilwenn checked her father's expression excitedly, trying to guess the clue he was giving her. He got onto his hands and knees, and swayed from side to side, his mouth sagging, his eyes blinking lazily.

"The Cow!" she shouted, clapping.

Edlin nodded dejectedly as Domhnall picked up his little girl and spun her around and around. Edlin slapped the cards one on top of the other, giving her a sour look.

"Off to bed now children," Inry said gently.

She smiled at Sybilla but it was doubtful whether Inry placed any real importance on their scheduled discussion.

Two Attendants appeared at the door and gathered the reluctant children out of the room.

Domhnall sat himself at the head of the table, the cushion letting out a puff of air at his sudden weight. He reached for the decanter, slopping wine into four glasses. Raising his own, he made a toast. "To the bounty of Velspar! May we live richly and well, in peace and unity." When he smiled, his ruddy cheeks shone, and at first gulp he had finished half the glass.

"Well said," Sybilla replied, holding up her glass before putting it to her lips.

"I understand you have some important matters to discuss?" Inry said.

Inry may have settled into motherhood, but she still aspired to be a Skalen of fine standing. She pursed her lips prettily as her husband slumped back in his chair.

"Thank you Inry and Domhnall for receiving us. I wish to ask your opinion of the situation in Brivia," Sybilla said.

"Situation?" Domhnall frowned.

Sybilla patted Gavril's knee, urging him to speak.

"Skalen, there are rumours that Sidney Karasek plans to stir rebellion against the Council of Skalens," Gavril said.

Domhnall's head jerked back. "No. What madness is this? My sister Olinda keeps me informed of affairs in Brivia, and writes to me every season. Sidney Karasek is an outcast of his own choosing. He poses no threat to the Council."

Gavril's face was impassive. "I understand it has been a while since you last visited Brivia?"

"A while?" Domhnall said, heat entering his voice.

Inry stood abruptly to refill everyone's glasses.

Sybilla was not in the mood for games. "Domhnall, we know quite well that you have not been to Brivia for more than six years. I understand you place great trust in your sister, but is it not possible there is something happening there she may have missed?"

Domhnall took another long sip of his wine, glaring into its scarlet depths. "Shall I have him executed?" he asked without looking up.

Sybilla sighed, knowing that he spoke in jest. "Sidney is one man. But if he sows hope in Brivia... if he confuses his loyalties, then we should be ready to act." She leaned toward him. "I want you to make sure the Maglorean Guard has not been corrupted." Sybilla held his gaze and Gavril sat straight-backed and still.

Domhnall's face purpled and Inry glanced from him to their guests in alarm as her husband leered drunkenly at Gavril. "And what of the Vaelnyri Guard? I hear they are a lusty bunch. That they indulge their every desire. Not like the old days, oh no." He laughed, liking his retort, but Inry had gone deathly pale.

Sybilla dug her fingernails into Gavril's hand to stop him from shearing the boor's head from his shoulders. Taking a deep breath, she calmed herself. Of course, Gavril would do nothing of the sort. She focused on the tranquil weight of her Meridian and came to stand. Gavril and Inry joined her a moment later, but Domhnall remained in his chair.

Sybilla looked down at him. "If we turn a blind eye to this, lives will be lost." At this, Sybilla gave Inry a pointed look, and the woman inclined her head, knowing that she spoke of the children.

"I thank you for bringing these rumours to our attention. Be assured that we will do what is required to maintain peace in Velspar," Inry said as she led them to the door. "Your rooms have been made ready–"

"That will not be necessary, Skalen," Sybilla said. "We will return to Vaelnyr directly. We have a carriage awaiting us outside."

"Very well." Inry smiled as she escorted them to the hall. "Next time you visit, you must stay longer."

Sybilla mirrored Inry's show of graciousness. "Thank you, Inry. And please thank Domhnall for his hospitality and the wine."

Inry giggled uncertainly. Only Domhnall had finished his glass.

Just then, two members of the Guard appeared to escort them to their carriage and the unfortunate exchange was ended.

When the carriage door closed and the cloy of lilies had passed from the air, Sybilla caught Gavril's gaze. She longed to fall into his arms, but the weight of the task before them loomed darkly in her mind. If Domhnall did not put things in order, then all of the Southlands would be in doubt. A heavy weight fell upon her chest. A feeling that came to her often these days. It was the weight of knowing that after all she had done, it had not been enough.

If Brivia had turned, then Avishae would be next. The Regents of Lindesal were an unknown quantity and would likely retreat to Seltsland and Nothelm, from whence they hailed. Sybilla could not do it again. She would not survive it. She was weary of hot words and blood, of smoking pits and raining ash. Of the endless lists of red deeds, and the smell of meat in the air. As the carriage drew them down the track, she felt that she was being wound on a reel toward some terrible fate. She leaned her head on Gavril's shoulder and he put his arm around her. At least this time, she would not face the darkness alone.

The carriage did not pass into Vaelnyr but took the south road at the fork. Through the night they clattered on beneath the silent mountains of Jokvour. The previous night they had camped in the forest rather than risk one of the inns on the Nanthe's east bank. Gavril assured her their Vaelnyri escort had not informed Peran of the second part of their mission. Still, she kept her eyes away from them, afraid of testing the oaths of secrecy they had made to Gavril in her name.

When Thrale Forest became visible in the distance, Sybilla and Gavril changed into peasant's clothes. Sybilla removed her cloak and Skalens' Star, swathing herself in a rough grey robe. Gavril unfastened the gilt buttons of his crimson vest, swapping his Vaelnyri sword for an iron blade bound with black leather at the hilt.

Just before they reached the Brivian border, the carriage stopped, and they stepped out into the mauve light of dawn. The Vaelnyri guards clapped the door shut and bid them farewell.

Gavril surveyed the hooded figure before him, and gave her an odd look.

"Good day sir, what may I call you?" Sybilla said with a curtsey.

Gavril looked about him, thinking, and then bowed. "Hamil, Miss, and what may I call you?"

Sybilla paused, smoothing her robe, and stretching out her hands. "Cecily."

Catching her around the waist she laughed as she never did. "Hamil and Cecily," he said, swinging her hand as they walked.

She looked into his eyes, which were Hamil's now – of course – and Miss Cecily skipped her feet. "Hamil and Cecily," she said, and on they went to Brivia.

51

SYBILLA

Fourteen Years After The Fire

THE MOMENT OF LEVITY WAS BRIEF, as she knew it would be. They had journeyed but an hour when they were spotted by a pair of guards, who signalled for them to stop.

Gavril noticed them before Sybilla did and whispered under his breath. "Cecily, what is the nature of our acquaintance?"

Sybilla bit back the words that came to mind and tried to think sensibly. "You are my brother."

"We do not share resemblance for that," he said, a clip of annoyance in his tone. He stared across the yellow field. "Your father, Senton Durrel, is ill. He has sent us to find his friend, a Brivian man named Ansil, whom you met as a child. I, Hamil Smithson, accompany you as your escort. We hail from upper Vaelnyr, close to the Seltsland border," Gavril said coolly.

Sybilla nodded, sensing his silent rebuke, that she would not admit – even here – that they were lovers.

The crunching sound of their footsteps went on as the riders drew near, two guardsmen in Maglorean garb.

Sybilla took a slow breath.

"Good day," the first said. He was a slender, humourless man with a thin black beard. His companion idled behind him showing little interest in the exchange, and coughed heartily into his hand.

Sybilla bowed.

"Mornin', Guardsman!" Gavril's posture was looser than normal, his head tilted in subservience.

"What is your business on the Brivian Road?" the guard barked.

"Miss Cecily and I come in search of a man by the name of Ansil. I understand he lives near Thrale Forest," Gavril said.

The man turned to his associate. "Ansil? Do you know a man named Ansil?"

The other guard shook his head.

The first turned back to Gavril. "No one here by that name."

"That may well be, but we have journeyed here to honour the wishes of a dying man. Miss Cecily took a solemn oath, in Velspar's name," Gavril said.

There was a moment's silence, and Sybilla did not dare look up, lest one of them recognise her.

"Very well. Once we have checked your Meridians, you may proceed." The first guard clicked his tongue, signalling to the other with a jerk of his head.

Reluctantly, the second dismounted and ambled over to them. "Hoods off!" he called.

Sybilla grasped at the cloth, pushing it back with a clammy hand.

"On your knees, then," he said.

They knelt, and the guard approached Gavril, bending close to him, inspecting and tapping each stone. He tapped the one on Gavril's forehead sharply enough to make him flinch, which sent the man laughing, and from laugher came his retching cough.

Next, he inspected Sybilla's Meridian, starting at her neck, breathing his ale-fouled breath into her hair. She could feel him behind her as he smoothed her crown stone with his finger, tickling the small hairs atop her head. When he made his way to the front, Sybilla kept her eyes fixed on his boots, trying not to inhale. The bulge of his pants loomed before her. Overcome with revulsion, she fought the urge to rise and slap him across the face.

He leaned down, his whiskers almost touching her cheek,

glancing up and down between her averted eyes and the stone at her forehead. Then, his grubby finger touched the stone, pressing lightly for a moment before he stood.

"You pair have a fine set of Meridians," he said, spitting into the dust.

Getting to her feet, Sybilla brushed the dirt from her sleeve and glared at him.

The guard rocked on his heels, staring at her, seeming to consider his next move.

With a tilt of his head, the guard gestured to his partner and whistled for his horse. "On your way then, Miss Cecily," he smiled in mock civility.

Mounting his horse, the man coughed again and spat.

"Velspar's blessings upon you," the bearded one called, giving his stead a rousing kick.

Once the riders were at a distance, Gavril chanced to speak. "You acted like a noble woman back there. You need to give them the upper hand, to show that you fear them. I know guards like that and what it takes to get them off your back." Gavril's look was dark as he scanned the horizon for signs of movement, signs of danger.

Sybilla was not used to such degrading treatment, and dug her fingernails into her palms, irritated by his comment. She disagreed with him entirely.

They walked in silence and Sybilla stared at the path's vanishing point.

"We are here for Sidney Karasek, and that is all." Gavril spoke formally, as if they were in the council room.

"I have not forgotten the purpose of our mission," Sybilla said with a sudden feeling of dread. She wished Peran could have taken care of this himself – as he took care of everything – but Sidney's death was not a part of his larger plan.

Sidney would draw the traitors out into the open, Peran said. They would gather around him as Intercessors have always done, seeking out a weakened mind, a powerful title to subsume for their own purposes.

Every time they spoke of the Southlands in Council, he dismissed her concerns. He did not understand that the Purge had taken every-thing she had. If Sidney drew allies, if he consolidated the Brivian Regents to his cause, she could not bear the bloodshed that would follow.

No.

Sidney had already given himself over to madness. With Gavril's sword, she would put his spirit to rest.

"This will set things right," she said, her eyes drawn to the great expanse of green in the distance, the place where they were headed. Thrale Forest.

52

SYBILLA

Fourteen Years After The Fire

THEY REACHED THE NORTHERN TIP of Thrale Forest at sunset. Though the path was right there, they were forced to lie in a ditch by the road-side for more than half an hour, waiting for a band of guards to pass. Sybilla knew from their last visit that if they crossed any part of the winding track that led to the Skalens' House, they were bound to encounter people who would recognise them. Instead, they moved southward across unploughed pasture. The farms were abandoned, and they passed easily through rotted fence lines that had once sepa-rated arable land from the encroaching forest.

When they were beneath the canopy, Sybilla felt better protected. The branches hung heavy with leaves, their trunks twisted with climbers. Everywhere she looked, there were shadows in which to hide. They were losing light, and so made camp, sketching the trail they would take at dawn. They ate dried provisions, and huddled close, forgoing the comfort of fire.

"Where do you think he will be?" Sybilla whispered.

"My guess would be on the south side of the Skalens' House."

"He will not know our faces," Sybilla said, partly to assure herself of the fact.

"Nor will we know his, but I think we will recognise him."

Sybilla sighed and lay on her back, looking up at him. Gavril came in beside her, and she snuggled into his chest. She looked up, making out patches of sky beyond the canopy. There were little stars up there, peeking, winking, their glinting bodies moving this way and that.

She closed her eyes then, lulled by the warmth of him and the rhythm of his heart. Willing the trees to cover them, to keep them safe till morning.

But only part of her knew rest.

Hours later they awoke to a wet thump somewhere in the forest, to the sound of birds scattering. A damp mist hovered about the trees, which were themselves barely visible in the grey light.

They gathered their belongings and pressed on, making good time on the downward slope.

As the day elapsed, Sybilla forgot about Sidney. She marvelled at the purplish beetles trailing from tree hollows, the knotted vines bobbing with waxy leaves, the ragged golden moss, and branches adorned with lichen. The wilderness expanded around them in an endless sea of ferns, and she did not have the faintest idea which direction they were going.

"Gavril look!" Sybilla called, as a bird of red and blue cawed past.

He laughed, but held his finger to his lips, reminding her to be quiet.

Sybilla walked on, listening to the crunch and squelch of their boots, the pit-pat of water. She stood on a log and stumbled as it came apart underfoot. Gavril turned, but she waved him off, finding another way around.

The sunken earth was spotted with warty mushrooms, and by the time Sybilla had passed them, she looked up to find Gavril gone. She scanned the forest; felt a sickening tug, the shiver of space behind her. Moments later, a dark shape moved in the distance, and Sybilla widened her stride to catch up.

When she reached him, she was panting. "Oh, Gavril, I thought I'd lost you!"

He smiled and offered her some water. "I knew you were behind me, but I should have waited. I just wanted to see if this was the best way to get through."

There was a leaf in his hair, and she reached up to brush it away. Her hand lingered, traced his jaw. The green of his eyes took on a deeper hue and she pulled him closer. She could taste his breath on her tongue, sweet as river water.

Gavril brushed his lips against hers, and then kissed her. Sybilla's thighs flushed, and she drew him close, seeking the laces of his pants.

He pulled back, fighting to keep the smile from his face. "What is it about the forest that moves you so?"

"It is not the forest that moves me," she said, and kissed him again, the nervous energy that had been building in her, seeking release.

Gavril pulled her close, kissing her more deeply still, the pommel of his sword cold against her stomach.

Abruptly, he stopped, his eyes sharp as he scanned the trees behind her.

She stared up at his face, chastened by his alarm, by her reckless stupidity.

He exhaled, relaxing somewhat. "It must have been a bird. I thought I heard something."

"I'm sorry." Sybilla pressed her palms to her eyes, shaking her head. They were not in Atilan. This was not one of their escapes. They had come here, by stealth, to kill Sidney Karasek.

"We should be quiet now," he said.

They walked on, Sybilla keeping pace, her ears pricked for sounds, her eyes darting where branches cracked. She was only distantly aware of the passage of the sun but guessed they would make camp once they reached the area south of the Skalens' House.

As they ascended a small rise, Sybilla began to feel hot and dizzy. A high-pitched noise sounded in her ears and brightness clawed at the edge of her vision. Steadying herself against a nearby tree, she tried to calm her breath. A cramp seized her belly, and when it eased, she was struck by a thought that should have occurred to her by now.

Gavril appeared in front of her, eyes wide with concern. "Sybilla?"

"I'm fine. I just need to rest for a moment."

Gavril sat her down and touched his hand to her neck, checking her for fever. The moment passed, and they continued on, but Gavril insisted on holding her hand until he was satisfied she was not going to faint.

Sybilla tried to feel the comfort in the gesture, but her mind was too busy calculating days. Her thoughts settling on the unused linens that all women must keep ready to hand when on a journey such as this. At the realisation, the blood seemed to retreat from her limbs, leaving her weightless and unfettered. She felt the serpent's eye upon her. A feather falling fast. And all about her the drip-drop of water in the forest.

53

SYBILLA

Fourteen Years After The Fire

"THERE HE IS," Gavril breathed.

Sybilla's heart thumped into the earth where she lay behind a low fern. Her eyes strained to see him more clearly. Was it him?

There was a man below. He moved silently among the trees, collecting things in a sack. At this distance, she could not tell if he wore the Meridian or not. He was tall, with long dark hair and a beard. His ragged clothes were loose, his pale feet bare.

The man disappeared into the abyss of a nearby cave.

Sybilla looked at Gavril, her mouth set, thinking.

When she did not speak, Gavril said, "He is alone. You wait here, Skalen."

Sybilla grasped his arm. "Wait. If we kill him now, we will not know who is helping him."

Gavril was not pleased. "If others come, I may not be able to fight them all. We may miss our chance."

"I need to know."

Gavril saw that this was a command and smoothed his face of emotion. "Yes, my Skalen." He looked about, searching for a better vantage point. "Stay close to the ground. We should move over there."

He pointed. "While he is inside, I will make a shelter of palms behind that rock."

They made slow progress in an effort to maintain their camouflage. If Sybilla was not so consumed by dread, she might have laughed at the sight of Gavril shifting the palms into place. He covered his body in broad leaves, shuffling along the ground with an expression of utmost seriousness.

Once they were safely tucked beneath their shelter, there was little to do but lay there, looking out. For the first time in years, she thought of Lucinda and the secret places they would find about the Skalens' House. How they had circled themselves in the dark drapes, listening to the Attendants chatter as they cleaned. She smiled sadly to herself.

Gavril stared at the cave's entrance and did not seem to notice her departure into memory. "Sleep now, Skalen," he said without turning his gaze. "You will need your strength for our return."

Sybilla squeezed his arm in thanks, and shuffled deeper, making a pillow of her satchel. The world spun when she closed her eyes and she knew that she was moments from sleep. She sought the scent of her sister's golden hair, her sparkling eyes in the darkness – remembering the two of them doubled over with silent laughter when the Attendants noticed the lumps along their parents' pillows. *What's this?* The older one had said, reaching her hand gingerly inside. *Rocks!*

Fingers dug urgently into her flesh. Sybilla opened her eyes wide, adjusting to darkness. Silently, Gavril pointed down the hill to where the man sat together with three others around a small fire. Sybilla stared at the figures, noticing their shabby dress, and yes – it was as she had suspected! They wore no Meridians.

One was tall, broad shouldered, and hunched in the neck – an old man. He prodded the fire and moved little, but spoke often, while the others listened. She strained to hear his words, but all she could make out was the depth of his voice, its sermonising tone. A plump woman with trailing grey hair meddled with the cooking pot, adjusting skewered meat about the flames. Sybilla squinted, finding something familiar in her motions, but did not think on it long, because – there he was. This time she was certain. Sidney Karasek, the mad Skalen of Brivia.

Another man moved about, traipsing in and out of the cave before coming to sit, facing her vantage point. His face was clear in the firelight. He wore no beard and his hair was cropped short, giving his broad face a youthful look, but the set of his features suggested he was about her age.

The man cast something into the fire and it flared briefly, before subsiding. Sybilla's eyes were riveted to him as he stared into the flames. The smell of their cooking made her mouth water, and she bit down on a strip of dried fruit, willing her stomach to accept the paltry offering. Then, she caught scent of the Alma. Taking a great breath of it, she turned to Gavril, eyebrows raised.

Gavril brought his steepled hands to his lips and frowned. Whispering, he said, "They will be more relaxed this way, and less likely to notice us."

Sybilla nodded but did not feel comforted. Her blood coursed in anger. What were they doing out here? Was this the serpent's nest – the band of traitors – that planned to move against her? She needed to know what they were talking about.

She met Gavril's eyes and tilted her head toward the black hearts and their fire. His face stiffened and he shook his head. He would not do this for her? What defence could they mount against a man of the Guard? Sybilla's throat tightened along with her fists.

He looked down, his brow furrowed. "Sybilla, I am yours to command, but let us first consider. If I kill them all, it will be with a blade, and it will not look like an accident. Are you ready for your will to be known? Do you know what it will mean for Velspar if you break allegiance with your own Head Guard?"

Sybilla's mind swam, feeling herself at the edge of a precipice. "Were you not always going to use the sword?" she said, to buy herself more time.

He exhaled in frustration. "I was to drown him in the river. It was to look like an accident."

She had forgotten this. "Yes, but we cannot let the others go free," she said, feeling the urgency of their task, afraid that if she looked away from the campfire, the three mysterious guests would vanish.

Gavril chewed his lip. "Let us wait until they are asleep. I will try to take Sidney without waking the others. And if they do wake, I will take them all."

Sybilla nodded, feeling a little sick even though she had finally gotten her way.

"We will need to hide the bodies," he said. "We should dig the hole while they are eating."

Sybilla nodded.

Carefully, Gavril removed the palm fronds, placing them near where he had picked them, so there would be no sign of their shelter. Then, moving at an excruciatingly slow pace, they crept northward, collecting stones to dig with, looking for a place to bury the rebellion before it had a chance to begin.

54

SYBILLA

Fourteen Years After The Fire

SYBILLA GRAZED THE DAMP EARTH with the sharp edge of a stone. Sweat trickled from her armpits, and her stockings were sodden. On Gavril's side, the grave was deeper, his muddied hands scooping the earth into a mound beside him. Their movements were smooth, their breath quiet, and so their progress was slow.

Her fingers found a root and with a snap she pulled it free. The leaves above them dripped, and after several hours they were both soaked to the skin. Sybilla's arms shook with fatigue and her senses grew dull as her body yearned for sleep.

Gavril must have noticed, for he came to sit beside her. She leaned into his chest, twining their dirt-encrusted hands together. The smoky smell of his skin filled her and her heart ached for him, knowing what he was about to do in her name.

"It is deep enough," he said.

It wasn't, but she was not about to argue.

"Have you any more food in your satchel?" Gavril said.

Sybilla pulled herself away to retrieve the pouch of shelled almonds she had saved for the morning. As she stood, she noticed a muffled glow over the rise, and wondered if she had become confused about the direction of the camp. But as she stared, she saw that the lights were moving. Sybilla dropped down behind the tree; her blood turned to acid.

Gavril scrambled in beside her.

She clutched his arm in the excruciating silence, and they waited.

They could hear footsteps now, drawing closer by the second. Gavril's hand moved to his sword, drawing it out with a low rasp.

Pass us by, she prayed.

"Sybilla Ladain! Show yourself!" The voice boomed from the shadows, impossibly close.

Sybilla pressed her back against the trunk of the tree, watching in horror as black figures materialised from the darkness.

How did they find her? She could not breathe and did not answer. Gavril had moved his body between her and the shadow men, as if he might make her invisible.

"Guardsman! Give her up!" the voice commanded.

Gavril remained where he was.

Torches fell to the wet earth but continued to hiss, the men's faces hideously underlit, their unsheathed blades glinting with reflected flame. She counted them. Six.

It all happened in a moment. Gavril charged, he hurt one of them, he was struck, the shadows grunting to the clatter of steel. There he was! Gavril's blade shone bloody. A gurgling cry–

A thick arm encircled Sybilla's neck from behind. She jabbed him in the ribs, but he did not buckle. Where was Gavril? She heard him cry out in pain, but the torches had gone out, and she could not even see which one he was.

The man that held her panted in her ear.

"Show us your true face," the voice said, and she felt her Meridian snap.

In a rush of sensation, she felt their desire. The many ways they wished to mangle her body even as they committed themselves to the civility of the sword.

They could see her, see within. She shrank back, too terrified to concentrate.

"Gavril!" she cried.

Before her, the clash of blades had ended. She watched the man's back, a man with the muscles of a bull, his fist thumping down, the sound of contact, the others holding something still – by outstretched arms – the black shadow of the man's back, the arm raised for another blow.

She panted, closed her eyes, "Gavril, no."

Gritting her teeth with defiance, she cast her spirit where all of them could see, she yearned for him, searched the bodies with her mind's eye.

Love gushed from her as his soft presence merged with hers, but his spirit was thin, and could not hold her.

She clung to him, his splayed consciousness, the screaming pulse that ran through him, the shock of his own weightlessness.

He was drifting, becoming lighter, misting...

A howl of agony sounded from her mouth. Her heart fled after him, but his will had slackened and the wind blew him elsewhere and on, away from her. He was among the trees! She chased him, and just like that, he slipped away and was nowhere.

Sybilla sobbed, hanging limply against the body that would take her, but not soon enough.

"Do it," she sobbed, "Do it, do it!" Her scream pierced the night, but nothing happened.

The shadow men dropped Gavril, kicked his body flat, and made their way to her. The voice repeated its command once more, and as it neared, she saw that it had a face.

"So," he said, looking her up and down. "You've come to Brivia, 'ey?"

He made to tilt her chin so she would meet his eyes, but she turned her neck to iron.

"The girl who killed the gods."

His smug expression changed suddenly. His eyes bulged as the blade entered his flesh. In the confusion of minds, Sybilla felt the dying man's knowledge of betrayal, and then another fell, slit from ear to ear. The arm about her throat tightened and she grew steadily faint, still following the dance of shadows, blood and groans, of missions failing, of brother turning against brother.

The one strangling her stiffened with a sharp strike to the head, and as he collapsed, she fell forward, his enormous bulk falling on top of her legs. She ripped herself free, stumbling as she ran, bodies writhing wetly on the ground.

The voices were growing dim, and as the last man died, the turncoat stood before her, his blade swinging like a pendulum. His Meridian was perfectly in place. She stared at him, unable to guess what he might do.

The man sniffed and returned his sword to its scabbard. "Peran sent me, Skalen. I will keep you safe on your journey to Nothelm."

"Nothelm?" she said numbly.

"Peran has secured safe passage."

"I don't understand..."

The man kept his distance and did not comfort her. "We must go now," he said flatly, and began to walk away.

"Wait!" she cried.

The man turned his head, but not his body.

"Gavril!" Her throat convulsed around his name.

She fell to her knees, and crawled to where he lay, putting her forehead to his. She took his broken face in her two hands, but hesitated then, feeling the horror of his lips. His eyes were glazed with death's ice, choking the river of his spirit, so it flowed no more.

"He is gone, Skalen. Let us move to safer ground."

55

SYBILLA

Fourteen Years After The Fire

Sybilla did not remember how she reached the boat. Moments blurred meaninglessly together. She walked, fell, scraped elbows and knees, juddered along in the back of wagons, among potatoes that thumped her face, and rolled off again.

The Meridian she had been given was poorly fashioned, and now, she supposed, she truly looked the commoner. The guard who escorted her cleaned the dirt from her body with the same cold industry as an Attendant would a chamber pot, but her nails were circled with grime.

How could they have laughed, but days ago, upon the road? Was it days? Hamil and Cecily... she could not stand it. Her escort had imparted whispered commands to the ship's captain and had gone northward on horseback. She could not be sure if they knew her, or whether she was to play peasant, so she averted her eyes, and spoke to no one.

Men were shouting, uncoiling the rope from the dock, setting muscle against the wind's tide as they pulled other ropes to stiffen the sail. Waves slapped against the boat, gathering foam. Sybilla pulled her cloak tighter around her and stared, moribund, into the swell.

The sea was a brackish green, bruised with patches of dark seaweed. It disgusted her and she wanted to throw up. She focused on the stone. It offered its particular brand of dullness, but was a tool fashioned for another – perhaps its original wearer was now dead.

And death was right there in the water. She could slump forward a little further, and fall, headlong, hands in her pockets and dissolve into nothingness. She had not allowed herself to think of the Stream since the fire. She dallied at the edge of the question now, wanting to dip her toes into that dreadful truth. She felt him go. She felt him dissipate and come apart. Was he gone?

She had flung herself toward him and felt him in his dying breath. Why had she not done so when her parents had burned? When her sister had cried out? Why was Peran always tearing her away from the people she loved?

Well, he could quash the rebellion himself. He had no need of her. She imagined him, Skalens' Star about his neck, holding Council. She felt suddenly breathless, squeezed between the ambitions of two men, one long dead, and one carrying on his legacy.

Without warning a stream of vomit surged from her mouth, splattering the boat's port-side. She remained there, watching the sea turn blue as clouds scudded past and were washed from the sky. The smell hit her occasionally, souring her guts, so she made her staggering way starboard. The crewmen drew back as she passed as if she was a contaminated thing.

Sybilla sat, this time, and watched the Brivian coast in its slow undulations. The unbroken stretch of green looked to her an unpeopled land, and she realised that she had never seen Velspar from this vantage. She knew the ways of river boats, and the passage to Avishae. The port-side view flashed through her mind and she felt the chill of endless ocean. The things it concealed.

Gavril's face came at the heels of that thought, and moments later, her mother's arms filled with wine-red roses. She stopped breathing as if this would cease the flow of images that emanated from some hot pool in her chest. Behind the milky blue above her loomed some eternal chasm, the place where spirits scattered. They called her to relinquish herself. For Gavril was nothing now, and so she must also be.

She felt a ghostly arm wrap around her neck; felt it squeeze. Blood tightened in her face, making her eyes swell like grapes. Rage pulsed within her, gathering charge until it cracked like a lightning bolt, and the arm was gone. She gasped for air. If she were to die, it would be by her own hand.

Still buzzing with energy, Sybilla stood and lifted her leg to cross the railing. Within seconds, two men were dragging her back down with rough hands. She screamed, thrashing as they stood away from her, looking down at their Skalen – or some madwoman – that they had been tasked to deliver to Nothelm.

Boots sounded on the boards, and an older man looked down on her. Sybilla turned her head away as the sun seared her eyes with its whiteness.

"She will have to be kept below until we come to dock." He spoke softly to the gathered men, but she heard him clearly enough.

Sybilla let them carry her as if her body were dead and she was just some lingering glimmer of consciousness, there to witness the finality of the pyre. They tied her wrists and ankles to the bed and tended to her body with clean cloths. She would wake for the burning, she thought, dizzied by memories, by screams and fire, as she closed her eyes to sleep.

56

SYBILLA

Fourteen Years After The Fire

A LITTLE GIRL SAT ON THE EDGE of a large chair, feet dangling. Her hair was short, her dark fringe cut straight. Dappled sunlight moved across her face. The child looked up, her eyes livid. Sybilla shook her head but could not quite hear her words of reproach. With some effort, she found a precise point just north of the girl's shining green eyes and the words became audible.

"How can you not know my name?" the child cried.

Sybilla did not understand the question. Could not form her own. She just stared at the girl, her posture forming a silent apology.

A loud thump awoke her as a wooden box fell from the shelf and the world tipped. With a rush, the room flattened, before teetering the other way. A man stood in the doorway, meeting her glance by accident. His face was pale, and he gripped the door frame as the boat continued its torturous game of see-saw.

She did not care what became of her body. But her spirit shook violently with fear. Sybilla's exhalation was guttural with rage. They must have given her a false Meridian made of some other stone. She felt for the cool silence, and found it, at the three points. It made no sense. How could she dream?

As her awareness of the room and her present situation dawned, small details sharpened around her. The man tasked with her well-being stared resolutely at the wall. She did not care to pull on her restraints, there was nowhere she wanted to be, no posture superior to the one she found herself in. But curiosity called, like hope's mirage. She closed her eyes and stilling her mind, listened for the girl, searching for her incredulous eyes.

Sybilla's breath became quiet, as if she held a sleeping bird. The girl was there once more, or, more precisely, her presence was there. Sybilla could not summon the figure from her dream, but something reminiscent of the girl was with her. Eventually Sybilla withdrew her awareness, returning to her own mind, her own thoughts. She counted the days, and found them falling still, far past the waxing of the moon. The thought trembled through her, lightly at first, a curious happening. But then she dragged her wrists against the ropes.

A mad laugh erupted from her throat as a creature bursting clumsily into flight. The laugh chugged on, rocking her chest, becoming wet with tears. Her mouth was a well glutted by rain, the whole world crashing down upon her in sweet, wet kisses, soaking the mattress, the belowdecks filling with water, until only her face remained above the rising lip of the flood.

She wanted to put her hand to her belly, but she knew what she would find. It was too late. And with dreadful certainty she recalled her face – the girl – how she resembled him. Oh Gavril.

And through gritted teeth she swore it, that this child was hers, a child of love, that would pay no tithe to Holy Ones. Her life would be different. She would be safe from it all.

A child of the Meridian.

57

WALDEMAR

Fourteen Years After The Fire

AROUND THE FIRE, *Sidney tells us of his dream. It returns, self-same and unchanging. He wants us to use Intercession to unlock its secrets, and so we listen.*

His mother, Emryl, reaches into the wet earth, and draws out a stone. She washes it in river water then holds it to the light. It is a black stone, of many colours.

Emryl's hair is long with wisdom. She takes the stone and draws it to her forehead. Her husband joins her, and they pray.

The world spins around them, Emryl's face thickening with bristles, Medard's hair flowing the length of his spine. Their fingers intertwine, lithe and furred; their chests flatten and swell with many breasts. Other parts lengthen and recede, seeds scatter the many wombs. A singular light emerges, hovering between them...

Amand is excited, Maeryn is troubled, Sidney is hungry for the scent of the dream.

"Sleep again, dear Brother," Amand says, "so I may see through your eyes." For in that shining stone, he sees the promise of the Eighth Gate, he sees his second chance.

Maeryn strips skins from the rabbits and does not speak.

Sidney is haggard and thin.

"My Skalen," I call him, and he shudders. "Heed my wisdom for I am your Intercessor.

We do not speak to the dead. Whatever their treasure, it is for Velspar to bestow.

We do not steal treasure from the dead.

In death there are no forms, only fragments. What glitters is but a lure.

The stars deceive, and so do the dead.

If you call to your mother, it is not she who will return.

It is said that those strong of will hold their forms.

That they pass quickly into death with eyes shut tight, so strong is their wish to return.

If you call to your mother, she will not be there."

(And, my dear brother Amand, neither will those treasured spirits that we have lost.)

"For in death, all are lost to mystery."

My Skalen stares at me with hollow eyes. His cheeks are dark with hunger.

"The Stream purifies spirit from earth, drawing like among like. The current is strong. There are no people in the Stream. But hear this, my Skalen, the dead see only silver threads. If you call them, they will come. They will be as shimmering fragments all mixed together. They come with many voices, to draw you near."

My Skalen stares into the fire. Amand turns the stone in his mind. Maeryn turns the rabbits on their spikes.

I hear death's roaring tide in my Skalen's ears, the stone's moaning call.

Emryl's tongue is poised at the back of her teeth. Her lips part. To tell my secret, perhaps. To tell him of the plans she set in motion.

I soothe the desire of his listening. I draw the redness out.

Listlessly, his shoulders slump.

My Skalen's eyes are heavy now.

INTERCESSOR WALDEMAR RASMUS OF BRIVIA, 714.

PART III

BRIGHT FLAME

58

ZOHAR

Fourteen Years After The Fire

ZOHAR STOOD AT THE PROW of the ship with the wind in her hair. Sun glittered on the water's surface as they made their way across the strait. Her heart faced Brivia, and the sight of Port Innes made her want to bounce up and down with excitement. Behind her stood twelve guards.

She could hardly believe she'd managed to convince her parents to let her go, but for all the reasons she gave them to account for her interest in the mainland, in her mind, the ship was taking her to Illiam. Following their first meeting, there had been a second, but they were not given a minute alone. Zohar and Ambrose had stood either side of their parents as Illiam recited figures from his scroll. She kept looking at him, trying to study his face without drawing attention. He was far less intimidating than she expected. He looked nervous, actually.

When the word *barley* left his lips, her palms grew damp, and she hid them among the folds of her skirt. He gave her a little bow of greeting, but it did not have the startling impression of his first farewell. Her father appointed Ambrose as his guide during that visit, and she burned to know the nature of their lengthy conversations.

She behaved. Made sure to give the impression her previous lapse in judgement had been an honest mistake. Of course, she would come to her parents with any change of plan that might arise during a diplomatic visit. She had learned her lesson.

When he returned to Brivia, Zohar felt the noise of her heart grow still. She busied herself with ordinary things, each day as unremarkable as the last. But out there was Illiam and she had to find a way to see him. Unexpectedly, it was Ma Bet who gave her the push. One idle day when Ambrose was off doing whatever Ambrose did, she sat by the old woman while she worked the loom. Zohar's thoughts skittered across the surface of her mind and she made no attempt to hide them.

"Brivia," Ma Bet intoned, giving the name fond resonance.

Zohar raised her hands in admission – for her guess was right.

Ma Bet looked into the middle distance. "You have not walked in Velspar until you have walked the seven gates of Thrale Forest. Until you have climbed the Aldberg Mountains and looked from there to Jokvour's black peaks. Until you have waded knee-deep in the eastern shoal pools, where the fish come to tickle your toes..."

Zohar raised an eyebrow. "You are merry today."

Ma Bet curled the last of the blue yarn into a neat ball before starting on the burgundy. "It was my home, Zohar. I did not grow up here. I miss it, and I do not know if I will ever see it again."

"But I thought you were a Raeburn," Zohar said, puzzled.

"I fell in love with a Raeburn. But he entered the Stream along with the others."

Zohar swallowed. She did not have to ask when.

"I am a bitter old woman now," Ma Bet said, squinting for effect. "But once I was young – like you – and I did not care for consequences. My parents forbid me from visiting Avishae, so I swam the strait and courted my dear Edward, emerging from the waves like a drowned rat."

Zohar laughed at the thought. "And you stayed here?"

"I stayed."

Zohar felt two questions tugging at her but did not wish to ask them.

"I did poorly by my parents, yes. That I do regret," Ma Bet prattled on.

Apparently, something had loosened her tongue and her manners besides.

"Do I wish I had entered the Stream alongside him?" Ma Bet said, peddling the loom. "I don't think the dead know anything of time. Your grandfather had a plan and he convinced me that it was possible – that things could go back to the way they were. Edward will know me when I cross. And he will forgive me," she said without looking up.

Zohar's hands curled into fists. "If I am not given the chance to speak the questions of my mind, you may as well whisper your answers into my dreams!"

Ma Bet smiled smugly. She liked playing witch.

As Zohar looked to the Brivian shore, she imagined a sea-drenched Ma Bet stumbling from the waves to declare her love to some tight-lipped Raeburn. Zohar kept her back to the guards, a smile playing at her lips. She breathed deep, catching the faint scent of the tannins that tinged the strait. White fisher birds plunged into the water, emerging victorious with their catch, and as they neared the coast, Zohar marvelled at the wilderness before her, the forest extending to the limits of her vision.

"Prepare to dock!" came the captain's call.

Zohar smoothed her skirts, wondering what Illiam would think of her ensemble. It differed greatly from what she had worn during his previous visits. Back then she had worn a tunic and skirts in the colours of her house, and a plain grey bodice, her hair flowing free in the manner of young girls. On this, her first journey to the mainland, Zohar wore twin braids threaded with silver. Her blue damask gown drew in neatly at the wrists, revealing the silk of her blouse in puffs along the sleeve. The neckline glittered with innumerable glass beads that trailed down in decorative curlicues to the fringe of her skirt.

It had taken Elspeth weeks to complete the embroidery alone. Together they studied books from the library, anything that described or pictured the mainland fashions. Though the books were old, Elspeth took inspiration from what she saw, creating styles that no one had yet seen. All the while, Zohar washed herself, emptied the chamber pot and made her own bed, bidding Elspeth to focus on her stitches. It was perhaps for this reason that her mother did not comment on the dress, though Zohar could tell from her expression that she thought it extravagant.

When the crewmen set down the gangplank and gathered her luggage, Zohar stood tall, walking with all the majesty she could muster. The guards, who were natives of Avishae, cast spurious glances to the thick forest towering behind a smattering of thatch huts. Five Brivian guards stood beside a string of carriages, transport for Zohar and her entourage. She tried to ignore their stifling seriousness as they exchanged greetings, passing them with a smile.

The best she received from the Brivian guardsmen was a tight squeeze of the lips. Upon second glance, she realised the one helping her into the carriage was a woman. She wore heavier armour than Zohar was used to seeing, and she flinched when she noticed the woman's left hand was missing a finger.

The guardswoman glared at her. "Now, Miss," she said, head inside the carriage, "before we depart, I must check your Meridian."

Zohar thought it was a joke and gave a nervous chuckle, but then recoiled as the hand reached in to touch the stone at Zohar's forehead with finger and thumb.

She smiled at Zohar's reaction. "Don't like that one 'ey? Bow your head, Miss, I will use the other."

Zohar bowed, her face in her skirt, where Elspeth's beadwork glittered primly. The guardswoman smelt of herbs, and though she frightened Zohar, her touch was gentle enough. When the woman reached the back of Zohar's neck, she paused, pinching the stone, drawing long deliberate breaths.

"There is a crack in the nape stone," she said so only Zohar could hear. The woman looked at Zohar, searching her eyes. "You must get it replaced as soon as possible. Do you understand?"

Zohar nodded eagerly, and was about to thank her, when she pushed herself out of the door, thumping the roof of the carriage with her fist.

"Move out!" she shouted, hopping from the step.

Zohar, somewhat shaken, resumed her seated position, touching her braids to check nothing had come loose. She fingered the nape stone but could find no crack. Her brother made this Meridian as a gift. She was under the impression he was a skilled craftsman. The silver embellishments had been added later and merely framed the stone. At the thought of her brother, Zohar's temper flared. Surely he wouldn't have done anything to ruin her trip? A litany of childhood pranks came to mind, but she did not think him capable of this. She tried to put it from her thoughts.

With a snap of the reins, the carriage lurched forward, heavy with the guards that sat on its outer ledges, front and back. A carriage travelled both before and after, filled entirely with guards, completing the chain of protection. From what? She wondered. She was not made to travel this way in Avishae. There was no one to ask, so she pretended Ma Bet sat beside her, telling her the names of the orange flowers that clung to the tree trunks, the uses of speckled mushrooms that she glimpsed on the forest floor. There were staghorns here, she noticed. They also grew north of the Raeburn camp, as Edith had shown her on one of their walks, but she had never seen so many in one place.

Abruptly, the carriage stopped, and after a minute of deep whispers, she caught the word – *snake*. She peered out the window but could not see what was happening. Then, there was a sharp clang of metal against rock, accompanied by a satisfied grunt.

"Carry on!"

The carriage wobbled as the men climbed back on top, and the horses trotted forward. Zohar watched the trees, daydreamed, dozed, and awoke to that same unchanging procession of green. They reached the waypoint at sundown, where a small company of guards were garrisoned. They presented simple fare, a porridge of grain and stewed meat that Zohar ate with caution. The guardswoman showed her to her room. It was tidy and secure, but Zohar kept herself high on the bed, considering the approximate thickness of snakes and whether they were likely to fit beneath the door.

She removed her finery, segment by segment, draping them so they would not touch the ground. Beneath rough blankets, she curled herself into a ball, drifting at the edge of sleep. The sound of dripping leaves and the scent of damp earth drew her near the surface, for these were not the sounds and smells of home. She looked out the window – it was dark. Over and over, she awoke and looked. Then, finally, the sun trickled through, drenched in green.

She dressed herself without too much difficulty, though the lace-work took some time to refasten. She stepped into the clearing, and set out for the Guard's mess, where she had eaten dinner the previous evening. Smoke rose from the chimney, so she knew she was not the first to rise. Zohar held her hand on the doorknob a moment before turning. Five sets of eyes roused to where she stood, guardsmen sitting about the fire eating breakfast.

Her presence caused several to remove their feet from adjacent chairs and offer her a formal greeting. One of the Brivian guards stirred the pot, and took the liberty of ladling her portion, placing it on the table. Zohar nodded silently and sat down to eat. When the door opened next, she saw the familiar faces of the Avishaen Guard and her shoulders relaxed. John came to whisper the plans of the day, and she nodded, reassuring him that all was in order.

The second day of travel was much like the first, but by this time, her excitement had subsided. After a terrible night's sleep, she closed her eyes, relaxing into the languorous rocking motion of the carriage. Sometime later, she jolted awake to find a patch of drool upon her blouse and blotted it anxiously as she tried to determine how far they had left to travel. Behind her, she glimpsed a gate but did not know if it was the first or the last. Bringing herself to attention, she practiced a smile and took a deep breath that extended her lungs upward and down about the confines of her corset. At the next gate, the carriage halted.

"Seventh gate!"

The carriage door burst open and Zohar was pleased to see that it was Elis, one of the more pleasant guards in her troop. He smiled, and though she avoided him in Avishae, here, he seemed a bosom friend.

Emerging from the carriage, Zohar took a moment to admire the steadfast form of the stone arch that was the seventh gate. Its surface was intricately carved, but she was not able to inspect it properly, as they ushered her on.

Zohar's skirt caught on damp leaves, and she hoped they would not have to walk for long. She was quickly distracted from her concerns by the eerie tranquillity of the place. The air was heavy with silence, and sunlight filtered down in soft shafts. The Skalens' House door was covered by a wrought iron gate, the House itself seeming to disappear into the forest, built as it was, of moss-furred stone. Two figures stood at the gate, and neither of them were Illiam. Her heart sank.

As she approached, the woman gave her a weary smile, her eyes darting quickly over her dress, as the man opened his hands in welcome.

"Miss Elshender, we are so pleased that you have come to Brivia. I am Jemryn, and this is Olinda, of the Greslet clan."

"Pleased to meet you," Zohar replied, falling short of anything else to say.

Olinda tipped her head in the direction of the guards. "You have brought a fine force with you, Miss Elshender. Are you expecting trouble?"

Zohar laughed with some embarrassment. "My parents. They have not visited the mainland for some time."

Olinda nodded, her expression unreadable. "Well, dear girl, you may have the entire East Wing. We have no other visitors, and it is just us, and our son, Illiam. Whom you have met, I understand?"

"Yes, my lady." Zohar cringed. "Forgive me – Regent Greslet."

Olinda laughed, and Jemryn feigned to scratch his forehead to hide his smirk.

Zohar's ears burned.

"Let us not speak in titles," Olinda said. "You are our guest, and we ourselves are guests in this land. We are fellow travellers, passing through Brivia. May I call you Zohar?"

Zohar nodded.

"Then you may call me Olinda. The guards will take you from

here. And you should know, we have some Attendants, but not many, and they go home at night. Consider what you will need before sun fall."

"Thank you, Olinda," she said haltingly, "and you, Jemryn."

They smiled and ushered a single Attendant to take Zohar and the Avishaen guardsmen to their quarters. Walking down the dimly lit hallway behind a young girl in a simple brown tunic, Zohar's majestic sky-blue gown seemed quite ridiculous. The other clothes she had packed were not much better, and she would have to make do by shedding the most ostentatious outer layer.

The girl before her stopped and opened the door. "This will be your room, Miss. I've set your bed, and wash basin. You shan't need a fire tonight, as it is warm this time of year. Should you need anything else, ring the bell before seven."

The girl spoke sweetly and Zohar was genuinely grateful for the small sanctuary she had prepared. "Thank you," Zohar said, and took the key.

John and Elis set her bags down in the room, bowing as they exited.

As Zohar locked the door behind her, she heard the girl introducing each guard to their separate quarters. She stopped listening after the third.

The room was humble indeed. She wondered what it was usually used for. The guest rooms in Avishae were at least twice the size, including couches, sitting chairs, an ornately carved poster bed, a full-length looking glass, drawers, wardrobe, fireplace and other comforts. This was a small, low-ceilinged room with a cot and only the basic amenities. The single chair that sat by the window was wooden and unupholstered. She sat in the creaking thing, noting that there was a handheld looking glass upon the chest of drawers, but no other mirrors.

She began the arduous task of undressing, feeling each loosened lace, and every freed clasp as a kind of humiliation. Brivia was not at all what she thought. Zohar would not find what she was looking for here. Then she thought of Illiam – who was probably abroad, doing something important – and how she would seem, dressed as she was, in this place. If he returned before her departure, that is.

Zohar lay on the bed in her undergarments and wondered if they would think it rude if she simply remained here till morning. She was sulking. It was pitiful, and she knew it. A Skalen would not sulk. She got up and laid her week's clothing upon the bed, arranging them to create an altogether different impression. She was lucky Elspeth invested so much time in lacework, as most of her dresses had removable sleeves or top-skirts. When she had finished, she felt better about things.

Adopting a pair of black stockings, a blouse, embroidered vest and underskirt, she appeared elegant without looking overdone. She rang the bell. Not long after, the Attendant knocked lightly on the door.

"Miss?"

Zohar opened it. "Yes, I wanted to ask, when will the–" she paused to correct herself, "will Olinda and Jemryn be taking their evening meal?"

"Dinner will be served in the dining room at seven. I will come to escort you there so you can be certain of your way."

"That would be most helpful, thank you."

Zohar returned to the dark room and, with nothing to do for the next hour, she opened the window as wide as it would go and stared out into the thickly clustered trees. Her thoughts wandered to Avishae, and Zohar lamented that Ambrose had lost his passion for the mainland. She would gladly have had Edith by her side, or even Ma Bet, over twelve unspeaking guards. This is how it would be. A singular adventure she could not share with anyone.

Zohar spotted movement below, and watched lazily as a man emerged from the trees. At first, she thought it was a guard, but he did not adopt the choreographed postures of patrol, walking instead with particular purpose, straight for the front door. She knew that short brown hair, and the set of his shoulders. It was Illiam. She almost squealed, and her pulse rose to a canter. Dinner was at seven.

~

Zohar was spinning with wine. She lay on the bed, pulling the covers up to her chin, trying to rehash the conversation. To recall the details that swirled about her mind. The girl – the Attendant – had taken her down after the others were seated. Olinda and Jemryn were there, of course, but she hardly saw them when she realised that Illiam sat at the table.

Illiam glanced at her briefly, offering a look of recognition, but nothing more. "Good evening, Miss Elshender," he said.

At that, Olinda interjected. "This is not a diplomatic mission, Illiam. Let us all call each other by our birth names."

Illiam squirmed at the reproach, but obliged and uttered her name.

Then there were questions, answers, small laughter and the passing of plates. She found Illiam's father, Jemryn, the easiest to converse with, and was relieved to answer his mundane queries about the landscape and industry of Avishae. Olinda was trying to figure her out, dangling questions that made her reveal things about herself. But to Zohar's disappointment, Illiam did not seem to share his mother's interest in her character. He looked distracted, and his laughter sometimes missed the mark, coming a second after it should, following the lead of the others.

But it wasn't all for naught. His finger had brushed hers as he passed the water decanter, and she was certain he noticed it too. That was toward the end when the food was gone and her blood was sweet with Alma wine. When finally Zohar drew the courage to pose a direct question, she asked Illiam about the workers from Avishae. Illiam answered her with yet more details about crops and transport, frowning into his glass as he spoke.

Nobody lingered when the Attendants came to take the plates just before the hour of nine. Zohar watched Illiam depart, still shocked by the experience of seeing him in his own home. She stood and made her way back to her room, turning the key in the lock.

There she lay, a light buzz in her ears, unable to keep the smile from her face. Zohar breathed deeply, recalling his particular scent, the set of his jaw, the way his cropped curls sat about his ear. He was real. And tomorrow he would be taking her on a tour of Thrale Forest. She could not wait.

59

ZOHAR

Fourteen Years After The Fire

ZOHAR STOOD AT THE FRONT of the Skalens' House smoothing the small hairs that had escaped her self-crafted bun, wishing she'd packed more pins. Already, her blouse was sagging from the humidity of the place. On the ground she noticed several iron stars, obscured by the leaf litter that covered the forest floor. Upon inspection, she saw that they were drains. Unlike her own home that sat high on the verge of a cliff, the Brivian House had been built in a gully of sorts, where the land sloped upward around it, tall trees smothering the building from all sides.

"I did not know you had an interest in irrigation, Zohar." Illiam's voice startled her.

"I didn't see these before," she said, lifting her head.

"The House was built at the place where Skalen Karasek was born. Without drains, it would be a swamp. Perhaps it didn't rain as much back then," Illiam said as he walked. "The horses are over here. I will show you some of the places I mentioned last night," he said, his tone brighter than it had been last evening.

Zohar hoped he would not ask her to recall such details, as she was sure none remained in her mind precisely as he'd spoken them.

The horse he brought out was a grey mare, and he passed her the reins, departing for his own horse after she was in position.

When he led off, they went along at a slow pace. There was no path, and the horses meandered about the densely clustered ferns as they made their way south.

"Can you remind me where we are going first?" Zohar asked, keeping a casual tone.

"There is a small camp nearby where your countrymen have been working. I am sure they will be pleased to see a familiar face."

Zohar had hoped she would have some time alone with him, but the day was still young. The horses veered west when they reached a small stream, and they followed it for a while. Apart from the stream, the forest looked the same in every direction and she made sure to steer her horse close to Illiam's. Her eyes dazzled at strange species of flowers with speckled markings and long stamens. She yelped every time the insects landed on her, such that Illiam could not help but laugh.

"You'll spook the horse if you keep that up," he said, looking behind.

She gave him a haughty look but felt a tickle on her neck and flicked her hands wildly about her head.

His back chugged with laughter and he shook his head, the white tail of his horse swishing.

Zohar's heart was warm, and as they rode, she tried to think of a less humiliating way to gain his attention. With one hand upon the reins, she dabbed at the perspiration on her face and neck.

"Here we are," Illiam said, sooner than she'd wished.

Zohar looked around but could only see a dark cave and a few hand tools strewn about the remains of a fire.

Hopping off his horse, Illiam extended his hand to help her down. Zohar was so distracted by the burning of his hand in hers that she could not form the words to ask him where 'here' was.

Keeping her hand in his, Illiam led her forward, toward the cave. He did not bother to tie the horses. Zohar felt a charge running through her entire body. Was he going to kiss her? He had hidden his feelings so well. *This is actually happening*, she thought in eager fright.

Zohar let out an involuntary scream as an old man's face loomed from the darkness.

Illiam's hand firmed around hers. "It's alright," Illiam said, but she did not believe him.

The man was not wearing a Meridian, and was smiling at her, advancing still. Around him, other faces emerged. All naked of their Meridians. There were five or six of them – seven. And then another joined them – *Guardsman Elis.*

Zohar stumbled, snatching her hand from Illiam's. Was this a test? She had not arranged for the cracked stone to be repaired as the guardswoman had instructed. Was she to order them all to return to the House to face execution? Her hands shook.

Elis looked at her, red-cheeked. "Zohar. You are among friends."

Zohar whirled around, expecting to find Guardsman John and the remains of her escort, swords drawn, to save her from the renegades. But the trees were silent and all about her the forest glowed a radiant green.

Backing toward her horse, Zohar realised she was so very far from home. Even if she could escape, where could she go? She looked at Illiam, not Elis. "I am not going in that cave."

"Of course," Illiam said, focusing on her in a way that made her mistrust and desire him at the same time. Turning to the old man, Illiam nodded.

"Join us!" the old man called, his formal Brivian accent noticeable at once.

Illiam stepped toward her. "Let us all sit down together, as friends, and say what needs to be said. I won't let anything happen to you."

But Zohar felt that something was happening to her already.

Illiam sat on a log, and Zohar perched at the far end. The others, who stared at her like the shy children of Haydentown, gathered quickly, and seated themselves. The old man positioned himself opposite and she knew he'd be the one to speak, for the others set their eyes upon the earth.

"Dear child," he said, "I am a friend of your grandfather's. All these years I thought that Landyn Raeburn was dead. I knew your grandmother, Addy, had passed, but that was before..." Staring sadly into her eyes, he searched for the words, but she was not about to come to his aid. "The killings," he said finally with a sigh.

"My name is Waldemar. Intercessor Waldemar Rasmus of Brivia."

Zohar's heart thumped, the forbidden title stark in the air.

"My companions, Intercessor Maeryn Rosemond of Vaelnyr and Intercessor Amand Angenet of Seltsland – we are the last of our kind," Waldemar said.

Zohar glanced guiltily at a round woman with long grey hair and a man her father's age with wide, clear eyes. Both of them smiled.

"This is Sidney Karasek. The rightful Skalen of Brivia." Waldemar gestured to a dark-haired man whose bare arms were criss-crossed with thin white scars.

"Elis is known to you, I trust," Waldemar went on.

Zohar looked past Elis to the next person, unable to meet his eyes.

"Our other companions are all members of the Brivian Guard – Vincent, Martin, Bryce." He pointed to each in turn. "The world you have known is not the world as it should be, my dear. We are a people divided. If we cannot attain unity, we are nothing. Velspar is the sacred heart to which we are all connected. I have come to understand your parents devoted their lives to its protection, to give you and your brother the ability to change what they could not." Waldemar clasped his hands, his face entreating.

Zohar's mind swam, nauseated by the lurid glow of too many ferns. "I'm sorry, you must be mistaken," she stammered.

"About your parents? No. There is no mistake," Waldemar said with absolute confidence.

Zohar had just enough time to turn sideways before she vomited. It came out red, a rich berry stench ribboned with bile.

Maeryn made to help her, but Zohar pulled back.

Elis then stood, walking to her and offering his hand. Zohar wanted to tell him to go away, that she was tired of being watched, of being spoken about in private. But who else could she turn to? Illiam would not look at her so sweetly after seeing her retch like that. She let Elis take her hand and once standing, he let go, keeping a respectful distance at her side.

When they were out of earshot, Zohar expected Elis to reveal the truth in urgent whispers: that he had been captured, and how they were to escape. But he didn't.

"This will be difficult for you to hear. But I will say it plainly in the hope that you will understand," Elis said.

She looked at him, amazed that this silent sentinel of her youth had a voice and thoughts of his own.

"When we received news of the fire of Vaelnyr, I was still in training. I had joined the Guard as a boy, under your grandparents, Armin and Gosia Elshender. Many in Avishae succumbed to the same illness that took them, and your father received his Skalens' Star with a heavy heart. Your mother did much to cheer him, and when you were born, it was a happy time. It is a great shame that you were too young then to remember, but I am sure you yourself recall when Ambrose was born?"

Zohar felt her cheek resting on her baby brother's bald head, singing a silly song in his ear as he giggled and squirmed. That she would never forget. Though it irritated her to hear Elis reciting her family history in such familiar terms, adding odd twists that did not marry with her understanding of things.

"After Vaelnyr, everything changed. Your mother was with child as you know..." Elis trailed off.

Zohar nodded curtly.

"Your parents were faced with an impossible choice. Avishae would be taken by force if they detracted. They could not protect the Intercessors. But they sacrificed them in order to protect you."

She stared at him, anger reaching a low simmer in her empty stomach.

Elis went on. "It was your mother who persuaded the Raeburns to live. She did not convince all of them, but praise Velspar, the tide is turning now."

"My parents are murderers. And so are you! You and the other guards, always standing around, watching. How do you live with yourselves? The Intercessors died at your hands!" Zohar breathed heavily, nausea staunching the bitter flow of her words.

Elis blinked and pursed his lips, not meeting her eyes. "You may never understand the choice we were faced with. The Intercessors knew what lay before them. They prepared themselves to enter the Stream."

Zohar rolled her eyes.

Before she could say anything more, Elis held up his hand bidding her to be silent. "Listen to me. Things are changing. Sybilla was here just two months ago. She came to Brivia with her guardsman, we do not know if she had discovered us or whether she was here for some other purpose, but we almost had her."

Elis took the shocked expression on Zohar's face as a question, and continued, "We had her surrounded, but one of the Brivian guards sworn to our cause turned on our men. Put her on a boat heading north." A bitter expression passed over his face. "It does not matter. We have people in the north. For now, we focus on the Guard. If we can organise forces from Avishae, Brivia and Lindesal, then we have a chance against Maglore. Without Maglore, Vaelnyr will lose its grip on the Southlands."

Zohar could hear the excitement in his voice but did not share it. And with a rush of cold dread, she realised he would only share such dangerous truths if he expected her to play a part.

"I want to return to Avishae," Zohar said firmly.

"I'm afraid that will not be possible," Elis said, in that irritating tone typical of the Guard.

"You are at my command, Guardsman!" Zohar snapped.

"I am at my Skalens' command. And your parents want you here."

"But what of my brother?" Zohar said, a lump rising in her throat.

"Your grandfather will take care of him," Elis said dismissively.

"I want to be with my brother! You can't keep me here!"

Her mind raced and she imagined swimming across the strait like Ma Bet, crawling bare knuckled through the forest until she found Edith at the altar. Edith would give her water and help her down to the camp. Her brother would be there, leaning on the fence, chatting with Rowan. She would tell him everything that had happened. They would stay there, together, in Baden Forest, and never go home.

313

60

AMBROSE

Fourteen Years After The Fire

AMBROSE KEPT THE VOYANT STONE hidden in the sea caves, close to the
spot he had first discovered it. He could not visit it often – that would
arouse suspicion – but part of his mind was always there, attuned to
its particular vibration.

He had fashioned a new Meridian, Arthur's now hanging on its
rightful hook on the Raeburn camp wall. Ambrose had selected
broad-planed blinding stone that left three wide apertures in the
leather once removed. It had taken him the better part of a year to
muster the courage to cut the stone.

Ambrose made his way to the cliff, reaching his arm over the
edge, finding the worn strap of his satchel looped round a tree root,
just where he had left it. Slinging his satchel across his body, he
climbed down, finding the cave where his other things were hidden.
Removing the blinding stones from his Meridian, Ambrose felt the
familiar presence of the voyant stones.

With sweating hands, he inserted the three painstakingly
polished fragments into his Meridian band. His hair was stiff
following his morning swim, and he tried in vain to part it at crown
and nape, to give the stone good contact. Becoming frustrated, he

took out his knife and hacked at his hair until it was an inch short along the strip from forehead to nape.

Though his body had begun to tremble in want of the stone, he was dimly aware of what his parents might think if he returned in such a state. Dutifully, he grasped at his curls, slicing them off until the cave swarmed with shorn locks. The breeze tickled the light fuzz of hair that remained, but still, he felt it was an obstruction.

Carefully, he set the blade against his skin and moved it across his scalp, arms aching as he worked. Finally, his searching fingertips told him the job was complete. He had nicked himself several times, but not deeply. Filling his hands with water, he cleansed his head of clippings and smeared blood, exhilarated by the feel of the wind against his skin.

Only then did he place the Meridian band upon his head. Even without the Alma, he felt the swoon of contact. A deep chuckle reverberated from him as his eyes rolled to the back of his head. He sucked air sharply through his nostrils and expelled it, harnessing his will to the deliberate force of his breath. In time, the rhythm steadied, and feeling himself more in control, Ambrose built a small fire from the wood and kindling he had left on his last visit.

It required little thought, it was but a series of familiar motions his hands attended to almost of their own accord. He crumbled Alma over the fire, relishing its familiar sweetness. The cave grew heavy with smoke, emboldening his mind with leaden focus.

Soon, a pyretic buzzing arose in him. A hum that started softly, of bees in the flowerbed, or perhaps it was the buzzing of corpse flies. He felt the shuddering of deep earth, and the unholy shrieking of the stars. He could not lose himself so early. Closing his eyes, he brought to mind the silver thread. Followed it on and on, in silence, breathing into this single point of clarity.

It worked for a time.

But then, in his mind's eye, he caught the dancing colours of the stone. They pulsated in a language he could not decipher, though he strained to hear them. The hot breath of urgent whispers, words of imminent death, a lover's promise, the psst-psst-psst of children's secrets since the beginning of time. The hiss of Intercession, a kettle fiercely boiling.

Bile rose in his throat and his heart hammered, brightness closing in on him, eclipsing his inner vision. Voices, forces, and processes – endless in number – thundered through him. All things called to him simultaneously, threatening to split him apart so that he would not know himself.

Ambrose called weakly upon his hands to move. To tear the stones from his crown. Something erupted, streaming richness, saturating, clustering, fluttering, snapping, squeezing, pulsing, coursing, birthing, swarming, scintillating, scattering—

He opened his eyes and stared hard at his hand. It twitched, and he tried again, breathing furiously, in and out. Clenching his guts, he let out a sound somewhere between a moan and a roar, and his arm jerked to life. Clawing helplessly at the leather band, one of the stones fell away and the rush of consciousness returned. Desperately fumbling, the second fell, and when the third came free he flung it across the cave like an insect.

Leaning backward, he stamped at the fire, the prickling of pins and needles shooting up and down his limbs. As the air began to clear, he stared at the stones that sat where he had thrown them, so very close to the edge. Gingerly, he reached for the band, and drew them safely in. Then, cradling his head in his hands, he curled up in the farthest corner, and sobbed.

It was as if the stones knew he was spent, for he no longer felt besieged by them even though they were still near. Sunlight winked across them.

He spoke to them, within his mind. *Where is Sybilla?*

When no answer came, he thought bitterly of the blood-tie Mr Sherburn kept from him. The canny bastard.

Not Sherburn.

Ambrose jumped, eyes darting about the cave to find the source of the voice that spoke in splinters, like the groaning of wood. He stared at the stone.

Not Sherburn? Then where?

This time, it was an image that came. His grandfather's eyes took up the entire sky in a flash of lightning.

Ambrose felt a surge of anger so hot that he feared his flesh would blister.

He had her; his grandfather had the blood-tie there in the camp! Then he saw something else. A weaving of sorts, glittering almost invisibly, coming in and out of focus. A silver thread cast from the topmost tower of the Skalens' House, which led to his grandfather's hut. A thread from there that led to a sea cabin of blinding stone. A spider's web of secrets, trickling along sheer threads like dew.

He straightened himself, the poison he had just perceived beginning to do its work. They were shaping the world around him, making him walk the maze. They would never initiate him into the mysteries. His heart ached.

They kept him in the dark, he and Zohar, so they would not know what they had done. Zohar. They had sent her to Brivia. Ambrose sensed his grandfather's hand. The old liar knew Zohar was the only person who could see who he really was. Ambrose closed his eyes and felt for her spirit, and somehow knew she was alive, that she was safe. In his mind, he sought her sun-warmed hair, a brief embrace from a time long ago.

His pulse slowed, his awareness meandering in the golden fields of memory.

After a while, he opened his eyes. All was serene. The objects around him steadied within themselves, vivid in their shape, posture, and texture. The perfect order of things. And Velspar, the animating principle. It was everywhere, and he was a part of it all.

He smiled.

They had closed all ways to him, but he had found the hidden road.

61

ZOHAR

Fourteen Years After The Fire

ZOHAR SAT ON THE BED, staring at the heavy wooden door and its iron lock. She was no prisoner, but it would only take the turn of a key to change that.

Now that she knew about the rebels, they expected her to laugh along with them by the fireside drinking Alma wine. They expected her to remove her Meridian. This was not how she imagined it.

She and Ambrose had whispered of the Temple, had uttered the god-names and blushed, had stolen Alma and let it warm their hearts, but these were crumbs gathered from beneath a great table where a feast was laid, where they were never meant to eat.

It had taken her time enough to walk among the Raeburns without the help of blinding stone. Zohar feared to see what the Intercessors had seen. She did not want to know what lay in the memories of the Guard, what it felt like to slit a person's throat. The darkness within Sidney Karasek was palpable even with her protections in place. He looked as though he could bring sickness to all of Brivia with the potency of his grief.

Elis spoke freely now when she asked questions of him, but it did not feel natural that he should speak outside the formalities of his station. It was too much for her to comprehend. Despite her daydreams and secret wishes, she was not pleased to find herself caught up in the beginnings of what would likely be a violent rebellion.

These people did not know her. She was a daughter of Skalens. What value did she have? What loyalty could she expect from them when the boundaries of expectation and duty were quivering and about to break? She was not brave enough to be beaten, tortured and raped. She did not want to die. Did not know what happened after death, not now that the Holy Ones had fled, not now that they stood at the precipice for the second time in her short life, the fervour of holy truth gathering candescence.

She could not think about it. So she kept her Meridian in place, and when her mind wandered, she let it dally with Illiam. She had watched him closely these past weeks and had settled on a few sure impressions. He wanted her to join them, and to believe in their cause. He liked her enough to search a crowd to find her face, and to draw the ladle for her, to pass her the fresher bread. But he did not come close.

Sitting alone in her chambers, she resolved that they would never have her loyalty if they kept her from Ambrose. She did not care if the Avishaen Guard were at her parents' command. They had known her since she was a child. They should know better than anyone that this was wrong.

Putting her hand on the doorknob, Zohar hesitated, fearing that it would not open at her touch. The latch clicked open without resistance. Walking down the hall, she took herself into whatever room she pleased, finding dusty books on high shelves, cupboards cluttered with wine, and in a sunroom of sorts she found the painted portraits of Emryl and Medard Karasek, looking both ethereal and menacing in their likeness.

Perhaps no one had noticed her trespass, as nobody came to stop her, and no shadowed figures lurked behind. Not knowing where the others were, she headed outside, feeling in her every step the tug of invisible reins. Zohar walked quicker now, hoping she remembered the direction of the port road.

She had not expected to get this far, and wished she had brought her pocketknife, her fire-steel, and some dried fruit or meat for the journey. She looked about her, trying to imagine herself as Edith. On their walks, Edith was always the one on alert, her eye on the practicalities as Zohar unravelled the contents of her mind, always talking.

"Zohar!" the voice came dimly from somewhere among the trees.

Gritting her teeth, she looked slowly around, trying to decide if she could still escape. She dropped herself beneath the ferns at her feet, praying that she would not be discovered.

Her pulse quickened in the silence, and she hardly dared to hope.

But then came the crushing sound of boots, distant at first, but steadily advancing.

Zohar closed her eyes.

"Zohar?" It was Illiam, and near enough that he must surely see her now.

She did not look up.

She felt him crouch before her, place a hand upon her shoulder.

Slowly, she raised her head and looked at him. He, too, was wearing his Meridian. Zohar's smile was naked with sorrow. "Illiam, will you please take me home? I have to go home."

Covering his mouth with his hand, Illiam stared back with dark resignation. "You know I can't."

Zohar's face tightened. "I enjoyed Amand's speech last night. I especially liked the part where he spoke of liberty. Where he said that Intercession should be used to ease the spirit, but never to impose the will of one person over another."

"I know you want to see your brother, but now is not the time."

"Who gave you that order?" Zohar shot back.

"Your guards," Illiam said stiffly.

"I will suffer my parent's anger if I must. What fealty do you owe the Avishaen Guard when everywhere I look oaths are being broken?" Zohar watched him.

Illiam turned, looking over his shoulder and sighed. "Why will you not remove your Meridian at camp?"

"I do not wish to," Zohar said, unable to keep the scowl from her face.

"Then how can I know where your loyalties lie? Why did you come here anyway?" Illiam said sharply, losing his patience.

"That's none of your business."

"If you want my help it is," Illiam said, folding his arms.

"I just wanted to see the mainland!" Zohar winced at the frivolity of her own words.

"A nice little holiday, was it? That is all you care about?" Illiam gave her a look of disgust.

"What do you care about? All you ever talk about are crops and trade."

"I care about getting rid of these stupid things," he said, yanking at his Meridian. "We only have a short time to learn from those who still hold the wisdom of the past. We need to bring the Holy Ones back before they disappear forever."

Zohar thought of the kshidol, and nodded.

"We cannot simply make a ritual of our guilt," Illiam said. "Our side will not accept things as they are. We have to fight back before it is too late. If you join us, if you are truly with us, then I will take you to Avishae."

Zohar felt the barb that was aimed at her mother, but softened her features to show her sympathy, to give him what he wanted. She thought of Ambrose, who would have readily joined them. Who would have taken it further and made Illiam look the coward.

She steadied her features, for it was a fool's question. "I am on your side."

Illiam stared at her a moment longer. "Right, then I'll go and ready the horses."

62

ZOHAR

Fourteen Years After The Fire

ZOHAR WALKED ON WITH ILLIAM trailing behind. They were close now. She had thought they would have trouble obtaining a horse and would have to fashion a raft to pass by stealth across the strait. It seemed, however, there were many people Illiam could turn to lying, to keeping quiet.

A local woodsman covered them over in the back of his wagon, finding a fishwife willing to gift them a boat and two hooded cloaks. At the shore, a stripling lad hid his eyes beneath his cap and pointed down river to the little worn track that would lead them into Avishae. His father's cottage sat by the way, and he readily offered their only horse. She did not know whether these folk knew her and graced them by right of her parents' title, or whether they cleaved to Illiam, to Sidney Karasek.

They floated downstream beneath stiff cloaks reeking of old fish.

"There it is," she breathed, catching sight of the outcrop that heralded the hidden track.

Illiam grunted as he manoeuvred the boat. The current was strong today.

"Let me help you," Zohar said, only now feeling grateful for his effort, and his discretion.

Zohar pushed with the oar, and they bickered as the boat lost its course. She blushed, watched him closely before pushing hers into the water. This time, they moved onward to the banks, and with a bump, the boat hit sand.

Illiam stepped into the shallows and dragged the boat by its rope, tying it to a waterlogged tree. Removing his coat, he started for shore. Zohar stood to shed hers, and almost fell as the boat began to wobble. She was about to step in when he turned. "Do you want me to save your shoes?" he asked.

The journey before them was long, she knew, and she weighed her pride for a moment before nodding.

Illiam strode into the water, seeming younger all of a sudden. Like a boy playing rescue, not a man intent on orchestrating a holy rebellion.

Zohar tried not to smile as he braced himself to lift her. "Put your arms around my neck or I'm going to drop you!" Illiam said.

As her arm encircled his neck she felt the intoxicating closeness of his skin, though he would not meet her eyes. When he set her down, he took several steps back.

"I can see the path," he said brusquely, wet sand clinging to his shoes and trousers.

Once they were ashore, Zohar's anxieties melted away. She would see Ambrose. The Brivian plot was behind her. She was home.

She strode ahead, catching sight of the horse's swishing tail. Illiam squelched behind her, and she felt a little guilty about his sand-caked feet that would surely develop a rash. "I know the way from here," Zohar said, looking at the path ahead.

Illiam stopped, resting his hands on his hips. "You want me to go?" he asked, his head downcast.

When he looked up at her, Zohar searched his face but did not answer. "Why did you help me, Illiam?"

He brushed sand from his shoes. "Do you want my true answer?"

Zohar nodded, bracing herself for some awful revelation.

He folded his arms across his chest. "I want to know whether you can be trusted. Whether Avishae is on our side."

Zohar's expression soured. "I am not Avishae."

He swallowed uncomfortably, face reddening, but he stood his ground.

"So this is a reconnaissance mission," she said, and gave him a scathing look. "Well, you'd better keep watch of me then. And don't tarry, or you might miss something." Zohar turned on her heel, making her way to the horse, caring little if he fell behind.

63

AMBROSE

Fourteen Years After The Fire

AMBROSE TROD SLOWLY THROUGH the forest, walking without destination. In every place that he could go, a trap was laid. Did they know about the stone? He felt they would kill him for it.

His grandfather coveted the stone; that much was certain. The old man knew of its power. Perhaps he had foreseen everything. A vision of his grandson; those children he despised, born in the black house that claimed his daughter. Is that why he had spent so much time with him? Was that why he showed so little interest in Zohar?

He still felt bitter toward the brothers. Each time he considered going down to the Bay, he saw the three of them standing upon their raft, awash in a tide of blood. If they turned on him, he could not fight them off. And Mr Sherburn, he spoke in whispers to the Raeburns, of that Ambrose was sure.

They'd asked him to make the blood-tie, but it was not for Ambrose to wield, it was for his grandfather. The old man was patient. He did not send the Raeburn boys to hunt Ambrose with their spears and arrows. He did not ask Ma Bet to mix him a sleeping draught, to steal the secrets from his lips. No. For some reason, he waited.

When forced to consider his parents' role in all of this, a certain numbness came upon him, so that his footsteps were those of a being unanchored to the earth. He scratched his head where a leaf had brushed past, feeling the shame of his exposed skin.

Then, he stopped. The leaf was not a leaf at all, but a feather. His eyes shot up, searching the sky.

"Father Kshidol?" he called aloud.

Caressing the feather with calloused fingers, he brought it to his lips and inhaled.

He was not forsaken. But what should he do?

Ambrose sat where he was, and though he was out in the open, he believed the feather would keep him safe. The stones called to him from his satchel. Chewing his lip, he hesitated, fearing the dizzying height, the place the stones might take him. It did not matter. He had already opened the door; he could not turn back now.

His fingers trembled as he extracted the leather band, its apertures empty of stone. Swaddled deeply in the bag, he found the three fragments and pushed them into place. Before he started, he set the blinding stone about him in a triangular shape, as if these small wards of silence would protect him from notice.

As the voyant stones touched the three points, they cleaved to him, ready to impart things of great significance. He swallowed the shudder of brightness, felt the flashing colours of the stone lance the marrow of his bones. Then, the intensity tapered off, giving way to a thick and joyful pulsation extending the length of his spine, flowering at the base of his neck.

For a little while, he let himself exist as pure sensation. Everything slipped away, including his reason for engaging the stones. Tangled feelings that had seemed crucial but moments ago were now curious shapes, severed curls shining in the sun. One of the curls felt very much like a feather, and he ran his finger along its spine, wondering that it held its shape where other things didn't.

If he ran his finger from its sharp point to its soft inky tip, it made a sound. He tried it once more – it was the same sound. Moving his ear closer, he tried again – the sound had two parts like a rock broken in two.

Jaa-nek.

Ja-nek.

Janek.

"Janek?" he called, his voice disturbing a flock of ravens. For a moment they blackened the sky, their breathy wings stirring dust from the earth.

Though the birds were now gone, the dust shifted before him, forming and dissolving before his eyes.

"Janek? Is that you? Janek – I have the stone!"

The shape could not speak, and could only whirl around him, conveying the urgency of its message.

"What should I do, Janek?"

Ambrose crouched with eyes wide.

Sunlight gaped through the canopy above, flooding him in golden light. His muscles fell slack with the pleasure of it, the stones throbbing about his head. But it was too much. The stones pressed against him tightly, sucking at him like babies at the breast, pushing against him like the lover his body had not yet known.

Nausea rose in him, and through the crack in his will flowed a rivulet of fear. The feeling would pass, he told himself. He had been here before. Looking down, he saw that his heart bulged from his chest, swollen with nectar, red honey oozing down his ribs with each sickening thump.

Swallow them.

He shook his head.

Swallow them, Bright Flame.

He looked down at his trembling hand, and saw it was that of a young man. A choking sob burst from him. He was a being; he was somebody's son. The hand was dirty, the fingernails cracked and bleeding. The hand moved slowly, feeling the dew of his breath. The hand gripped the band and snapped.

The first stone fell, landing on the ground. Then the second and third, which he ripped from their bindings. The tripling of the stone dizzied him, making it impossible to focus. He looked away, trying to settle his vision on a steady branch, but the effect intensified, duplicating everything he saw into an impossible crosshatch.

Despite the leaden feeling in his muscles, he desired the stone. He lay down next to the three polished fragments. He held one up to the sun, watching its amber heart flare. He smoothed it on his pants, held it to his lips and extended his tongue. A charge shot through him, and he tasted fire and tangerines, honeyed sweat and raw flesh. Letting it slip onto his tongue, it seemed to drip with sweetness, urging itself to slip deeper, to lodge itself at the precipice of death.

Ambrose swallowed.

The cool ache sunk down his throat; slinking its way through a system of tunnels where it came to rest.

He had swallowed the stone.

A dreadful certainty came upon him. What had he done?

For a moment, he felt that he might live. He would put his fingers down his throat and get it out. His throat convulsed as he leaned forward.

But then the stone called to its other parts. He salivated, wanting it out and wanting it in at the same time.

He shoved the second stone into his mouth, swallowing with violent urgency. It left an aftertaste like claw prints in snow.

Ambrose barely looked at the third before taking it in his mouth, but once it was there, he did not want it to go. His tongue moved about it, left and right, and he pushed it toward the roof of his mouth.

His entire being throbbed in terror and tears streamed from his eyes as he waited to be ripped apart, but nothing happened.

Finally, calm came upon him, and the world around him was quiet. He stood, and walked, his mind empty and still. Soon, his mind began to chatter with the thoughts of Ambrose, to drift, as it normally did. He would say the Sherburns dared him to shear his hair – he had lost a bet – and his father would surely laugh. His mother would stroke his head in disapproval. But hair grows back, he would say.

He started to believe the stories as they wove themselves, and felt himself light of step, anticipating the sight of the Skalens' House when it would appear over the next hill. He thought he might just go down to the Bay in the morning and put down a wager with Gwyn, smooth this mess over, they would forget the—

The stone flared fiercely in his gut.

He heard himself moan around the fragment in his mouth.

Siatka have mercy!

The pain whitened everything around him so that he was alone in light, in agony.

Eventually, through hard blinks, he caught flashes of grass, a tall tree, black against blue sky, a thorn bush with red flowers. Panic shot through him.

He could no longer stand, but the grass gave his hands good purchase as he grasped the wiry lengths, dragging himself along. It seemed an eternity, but he found it, the tree they had climbed as children. It was a magic tree. He touched the roots of it, and they were just as he remembered, elegant and strong.

The tree had a hollow, and as he clambered to his knees, he reached inside. It was littered with dry leaves and small things that tickled his fingers as they fled. His breath hitched, fearing that it was gone, that some animal had taken it. But then he felt it. He sobbed through the pulsing light that stole his vision. Feeling with his fingers the small length of plaited hair.

Though he could not see it, he knew what it looked like. Zohar's red-blonde hair, striped with Ambrose's dark. She had made it just for fun because it was a sunny day and she was bored – because Ambrose wanted to cut something with his new hunting knife. He held it tight now. He would never let it go. It would be his talisman. It would carry him through death, to the other side.

Something inside him burst, and his body succumbed to violent spasms. His awareness moved outward, held together by the tug of plaited hair. He was dying. Yellow liquid oozed from his mouth. Black veins spidered his flesh like lightning. Soon it would be over. The pain of it broke away from him, and dimly he saw his own body, slumped against the tree. His eyes were open, but they did not blink, not anymore.

Silence flowed from the moment when his heart stopped, blanketing the place where he lay, stretching out to swallow all of existence; a stretching tide that would reach eternity and never draw back. But something of him witnessed this. He could not bear to witness this without end.

In whiteness and in silence he felt something shift behind him.

A presence descended close by, hopping on ghostly talons, with wings clear as water. Another came, and more followed, falling like washes of rain from laden branches. He saw them nestle their beaks into his body, nudging and nibbling, pulling and tearing. But his flesh remained unmolested. His body was whole.

Where one swallowed, it took his jealousy. The heavy plumed one gulped down his laughter. A small one burrowed into his side, taking learned things, the knowledge of his muscles – how to hold a bow and shoot an arrow true to its mark. For all that he saw, he felt strangely impassive, knowing that they would take all of him. They would split him apart until nothing remained. Until there was nothing to see them with, and no one to speak their name.

A glassy eye shifted over him, and started its meal. He wondered what this one would find, what it would collect. It pushed its head so deep in his spirit that it disappeared completely. The feeling surprised him. This part hurt. He looked up at his mother's face, pawing at her breast, in the limitless safety of her arms. Her eyes met his and he felt her love, felt love flowing unhindered between them.

More memories like this were exhumed, beak and tongue drawing them from the depths. A faraway feeling of comprehension came, of how things were – how his parents were – when he was a child, but he was beyond sorrow, beyond regret. He was disappearing, and almost gone.

One of Kshidol's many bodies took flight. It took his name.

The next met His twin on high, dissolving the bond with his Birth-Kin, the day of his birth.

Three – Sister. Four – Father. Five – Mother.

Every kiss upon his brow, sticky hands holding his, the sting of salt water on grazed skin, lonely eyes gazing out to sea.

Six, seven, eight, all—

Gone.

64

ZOHAR

Fourteen Years After The Fire

"WHERE DO YOU THINK HE WILL BE?" Illiam asked. He held tight to the back of the saddle, his chest only occasionally touching Zohar's back, and when it did, it was accidental.

She had taken satisfaction in his expression when she beat him to the horse, claiming her place up front. "I will ask at the camp. Do you know the Raeburns?" she tried a friendly tone. The last mile or so had dissipated her anger, and when she gave herself the chance to reflect on his words, Zohar realised she didn't trust him either. She just didn't say it to his face.

"I know of them," Illiam said, a little defensively.

"We are almost there." Zohar caught a glimpse of the fence line through the trees. Giving the horse a little kick, the rickety old girl did her best to break into a gallop. Illiam's body collided with her back and he grabbed at her waist to prevent himself from falling.

"So sorry, Miss Elshender," Illiam muttered.

Zohar grinned. She could see Rowan was atop the watch post, staring listlessly through the treetops and broke into a broad smile.

"Rowan!" she called, waving.

"Zohar – who is with you?" Rowan's hand moved surreptitiously to his bow.

"Illiam Greslet of Brivia. He is a friend." She did not know why she added that last part, for he was not her friend, but the words served to open the gate.

When they had dismounted, Illiam readjusted his clothing, smoothing his hair.

"Meridians on the wall," she instructed him, enjoying his look of uncertainty.

Illiam stared in disbelief as she removed hers. "But – you would not do that in Brivia!"

"I didn't feel like it." She shrugged, searching for Ambrose or someone who might have seen him. "Edith!" Zohar ran over to her, leaving Illiam gawking where he stood, removing his Meridian slowly, and with ceremony.

Edith raised her eyebrows, never quick to smile.

"Where's Ambrose?" Zohar asked breathlessly.

Edith's face darkened a little. "He's not here. Your parents are looking for him."

Zohar felt a lurch of dread. "What do you mean?"

Edith wiped her palms on her britches. "Cousin, he has been missing for two days." Edith could not keep the concern from her voice, but Zohar could tell that she knew nothing more.

Her mind raced, imagining that he had broken his leg and was stranded, that he had gone diving without checking the tide, that he had fought with his parents and was hiding somewhere. But with sudden sharpness, she thought of her grandfather.

Slowly she became aware that if her grandfather chose that moment to focus on her, he would read her plainly. She did her best to silence her mind, grasping Edith's arm in acknowledgement as she moved to leave. When she turned back to the gate, she saw Illiam smiling hesitantly at a tribe of Raeburn children.

Heading straight to the wall, she picked up Illiam's Meridian along with her own. Illiam frowned at her in confusion but followed when she gestured to him urgently with her hands.

"Why are we leaving?" Illiam jogged to keep up with her, looking disappointed by their sudden departure.

"Ambrose is missing." The words came out in a croak.

"Would he have left the island?"

That had not even occurred to her. But no, he would not leave the island. "I feel something…" Zohar said, trailing off. She could not put her finger on it. It was a dark throbbing in her chest.

Ambrose, she called him with her spirit, trying to think of places he might be.

She would try the sea caves.

"Wait!" Illiam called, but Zohar kept going.

She was halfway there when she was forced to slow, her lungs burning. Her head swam and she could not think clearly. She needed to concentrate.

Zohar let her feet carry her along a meandering path toward the cliffs west of the Skalens' House. Her eyes caught something pale, out of place, and she glanced over to see what it was.

A bare-chested man with shorn hair lay slumped against a tree. She stared at him, unable to comprehend what she was seeing. Each step threw the ghastly image toward her, where it shifted and trans- formed – her brother – a stranger – old – young – no. It *was* her brother. The image steadied and a shock of air hit her throat, catching there as if she had breathed poison.

She screamed his name, running to him, to help him up, but when she reached him, she saw. Zohar's heart constricted. His chin pushed into his breastbone, his arms stuck out at his sides. His unseeing eyes, still half-open, looked a different colour, as if twilight had fallen over him, turning him grey.

Illiam approached, crouching cautiously behind. *Ambrose.* What had happened to him? She witnessed the crime of his scalp, and the youth of his chest, crying so hard she could hardly breathe.

The tears stole the image of him, submerging him in deep water. But from the blurred crack of vision, she saw him anew. She learned of his death over and over, moment after moment, unchanging, unchanging.

She had to wake him, she had to bring him back!

Firm hands grasped her shoulders.

No. Illiam said.

His voice sounded inside her mind, clear as a bell. Without understanding how it was so, Zohar felt the streaming of their spirits, the intermingling of tides. Illiam went into her grief and suffered there, his own spirit screaming for Ambrose as if he had loved him. His hands were fists, he could not stand to see Ambrose like this...

Zohar turned to him in horror and fascination, her mind drifting close. She slipped through the gauze of him, his flesh like her own, his memories familiar, his hopes and fears anchoring themselves in the centre of her heart. He was Illiam, she was Illiam, she could not keep him from her, from the naked terror of Ambrose, of her brother, blood of her blood, lying there dead. It was too much.

She tried to shut him out, to bear him away. She searched for Ambrose, focusing on him, urging him to return, *come back*. There was nothing there, no sense of him. This body was devoid of spirit. A body holding a piece of plaited hair in its hand.

Zohar reached for it, prising the plait from her brother's grip. Her thumb moved along it, the pearled bumps of this-way, that-way, that were she and him, she and him. The memory filtered in, awash with sunlight, but then Illiam noticed something.

There is something in his mouth.

There is something in his mouth, she echoed.

Zohar looked at Illiam, feeling herself melting into him in a confusion of sensations.

Illiam's eyes were wide.

In her mind she spoke, *will you take it out?* She could not bear it.

He moved forward and reached his fingers inside. Zohar felt a wave of nausea as the smell of fouled saliva met her nostrils. Gingerly, Illiam pulled the slimy thing – a black stone. Much larger than she first thought, glinting green in the fading light.

Illiam poured water over it, his trembling hand turning the stone. Drying it on his tunic, he passed it to her, but seemed to have trouble letting go.

It was a dread thing. Heavy. It burned black. It shone with living light of every colour. She felt herself fascinated, being drawn toward it, meeting its predatory gaze. Feeling at once known and knowing.

She looked up at Illiam, sunlight about his head. His beauty opened a string of thoughts like cherry blossoms bursting along a hardwood branch. His breath on her neck, his hand smooth on her thigh. But Zohar did not laugh or try to hide her thoughts away.

Illiam saw all of this, accepting it as an effusion of light. Then, Zohar saw herself through Illiam's eyes. How different she looked... and then there was Ambrose. There her brother lay. His form incoherent, a memory in flesh, of someone now gone.

65

ZOHAR

Fourteen Years After The Fire

ZOHAR STEPPED AWAY FROM THE BODY, holding the stone. "Illiam," she said, as if through water. He did not respond. Just stared at the rising moon, his arms moving toward it as if to pluck it from the sky. They had lost time.

"Illiam!" She caught his eyes. "This." She held out the stone, struggling to form words; *killed him*, she said silently.

Illiam nodded, staring at her.

Using what strength she could muster, Zohar sought the familiar feelings of seclusion, of secrecy, of solitude. It helped.

Zohar picked up her Meridian and put it on, feeling like her hands were made of butter. Once it was secure, she flexed her fingers, testing that they were still within her power. Dragging herself to where Illiam was, she set his Meridian upon his head, stones slipping sideways as she struggled to find his centre.

When the three points were concealed beneath the quiet of the blinding stone, Illiam seemed to come to his senses.

"Stand away from him," Illiam said.

She did, but then realised her other hand still gripped the black stone. Its glassy surface winked through the gap between forefinger and thumb. Zohar tried to let go, but her hand was rigid. She knew it was turning her to crystal and she was not afraid—

Illiam hit her hand sharply with his own and the stone skidded into the shadows. "Stand away," he said, pointing to a clearing bathed in moonlight.

Zohar fell into him, and they linked arms, trying to regain their footing as they stumbled to the clearing. She felt blood returning to her body in waves. "We need blinding stone." She nodded in the direction of the Raeburn camp.

"Yes," was all he could manage.

The two of them ran, at times a four-legged creature with a single beating heart. At times, two strangers, with a common destination. It was difficult to hear each other's breath without wanting to wrap their linked arms around one another, to consume each other and be consumed.

As they drew closer to the camp, this desire began to ease and they unlinked their arms, running side by side. Rowan had fallen asleep at his post but wore a frown as if dreaming.

Zohar and Illiam beat on the gates, but Rowan did not wake. They beat harder, shouting for anyone with ears to hear.

Moments later, Ma Bet wrenched open the door, her eyes bloodshot from sleep. At the sight of them, her mouth went slack. "What has happened to you?" She made to gather them in, but Zohar pushed past, heading straight for the Meridian wall. "What do you think you are doing?" Ma Bet shouted, gripping Illiam with a surprisingly strong hand.

It took too much effort to speak and her head was swimming. Zohar shoved the old woman and Illiam broke free, both of them scrambling for the bands, stones clobbering to the floor where they fell.

Before she knew what was happening, Ma Bet was standing livid beneath the night lamp, clanging a huge copper bell. All around them, people were waking.

Chief among them, her grandfather. She felt him prickle to life, his senses coursing outward for signs of intrusion. Still wearing his night clothes, he emerged in the doorway of his cabin and marched toward them.

"Is it Ambrose?" His rasping voice betrayed his apprehension, his fear.

Zohar almost collapsed, an ocean of tears stirring inside her. But she could not say the words.

Her grandfather looked into Zohar's eyes, nodding as his own turned glassy, his face contorted with pain.

How could she have doubted his feeling? In Zohar's eyes her grandfather searched for Ambrose. The last image of the boy – which his granddaughter held – just there, behind her Meridian. Zohar felt him tugging at her, like a child at her sleeve, begging to know, but afraid to see.

She let the image float upward, let it linger there. Her grandfather's hands reached into her, lifting the drowned boy, white as bone. Zohar stood face to face with her grandfather, as the entire encampment looked on.

"We need blinding stone. All of it," Zohar said.

Her grandfather nodded. "Rowan! Get word to the Sherburns. Tell them to bring all of their stores to Baden Forest. And send a messenger to my daughter – to the Skalens," her grandfather instructed.

Zohar and Illiam gathered the fallen pieces from the ground, and with arms full of soothing grey stone, they ran back into the night.

Finding the tree, Zohar saw her brother's body. Illiam was close and held her so that she would not fall apart. "I will lay the first stone," Zohar said, passing her bundle of Meridians to Illiam.

The first stone, she brought to her lips, blessing it with a kiss before placing it on her brother's forehead. After that was done, Zohar and Illiam positioned gentle stones upon his palms, his heart, his feet, the hollows of his chest, until the stones formed a patchwork shroud.

They sat beside, silently, feeling the muted effects of the stone. The moon was small and high when the others came. All of them came, their rustling footsteps coalescing in that one place. Her parents pushed to the front, her grandfather in solemn step advancing from the other side.

Zohar looked up and saw her father as his face broke. His legs buckled and he staggered to his son, reaching to tear away the stones. Her grandfather caught him from behind and pinned his arms behind his back.

"Don't you keep him from me, not now Landyn!" her father shouted.

"Ulric! He is dangerous, there is something in him," her grandfather said, his breath coming sharply through his teeth.

Her father rammed his elbow into the old man's ribs, breaking his grip. "I am sick of you telling me what is good for my son! He is dead! You did this to him. You!" Her father roared, his eyes savage.

Her mother took his arm, pressing her nails into his flesh. "Stop. We will not surround our son with red thoughts while he stands at the shores of the Great Stream!"

He shook her off. "It didn't work, Rebekah. All those years, drawing poison, spending every waking minute in that Tower, playing Intercessor. It didn't work! It was your father's way of imprisoning us, of punishing us for what we did!" her father cried, oblivious to the people listening.

Zohar heard his words, but with all that had happened, she did not care to know what he meant.

Mr Sherburn and his sons pushed through the crowd with a wagon full of stone, bringing a cavernous silence into the fray.

Zohar stood numbly and walked toward the wagon. Her mother looked at her aghast, not understanding how she could be here. When her father saw her, he made a sound of exclamation, as if she had returned from the dead.

But Zohar could not stop to look at them, could not open her mouth to speak when the river of words would flow for days.

When she reached Rob Sherburn, the eldest, she put her hand on his. "This way," she said.

All eyes followed as Zohar led Rob to Ambrose's side.

Zohar raised her voice up, speaking with the music of her soul, clear and bright, so everyone could hear. "Ambrose, my brother, is dead. Though we are not at peace with one another, he will need all of us to soothe his spirit, so he can be at rest. Take a stone from the wagon and lay it upon his body. This is how we will say goodbye."

Her parents looked at her as though the Skalen's burden were being lifted from their shoulders and set upon her own.

Rob removed his Meridian and stepped forward. He closed his flickering eyelids, searching the rubble for a stone befitting of his tribute. "This is one of his," Rob said, choking on the words.

The Sherburn brothers and their father shuffled in behind; Mr Sherburn's face tough as driftwood, Gwyn's head bowed low. Rowan took his place behind Allen, nodding to one of the Raeburn children to come and hold his hand. But the Skalens' Elshender stood stock still, watching their son disappear, stone by stone.

Her mother gasped as a blanket of cloud stole the light of the moon. She launched herself toward Ambrose's body, ripping off the stones. Illiam made to stop her, but Zohar shook her head, feeling possessed of some superior wisdom, a tide that pulled her steadily on.

Her mother pulled her hand away as if bitten. "What is this?" she whispered, her eyes round with terror.

Zohar caught her mother's gaze and moved close to her spirit, to comfort her, to let her know that whatever poison was at work, Ambrose was no longer here.

Her mother closed her eyes and lay her palm flat against Ambrose's belly. She was quiet, absolutely still. Then, with sudden ferocity, her eyes cast about the shadowed crowd.

"Where is my father?" she said, staring in but one direction.

Then Zohar understood. Quietly, she motioned for Rob to come close. "Take care of my brother's body. Cover him with stones, and do not let anyone disturb him."

Rob nodded.

Zohar took her father's hand that hung limp at his side and spoke into his ear. "Father, Ambrose must be protected. Some of us must go. Mother will come with us. Keep him safe."

Because Zohar had spoken with the voice of the dream, her father saw in her the certainty of holy vision, and heeded.

66

ZOHAR

Fourteen Years After The Fire

ZOHAR AND HER MOTHER WALKED hand in hand, their bodies still tingling from the charge of her brother's skin. Illiam and a company of guardsmen trailed them, eyes low, following the moonlit flow of auburn hair, the deep and the fair.

They knew where he would be, for they all heard the song of the stone. In flashes, Zohar saw the old man, running, black fire burning in his hand. Saw him barring the gates, locking himself inside his cabin, searching for something, something he had hidden there.

The perimeter was made of wood now, and as they drew closer, she rode the strength of her mother's vision, moving like vapour through the camp perimeter. The guards made short work of the fence itself, stepping over splintered timber and clearing their way.

With Raeburn axes, they penetrated the heart of the door, leaving its locks intact.

Over her mother's shoulder she saw him, crouched and shaking as he fumbled with the clasp of a small box. His breath was ragged with effort and he could not stop his hand from shaking as he held the wild black stone.

341

Zohar did not flinch when her mother pulled the axe gently from her guardsman's hands, tightening her own about its handle.

"Let go of the stone, Father."

His breath quickened, and with a cry he freed the latch from the box. Zohar glimpsed white fabric with its stain of blood, and knew what he meant to do. She saw Sybilla's face set tight within the box, as if she had been imprisoned there since last she came to Avishae. Her cheeks, forehead and chin pressed against the box's sides, her jaw fastened shut.

Zohar's heart raced.

"Stop!" her mother cried as her grandfather's hand moved wildly from side to side, unable to control the stone, to force it into the box.

Her grandfather whirled, still clutching the box and the stone in his trembling hands. "Why would you protect her?" he demanded, through gritted teeth.

"The tide is turning, you told me this yourself. She will burn. But what will become of you? Of our people?" her mother asked.

Her grandfather seemed to fall momentarily into a swoon, gathering the stone to his chest.

Without warning, one of the guards shot out from behind Zohar, kicking the stone from her grandfather's grasp. In the shocked silence, the stone shot beneath the bed, and her grandfather made for it, scuffling on his belly.

Zohar picked up the box, and without thinking, gathered the cloth into her mouth, swallowing hard against its retching dryness.

Her grandfather's arm extended beneath the bed, fumbling for the stone, but when the blood-tie passed into her throat, he squeezed his eyes shut as if in pain.

"Restrain him!" her mother called, readying herself with the axe.

Her grandfather's face was a contortion of bitterness and rage. "You stupid girl," he spat. "What have you done?"

The guards moved impassively toward him, easily overpowering the old man and tied him to the bedpost.

"Rebekah," he breathed, "You have lost so much. But you must let me make this sacrifice. It is past time that I joined the Stream."

Placing the axe on its head, her mother looked at the floor, choosing her words. "I bear the Skalen's burden, Father. As you have never let me forget. This evil that has taken my son, I will not let it take you too." She stared at him with hard eyes. "For it would not end there. There are no holy men in Avishae. Those who seek consolation, come to you. Every last one of them took their oaths at your behest. I forbid you to abandon them."

Her grandfather looked suddenly weary and Zohar saw the weft of pain between them that hung like tattered rags.

Her mother did not give him the opportunity to answer, shoving the bed away from the wall, and snatching the stone into her hand.

Holding it in her fist, her mother pushed through the door, splinters clawing at her dress. Zohar watched her leave. Watched her as she passed the last light of the Raeburn camp and disappeared into the forest.

67

WALDEMAR

Fifteen Years After The Fire

An Intercessor does not know. An Intercessor is given permission by the clans to cast themselves into mystery. To do so on behalf of those who cannot make the journey, who have not the ears to hear. An Intercessor goes many places, and never knows where they will land. And so we listen, so we open ourselves, to the great and shining voice, flowing onward with the revelation of the Stream.

But truth is laced through the flesh of falsity, and all, even the wise, are prey to the corruption of earth. It is the force that pollutes, that perverts. That has led our brethren to dust.

We three, the only ones who heard the call to remain.

But Velspar sings, and Velspar draws its spirits near. Even in this silent age, when the beacons of our faith grow dim, Velspar draws its spirits near.

On Avishae, a child of Velspar gave his life. Let this be remembered.

And let him be remembered. Intercessor Ambrose Elshender, this, his rightful name.

He, whose heart called to Velspar – in solitude and desolation – and was heard.

When there were no elders to initiate him, he looked to Velspar for initi-

ation. And he tore the Meridians from his clansmen as he opened their hearts in grief. Opening the way.

Avishae – little island – teaches us, teaches the mainland, as a child teaches his father the joy of crunching autumn leaves.

And precious is his wisdom. A beacon, dark and shining.

Our hands surround his flame.

INTERCESSOR WALDEMAR RASMUS OF BRIVIA, 715.

68

SYBILLA

Fifteen Years After The Fire

Sybilla remembered little of her first days in Nothelm. Interspersed between fevered memories of Gavril, were concerned faces, condescending faces, cunning faces. There were elegant towers of grey stone, sparse trees, and foliage that kept itself near to the ground, holding tight against the salt winds that blustered in from the north.

It was Peran's will that she remain in Nothelm until the babe was born. Things were becoming dangerous in Vaelnyr, spies from the rebellion emerged like termites throughout the Seven Lands. It was Sybilla's sacred duty to protect the Ladain line, to deliver her heir. She was to eat well and rest. His correspondence said nothing of the guard who had been slain. Nothing of her lover, the father of her child. The omission scalded more than anything.

The Braedals gave her fine clothing, respectably altered to accommodate her changing shape, and living quarters as fine as any Skalen could expect. Though she was free to mingle in the town, Sybilla did not feel safe outside of the Skalens' House. Her routine took her from one room to the next, and for a turn in the garden in the afternoon when the sun came to drench the courtyard with its nourishing light.

The gardens themselves were flowerless and austere, featuring rows of clipped topiary hedges.

And this is where she sat, in chill shadow. The time of day when she customarily took tea in the library. Re-entering the House, her heart sank at the sound of approaching footsteps. She tried to hold her head high, though her belly was now round enough to make her waddle.

A tall guardsman rounded the corner, his eyes flicking in her direction. It was Edric, Nothelm's Head Guard. His face had grown older, his beard streaked with grey, but he was that same man who had stood by her side as the Gulf turned red with blood. Fifteen years had passed since that dread day.

"Skalen," Edric said with an automatic smile that evaporated as he continued past.

"Guardsman."

It shamed her that Edric had been the one to escort her to her chambers the day she arrived. He had seen Sybilla raw in her grief. She cried and cursed, tore at her hair, and begged for death. If there was one thing the Guard despised, it was unbridled feeling. Away from Vaelnyr, they regarded her with apprehension. They did not see her as their leader but a weapon that had been discharged to eradicate a greater pestilence.

Continuing down the hall, Sybilla's mouth tightened with resignation. There was a time when she had sought kinship among them, imagined herself as part of their ranks. Even dressed like them. Her humiliation would not end. Her misshapen body bore witness to her disgrace. She had lured a man of the Guard to break his sacred oath, to give his heart to love. Had taken his face in her hands and turned him from his duty. Sybilla walked quietly now, praying she would not encounter anyone else before she reached her soft velvet chair by the fireside.

Entering the library, Sybilla found it as it always was. The golden light of late afternoon illuminated tall shelves filled with leather-bound books. Her shoes clipped across the tessellated tiles, the fire's soothing warmth, fond in its welcome. She sat, and gazed into the fire. The iron grill bore the Skalens' Star. She stared at its centre – the hollow that signified the penetrating insight of the Intercessors. It had been filled with a blot of smooth iron. The Nothelmites were not known for their subtlety. The seven diamonds representing the Seven Lands were absences through which orange flames danced. Its outer edge represented the Skalen's Guard, and had been inlaid with shining copper. She smiled wryly, wondering whether it was Damek's idea to flatter the Guard, or the demands of Edric's shining pride. Perhaps they would now call it the Guard's Star.

Sybilla was startled then by a sudden coolness, looking up to find an Attendant standing between her and the fire.

"The meal will be served now, Skalen Sybilla," the old woman said, dropping into a curtsey.

"Thank you," Sybilla said, recovering herself.

At the thought of food her stomach began to churn, and through the open doorway she caught scent of roast lamb, potatoes and bread. Using the arms of the chair, Sybilla pushed herself to the edge of the cushion and tipped her chest forward to gain the leverage to stand. Thankfully, the dining room was close by.

Lenna and Damek sat at the table, a single place-setting opposite them. It appeared their daughter, Voirrey, would not be joining them tonight. No doubt she was out in the village tending to the sick. Voirrey was a little younger than Sybilla but her heart was as light as that of a maiden. Sybilla felt dirty with guilt the longer she sat with Voirrey, hearing stories of her many acts of humble heroism. But still, she preferred Voirrey's company to that of her fellow Skalens, who itched for her departure.

She lifted her eyes to meet them.

"Ah, good evening, Sybilla!" Damek roared.

She hated it when he was over-friendly, as it tended to fore-shadow some small act of cruelty. "Good evening, Damek." Sybilla managed a small laugh. "You are in good cheer."

"I have had a most interesting day, Sybilla. Things are progressing very well indeed." He smiled into his glass of brandy, relishing its candied bouquet.

She inclined her head and smiled. "Lenna."

"Evening, Sybilla," Lenna replied, pushing a potato segment through thick pan drippings and popping it in her mouth.

"Damek, what is it that has pleased you so well?" Sybilla asked. She cared little for his answer but preferred small talk to the clack of cutlery in the cavernous hall. She pressed her hands into her lap as she waited for her meal to be served.

"Many of my guardsmen have become expert sailors, as you well know." Damek paused to fold a slice of lamb into his mouth. Chewing, he continued. "You may not know that one contingent has been working exclusively on the development of an apparatus that will enable travel far beyond the waters of Velspar, and navigate our safe return. I spent much time examining the instrument today, and it is quite extraordinary!"

"How does it work?"

Damek pointed his fork at her. "Its coordinates are determined by the stars."

Sybilla raised her eyebrows slightly to show that she was impressed but could think of nothing to say. The man was a fool.

Despite herself, Sybilla thought it heresy to put faith in the stars. What would her father have said? She knew without a doubt he would have demanded an end to their boat building. He would have taken Damek's seaward gaze and turned it back to Velspar. But she no longer wished to turn anyone to her cause, her faith shook like a mouse, and she took the crumbs her position afforded her, feeling all of its fragility.

They were so different here, so free of superstition that she could not imagine the kshidol ever set down upon the Stetlan Mountain's pristine peaks. And when Damek took her to the port town where the Temple once stood, showing her the great hole they now used to bury their refuse, she trembled. It was disconcerting. In all the lands she had visited, it was she that held them to their word, who drew them back from the brink of heresy. But in Nothelm, she was heathen. When Sybilla had asked for Alma wine to help her sleep, Damek had laughed.

"We have pulled the weeds from our garden, Sybilla. The Alma makes men soft. It stupefies. You have only to look at Domhnall to see

349

that. Vaelnyr will never prosper if you allow your people to comfort themselves with the Southland's snare."

She had not argued, but knew he was wrong. And in such moments, she saw herself as a relic from a bygone age, holding stubbornly to the past.

A steaming plate arrived before her, and Sybilla began to eat. The meat was dry, but drenched as it was in fat, it revived in the mouth, giving the impression of a much finer cut of lamb. It was delicious, she thought, and the babe began to push and kick, demanding more.

"You have nothing to say on this, Sybilla?" Lenna asked, her pursed expression accentuating the hollows of her cheeks.

Sybilla's thoughts came slowly these days, and it took her a moment to respond. "This apparatus sounds very useful. I am sure it will also be advantageous for the fishermen of Velspar," Sybilla said, addressing Damek.

Lenna leaned toward Sybilla. "You do not think there are undiscovered lands beyond our coast?" Lenna enjoyed moments like this, the twitch of a smile forming whenever she succeeded in intimidating Sybilla into silence.

Sybilla looked at Damek when she finally spoke. "If anyone is to discover the new world, it will be you, Damek."

He gave a satisfied chuckle. "This one is smart," he said to his wife.

Lenna took a sip of wine to loosen the morsel that stuck dry in her throat, and spoke no more that evening.

Sybilla smiled to herself, ever grateful for her Meridian, and flattery's saving grace.

69

SYBILLA

Fifteen Years After The Fire

IT WAS MORNING. Sybilla knew not what day, but frost formed brittle stars upon her windowpane. The skin of her belly had grown tight, and all her days were spent waiting for the little jabs of elbows and knees that told her she was not alone. She still drifted often into dark forests where Gavril screamed her name, but when she felt her baby turning, a little bird flew down to sing its song. A song that knew nothing of cruelty, nothing of loss.

It was a soft feeling, nothing more, but it was as breath to one who was suffocating. These past days, the child's movements brought pain, but with that pain, she felt her daughter's presence. Sybilla feared this knowledge, that her child would be a girl. A child of Siatka. So, she pretended not to know.

There was a knock at the door.

"Hello?" Voirrey's fluting voice sounded through the door.

"Come in!" Sybilla called, shifting herself into a seated position.

"How are we?" Voirrey asked, her bright eyes twinkling.

"Quite well," Sybilla said, discomforted by the attention Voirrey bestowed on her.

"Skalen, may I examine you?"

Sybilla winced, wanting to refuse, but did not wish to estrange the one person in Nothelm who cared if she lived or died. Sybilla suspected that if she were not with child, Voirrey would not have come with her on her walks, would not have attempted to come near the Skalen so wild with grief that she arrived in Nothelm in restraints. But Sybilla was a mother, and to Voirrey, there was no greater joy in life than to deliver a child into the world.

So Sybilla lifted her nightdress and Voirrey washed her hands in a pail of clean water that she had set by the bedside. Voirrey's hands were cold but her touch was gentle. Sybilla smiled as the baby kicked where she touched.

"The position is good," Voirrey said, nodding. "It will not be long now," she added excitedly.

Sybilla tried to laugh but could not hide her apprehension. A woman of her age should have seen childbirth many times, but she was a Skalen, and a novice in these matters.

Voirrey smiled down at her. "All will be well."

"Thank you, Voirrey."

"Now then. Shall we take a walk?" Voirrey said, pulling down her shift.

This was not a question, and slowly Sybilla nodded.

Voirrey smiled. "Would you like help with your gown?"

"Oh no, Voirrey, please. I am fine. I will join you shortly."

When Voirrey closed the door behind her, Sybilla felt a certain heaviness return to the room. A lurking feeling that her bright-haired companion alleviated when she was near.

Removing her night cap, Sybilla slowly unwound her hair, reaching to the bedside for her comb. She no longer bothered to weave horsehair into her braids, adopting a style worn by old women and spinsters – a loose, side-parted bun.

The Attendants had been kind to her in fashioning clothing with few laces or clasps. Today she bulged beneath layers of crimson silk and soft woven wool trimmed in green. She smiled ruefully at the green ribbons that circled her neck and wrists, the colours of Nothelm. The Attendants had such a sense of humour.

The looking glass told her she was ready now for her walk. She did not listen to the other things it had to say. If she looked too long upon her own reflection she would feel her own sorrow, she would see herself in Gavril's eyes. A person deserving of judgement. She much preferred to focus on other things, to witness things outside of herself, and simply be the thing that saw. Not Sybilla, not the Skalen of Vaelnyr.

Not anyone.

70

SYBILLA

Fifteen Years After The Fire

THE PAIN BEGAN TO BUILD once more. Sybilla counted the stitches on the hem of her nightgown as her belly tightened, withstanding it... and then the wave petered out.

"Please, Voirrey, put out that fire." Sybilla wiped the sweat from her forehead, slipping the cloth beneath her Meridian to cool her skin.

"I will lower the flame, but the little one will need to be kept warm. There is frost upon the window, Skalen," Voirrey scolded.

Sybilla was about to argue, but the next wave made it impossible to talk. The intensity was intolerable. Cruel images came to match the pain in her body. Here, Siatka wrapped herself around her belly and squeezed...

She panted, searching the room for the one who was not there, and tears trickled down her cheeks, building to short, gasping sobs.

It came again, clawing at the base of her spine, and she felt herself losing control.

When the talons finally released her, Voirrey approached her with a small vial. "Open your mouth, and lift your tongue," she said.

She did as she was told and Voirrey dripped a distilled substance into her mouth that burned and tasted strongly of Alma. Sybilla closed her eyes gratefully and swallowed. "Bless you, Voirrey," she managed before the pain took her once more.

Soon, however, she found that she could breathe. Her breath began like a girl standing tall by the lakeside. Then it dove in, gliding all the way to the bottom until the sky above called her back.

Through the delight of her breath, she began to harness the sensations of her body. She imagined she held reins about herself, and that she was the one pulling them tight, testing her own strength.

Time was breath, the rise and fall of agony. Voirrey came, and Sybilla opened her mouth, taking more of the Alma. She did not fear. And when the baby moved down, Voirrey gave her body the instructions it needed until she could feel the moist and fuzzy head when she reached her fingers down.

Sybilla heard the cry. Voirrey's eyes were set upon the child, and Sybilla watched her, wanting to see what she could not. Then with a rush, the child was free, and Sybilla felt her for the first time, warm upon her chest. Her little girl, reaching tiny red hands, resting her tender head upon her breast. Sybilla protected her with her palms, large enough to cover her, her heart bubbling over.

But when the Alma began to fade, she searched for her child – the feeling – that presence that she had known when she was yet unborn. It was distant now.

Voirrey wrapped the babe and returned her to Sybilla's arms. "What will you name her?" Voirrey looked longingly at the child.

Sybilla stared at her baby's face, at her scrunched skin and barely opened eyes. She tried to imagine how Gavril's features would merge with her own, to form a face that would forever express the unity of their love. How could his parents have abandoned him to the Guard? A baby as fragile and perfect as this.

She ran a gentle finger along her baby's cheek. "Davina."

Voirrey smiled. "Davina, what a beautiful name. Does it come from your family?"

It was the name of Gavril's elder sister, whom he had loved. It was the only girl's name Sybilla had heard him utter in tenderness, aside from her own. She journeyed back to that moment, his face, the sound of his voice. *Davina*, he'd said.

"Yes," Sybilla replied.

Voirrey nodded and moved away to busy herself, cleaning the floor of Sybilla's blood.

Look at her, Sybilla thought, drawing Gavril's memory near.

The babe strained to open her eyes and Sybilla kissed her.

My beautiful one.

71

SYBILLA

Fifteen Years After The Fire

Sybilla awoke to the sound of whimpering. She made to hoist herself up on her elbows but was much lighter now. She touched the dough of her belly with a curious hand. From the shadows came an impatient cry.

"Shh, Davina," Sybilla cooed softly, as mothers do, making her way across the room.

She picked her daughter up and came to sit by the fire, bringing the child to her breast. But her baby writhed and shook her head from side to side. Sybilla tried to guide her breast to her baby's mouth, afraid the milk would not come.

The child began to cry in little mewling gasps that made those tiny ribs heave. Sybilla tried again but could not get Davina to feed. Tears of frustration coursed down her cheeks as she stared at the baby's fists that shook in rising angst.

There was a knock at the door. "May I come in, Skalen?" Voirrey's muffled voice was tentative.

"Yes, Voirrey, please come in," Sybilla said, trying to bring evenness to her tone.

Voirrey entered wearing a light cloak over her nightgown, her pale hair falling in wisps from her cap. When Voirrey neared, she held out her hands for the baby.

Sybilla handed Davina over, feeling the shame of her failures, knowing that after all she had done, she could not expect a child to love her. She was a monster, and innocence rightly recoiled at her touch.

Voirrey hummed a tune, holding the babe against her with one arm. Before long, the crying ceased, and then Davina let out a satisfied huff, deciding she liked this one much better.

Sybilla stared into the dwindling flames, knowing Voirrey would tell her now of wet nurses, or would take the babe herself to tend to by night.

"Open your arms, Sybilla." Voirrey motioned to her.

Moving with reluctance, Sybilla did as she was asked, bracing for the sound of crying. Davina wriggled at first, but then softened into the crook of her arm, blinking her hazy blue eyes.

"May I speak to you plainly?" Voirrey said, putting her hand upon Sybilla's knee.

Sybilla nodded, afraid of what she might say.

"The problem is this." Voirrey tapped her finger against the stone of her Meridian.

Sybilla frowned and shook her head.

Voirrey sighed, looking far away. "I have no doubt that it helps you. We all know the peace the Meridian can bring. But a child needs its mother, there can be no barriers between a mother and their child."

Sybilla gave her a tight smile. "You are very kind, Voirrey. Thank you for calming her. We will be okay now." Sybilla set her eyes upon Davina's face that crumpled into a frown.

Sybilla listened as Voirrey stood and walked to the door, closing it softly behind her.

Stubbornly, Sybilla rocked the baby as Voirrey had done, but could not think of a tune. As she began to cry, Sybilla felt the pricking of ears all about the Skalens' House. "Shh, Davina, shh…"

It was not working. Panic rose in Sybilla's chest, and she placed Davina in the crib, which only served to louden the babe's cries.

Struggling to keep her thoughts straight, Sybilla hurried to the door and turned the key so no one could disturb them.

In a cold sweat, she considered Voirrey's words. She could do it. This was Gavril's child; this was *her* child. But still, her hands were slow to the strap, hesitant.

Sybilla checked the door again. Then, to be sure, she wedged a wooden chair beneath the handle. The babe was squalling.

She undid the buckle and eased her Meridian away from her skin, feeling the air tingling about her head.

"My little Davina," Sybilla breathed, gathering up her child, who still sobbed, but more gently now. Then, bringing their foreheads to touch, she let love pour from her. She thought of the smiles Gavril drew from her that, years later, gave way to real laughter. She told her daughter, *this is your father.*

Davina's tiny hands pawed at her cheeks, and her blind and hungry mouth began to grope the tip of her nose.

Sybilla giggled, tears starring her smiling eyes.

She sat down by the fire, drew Davina to her breast and helped her find her way. This time, her daughter suckled, drawing milk. The sensation was strange. It stung and tugged unpleasantly, but inside Sybilla was glowing.

The fire crackled and hissed, and in the quiet, she felt that familiar feeling return. Davina was here with her once more.

72

SYBILLA

Fifteen Years After The Fire

"She has emerged!" Damek's voice boomed through the stone hallway.

Sybilla stared at him, but before she could respond, she heard Voirrey's light step coming down the hall.

"Father," Voirrey said, inclining her head.

"You do not take meals with us anymore, Sybilla. Are you ill?" Damek asked, ignoring his daughter.

"Sybilla is quite well, as is the baby," Voirrey informed him in a clipped tone.

"You are the expert in these matters," he said, smoothing his surcoat, his eyes flicking to the window. "Let me show you something." Damek gestured for them to follow him to the window. "That," he said, "is the future of Velspar." His thick finger pointed to the sea, and Sybilla peered through the glass.

All along the coast, half-built boats lay upon the sand, their ribbing exposed like so many carcasses. If she squinted, she could see crafts of many sizes bobbing proud upon the wind-grazed sea, their green sails in flight.

"I have you to thank for this," Damek said, looking at Sybilla. His words did not match the look he gave her, which was one of mild disgust.

Sybilla smiled weakly.

Beneath her cloak, Davina let out a sigh, shifting in the sling that bound her to Sybilla's chest.

"Oh!" Damek gave a startled chuckle. "I wonder that the child can breathe under there!"

"This is how the villagers carry their babes. It is quite safe." Voirrey backed away from the window, taking Sybilla's arm.

Damek looked as though he would say something, but merely made a clicking sound with his tongue, before wishing them good day.

Sybilla held Voirrey's arm and thought with a pang how she reminded her of Lucinda. It was something in the way she stood near Sybilla, and the brightness of her hair.

When they reached the outer doors, Voirrey released her, waving to her Attendant. "You will love the mountains, Sybilla, it is so beautiful there."

Sybilla nodded, still feeling nervous about their outing.

The Attendant stocked the carriage with food and blankets and all the things they would need. An elderly stableman held the reins, the straps sunk deep into his wrinkled hands.

The wheels lurched into motion, and they passed through the noisy part of town, where men barked as they fell from the tavern door, and children ducked into alleyways. Behind the jumble of shopfronts, the docks showed hazily in the distance.

Sybilla set her eyes ahead as the carriage wended beneath winter branches stippled spring-green. Travelling inland and eastward to the foot of the Stetlan Mountains, the landscape sprawled in wide grassland where thick-horned cattle chewed and watched them pass.

The motion of the carriage kept Davina sound in her sleep, but even as she held her child close, Sybilla felt the effects of her Meridian. Voirrey had fallen into a doze, her head bobbing lazily as the wheels jolted over roots and rocks. The road only got worse as they went along, for the pilgrims no longer came with their three drops of blood or their smoke-scented hymns. Sybilla heard the driver talking to the horses, "Easy, easy now." Slowly, the carriage rose up on one side, and with a crash, the wheel came down, waking Voirrey with a fright.

Bleary eyed, she looked out of the window, getting her bearings. "We are almost there, can you see the house?" Voirrey smiled. "Look at the starflowers. They are everywhere. Do they grow in Vaelnyr?"

It was an idyllic vision. Starflowers swayed in mauve and white across the sweeping pasture, extending into woodland and snow-peaked mountains. The little house was made from grey stone and its squat chimney smoked.

"Sometimes... Voirrey, I thought we were coming here alone. There is smoke coming from the chimney," Sybilla said.

A bond of trust had developed between them, but Sybilla had only to detect the smallest sign before she feared treachery.

"You have nothing to fear, Sybilla. The resistance is weak in the Northlands, you know that. It would be the farmhand that lit the fire. His name is Menton. He has worked for my uncle since I was a girl. But he has his own quarters behind the house. He will not bother us." Voirrey patted her arm.

Sybilla took a deep breath that smelt of woodsmoke and sweet-grass. "I'm sorry, Voirrey."

Voirrey turned to catch a peek of Davina who slept, squash-faced against Sybilla's chest. Not wanting to wake her, Voirrey wrinkled her nose at her sweetness and kept quiet for the remainder of the journey.

73

SYBILLA

Fifteen Years After The Fire

Darkness fell, and stars showered night's black shore. Though, the longer Sybilla looked, the brighter the sky became, until it seemed to glow in indigo. The fields and mountain peaks sat in muted shades of grey, utterly still.

Inside, the fire sputtered, and it was warm.

Voirrey held Davina, and kissed the child's forehead. "La, la, lah..." Voirrey babbled, pulling faces that made Sybilla smile.

"Would you have one of your own?" Sybilla asked.

Voirrey gave Davina a squeeze. "I am not sure that is my fate." Voirrey paused. "It is strange that people still believe the Skalens' blood to be holy. They put so much weight upon a title and a name when the spirit can be reborn anywhere. What was your name before you were Sybilla? And what was mine? I do not think it matters what becomes of the name Braedal. We are everywhere."

Sybilla took this flight into philosophy as a sign of some other problem her friend did not wish to discuss. Davina must have sensed it too because she began to cry, reaching her arms out to Sybilla.

"She is hungry," Voirrey said, passing her over.

Sybilla's breasts prickled with fullness, and she wanted to remove her Meridian as she did by night at the Skalens' House in Nothelm.

Voirrey walked to the other side of the room to busy herself with something. Sybilla felt safe here, and should not have doubted her friend. Voirrey had been nothing but kind to her. Had been as family when Sybilla had none of her own. Swallowing nervously, Sybilla removed her Meridian, placed it by her side, shifting the cloth of her dress to feed her child.

Sybilla felt the closeness of her daughter, but this time, she also felt the exhilaration of her daring. She could hear Voirrey moving things about in the kitchen, preparing them a simple meal.

Bowls rattled on the tray as Voirrey walked, steam curling from the broth. Setting them down on the table, she broke a fragrant loaf of bread, fresh baked that morning, and set out a pat of butter.

"Dinner is on the table when you are ready–" Voirrey stopped, staring at her forehead. "Sybilla!" she breathed.

Sybilla smiled, both happily and with shame.

Voirrey clasped her hands to her heart, her head sinking low. As Voirrey unbuckled her own band, she laughed as if in victory.

Then they were both laughing, and Voirrey rushed to embrace her, leaning awkwardly over Davina. As Voirrey drew back, she held Sybilla's head in her hands and pressed their foreheads together. Sybilla's heart seemed to crack and give off liquid. She tried not to move, keeping her eyes shut, smelling the chamomile of Voirrey's hair. The moment passed and her friend let go, moving back to her seat, eyes bright with joy.

She felt a pulse of sweat, and looked down at Davina. Asleep, now. As Sybilla stroked her brow, Davina's mouth fell open and she began to snore. Reluctantly, Sybilla set her down, then smiled at Voirrey, and sat opposite her at the table. She tried the soup and Voirrey spread butter on the bread. As she ate, she noticed all the little knick-knacks about the place. Sleeping animals carved from scented wax, baskets of wool, half-finished lacework folded beside a box of coloured thread.

After their meal, the two women sat by the fire in the generous armchairs intended for the house's usual inhabitants – Haldi Askier and Moriel Braedal. The pair would keep their clan names, even in marriage, for they were equal in the line of inheritance. Only the death of a sibling would set their place among the Seven.

Sybilla smoothed her hand along the worn velvet, wondering who sat where. But in truth she wished she could call it her own.

"I too would love to remain here," Voirrey said wistfully.

Sybilla smiled, but felt her stomach grab, forgetting that her thoughts flowed unguarded.

Voirrey leaned forward. "I have been meaning to ask you, do you intend to take Davina back to Vaelnyr for Festival?"

Festival was a while away, but the thought did not please her. Sybilla knew her time in Nothelm must come to an end, but did it have to happen so soon? "No," Sybilla said with certainty.

At the thought of Vaelnyr, her blood surged as if Peran had just entered the room. Her mood shifted, and she stared into the fire. With a great crack, one of the logs splintered, and she jumped. Eager flames scurried up and down the blackened shards, reminding her of home. Vaelnyr had never stopped burning. She did not want Davina to see it.

From the corner of her eye, she saw Voirrey's blonde hair hanging down – just like Lucinda's – the way she leaned, her elbows on her knees...

"There is so much that I fear," Sybilla said, her eyes stinging at the fire's brightness. "I want Davina to be safe."

"Do you fear the rebellion?"

Lucinda vanished, and there was Voirrey, speaking of things that were happening in Velspar, right now.

Sybilla shook her head.

"You fear death?" Voirrey said, her words hanging starkly in the air.

Sybilla looked at her friend, feeling a chill as she glanced at Davina. They were having a different conversation now, one that she had known would come. "Have you come to kill me?" Sybilla whispered, feeling the stirrings of fate surround her.

"No, Sybilla." Voirrey sat close to her but did not take her hand. "Though I know someone who can help you."

Sybilla glanced at the empty bowls upon the table. They contained nothing now but small salty pools. "What is this person's name?" Sybilla asked, watching Voirrey's forehead, but also looking through her. The shadows of the fire made mountains about her hair, great black mountains, soaked in the blood of her forebears.

Jokvour.

"Amand," Voirrey whispered, softly, so the vision would not break.

Dawn spilled over the peak, revealing figures made from shadow, gathering to meet them on the summit. Some were men, and some were women.

"There is more than one," Sybilla murmured.

"Yes," Voirrey said, a single tear slipping down her cheek as the vision darkened into dust.

74

SYBILLA

Fifteen Years After The Fire

SYBILLA WATCHED VOIRREY with the farmhand and stableman as they prepared the carriage for their departure. She did not like that these men knew her whereabouts. Though she did not trust them, she trusted that Voirrey cared for her child. Whatever was to happen to her, Voirrey would protect Davina.

The old man pulled himself atop the carriage and sat there, head bowed. The farmhand tipped his hat to Voirrey and walked briskly to his cabin. Sybilla moved away from the window as Voirrey opened the gate that framed the country house and its garden.

Moments later, Voirrey entered, bringing a gust of cool air from outside. "Are you ready?"

"Yes," Sybilla assured her, moving to collect Davina from her crib. Her daughter yawned, stretching her fists in the air. It made both of them smile.

When they had climbed aboard, Sybilla focused all her attention on Davina, not wanting to acknowledge the journey they were embarking upon.

Voirrey smiled, her cheeks ruddy in the chill morning air. "We travel to Jokvour," she said, her eyes upon the white peaks of the Stetlan Range.

The word sunk like a rock in Sybilla's stomach, but she did not protest.

"There are two paths that we can take. We can travel the Seltsland way by road and down through Lindesal. If we go that way, we would need to seek the hospitality of the Askier, but in Lindesal, my uncle will make us welcome."

After having stayed in Moriel's house, Sybilla felt she knew the kind of man he'd be. The Regents of Lindesal were one thing, but Sybilla had no doubt that if they sojourned in Seltsland, they would never reach Jokvour. She thought it an unnecessary courtesy on Voirrey's part to pretend she had a choice.

"What is the other path?" Sybilla asked.

"Soon, we will meet the waters of the Kelbourne. If we travel by river, we can pass through Seltsland and Lindesal without touching dry land."

Sybilla paused, thinking of Davina. "What manner of craft have you secured?"

"A Nothelm river boat, with comfortable lodgings under deck. They are common on the Kelbourne and will not attract notice."

"What of the crewmen?" Unpleasant memories of Sybilla's journey to Nothelm returned to her.

"They are my men."

Sybilla scanned the fields, fearing Peran would find her, even here. "Then we go by the Kelbourne," she said, sadness gathering behind her Meridian.

The boat was docked in an obscure mountain inlet. They boarded with only the starlings to witness their passage. The crew were northerners, marked by their accents, but she did not know if their fishing garb was merely for appearances. She kept clear of them, holding her baby close, as if Davina's innocence would protect her.

Sybilla kept below deck when they passed through peopled areas. Cloak-shrouded in the shadows, she heard the thwack of fishing nets and the rough banter of the menfolk interspersed by the quacking of cormorants. The reek of fresh and fouled fish intensified, and then dispersed, but she did not emerge from the cabin. Voirrey often came below, imploring her to stand in the sunshine and to get some fresh air, but Sybilla refused.

When her baby needed her, she could keep her thoughts at bay. But when Davina slept, the torrent came. Her mother stripping roses, threshed thorns about the floor, Attendants sweeping, listening, guards with messages for her father, Lucinda rolling an apple across the floor. Her grandfather, long ago, high upon his chair, Sybilla and her sister among the scuff-kneed boys. Young eyes, sneaking glances... finding the pause... searching, retreating, from white-robed devils, from weavings and game, from the boys and their stick wars, tadpoles and slime... her grandfather's smile. The bells, always chiming, window smoke, thick-bodied smoke, the blood-gullies that ran to the Gulf, Lucinda rolling an apple across the floor. Empty hallways, Lucinda out walking, a cough, red thorns and wine roses, serpents thick as a Skalen's throat—

Sybilla shifted her eyes to the ceiling. The cabin creaked. About the dark and fetid chamber, dust motes shimmered in the gloom. She wrinkled her nose as she changed Davina's soiled garments, wanting nothing more than to feel the breeze on her face. As she fed her daughter, Sybilla listened. There was nothing but churn, the tink of the sail's metal rings, and the steady hush of the wind.

When finished, Sybilla looked down and smiled. "I think we can come out now. What do you say?"

She secured Davina in her sling and opened the door, bright light flooding her vision. The wind blew, and through the tangle of her hair she saw Voirrey. They had reached the wetlands. Thick reeds stretched as far as the eye could see. Here and there, the sun glanced from sky-blue pools.

Davina fussed in her sling.

"I can take her so you can get some rest," Voirrey offered.

Sybilla's head swelled with fatigue, but she did not want to release her child. She breathed deeply, taking in the vastness of the landscape. "We are fine," she said, looking in at her baby, her gums exposed in a wide mouthed grimace.

Sybilla took Davina back below deck and settled herself in the corner to feed. The baby pushed herself away from her mother with stiff fists. Sybilla covered her breasts and removed Davina from her swaddle. She shushed, changed positions, walked up and down, rocked, swayed, and held her with one arm facing outwards as Voirrey did. Nothing worked.

She considered removing her Meridian, saw the folly in it, and left it on. But the crying continued, going on and on so all she could do was count the wooden slats to keep her sanity. In a moment of pity, she felt that her child must miss her, and Sybilla let the impulse take her. She undid the strap.

"There you go," Sybilla whispered, allowing her cheek to drift softly against the down of her hair.

The child took in a shuddering breath and exhaled. She was quiet. Davina clung to her with eyes closed, her breath hitching here and there in echo of her previous cries.

Sybilla sat carefully; Davina's heart a butterfly coming to rest.

She felt herself relax, but as she touched the edge of sleep, Davina stuck her arms sharply into her mother's ribs and wailed. Sybilla's heart sank and became a compressed thing that tightened with the rising pitch of Davina's screams.

Without her Meridian, Sybilla felt an uncontrollable urge to wail with her own voice, to push with her fists, to kick and twist, to cry with racking sobs. The urge came on in waves, like a thousand cloying hands coming to caress her. She counted the boards again, her ribcage stiffening, her fingers curling in.

Sybilla locked her arms, making them a cradle, stepping stiffly up and down the length of the cabin. Pet names formed between her teeth, as the child tried desperately to break free. She set her down in the cot and stepped backward. Arms, legs and mouth searched the air, incensed by the sudden emptiness surrounding her. The baby retched, surging with want.

She reappointed her Meridian and breathed, staring at the child impassively as she reached into the cool solitude of Hiatus. The came Voirrey's hesitant footstep descending the stairs.

"Sybilla? Let me help you," Voirrey said, her resolve only lightly disguised by the gentleness of her tone.

Her shoulders fell, and she stepped aside to let Voirrey past. The child cried as a new set of arms encircled her. Sybilla went above deck and tried to clear her mind.

They had passed the marshes of lower Seltsland and were now in upper Lindesal. Here, the riverbank formed a more definite boundary between water and earth. The early buds of spring dotted broad green hills. Cattle roved in flocks where the farmland began, but the villages were still too far off to see.

The boat jostled her as the river suddenly widened, flowing now with the combined waters of the Kelbourne and Samlae. The turning craft opened up the southern tip of the horizon, where a great cluster of red-tiled roofs gathered heat in the afternoon sun. She stared, watching for the movement of people, but all she could make out was the etched line of the road, and a hint of the Skalens' House turret, flying the burnished flags of Lindesal.

The road drew her down a path of memory, through the town, toward the Sea Altar. She had not seen the bloodied women, or the marks the Maglorean Guard left upon their breasts. Had not seen the crowns of Alma the Attendants had worn as they stamped upon the earth in their ecstatic dance. She had no way of knowing whether Siatka received Skalen Jagoda Hirvola through the proper rites, or whether their spirits were now one. So when Neilan and Orane drowned at the Sea Altar, Sybilla could not say what became of them...

She wondered why the Sisters of Jagoda haunted her after all these years. That the women who served Jagoda could be so drunk with adoration, with the fever of their faith, that they would strip themselves to the flesh just to dance. That their joy extinguished all fear of death. Neilan and Orane seemed men when she was a girl, but now she saw them truly. Their mother six years dead, and still they followed her through the mouth of the serpent. Would that she had the courage to do the same! The heretical wish floated past her, tantalising in its simplicity.

But as the current dragged her on toward her destiny, she allowed her thoughts to come. To cast their shadows against the wall of her mind before all went dark. She wanted to die as Gavril had died, his spirit awake, alive at the last. She must not spend her final days in Hiatus.

The scent of cooking caught her, and her mouth watered involuntarily. It smelt sweetly of root vegetables and beef fat. Making her way across the deck and down the stairs, she noted that Davina had stopped crying. She kept quiet so as not to wake her daughter. Ducking her head, she was surprised to see Voirrey standing in the corner. Sybilla's heart quickened as she noticed her peculiar stance. Davina lay on her back, naked from the waist up, and above her small round belly hovered Voirrey's outstretched hand.

Her thin hand was red, and her eyelids flickered as if she were in trance. Sybilla stood frozen on the stair as Davina lay there, calm, as if beneath the soaking warmth of the sun.

A loud clatter came from the kitchen where the shy-faced crewman prepared their dinner. Sybilla kept herself rigid, praying Voirrey wouldn't notice her. The sound, she saw, had broken her concentration, as Voirrey took a sudden breath, bringing her fingertips to her forehead in a small bow, before reaching for her Meridian.

Sybilla waited several moments before taking the last three steps. "Something smells good," she said, pressing her lips into a smile.

"Oh! Sybilla, you startled me!" Voirrey tucked her hands behind her back, her freckled cheeks darkening.

Sybilla moved past her. "Davina, you are so happy now," she cooed in soft tones, reaching her hands in to draw her baby to her chest.

"I believe dinner is being served. Come along when you are ready," Voirrey said as she exited.

Davina nuzzled into her mother's neck, her body utterly relaxed now. Sybilla brushed her lips across her head, avoiding the small depression in front of her crown. She wanted to fill her heart with her child's particular scent, now they held each other so. But it was mingled with chamomile, sweat, oil of almond; the scent of blonde hair and thin red hands, a scent that unsettled her thoughts, and made her think of the morrow.

75

WALDEMAR

Fifteen Years After The Fire

THERE HAVE BEEN MANY TIMES *when doubt has stuck its swords in me, weakening my resolve. But Velspar is generous. Unwavering. Velspar sees us when we cannot see ourselves. And Velspar guides me still.*

I feared our number were too small, that even if we overcame our enemies, we would remain lost. Forever, the people of Velspar would remember, and they would mourn. Their worship given to nothingness, given to gods that would not return.

They would sanctify the Temples, and make frescoes of their forms, Mother Siatka, the graceful one, Father Kshidol, thick plumed and wise. The last of us to remember their image, as seen with our own eyes, would perish, their scent extinguished, their call unheard.

But I have seen the shining furnace of Intercession.

The dark and snaking seam from which the Holy Ones were born.

The shimmering place.

The place of changing.

INTERCESSOR WALDEMAR RASMUS OF BRIVIA, *715.*

76

ZOHAR

Fifteen Years After The Fire

ZOHAR WATCHED HER MOTHER'S FACE as the strangers approached. The Attendants had braided Skalen Rebekah's hair, as she would not let them wash it. Piled as it was in tight nubs atop her head, her tortured face stood perilously exposed. Zohar's father was flushed, his eyes darting from beneath lowered brows as if seeking escape.

The Intercessors did not wear white. Their robes were tattered things that passed as blankets by night, and kept the weather off them by day. As they approached, Zohar noted they had made use of their journey by river, for their skin was cleanly, and their eyes shone bright.

When they crossed the outer threshold at the gates, her parents bowed. Zohar followed, moments behind, and rose to find Maeryn smiling at her. Waldemar's eyes locked upon her mother. The nod of welcome Waldemar gave was not quite a bow, and though he also met her father's eyes, he did not grace him with a smile.

Behind her, and on either side, Zohar sensed the guards standing at attention, but if they felt something about this portentous moment, she could not tell. Zohar knew what her mother felt – she was a marble statue weeping blood. And her father held his centre tight like a fist, holding something dark and shameful within.

Amand stepped forward to break the silence. "Skalens," Amand said, bowing, "we come in friendship."

Her mother unstuck her lower lip, her words coming slowly. "We welcome you to Avishae."

"Come in, it is cold out," her father added brusquely, tightening his cloak.

With a creak, the heavy wooden doors of the Skalens' House opened behind them. The winds of late autumn brought yet another gust of red leaves about their feet, and a flurry of Attendants rushed to sweep them away. Zohar saw Elspeth among them, her eyes following their guests while her hands worked with brush and pan.

They entered the main hall, and once the six of them had filed in, the guards fastened the door. Though the wind blew fiercely without, inside, the pall of silence was unbearable. Chairs creaked as they sat around the table, and Zohar waited for one of them to speak. Eventually, Waldemar, who sat opposite her parents, opened his palms. He stared at his hands for a moment before raising his head. His eyes marbled with tears, and Zohar heard her mother gasp as she joined him, her body convulsing with sobs he seemed to draw from her. Zohar stared, unable to look away, as her mother heaved, her body curled in as if her heart burned in her chest.

Amand stood and walked slowly around the table and held his hands above her father's head. He went very still. Then with widening eyes, he began to shudder. His lip trembled, but he held his teeth tight against the storm that rose within. Amand stood behind him, clicking his fingers at the three points, humming low as he worked, then placed his hands on her father's shoulders, his skin reddening halfway up his forearm. She felt her father losing his grip, and within him, something slipped away.

Without warning he let out a terrible sound. A grating howl, impossibly deep, that seemed to come from a yawning slit in his throat. Zohar wanted to cry out, to gather him in, to stop the air from playing about the gash in his neck.

But as her heart raced, Maeryn caught her eye and nodded. *Walk with me*, she seemed to say. Her face was soft and kindly as she rounded the table. When Maeryn clasped her hand, Zohar found that she could no longer hear her parents. A profound feeling of peacefulness blossomed about her forehead, swelling atop her crown like a flower. A delicious feeling, like honeyed wine, both warm and refreshing.

They stood at the window where the wind ruffled the surface of the sea. In the distance she saw a raft. Ambrose was there! *Ambrose!* She gasped, reaching her hand to the window. She turned to the woman beside her; *my brother is here*, she said in her mind. The woman nodded. Zohar's heart swelled with excitement. Then her thoughts fell in a jumble as she tried to tell her everything about him. And everything she brought to mind radiated with joy! That joke he used to tell – she laughed so hard that the tree of her memory lost all of its leaves. She lay down among them, fanning her arms out, hearing them rustle, kicking them into the air with bare feet.

A leaf, all yellow and scarlet, fluttered down and she caught it. This one. She smiled. Down at the beach, drawing secrets with sticks into wet sand. Laughing as the water washed them away. It was her turn. She drew her mother's fat belly. Ambrose laughed and poked the stick for her navel. Then came the tide, catching and melting her away. Ambrose drew a snake, long and twisting, its jaws open wide. He wrote Her name. Zohar licked her lips nervously, glancing to the guard. The waves were slow to claim this one. Ambrose leaned upon his stick, casual as could be, dark curls dancing in the wind. That face. How she loved him.

The winds came on strong, sharp with sand, and she squinted to see him. *Ambrose!* She called. Sand was everywhere. She looked down and saw that her feet were deep in the tide-wet shore. It sucked at her legs, gathering about her in a ferocious storm of needles so she had no choice but to close her eyes. *Ambrose!* she cried, scared now. The sand was tight about her body, up to her neck and bearing down. If she exhaled now, the sand would follow the breath inward so that her chest would never expand again. She stopped. Froze herself. Willed herself not to think, feel, sense, know...

The soft, elderly hand squeezed hers. The room began to come back into view. Zohar's bodice was drenched with sweat, her neck, armpits and groin burning as if she suffered fever. Remembering her parents, she searched for them in sudden terror, expecting to find them mangled by their pains. They were not. They sat calmly and looked toward her with generosity, with sympathy. She shook her head as if they, too, were apparitions, too perfect to be real. The weightlessness of their hearts was too ancient in her memory, trapped in a time of games and spinning tops, grazed knees and saddles too big for her to ride.

"Is this real?" Zohar asked numbly.

Her parents opened their arms to draw her in. She staggered to them, falling into their embrace, surrounded by their scent, their hands upon her hair. Zohar felt her breast warm against them, the small space between them a sanctuary light with rain.

77

ZOHAR

Fifteen Years After The Fire

THE INTERCESSORS BROKE BREAD with them. They laughed, and the food tasted good. Zohar's father raised a toast to Velspar. The air was sweet with smoke. She did not know how they arrived at this moment, but it shined, and she wanted it to keep on shining. Zohar had drunk enough wine to bring heat to her cheeks, and sat back in her chair, thinking for the first time since the meal began, of Ambrose.

When she looked up, Waldemar caught her eye. "There is something that we must discuss," he said.

Her parents both looked at him, chastened by the breaking of their reverie.

"Rebekah, Ulric," Waldemar said, looking at them in turn. "I have seen your guilt and how it plagues you. But none of us who survived the Purge are innocent."

Zohar tried to see the man clearly, to detect what shame lay hidden behind his eyes.

"You wonder at me, child," Waldemar said, turning to Zohar.

"Apologies, Intercessor, I–" Zohar began.

Waldemar waved his hands. "No, no – we come here with open

hearts."

He swallowed, narrowed his eyes. "You, the Skalens Elshender, sent many innocents to the pyre. But beneath your red deeds there was the spark of good intent."

Zohar looked at her parents, their faces turning grey.

"And so it was with me," Waldemar said. "It was my good intent that brought fire to Sybilla's door. It was my red deed that brought ruin to Avishae. Mine." He thumped his fist to his chest.

Maeryn and Amand glanced at the man from either side with expressions of pained sympathy.

Her father's eyes widened. "Then you are to be praised, Intercessor! It is not your fault the fire did not finish its work. You saw what Sybilla was long before the rest of us."

Waldemar chuckled darkly, shaking his head. "No. I allowed red thoughts and the ambitions of others to guide my hand. Whatever Sybilla became, I must take my own share of responsibility for it. Her monstrosity is of my making."

Her mother clenched her hands.

"Rebekah." Maeryn tilted her head and waited until she looked up. "We have seen the other lands. Avishae would have been taken, just like Brivia and Lindesal. The faithful would have been executed, and you with them. Your sacrifice was not made in vain."

Amand nodded, looking eagerly to Waldemar.

"This," Waldemar said, "is why we have come. Your son, Ambrose, he uncovered an object of great power."

"What do you know of it?" Her father's brow furrowed.

"I know that it also exists in Brivia," Waldemar said.

"It is in your possession?" her mother asked, breathlessly.

"With the proper tools, and labour, we will be able to unearth it," Waldemar said.

"Then it must be destroyed," Zohar said, forgetting all decorum.

"Destroyed?" Waldemar gaped. "No, child. The stone is the blood of Velspar. It is holy."

She stared at him dumbfounded, the hairs of her arms prickling in anger.

Looking back to her parents, Waldemar continued. "We know

379

from recent visions that the piece held by your son was fragmented, and that Rebekah has hidden one of the three. The other fragments are…" he searched her mother's face.

"You can't!" Zohar shouted, but her parents merely sat, staring at the old man. Zohar pulled at her father's arm. "No, Father, don't let him!"

Slowly, her father came to look at her, and clasped her hand, but his eyes were milky, his spirit traversing some place beyond sight.

"Mother!" Zohar beat her fist on the table to rouse her. Her mother's body was entirely rigid, such that she did not blink, her pupils loose with Alma.

Before she knew what was happening, Amand had grasped her head, and with firm hands pressed his forehead to hers. He smelt of earth and lemon thyme, his breath like salt water. He reached into her, found the feeling of the stone, the way it had run thick through her spirit, coursing with blackness, speaking in a thousand tongues. He made her feel it again, she and Illiam merging and coming apart, her grandfather hungry with bloodlust. The body of her brother, smooth as an egg in the moonlight. The stone throbbing in his belly, like a bird wanting to be born.

But it did not burst forth… It nuzzled deeper, exiting her brother's back, pushing down into the earth. It called to the Stream, finding, furrowing. For an instant she saw it, a lightning flash, a snaking river of black stone, deep within the earth. Its colours looked into her like so many eyes. She shook, transfixed, unable to call herself back.

Suddenly, she lurched, as if emerging from deep water. Amand stood back from her but still held his hand to her face. His pale eyes harboured many colours, and if she looked too long upon them, she felt she would come apart.

"Hush," Amand said in a whisper, remaining completely still.

Zohar stretched her fingers out by her sides, trying to remember her body. Slowly, the room about her solidified, becoming real.

Amand let his hand drift down, and nodded, confirming that she was okay now.

"The seam runs beneath us, the Bay, and the east coast of Brivia," her father said, matter-of-factly, for all had seen the vision.

"It runs also through Jokvour," Waldemar said wryly.

Amand joined him with a wide smile. "It hides well beneath the blinding stone, so deep that none would find it."

Zohar felt these revelations teeter in her mind, finding little purchase. "Then it is our job to keep it hidden."

Waldemar pressed his lips, choosing his words. "My child, you are too young to know what is best. You fear the stone because of your brother's death, but if he were joined by other Intercessors, he would have wielded it and found great insight. Do you curse the fire because it burns your hand when you hold it to the flame?"

Zohar caught a fleeting expression on her mother's face.

"Intercessors," her mother said. "I honour your wisdom, but there are but three of you. There are no initiates in Avishae."

"This is the case, Rebekah. But I do believe the three of us can channel the power of one stone. Those that your son still holds will not be taken from him," Waldemar assured her.

At this, her father nodded strongly, and Zohar's stomach unclenched.

"What do you plan to do with it?" her mother asked.

Waldemar looked at them darkly. "If there is one thing I have learned, it is that the Great Stream does not quench the passion of evil. It will return. If Sybilla dies without receiving Intercession, she will be birthed somewhere else, drawing blood from her mother's breast until she is old enough to bring her wrath upon us once more."

Zohar began to laugh uncontrollably.

Her mother steadied her with her hand, but no one paid Zohar any heed. They wanted the stone, and only her mother knew where it was.

"Do you know where Sybilla is now?" her mother asked.

"We have her. She will be brought to Jokvour," Waldemar said, fixing her parents with his feverish stare.

Her mother straightened in her chair. "It was my son who found the stone. It was my daughter who shrouded it and in doing so, liberated us of the Meridian. If it were not for my children, you would not have received our visions." The fire crackled as she paused. "The Elshenders are a part of this stone. It is an Avishae stone. If you want it, and if this is your mission, then you must take us with you. Those are our terms."

Zohar could not believe what she was hearing, and felt violently opposed to the idea.

Maeryn glanced at Zohar and then whispered something in Waldemar's ear. When Maeryn was finished, the old man looked at Zohar with keen terror.

Waldemar pointed his bony finger in Zohar's direction. "She has made herself dirty with blood magic. She must remain in Avishae."

Her mother faced him. "All of us, Intercessor. Or you will leave this place with empty hands."

78

ZOHAR

Fifteen Years After The Fire

"CAN YOU FEEL ANYTHING?" Illiam stood beside her, his hand upon her shoulder.

Zohar closed her eyes, spray from the hull clinging to her eyelashes and hair.

Her mother squeezed her hand. "It is alright if you don't, darling."

Zohar searched her spirit for the foreign thread and followed it once more. "I do... I just can't hold onto it," Zohar said, still seeking the meandering strand.

"Let go, child. Velspar will guide us." Maeryn's voice came from behind her.

Zohar abandoned her pursuit, searching the heavy canopy that crested the Brivian coast for signs of life. They travelled with the stone. It lay silently, encased in a chest of blinding stone. There were locks upon it of many kinds. The Sherburns had crafted the chest, working fresh blinding stone into interlocking tiles that left no fissures for the stone to speak. Mr Corbin gifted locks from his collection to protect the holy relic. It sat below deck – unguarded at present, for all were in sight.

Though her father's presence was part of the bargain her mother had struck with the Intercessors, he resolved to stay behind. Zohar knew what he feared. She saw the flash of it in the dark of his eye. Townsfolk and villagers clawing up the mountain to tear her brother apart, to wrest the stone from him. Her grandfather, for his part, seemed much chastened since the arrival of the Intercessors. Zohar saw him so clearly now. He burned the Alma, he tinkered at the edges of Intercession, but he could not find his way into the heart of it. Now that Zohar knew how it felt, she understood why the Intercessors had stood above them all, the font of holiness and dread.

They had set forth for Jokvour, but Zohar knew her mother's thoughts, like her own, remained in Avishae. The cairn would be protected, day and night. Her father had chosen the guardians: Edith Raeburn, Patrick Milwain, Robert Sherburn, and Head Guardsman John. The others from the Raeburn camp had been sent to shepherd the people of Avishae. Ma Bet went door to door, looming over housemaids and stiff-jawed farmers giving them licence to be rid of their Meridians. Many did not believe. But her father helped them build a second cairn in the valley where they gathered to pray.

As the boat neared Port Innes, Illiam went to help Amand with the sail.

"Are you afraid?" her mother asked.

Zohar felt her mother's exhilaration. "I don't know. None of this seems real." The current drew her on, but she did not know where it was taking her.

Her mother nodded, trying to still the smile that played upon her lips.

Zohar realised this was the first time her mother had been to the mainland since the Council of Vaelnyr. How strange to think of that time. Creeping on pad-foot down the sombre halls of their House, Zohar and Ambrose meeting eyes at the whispered name, *Sybilla*. And now her mother was returning, three Intercessors by her side, to face the one who started it all.

At the dock, a party of guards awaited them. The three-fingered guardswoman was among them, but this time, she did not inspect Meridians. They mounted double-saddled horses and moved out, Waldemar and Amand up front, her mother and Maeryn next in line, and Zohar with Illiam at the back. The journey commenced in silence. The canopy rushed high above them, and deep among the leaves, birds sounded their call, triangulating the presence of horses, of riders, of warm-blooded creatures working their way deeper into their verdant realm.

Zohar hugged Illiam's waist, feeling his breath as her own. Her fantasies seemed so frivolous now. His skin did not steam with passion's mist, his hair did not glow. Since that night with the stone, she knew all his many embarrassments, his fear of singing, taunts from his uncle, the webbing on his little toe. She knew the scald of a pustuled rash that had raged on his arm for weeks. She knew the chore of bathing, of washing parts of his body that had once made her blush. With weariness, she knew the foul smells that sometimes came from him, the habits, the pickings and scratchings.

The smell of oranges now reminded her, not of Ma Bet's cabin, red twine and pushed cloves, but of being a small boy, walking at market in Maglore, catching an orange thrown by a girl with pigtailed hair. His portrait was so full it lost all of its art, and she knew her luminescence had also faded. Illiam knew her petty jealousies, peacocking about in her room, wishing and wanting, pimples and all. He knew how she hid from the fires of her childhood though she was old enough now to recall. How many years would it have taken to know each other this way without the stone? There was not even room for the shame of it, for at the bottom of it all was Ambrose, the horror they shared – Zohar and Illiam, Illiam and Zohar – their eyes wide to the rift that gaped before them.

The person she used to be understood the push and pull romance asked of lovers before consummation. Dimly, she regretted losing all of that, for even as she held him, the flame of desire would not catch. It seemed they would not pine for each other in solitude, would not retrace memories of their last meeting trying to solve the puzzle of words and gestures. They would not mistake one another's intentions and close themselves away. They would not reunite and realise their folly in a shower of kisses. They were as two rock pools, relieved of their dividing wall. But still, they held their waters back, out of habit more than anything, enforcing the memory of separation.

On the first day, and the second, she watched Waldemar and Amand rock upon their horse at the front of the line, Amand's brown cloak ragged at the edge. Her mother rode with Maeryn just ahead of them, and Zohar wondered how she could hold the old woman about the waist as if they were kin. Did her mother fall guiltily into the faith of her youth? Or had she strayed too far for that? Before Zohar's thoughts could go any further, Illiam's presence wafted into her, his silent touch a warning. He was right, she should not think so freely now.

"We are almost there," Illiam said, his muffled voice vibrating through his back and into her chest.

She lifted her head, recognising the place, and feeling it as familiar as home. The horses passed into the forecourt of the Skalens' House, following its paved circular ring. Rivulets of water funnelled into the central drain, filling the forest with a wet-throated sound. Jemryn and Olinda stood smiling at the entrance, and Zohar waved, for now they seemed blood of her blood.

Illiam hopped down, then held his hand to Zohar. Then the two of them walked, arm in arm.

Jemryn stifled a chuckle. "Well, what do we have here?"

Olinda looked from Zohar to Illiam and back again.

Zohar laughed. It was infectious. Within seconds Illiam was laughing too, and heartily at that.

Her mother strode toward them, smoothing her hair for a Skalen's introduction. But these were dizzy times, and Zohar put her arm around her mother. "These are Illiam's parents, Olinda and Jemryn."

"I see you have taken my earlier dismissal of titles to heart, Zohar." Olinda bowed. "Welcome, Skalen."

The awkward moment ended as Waldemar strode toward them, Maeryn and Amand in tow.

"Intercessors." Jemryn and Olinda greeted them with heads low.

"It is good to see you again, my friends," Waldemar said with a sigh. "All is well in Brivia, I trust?"

"All is in hand," Olinda assured him.

The Attendants met them in a flurry, tugging at cloaks so they might be hung to dry by the fire. Her mother walked beside Olinda, and the Intercessors followed, garnering details about what had transpired on the mainland during their absence.

Zohar walked behind, caring little for their conversation. Feeling a pull on her hand, she turned.

Illiam smiled. "Follow me. They won't even notice we are gone."

For a moment Zohar felt a spark of excitement, uncertain of what he had planned.

He ran down the hall and she followed breathlessly behind. They had turned so many corners, that Zohar lost her bearings. Finally, Illiam stopped and opened a small door. Catching up to him, Zohar inclined her head, and passed through into a tiny room with a maroon settee, a wooden side-table, and a desk strewn with books.

"What is this place?" Zohar asked, noticing the movement of foliage through the window.

Illiam grasped her by the shoulders and gazed at her with intent. Zohar noticed the shape of his shaven face, his short, curled hair, his eyes the colour of oiled wood.

He kissed Zohar full upon the mouth. It felt good, but the little spark had gone out. The glittering thing had rolled into some dark corner where she feared she'd never find it.

She ran her hands beneath his shirt, trying to find undiscovered territory, but his skin felt too familiar, too much like her own.

Zohar pulled away and looked at him. "This isn't working."

Illiam sighed. "I know."

Zohar shivered. "It is freezing in here."

Illiam wrapped his arm around her shoulder and they sat together on the settee. They sat in silence for a while.

"What will we do?" Zohar asked, tracing the scars upon his hand.

"The stone has made us old," Illiam said, a scowl forming on his face.

Zohar shared his sentiment. "There has to be a way to fix it," she said, holding little hope.

He placed his finger to the disc of blinding stone at her forehead, pushing it upward so her Meridian fell to the floor. Removing his own, he drew their foreheads together. His hands were warm and he wanted this so much. She ran her hands up his thighs. They breathed into each other, their lips almost touching. A shiver coursed through him, through her hands. She persisted.

Then, after a time, Zohar felt a stranger enter the room of his mind. The maiden walked upon grey sand, night's water tugging at her gown. He reached out to touch the soft waves of her reddish hair. She stood in the forest, removing her bodice in the afternoon sun. Her naked flesh pressed against the pine, hands slipping over skin. Zohar gasped, in the darkness she found it, sharp and bright.

How he had kept this from her she could not fathom, but this time she did not know what would happen next. This time, she kissed a different Illiam.

79

ZOHAR

Fifteen Years After The Fire

THEY STOOD UPON THE PEAK watching the women in their slow ascent. Zohar felt a sudden thirst, and swallowed dryly. To one side, her mother stood, her eyes flickering as if she meant to blink. To the other stood Illiam, the corners of his mouth wound down in an apprehensive expression. But the Intercessors were calm and slate-faced as the hulking ridges of black stone that surrounded them. The unnatural silence of Jokvour seemed to quiet the wind, to swallow the bird's call. As the women emerged from behind a jutting slab of rock, Zohar saw their faces, dour in the dawning light. One was slight of build with pale hair – Voirrey. The other, was Sybilla. For a second Zohar felt nothing, but then it was as if a gust of wind had washed her legs away, and all her blood was in her chest. She blinked to clear her vision, but Sybilla seemed a shimmering thing reflecting too many impressions at once.

She looked strange. Her face was fuller, and she looked as though she had aged ten years in the two that had passed since Zohar had last seen her. Sybilla walked awkwardly with her arms bundled under her cloak, and her guardsman was not with her. Zohar tried to sharpen her anger but felt only a kind of pity or disgust.

As she stared, Zohar sensed Sybilla's grief like a foul odour on the wind. The sensation gave off images, of lover's blood soaking black soil, of screams and ash, of blonde hair clinging to a charred branch of thorns. She felt the woman's confinement, death hovering close, and uncertain fragrances mingling all together, of chamomile, oil of Alma and the downy scent of the babe. Zohar recoiled, and clung to Illiam's hand, focusing on him, the blisters on his palm and the keen simplicity of his moral stance – this woman was a murderer.

Zohar waited for the silence to break.

"Sybilla Ladain of Vaelnyr," Waldemar's voice rang out. "You have been called to Jokvour to receive holy judgement."

A gust of wind came, casting her cloak to one side, revealing the child.

Amand approached Voirrey and whispered something in her ear, who turned to Sybilla, asking for the baby.

Sybilla began to cry, fast tears slipping down her cheeks as she tried to harden herself, to remain strong. But as the child left her arms, she gaped at the hollow, and clutched her chest. Zohar winced as she felt the pang, the tug of loss, all over again.

Sybilla stood on her own, pressing her fists into her eyes. Then, with her hands now hanging by her sides, she looked up. Zohar felt the surety of her death, felt her standing at the edge of the Stream, the wetness of it at her feet. Sybilla's eyes moved along the line, but she did not appear surprised, and Zohar wondered if Voirrey had told her everything, if somehow she knew what had happened to Ambrose.

Waldemar led them into the cave. He pointed to a place by the fire, and Sybilla sat, the others standing around. Voirrey and the babe did not follow.

Sybilla's head hung low, and Zohar noticed the rush of silver that spread from her crown, the worn leather of her Meridian.

"Skalen, arise," Waldemar said.

Sybilla did so, her eyes sliding dully to the side.

"Do you recognise Intercessor Maeryn? She is from your birthplace of Vaelnyr." Waldemar spoke slowly as if Sybilla had suffered a knock to the head.

Sybilla moved her dark eyes toward Maeryn, but could not quite look at her, giving a small nod instead.

"I am Intercessor Waldemar Rasmus of Brivia." He gestured to his left. "This is Intercessor Amand Angenet of Seltsland."

Amand's face crinkled sourly.

Then, Waldemar pointed to her mother. "Skalen Rebekah Elshender of Avishae, her daughter Zohar, and Illiam Greslet of Maglore."

Sybilla frowned slightly, and then the expression was gone.

Waldemar paused, thickening with presence as the rest of them listened. "I never met your father, but his name is legend. It was he who named the First Heresy, was it not?"

Sybilla glared into the flames.

"It was he who started this bloodshed. And you, the grieving daughter, took up his mantle. You, and – Peran, the guardsman."

Waldemar removed his hood, as the fire had grown hot. "Sybilla." He brought his gaze level with hers. "Are you a woman of faith?"

Zohar felt a tiny buzz, like insects scurrying from water. Sybilla's eyes darted around, but her lips remained tightly shut.

Waldemar nodded to himself. "Well, this will be the test of your faith. Of Velspar's faith in you. Today you will perform the Blood Call," he said. "Take her to the circle."

Sybilla's neck stiffened, but still she looked down.

Maeryn came to Sybilla's side, linking arms with her. Amand guided her other shoulder, pushing her slightly as they emerged from the cave. A brisk wind greeted them. Zohar watched Sybilla, deformed by guilt, wondering what the stone would do to her.

They had built the circle on a wide outcrop. At home, and along the way they had spent countless hours touching the stones, caressing them, rubbing their bodies to life. Their silence was attuned to the living now. The circle smoked with Alma. Within it sat the box, and Maeryn guided Sybilla to the centre before stepping back behind the line of blinding stone.

Sybilla breathed, sharp and shallow, trembling whenever the wind came as if it might send her crashing into the chasm below.

"Sybilla," Waldemar said, "Velspar has given us a great gift. A gift that may yet prove your part in Velspar's plan."

She stared at him as he pointed to the box. Sybilla crouched, pressing her lips as she turned the key. She glanced at the knife.

"Remove your Meridian, and cast it out of the circle," Waldemar instructed.

Sybilla slipped her Meridian from her head, squeezing it in her hand a moment before casting it out. She went to the box, and opened its heavy lid, frowning at the dark and glistening thing inside.

"Make the cut, and then take the stone in your hand," Waldemar said.

Sybilla took up the knife. Closing her eyes, she pushed the blade across her palm, laying the stone upon the mess of blood that darkened her skin.

Moments later, she began to shake.

"Form the circle," Waldemar commanded.

The circle closed around her, palm upon palm.

Zohar watched Sybilla as if she watched herself, knowing all the sensations that wracked the woman's body, that sought to tear her apart. Her eyes rolled back, her mouth a grimace.

"Call Him," Waldemar said.

Sybilla did not seem to hear and was now emitting throat noises that came in their own nauseated rhythm.

"Call Him now Sybilla." Waldemar's words vibrated through the circle and seemed to penetrate the Skalen's mind, as she looked at him fixedly now.

She looked skyward. "Father..." The word-moan barely made it from her lips. Sweat slipped down the sides of her face. "Father!" This time her voice rang clear through the mountains.

"Use the god-names," Waldemar spat.

Wavering where she stood, Sybilla clamped her lips shut and looked as if she would be sick. "Kshidol!" She buckled and held her arms across her face.

"Call The Mother," Waldemar urged.

Sybilla's head rested on its side like a flower on a broken stem.

"Siatka..." she whispered into the dirt. A mad spark came to her eye. "Siatka…" she whispered again, barely audible this time. She put her ear to the ground, her closed lids flickering in the silence that followed.

Then without warning, she heaved, throwing herself backward, her face rigid.

"Sybilla," Waldemar said, the whites of his eyes showing. "Sybilla, what is your vision?"

Her body remained frozen, her mouth agape.

Zohar watched Sybilla, distantly sensing what flared within. She stared at the woman's open mouth, a queasy tugging sensation in her belly. The feeling sharpened and as she stared, the mouth began to change, the world around her falling dim.

A deep, wet abyss opened up, framed by ceremonial daggers. Sybilla was driven into it, blades dragging as she passed through. She slithered from the sun, deeper into darkness. Sliding through rough tunnels where the water ran thin. Her arms and legs were gone, she was hairless and scaled all over, she felt the god-name rise in her throat, filling the tunnel that ran deep beneath the mountain.

She was being sucked, the threads of her, through endless rock, and she felt Siatka coming, slipping in and out of Her muscular rhythm, the creature's body given slide by the gloss of Her own blood. She could sense Sybilla, and the others up above. She would find the deep pool in the belly of the mountain, She would press Her tongue to the cave wall where the stone ran bright and black, She would draw the spirit down, silver threads sweet with smoke.

Zohar felt pain in her hand and looked at it, curious to find that she was still standing between her mother and Illiam, a part of the circle. Illiam hurt her hand again and she frowned at him. He seemed to travel up her arm a little way, moving like blood into a sleeping limb. The tingling sensation flowed through her shoulder and into her face. When it reached her forehead, her mind cleared a little.

She focused on her feet, her body, on Illiam's hand. "She is trapped in vision. She is dying," Zohar said in a faraway voice.

Waldemar turned to her, teeth bared. Then Maeryn caught his eye, and nodded.

Smoothing his features, Waldemar smiled at Zohar. "Have you the courage to bring her back, child?"

It was not a question.

Zohar stared at the figure before her, unable to prevent herself from seeing Ambrose in Sybilla's place. The skin leeched of colour, the stiffness of those limbs. Letting go of her mother's hand, Zohar removed her Meridian, dropping it on the ground. Her other hand still held Illiam's as she stepped inside the circle. She felt Illiam drift close, flowing around her. Zohar did not know if it was him who buffered the power of the stone, or if it was spent on Sybilla, but she found that she could think. Her thoughts, when they came, were exceedingly vivid, rich with scents, extending the bounds of her body, but they did not overwhelm her.

Zohar knelt beside Sybilla, observing the terrible arch of her back. She looked at her as if she had come upon a horse ravaged by wolves, looking calmly at the fearful rolling eyes, and more calmly still at the unstitchable gash from which its entrails hung. Cradling Sybilla's head in one hand, she eased it forward, the tautness of the woman's form giving way in little jolts. Zohar managed to shift Sybilla so the Skalen sat, though her head still slumped to the side, her eyes vacant and unblinking, her fingers curled into tight-boned claws.

When Zohar closed her eyes, the power of the stone surged through her. She lost her bearings. The stone tasted of her brother's hair. Tears rose in her throat. It knew where he was. It would show her. Zohar could see him, his wild hair, his brooding look, right there in the deep of Sybilla's left eye. The stone urged her on, and Zohar brought her brow to Sybilla's, searching for him. Forgetting where she was or how she came to be there, Zohar gripped Sybilla's skull and pushed herself through the three points. *Where is my brother?*

Raft, Bay, Avishae – Zohar slipped into a gust of memory that was not her own.

Ambrose looked at her with strange eyes – reserved – he laughed – falsely, nervously – his eyes flicked – noticed her body – his shoulders braced against the pounding surf. His hair shook in the wind, and then he dove in. Zohar followed him down – water deep, his body upside down, the pale blur of his skin – she pushed, came closer, almost burst – her fingers traced the blistered stone – he cut her!

The cloud of blood darkened her vision, and when it cleared, there was only Sybilla, her hair twisting like a rope around Zohar's ankle, dragging her swiftly down. Above them, on the surface, ash rained down, sparks sizzling as the whole world burned. The silt was blinding. And in darkness they landed. Their bodies thudded softly, one after the other onto the ocean floor.

Ambrose, Zohar thought, but Sybilla was stronger – *Gavril*, came Sybilla's husky groan. A sucking current dragged the woman away, the coil of her hair slipping silkily from Zohar's ankle – taken off somewhere in the darkness.

Zohar remained where she was, the black water becoming silent and still. She moved her hands along the seabed finding only rippled sand. Her fingers grew numb. She was so tired and thought she might rest here, and close her eyes. Her body was like lead, the curve of her hip and her jutting arm creating depressions in the sand. Her cheek sunk down, her jaw, her lips. Absently, her fingers stroked the sand.

Her forefinger discovered something hard and rough, returning to it, brushing it clear. It seemed to be growing. As she traced the shape of it, she realised that it was a branch and that at the tip of the branch were smooth green leaves.

She heard a watery sound. A voice.

Zohar.

The branch pushed up, lifting her shoulder.

Zohar, can you hear me? Don't let go of my hand! In a rush she recognised Illiam's voice, breathy like mountain wind, and the tree's thick branches lifted her up. To the strongest branch Zohar clung, the rush of distance passing her closed lids.

She fell and the air went out of her. Opening her eyes, she found herself at the foot of the tree, its branches dripping, the plait of hair still resting in the hollow.

You have to save her. Illiam's voice splintered.

She lay at the foot of the tree and looked down at her stomach. Somewhere inside, Zohar felt the thread. It tugged, dragging at the other end. Numbly, she followed it, its scent of blood, its shaking. She stood, sparks of ash singeing her skin as she squinted. From the blood, a glut of bodies emerged from the swamping sea. A man surfaced, a shadow, charred black, and rose into the sky. The Skalens' Star gleamed about his neck, his dead arms listless, a curse frozen upon his lips. The thread pulled taut. Somewhere down on the beach, Sybilla coughed, her red soaked tunic tight against her flesh, hair shrouding her face. She crawled toward another body, one that lay upon the sand.

Zohar drifted closer, curious, then closer still.

Her eyes moved behind heavy lids, dark lashes, roped hair. She felt the suck of the wet tunic against her, the grazed skin of her knees, but he was all that mattered. She knew the muscles of his arms, and traced them, the knuckles of his hand, his leather boots, dark beard, she would look into his eyes of green...

A rush like sweet autumn wind, and suddenly she was elsewhere, in another land, a woodland, by a babbling stream.

Zohar looked around, where was she?

At her feet, Gavril's blood soaked the earth. He would not open his eyes. The jewel of his soul was hidden and above was the sound of wings.

She was lost now. "Sybilla?" Zohar called.

The sound echoed through mountains she could not see.

Zohar walked on, scanning the trees, a thudding in her ears.

"Sybilla!" Zohar screamed, not wanting to remain here.

Sybilla's body lay upon the bank, her head fully submerged in the stream. Her hair snaked about her scalp. Zohar dragged Sybilla by the shoulders, but she was lodged there, in the mud. Zohar could not draw her out, only shift her sideways, withdrawing her head so she lay on her back.

Help her. Illiam's voice carried many passengers, among them Intercessor Maeryn, her presence soft and insistent.

Illiam? Zohar called, fearing for him now.

She stared at the body at her feet. Sybilla's body. Scarred by lacerations of beak and claw; bruises of constriction. The face was filthy. A school of fish shimmered past; gleaming sunlight played upon the water.

And then, somehow, she knew what to do.

Zohar stared at the sun, breathing its white fire and pressed her mouth to Sybilla's, filling her with light. The thread guided her to other elements, to the bright parts concealed within. Fluttering green leaves and their red stems, Zohar took them into her lungs, and breathed them into Sybilla's. The water that dripped from Gavril's hand and the print he'd made upon the rock.

Sybilla, breathing slowly, in and out, with her grandfather beside her. Building stick castles with Lucinda, gathering pebbles for the path. Her mother cradling her, laughing, a mangled wreath of blossoms held in Sybilla's chubby hands. She with her father, their faces pressed, the safest, warmest feeling... heart-beat, heart-beat, heart-beat.

On it sounded, heart-beat, heart-beat, heart-beat, his stern and bristled face melting into joy. Davina sucked the Skalens' Star that hung about his neck. He gave it to her, placed the Star on her chest, and blessed her. The colours of the Seven Lands soaked into her heart until they were a part of her heart-beat, heart-beat, heart-beat.

The body stirred. Sybilla opened her eyes.

Stay, Zohar said, breathing the forest in.

She brought her lips to Sybilla's mouth, filling her with the verdant hush, a man reflected in the stream. Their daughter in the rushes crying, his smile, there, in the water.

"Davina." Sybilla's voice was warm. She looked up and saw Zohar, trees and sky about her head. Sybilla opened her eyes, to find Zohar's face, close to hers, their hair mingling in the mountain winds, their hair, a shroud, sheltering their faces.

Zohar closed her eyes and pulled away, calling out to Illiam in her mind.

His hand gripped hers, and she felt the solidity of his flesh, that this was real.

Zohar saw the strain upon the faces of those surrounding them, and knew that they harnessed the stone.

"What did you see?" Waldemar spat, his face rigid with effort.

Sybilla wiped her face with her hands, a smile tugging at her lips.

"What is your vision?" he pressed.

She turned from him, and stared out across the range, her eyes clear and bright. "This vision is mine, Intercessor."

The anger on his face ricocheted through clasped hands like a static shock. Waldemar withdrew his hands from the circle, curling them into fists. He looked down, his lower lip buckling at the edges as he brushed the dirt from his robe. He glared at the back of Sybilla's neck. But Sybilla was smiling. A wide and joyful smile that transformed her face entirely.

Zohar's heart leapt, feeling all that she felt, and Sybilla closed her eyes as if she would fly.

80

ZOHAR

Fifteen Years After The Fire

THE STONE THROBBED FITFULLY, and Zohar could feel the others in waves. Waldemar stared at the back of Sybilla's neck, his eyes flicking to the knife. In his rage she sensed the blood-tang of Temple dungeons, marble white, the Alma coming thickly, the choking cries of the many throats he had slit before. The red deeds of the condemned, so brutal, so unforgivable, so adverse to the nature of spirit that they must be destroyed. Their animal nature bled out and drained to the sea, their flesh vanquished by fire, and scattered to the wind.

Sybilla stood before him, a corruption of fate. A wicked thing that had crawled from the fire and lived. That had sent her evil visions among his brethren, and led them to their annihilation. Had she done it? In his dreams he had been sure, but she did not seem so powerful now. He shuddered to think that Velspar had touched her womb, that there was a child in the world that had grown from her. Why had she been saved?

He thought of Emryl's voice in his ear before the Skalens' House burned. Of his journey by dark, his forehead pressed hard against the girl's, the Attendant with coal-bright eyes. The corruption in the West

Wing and East that she must cleanse away. First with fire, *first with fire*, then with water, *then with water*, then go down to the Temple, *go down there*, and be made clean again. He had to finish it.

Still, he stood there, unmoving. Why did he hesitate?

His arms felt limp at his sides, his strength given to the stone.

Was it the stone?

His chest and groin ached as if with fever, and he felt suddenly faint.

Waldemar centred himself, collected his will, and then he knew. Maeryn. Of course she would do this. He wanted to weep. She shadowed his desire, a persistent breath blowing his passions away like ash on the wind. He wanted to resist, to pursue his course unhindered, but he knew what it would mean. If he took up the knife, she would move against him, and he could not bear it. For he needed her, Maeryn and her voice of sweet silver, in this life and the next. In *this* life...

Amand waited, desperate for Waldemar to act, himself falling prey to the insidious subtlety of Maeryn's will.

"She does not give prophecy," Waldemar said, his voice catching as he moved his eyes to Maeryn. "She has brought ruin upon us. And for what? There is no reason, no purpose. I was willing to entertain it, Maeryn, to open my heart to the mystery of Velspar, but there is nothing holy in her. I must finish what I started. I have let this poison fester in the world for too long."

"No, Waldemar," Maeryn said firmly, and even from a distance, Zohar felt the old woman's power.

"Her spirit must be destroyed," Waldemar said, his raised brows quivering.

"All of our brethren went to the flames. Do you believe their spirits were destroyed? It is our faith that draws them back to Velspar," Maeryn said, her voice low. "Will you be the light for them, Waldemar?"

To this Waldemar had no reply, and his face contorted as if in pain.

All the while, Zohar watched Sybilla's face. Her eyes glossed with joyful resignation as she waited for the Intercessors to pierce her body like a wineskin and send her spirit like a breath upon the wind. For she knew the Skalens' Star about her neck would draw her upward, wherever her father had gone, and that Gavril waited somewhere close by to come and take her hand. She knew that if her death must come to pass that it was right for Voirrey to hold her child. That the future Skalen of Nothelm would guide Davina and keep her safe.

Zohar looked at her mother, recognising the stiffness of her posture. Her mother looked for a moment at the blood smeared stone that still sat in the centre of the broken circle. Zohar had been so long in vision, she had not realised the leaden weight that still hung about them. That she perceived so much and that none of them moved.

Waldemar and Maeryn were locked together in silent struggle, sweat trickling from the old man's temple as Maeryn's hands grew red and began to shake. Zohar's stomach flipped, recalling the sickening moment when she and Illiam had trespassed into one another's spirits. She could not watch it happen. And as the thought struck her, she feared that part of her would leak away into Sybilla, and Sybilla into her, that if they killed the Red Skalen, Zohar would be pulled so thin, she'd cease to exist.

Her palm was slick with sweat, but she gripped Illiam's hand harder still. With what strength she had, Zohar swelled the waters of her spirit toward him. He looked at her, gave the smallest nod. She felt him trying, felt the strain of his will, but his body barely moved. She concentrated, watching his teeth clench as his shaking arm reached for the stone. She gave more of herself, drawing small sustenance from the blood-tie. Sybilla held her hand to her heart and stared at Zohar; her brow creased, but her gift was given willingly. In a sudden motion, Illiam lurched forward and grasped the stone, flinging it with a wavering arm, losing his footing in the process.

Second by second, its weight upon them lifted, the headiness of vision dissipating, voices receding into the discrete boundaries of flesh. All of them felt it and all of them saw it go. A black star falling into nothingness.

Zohar stumbled to Illiam as he lifted his face from the dirt, a red smear coming from his nose. She pulled him close, not knowing what the others might do.

Amand went to the edge and stared down. Then his wide, clear eyes fixed on Illiam. In seconds, the Intercessor was on top of him, hands about Illiam's throat, pushing him closer to the precipice. Illiam thrashed, but Amand was stronger.

"What have you done?" Amand gasped, bearing down on Illiam's throat.

Zohar ran at Amand, tearing at his robe, but could not pull him off. Her mother came too, a rock in her fist.

"Amand? Amand!" Voirrey's voice was distant and Zohar heard the baby cry.

Her mother threw the stone at Amand's head but missed. Zohar scrambled for another, turning to find Sybilla standing stiffly against the cave wall, her eyes darting. Voirrey passed the child to her and ran over, face flushed.

"Stop this!" Voirrey cried breathlessly.

Zohar's heartbeat was otherworldly, thunderous and slow. *Illiam*, she spoke to him, but he was not there, and did not answer. Yet his muscles strained. His fists dug into Amand's ribs, his feet grazing the ground.

"Velspar decides when each of us must die, not you, Amand," Maeryn said, her voice ringing.

Amand's body stiffened and though he released his grip a little, he would not let Illiam go. Slowly, he turned his head, staring only at Maeryn. "And who of us decided to cast away the stone? It was our only hope. They worked together, I felt it, Maeryn. None of them can be trusted." Amand's mouth twisted in disgust, and he shoved aside the boy who had once been his ally, and stood.

Zohar scrambled over, and to her relief, Illiam was very much alive, his throat heaving as he spluttered for air.

"You would wield it over us, Intercessor?" her mother asked, her tone seething sharp.

Amand stared at his now empty hands, watching them tremble.

Waldemar drew him away from the edge, and put his lips to Amand's ear, speaking so quietly Zohar did not know if the others could make it out, but she could read the shape of his words, could

402

see the cunning that passed over his face. "Hope runs beneath our very feet, Amand. Our dark river of destiny," he said.

Amand's eyes took on a steely cast.

Zohar held fast to Illiam, listening to the rasp of his breath as Voirrey made her way to Maeryn in quick strides. The old woman nodded at her words, her steady gaze fixed upon Amand.

Eventually, Amand turned to Maeryn, his face defiant. "What would you have us do?"

"We came here to perform Intercession on a troubled soul," Maeryn said. "That it was done by this child of Avishae shows us that despite all we have lost, the holy gifts are yet bestowed by Velspar. When the forest has finished burning, new leaves shall always return in the spring. We need no stone, no prophesied Gate – we need only to remain true to our mission and make ourselves ready teachers for the young."

Amand laughed bitterly. "First it was Intercessor Ambrose, and now it is Intercessor Zohar? We do not know what has been done. She entered the woman by blood-magic, not by the will of Velspar. She is just an ordinary girl."

Zohar breathed slowly, keeping her body very still, and was relieved that none of them turned to look at her.

"Velspar gives back what has been taken," Maeryn said, coolly. "Is that not what you said to Intercessor Phelan before he let himself be burned? Did you not swear to remain so that you could illuminate the way?"

"I have always admired your faith Maeryn, but it is not possible without the stone. Be assured I will fulfil my promise to Phelan and all the others that perished at Sybilla's hands."

Voirrey came forward then, arm in arm with Sybilla and the babe. Sybilla still held the vacant expression of someone lost in a dream, and she gazed upon Davina's face.

Waldemar swallowed grimly as they approached, and could not meet their eyes. Amand stared at the child and blinked, his expression sour.

"Amand," Voirrey said quietly. "Who is this child?" she pointed at Davina.

Amand squeezed his eyes shut, pressing his palm to his temple.

"This could be Intercessor Phelan, or Ennis, or any of those we have lost," Voirrey said.

Amand looked to Waldemar with growing desperation, but the older man had gone silent, seemingly paralysed by his proximity to Sybilla. "You do not know that," Amand said. "You are blinded by compassion, Voirrey. You see what you want to see."

"You would kill a mother in front of her child?" Voirrey said, her delicate features rosy with indignation. "All those years ago when the fires were burning in Seltsland, you came to me, and I did all that I could to help you," she said. "Sybilla is not the answer to your grief, Amand. Her death will not bring anything but sorrow, to me and to her child, and to those you have gathered in Brivia. My father cares little for matters of faith but if Peran asks it, he will help the Vaelnyri and Maglorean Guard in their bloody work. And you should know the nature of your own Skalens best. Which way do you think the Askier will turn? This is not over. But we are not here to conquer. We are here to minister to Velspar, as we always said, one spirit at a time."

She put her hand on him. "Come with me," Voirrey said. "There is a village in the Stetlan Mountains. The people there are in need of an Intercessor. You and I were not put here to fight and strategise. We praise Velspar when we ease the pain of others. We must teach the rites of faith! This is how we grow our number. Not by bloodshed. The age of execution has passed."

Amand looked at Sybilla, who moved her lips across her baby's brow as if none of them were there.

"And she will return to Vaelnyr?" he asked.

"She will come with us, and the child too."

Amand laughed, but Waldemar began to nod.

"This would be a good life for you, Amand," Waldemar said, giving him a meaningful look.

Amand stared at him, the hardness of his gaze slowly softening as something passed between them. "Where will you go, Waldemar?"

"My Skalen needs me, in Brivia," Waldemar said, folding his hands.

"And you, Maeryn?" Amand said, looking coldly upon her.

"Dear one, do not despair," Maeryn said, her expression serene. "We will see each other again, in this life and the next. My visions call me to Avishae."

Zohar looked at her mother, wondering if Maeryn had told her as much on their way to Jokvour.

Her mother squeezed her hand but did not meet her eyes as she advanced toward Sybilla, her posture very straight. "Skalen Sybilla," she said, and the woman turned slowly. The Skalens' locked eyes. "Our business is not yet done. On this day I call a meeting of Council." Her mother's formal tone was stark. "Let us breathe of the Alma and speak our piece."

When Sybilla nodded, the Intercessors stepped back, keeping their eyes down, giving over to some mannerism of the past. Sybilla kissed Davina and gave her to Voirrey, who accepted the child with a nervous smile.

Then the two Skalens walked past the stone circle and into the cave, beyond sight.

81

ZOHAR

Fifteen Years After The Fire

ZOHAR STARED AT THE CAVE'S ENTRANCE but could not see them, the two Skalens, together inside. Illiam's temper simmered on, and there was no getting free of it. He glared at Amand, chewing his lip, glancing often at Waldemar, who would never again put his hand on Illiam's shoulder and call him a 'good lad'. His expression grew pained when he looked at Maeryn, who would not even turn in his direction. For it was she who could smooth things over, as she'd done in Thrale Forest when the rebellion was new.

At the crunch of footsteps, Zohar noticed Voirrey coming toward them. Davina's legs dangled either side of her hand, and yet she slept, leaving a wet patch of drool on Voirrey's woollen smock.

"You will not rush them. Why don't you take a walk in the mountains? Jokvour is beautiful at this time of day." Voirrey smiled.

Zohar found the black mountains had grown feverish in blood-hues, their edges sharp and golden. It was a beauty that made her want to turn her eyes away.

Zohar nodded, and Voirrey returned to her friends, both old and new, bouncing the babe and laughing at something Waldemar said. The Intercessors did not smile so readily, but the four of them were turned toward each other in an attempt at optimism. Zohar sat with Illiam, feeling the gravity of each passing moment that her mother spent in there with Sybilla, knowing she could do nothing but wait.

She looked at Illiam and they both came to stand. There was no sense in languishing here, and Voirrey was right, the walk would likely do them good. They trod the path the way they had come, and Zohar was relieved to find the horses were still there on the low rise.

"Distract me," Zohar said.

Illiam smiled, though his mind was elsewhere. He reached for her hands, looking down at them in order to hide the miserable look on his face. As he moved his fingers over the curve of her wrist, he frowned. "Do you feel different?"

Zohar closed her eyes and intertwined both of her hands in his. Slowly, she discovered his blisters and scars, his skin smooth where he'd held the reins, his palm soft, warm... and vaguely unfamiliar. Zohar looked at him questioningly. "Yes."

They stared at one another.

His look made her nervous all of a sudden. But even as she wanted to look away, to regain her composure, a smile spread across her face that made her cheeks ache.

Illiam chuckled, moving his head to the side, turning his eyes to the ground. "Do you think we are... as we were?"

Zohar reached to touch the livid marks about his neck. "I think so," she said, wincing at the pain he must surely feel.

There was a pregnant pause.

"What should we do now?" Illiam said, seeming little bothered by his injuries as his attention came to rest entirely with her.

Zohar pointed her toe, turning it this way and that in the dust. "Shall we start from the beginning, Mr Greslet?"

Illiam rolled his eyes, but moved closer, his hands encircling her waist. "Very well, Miss Elshender."

Their laughter fell away as he drew her close. She buried her head in his chest, relishing the sound his heart made, the scent of him, of clove and sweat and horses. Zohar looked up, Illiam's eyes warm and deep, and she looked upon him in fascination, that he was there before her, real and unknowable once more.

He kissed her. She closed her eyes, journeying on, travelling somewhere as tears slipped down her cheeks. She had nearly lost him.

Illiam laughed, heat rising in his face as he glanced aside.

She never thought she'd see him this way again. Her body tingled as it had that day on the Temple stair, but all about them the light was fading, and she remembered her mother. "We should go back."

Illiam took her hand and together they walked, not knowing what awaited them on their return.

When the circle came into view, Zohar saw that the others still sat alone. Her gaze darted to the cave that glowed with orange fire. A gust of Alma whipped past her face. She looked at Illiam.

It did not take long for darkness to fall, or for the wind to grow cold.

Zohar was huddled in the crook of Illiam's arm when finally the figures emerged. She shook Illiam awake, and the two of them stood.

Sybilla and her mother walked a small distance apart, their postures relaxed. Zohar stared at the bandages wound upon their left hands.

Sybilla spoke. "The night grows cold, let us take shelter together here tonight."

Nobody responded, such was the strangeness of having the Red Skalen speak to them in hospitality and sovereignty.

Her mother smiled. "Skalen Sybilla has provisions to share. If Illiam and Amand would be so kind as to collect them?"

Illiam looked at Amand uncertainly, but Maeryn gave the Intercessor a playful push and he stood.

"It will be alright," Zohar said to him, knowing no one would dare act until they had come to understand the nature of the Skalens' bargain.

Reluctantly, Illiam walked with head down, and the two men muttered among themselves, pointing and peering down the mountain.

Voirrey followed Sybilla into the cave, Davina's cries rising into choking screams.

Zohar went to her mother who looked unusually vital. "What

happened in there?" Zohar whispered, cradling her mother's bandaged hand.

Her mother pressed the reddening stain. "We made a Skalens' pact." She lowered her voice. "To protect the stone. To keep it secret."

Zohar nodded, picturing the cairn.

"Come inside now," her mother said.

In the cave, Sybilla fed Davina at her breast, her back to the fire.

Zohar sat and warmed her hands. A dizzy calm descended over her. Her mother was safe. For the first time in days, she let herself relax a little, the cosiness of the Alma making all of this okay.

Waldemar dipped his head to pass the low entrance and Maeryn followed, rubbing his back.

The flames danced, orange, red, yellow, white. Her limbs were heavy now, and she felt quite at ease. Zohar unwove her braids, shaking her hair out as if she were alone in her chamber. She saw the others moving about their private routines, shuffling, preparing their nests. Zohar choked back a laugh; she could not have dreamed a stranger situation.

Thin voices approached, and then Illiam was there, flushed from the mountain winds. He smiled at her as he unloaded his pack, Amand still talking, bringing wrapped parcels that smelled of cured meat, cheese and baked things.

With the food came instructions, to move here or there, to pass this thing or that, and in the end none of them were silent. They spoke of small things, where to find more kindling for the fire, the pattern atop the oat biscuits, and which herbs grew where. Where the chewing grew tense, Voirrey wove new tales together, of ailments she had tended, and places she had been.

The chatter was warm, but Zohar could not help but look outside, for the one who was missing, the one who was gone. She leaned against Illiam's chest, hearing the reverberation of his voice, but not his words. Zohar stared into the fire, her thoughts drifting to daybreak. To horses and strap-tightened packs. To the jolt of the saddle numbing her thighs. To black mountains giving way to an emerald canopy, expanding in all directions beneath a featureless sky. To the peering eyes of Maglorean guards, and the whistle of their arrows. To the scream and whinny of startled horses. To death's many doors.

Or perhaps it would happen differently. Their enemies would not find them, and they would reach the Skalens' House. The Brivian Regents would be waiting. Illiam would embrace his parents, eat his stew and melt into his favourite chair. Would he follow her to Avishae? Would he stay? In the back of wagons, under blankets, in fishing boats they would go. They would travel from Port Innes to Port Fallon, by Selbourne or the mountain way, but still they'd find the valley, yellow-green, sloping down to that grey and stony mound.

She would stand upon the cliffs of her childhood, breathing the salt wind. She would trudge pine forests misty with ghosts and find the Temple scrubbed clean. Among the sentinels, her father would be standing, in silhouette, his head bowed toward the cairn. At some point she would have to open her mouth to speak, to greet them, to explain what had happened, there in Jokvour.

Zohar would have to walk by the yard where nobody laughed, into the dining room, her heart calling down the halls, her footstep quick upon the flagstones, her hand poised upon the handle of his door.

Illiam kissed her hair. The mumble in his chest broke into a laugh. A twig snapped and smouldered in the fire.

She watched in silence as quiet tears leaked from her eyes, blotching the linen of his shirt.

Zohar moved to stand, and Illiam leaned back to let her pass. Hugging her arms around her waist, she walked to the entrance of the cave. Outside, her skin prickled, the howling wind coursing through caverns, screaming of loved ones long dead.

A spark streaked at the edge of her vision and she looked up, the sky awash with stars. Zohar noticed their shapes, the patterns they made, that seemed to hiss, distant and small, gathering together, gathering form.

82

WALDEMAR

Twenty-Six Years After The Fire

My BREATH GROWS SHORT *as the days grow long. I am alone here, and I know not the name of this place, for I have wandered far from home. I followed them across the ocean, following a trail of stars, but it has led me nowhere. As I lie in this sulphurous place where the bones of Siatka wash upon the shore and the Alma does not grow, I close my eyes and return to Jokvour. To black mountains that brought chorus to my solitary Call. That bid the birds be silent as I wept into my hands. That held the heat of day as twilight fell and Amand first found me on the rise. That sheltered us as we talked and talked into the night. Mountains that birthed small flowers among the dry and shaking grass, the flower that I was holding in my hand when Maeryn's voice filled my spirit.*

Skalen Karasek, the First Diviner, walked in Jokvour, but now his line has come to an end. And what am I, now that my Skalen is dead? What am I, adrift from the Seven Lands, without brethren or Birth-Kin, without the sweet comfort of Intercession, without Alma leaves to crush between forefinger and thumb, without another's hands to prepare my flesh for burial, without another's voice to sing the hymns of my crossing?

This is the work of my adversary. She keens my spirit to be bright, for only in brightness will I survive the journey. I know that when I enter the Stream, Sybilla will be there. She was the red thought in me, and yet she was more. In vision she was flagrant, but when she walked the holy mountains, how she hung her head and wanted for the knife.

My hand shook with readiness, but then came a voice of sweet silver. Maeryn dragged me deep into the well of my spirit and spoke such that I went deathly still, and listened.

"This life must be different, Waldemar," she said.

I stared at the small hairs fluttering on the back of my adversary's neck.

"You must enter the Stream with clean hands."

In the cave, that night, I watched Sybilla nursing the babe, her face turned away. The play of the fire made shadows on my hands, light and dark, just as Sybilla changed with the movement of the flame. She was the eternal mother, and the shrieking wraith of my dream, one in the same. Maeryn kept her hand on me, drawing heat and staying my intention. And when day broke, I watched her ride away.

Beneath Jokvour the voice of the stone murmured, and Amand and I followed its path back to Brivia. The Eighth Gate yielding nothing but memories and regret. The stone imparting songs of unity, songs of yearning. Long have I listened for its liquid voice. But listen as I might, I cannot hear it now. The silence is unrelenting.

So, in my dreams I go where my body cannot. I go far across the ocean and deep into the earth, along that black and shining seam. Its colours dazzle like garland flowers and it pulses with the heat of Festival. It is all variety of voices, talking all at once.

This is where the silver threads are gathered, ripped apart in their ecstasy, and twilled into new shapes. This is where I will go when the moon next turns full, and there is no place for me to rest.

To go there, I must pass through the wall of protection. I must exit the womb of life.

I must not look up at the stars above, but to the bright blood of Velspar.

Through the heart I must travel. And at journey's end, my eyes will open anew. In their arms they will hold me, helpless, as I shall be. I will drink of sweet milk, and life's joyous rhythm will sound in my ears. If I awake among the faithless, I shall not fear, for Velspar is known to me.

When you read my words, slow first your breath, and open your inner eye. Among my words is a silver thread. Follow it, and you will find Velspar. Return always to Velspar.

INTERCESSOR WALDEMAR RASMUS OF BRIVIA, 726.

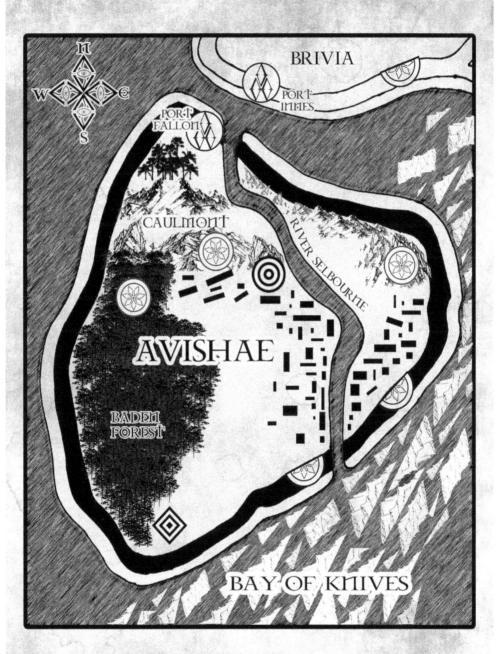

 KSHIDOL SKY ALTAR

 SKALEN'S HOUSE

 FOREST

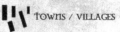 TOWNS / VILLAGES

 SIATKA SEA ALTAR

 THE TEMPLE

 MOUNTAINS

 PORT

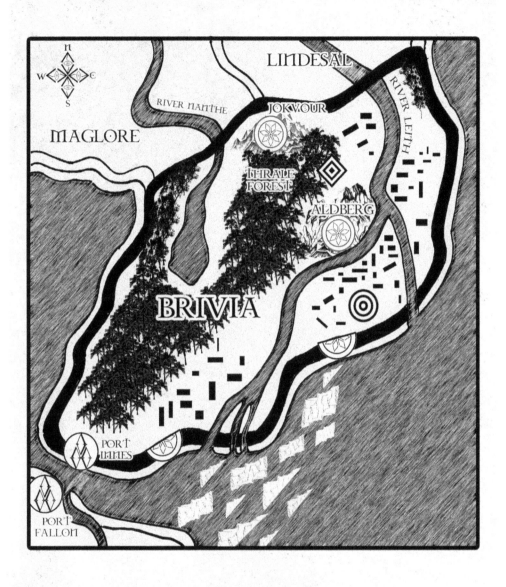

SELTSLAND

MAGLORE

LINDESAL

JOKVOUR

BRIVIA

LEITH

 KSHIDOL SKY ALTAR

 SIATKA SEA ALTAR

 SKALEM'S HOUSE

 THE TEMPLE

 FOREST

 MOUNTAINS

 TOWNS / VILLAGES

LINDESAIL

VAELNYR

FIELDS
OF
MARAIN

MAITHE

MAGLORE

JOKVOUR

BRIVIA

 KSHIDOL SKY ALTAR

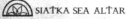 SIATKA SEA ALTAR

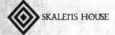 SKALENS HOUSE

 THE TEMPLE

 FOREST

 MOUNTAINS

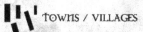 TOWNS / VILLAGES

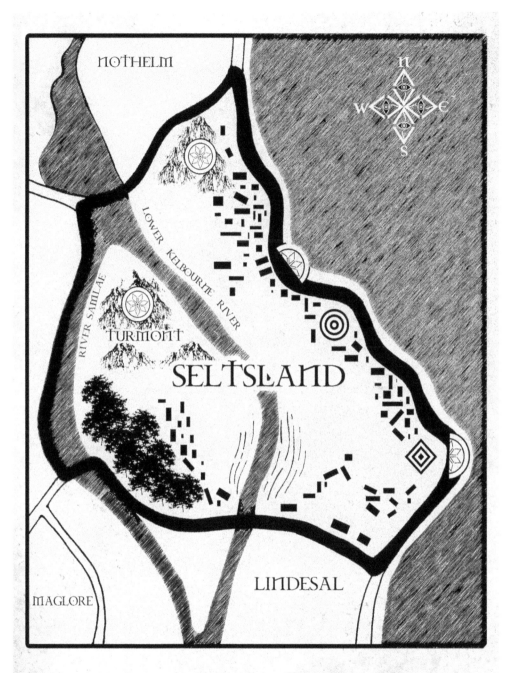

NOTHELM

n
W · · · · E
s

LOWER KELBOURNE RIVER

RIVER SAMLAE

TURMONT

SELTSLAND

MAGLORE

LINDESAL

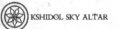 KSHIDOL SKY ALTAR

 KSHIDOL SEA ALTAR

 SKALETIS HOUSE

 THE TEMPLE

 FOREST

 MOUNTAINS

 TOWNS / VILLAGES

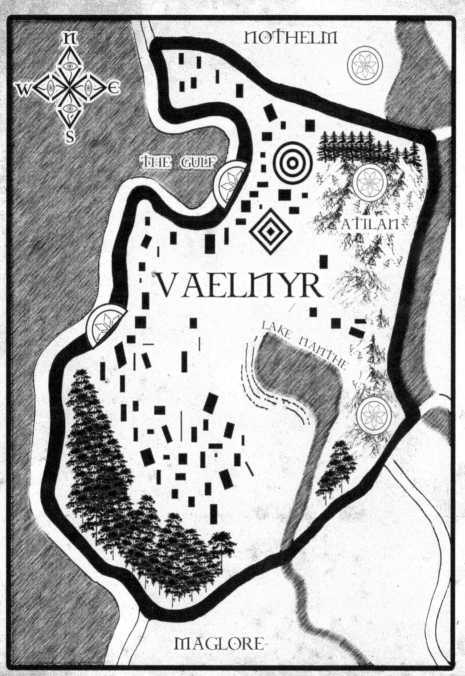

NOTHELM

THE GULF

ATILAN

VAELNYR

LAKE NANTHE

MAGLORE

 KSHIDOL SKY ALTAR   SKALEN'S HOUSE   FOREST   TOWNS / VILLAGES

 KSHIDOL SEA ALTAR   THE TEMPLE   MOUNTAINS

NOTHELM

UPPER KELBOURNE RIVER

STETLAN

VAELNYR

SELTSLAND

 KSHIDOL SKY ALTAR

 SIATKA SEA ALTAR

 SKALENS HOUSE

 THE TEMPLE

 FOREST

 MOUNTAINS

 TOWNS / VILLAGES

ABOUT THE AUTHOR

Sarah K. Balstrup is an Australian author of dark fantasy and former Religious Studies academic.

If you enjoyed this novel, please consider leaving a review on Goodreads or elsewhere online. Your support helps keep the words flowing and the wind in this author's sails.

For updates on Book 2: A Trail of Stars, sign up to Sarah's newsletter at sarahkbalstrup.com

Lightning Source UK Ltd.
Milton Keynes UK
UKHW040701160223
417122UK00001B/22